CARSTEN STROUD

THE RECKONING

Carsten Stroud is the author of the *New York Times* bestselling true-crime account *Close Pursuit*. His other novels include the first two volumes of the Niceville trilogy, *Niceville* and *The Homecoming*, as well as *Sniper's Moon*, *Lizard Skin*, *Black Water Transit*, *Cuba Strait*, and *Cobraville*. He lives in Florida and Toronto.

BOOKS BY CARSTEN STROUD

Niceville

The Homecoming

The Reckoning

THE RECKONING

THE
RECKONING

CARSTEN STROUD

VINTAGE CRIME/BLACK LIZARD
VINTAGE BOOKS
A DIVISION OF PENGUIN RANDOM HOUSE LLC
NEW YORK

A VINTAGE CRIME/BLACK LIZARD ORIGINAL, AUGUST 2015

Copyright © 2015 by Esprit D'Escalier

All rights reserved. Published in the United States by Vintage
Books, a division of Penguin Random House LLC, New York, and
distributed in Canada by Random House of Canada, a division of
Penguin Random House Ltd., Toronto.

Library of Congresss Cataloging-in-Publication Data
Stroud, Carsten, 1946–
The reckoning / by Carsten Stroud.
pages ; cm. — (Niceville trilogy)
I. Title.
PR9199.3.S838R43   2015
813'.54—dc23
2014047944

Vintage Books Trade Paperback ISBN: 978-1-101-87302-1
eBook ISBN: 978-1-101-87303-8

Map by Robert Bull
Book design by Virginia Tan

www.weeklylizard.com

Printed in the United States of America
10 9 8 7 6 5 4 3 2 1

For Linda Mair

The things we remember best
are those better forgotten.

—GRACIAN, 1647

Cruelty is not softened by tears.
It feeds on them.

—PUBLILIUS SYRUS, 1ST CENTURY BC

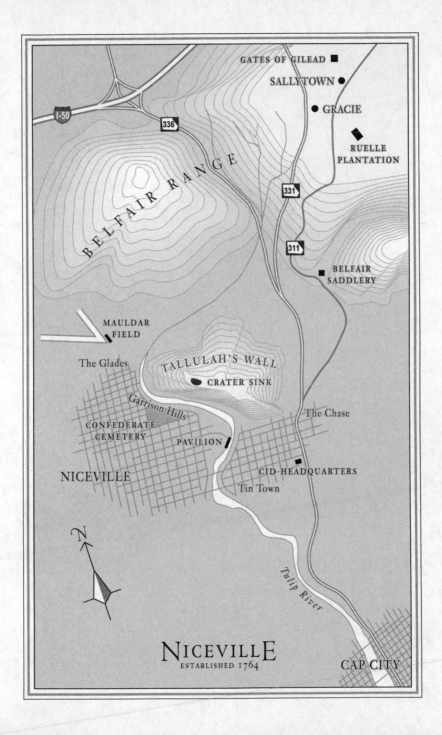

The Reckoning

In the fall of 1814, under a harvest moon, the people of Niceville came together on the banks of the Tulip to talk about the evils that had come upon their town and to consider what should be done about them.

Amity Suggs, the minister, said it was God's Holy Wrath. Dr. Cullen said there was something in the water. The mixbreed John Brass said that a Kalona Ayeliski, a Raven Mocker demon, had always been in this place and the town should be abandoned. The debate went back and forth.

In the end the naming calls God will be taken. Go about your ... two hundred years this covenant held up. ... on one rainy Friday night in October, it all went straight to Hell.

Friday night, nine-thirty, and everybody in the Morrison family was safely tucked away in their white stucco home at 1329 Palisade Drive in The Glades. The Glades was a prewar Art

Deco neighborhood in the northwest corner of Niceville. It had started out as Old Hollywood and gotten a lot older by staying there.

The Glades had shady curving lanes lined with palms and cypress and live oak trees. The rain streaming down put a misty halo around all the streetlamps and hammered on the red tile roofs of the houses. The gutters were choking on leaves and muddy water. A thick fog drifted through the trees. The warm air was heavy with the graveyard scent of wet earth.

Inside the Morrison house everything was serene and cozy, dinner done, the day ending well. Doug, the dad, was a short round man with a friendly streak, a forensic tech with the Niceville PD. Ellen, the mom, was a neonatal nurse at Our Lady of Sorrows down in Cap City. Jared, the eleven-year-old son—skinny, big-eared, with shaggy brown hair—was flat on his stomach in front of the 52-inch Samsung. An immense and overweight Maine Coon cat named Mildred Pierce was stretched out along his spine, the huge cat purring like a well-tuned motor.

And Ava, the fifteen-year-old daughter, was tucked away up in her shell-pink bedroom with the door locked, leaning in to her Mac, ~~~ing with Julia, her latest OMG-BFF, glee-fully sla~ing the ~ew g~~~ ~ their class at Sacred Heart High.

Ava, b~ck hair an~ ~~ their class at Sacred Heart High. God woul~ never have issu~~es, had a body that a loving was only d~mly aware of the p~~~ the cheerle~ding squad at Sacred Hear~ ~-year-old, and she players at the Sunday-afternoon football g~ ~~~ was on after school, she went out in the town with her fr~~ ing the Galleria Mall, riding the Peachtree Line tro~~. their navy blue Sacred Heart tunics and their scarlet blazer~ with the school crest. They hiked the tunics up too high as soon as they were out of school, showed lots of pale white thigh and knee socks, deliberately careless of how they sat, feeling all the eyes on them, savoring the burn. Well, everybody is doing it, aren't they, is what Ava would have said if you'd asked her, because she had no clue whatsoever about the risks they were running.

The cops figured Ava probably never heard what was happening downstairs—the doorbell ringing or whatever it was—because she was up in her room with the headphones on, busy with her Skype call.

Not to say that there was no sign of everything that happened that night, beginning with the front hall. The CSI people were pretty sure it started there, in the front hall, when Doug the Dad opened the door.

It went outward from the front hallway. Traces of what happened were all over the place—the walls, the ceilings, the living room carpet, the staircase. Signs were everywhere, but the worst of them were upstairs, in Ava's room.

Nine-thirty p.m. and up in The Glades, Hell was getting busy with the Morrison family. There were sounds, cries, pleas, but the neighbors weren't hearing anything over the pounding thunder and the lashing rain. As a result, what went on inside the house went on for two and a half hours. Shortly after midnight the lights flicked off and a kind of stunned silence came down inside 1329 Palisade Drive.

A few minutes later a large shuffling figure carrying a green garbage bag emerged from the door next to the garage, walked slowly down the driveway and off under the trees, moving into and out of the pools of light from the streetlamps, wrapped in a dark gray rain slicker. The figure reached the end of the block, stepped left into darkness, and was gone.

Five minutes passed. Then an old navy blue Cadillac Fleetwood rolled through the intersection of Palisade Drive and Lanai Lane, trailing a veil of rainwater. The Caddy reached the traffic lights at River Road, ran the intersection against a red—got itself duly snapped by a traffic camera—and accelerated south and east, disappearing into the southbound traffic on River Road, a shiny blue tank glittering in the streetlights, windows tinted dark, dashboard dials glowing, lighting up the face of the driver, his chest heaving, his heavy hands at the ten after ten position on the black leather wheel, heading out of The Glades as fast as that Caddy could go.

Never Get Out of the Car

Twelve fifty-five the same night.

Down in Tin Town, a Niceville police cruiser driven by a thirty-year staff sergeant named Frank Barbetta was rolling down the Miracle Mile, Tin Town's main strip.

Tin Town was Niceville's version of Compton, California, or Chicago's South Side. The Miracle Mile was called that because if you tried to walk it after midnight it would be a miracle if you got a mile. Tin Town people just called it the Mile.

Frank Barbetta was an amiable bulldog-type cop who had a reputation on the Mile for being fair-minded and likable, slow to anger; he never needed his gun, hadn't shot anyone in thirty years, and used his brains and his muscle and occasionally a nearby chair to get bad situations under control. In short, an old-fashioned beat cop who would never kick the living daylights out of anybody who hadn't been simply begging for it.

In Tin Town he was seen as a Wyatt Earp sort of cop who knew that the hookers and druggies and bikers and mutts and grifters were all part of the passing parade and they were his people to protect and care for.

This was essentially true.

In short, on this rainy Friday evening, Frank Barbetta was the benevolent God in his personal heaven and all was right with the world. Fate is drawn to that kind of attitude, finds it amusing.

The Tulip River had, in a way, created Tin Town. Broad and deep, the Tulip rose up out of the Belfair Range ninety miles north and gathered strength all the way down a wide grassy valley until it curved around a huge limestone cliff that dominated the northeastern part of town and powered through the center of Niceville like an interstate highway.

But the river had to make a sharp bend around a stony shoal south of the Armory Bridge. Here water roiled and rushed across a muddy flat where a cluster of tin-roofed fishing huts sat on pitch-pine stakes driven into the gravel.

Cattails and saw grass drooped down over washed-up garbage, beer cans, every kind of dead thing. At least once a week a stray corpse would get caught up in the weeds, a blue-skinned waxy blob, eyes and lips and ears torn off by the river carp. Smoke rose up from stovepipe chimneys on the roofs and the yellow glow through shuttered windows glimmered on the surface of the water. These tin-roofed shacks gave Tin Town its name, and in the fall, the warm days and cold nights gave Tin Town its mists and fogs.

The Miracle Mile reflected in the rain-slick windows of Barbetta's cruiser was lined with neon-lit biker bars covered in chicken wire, tattoo shops, Dollar Generals, and six different barred-up bunkers with bulletproof windows where you could get a payday advance at thirty percent interest compounded daily or a cash loan on somebody else's wedding ring provided there wasn't a finger still in it.

———

Halfway down the Mile, between the Piggly Wiggly and a Helpy Selfy Laundromat, there was a ten-floor brownstone hotel with spray-painted gang tags all around its base. A board above the entrance said in bold black letters:

CASH ONLY NO CREDIT !!!
NO DISCOUNTS FOR THE ELDERLY
YOU'VE HAD TWICE AS MUCH TIME
TO GET THE DAMNED MONEY!!!

The crumbling brick facade carried a neon sign shaped like a huge cross made out of the words *MountRoyal* and *Hotel*, the words crossing at the letter *T*.

In Room 304 of the MountRoyal there was a man who had a lot on his mind. A tall, lean, and big-boned guy with long silvery hair and a face that looked like it had been chipped out of sandstone, he was standing at the window and looking out at a Niceville black-and-white as it cruised south toward the riverbed. From the numbers on the roof he figured it had to be Frank Barbetta's ride. The man standing at the hotel window knew Barbetta from way back, when he himself had been a staff sergeant with the State Troopers.

Good memories, most of them, and some others best forgotten. Memories were on his mind tonight.

Mainly, where were his?

He could clearly remember the kick-ins, the bar fights, and the highway patrol car chases, the rollovers and the mangled dead and the occasional gunfight. He could recall many wild nights raising hell with Jimmy Candles and Marty Coors and the one and only Coker, and he had a crystal clear memory of the death of his wife, and he could remember all sorts of the scrapes and scandals and escapades of the typical cop life that he had lived, over thirty years of it.

But all that was in the past. He had a strong feeling that a lot had happened recently, important life-altering stuff, but when he tried to remember precisely what that might be, he got nothing. Nothing up to right here and now, standing at the window in Room 304 of the MountRoyal Hotel watching Barbetta's cruiser slide down the Mile. He wasn't even all that sure of his name.

He did have a big gold ring on the third finger of his right hand, with the crest of the U.S. Marine Corps on it. And he had a wallet with a whack of cash, maybe a thousand, a blue plastic bank card with the word MONDEX on it and a logo for some kind of bank, PNG Bank.

It had a microchip embedded in it, but the man had no idea what the hell a Mondex card was or why he had one. He'd have to Google it.

There was also an employee card from Wells Fargo. It had his picture on it—yep, it was him, all right—and the card said his name was Charles Danziger.

Then there was the driver's license with an address on Rural Route 19 in Cullen County and a picture that looked sort of like him only it was maybe taken after he died because he looked too fucking sick to drive.

It was *also* telling him his name was Charles Danziger, and that he had to wear corrective lenses while driving at night.

There was a third card that indicated that he was a fully paid-up member of the Retired State Patrol Officers Club with the rank of staff sergeant and a whole bunch of award citations listed on the back.

The man looked at these various pieces of official plastic and figured a reasonable man could draw the conclusion that his name really was Charles Danziger.

*Okay, I'm prepared to accept that my name is Charles Dan-
ziger, but what the hell happened to me? A blackout?*

From booze or drugs?

No.

Not him.

Never in all his wild years had he ever done drugs—
other than OxyContin for injuries acquired in the line of
duty, and his only weakness was wine. Now *Coker*, there was
a man who liked his pharmaceuticals, a risky hobby for a guy
who was a staff sergeant with the Belfair and Cullen County
Sheriff's Department and the most famous police sniper in
the entire state.

But not Charlie Danziger, who favored pinot grigio, and
no man with any self-respect blacked out over a couple of bot-
tles of pinot grigio.

The cruiser stopped at the intersection, and the light
from the hotel sign lit up the interior of the cruiser and the
driver, a big gray-haired Sicilian with deep-set black eyes
and a heavy jaw.

Frank Barbetta.

Danziger considered opening the window and calling
down to him, but for some reason decided not to. The cruiser
pulled away into the traffic along the Mile, tires hissing on the
slick pavement, trailing a veil of rainwater.

Danziger turned away from the window, feeling dog
tired and blue and cut off from real things. Also, right now,
his chest hurt like a bitch. It wasn't a heart attack; he'd had
one of those and there was no mistaking them for anything
else.

No, this felt more like he'd been kicked in the middle of
the chest. Twice. Two distinct sore spots. No bruises, but
pain, deep and aching pain. A puzzle, like the rest of it.

Well, he did remember that there was a cold bottle of

pinot grigio in an ice bucket on the dresser. He crossed the room, twisted off the top, took the plastic wrap off one of the cheap-ass paper cups the hotel supplied, and poured himself a stiff one.

Sleep now. Maybe the morning would bring wisdom. He was looking at the mirror over the dresser as he drank it down. Noticed something a bit unusual.

He wasn't in it.

Danziger stood in front of the mirror, stone-still, his breathing suspended. Instead of his reflection, he was looking out at a section of tilled earth that fell away toward a dense stand of pines and willows. From the way the shadows fell on the land, it looked to be nearly sunset. There were dark figures in the distance, working the field, digging in what looked to be trenches, shovels and axes working, the figures bent and somehow beaten-looking.

There was a wheeled cart being drawn by a brace of oxen. The cart was loaded with round white stones, or maybe melons. It struck him that they could be skulls, a dark thought not at all like him.

There was no sound coming from the scene, only this image floating in the mirror, the tilled earth, the bent black figures hacking at the ground. He put out a hand to touch the glass and the image went away.

He was looking at himself in the mirror, a picture of a worn-out hard-looking man with a lot on his mind. He turned away from the mirror, thinking *Forget it, just go to sleep*.

But sleep did not come.

Instead Danziger lay there in the dark, listening to the rain lashing against the window, the sound of the street below, seeing that mirror vision in his mind, the farm field at sundown, the workers, the sled piled with round white stones that made him think of skulls.

He had seen that field before somewhere, and down in his lizard brain he had a feeling that he'd see it again.

Back out on the Mile, things got downright dismal. A few people were wandering about, drunks and addicts and mopes and the feral kids who preyed on them. Most people with ready money and a choice in the matter were still in the bars getting rid of it, and the few hookers with a serious work ethic were over in the MountRoyal, earning their cut the hard way.

"A typical Friday night in Tin Town," said Barbetta to no one at all. Barbetta was alone in his Crown Vic Police Interceptor because Little Rock Mauldar, Niceville's Mayor for Life, was up for reelection and he was shaving the corners on nonessential services so he could bribe the voters with property tax cuts. Apparently keeping a patrol cop alive while policing a part of Niceville as dangerous as Tin Town was a nonessential service.

Barbetta had reached the end of the strip and was turning left onto Scales Alley to check out the Shore Walk down by the Tulip when his lights raked across a scruffy parkette next to a boarded-up gun shop.

The parkette had a cluster of raggedy-ass palm trees jammed into it. They were surrounded by a chain-link fence that made you wonder what terrible crime the palm trees had committed.

Barbetta caught a flash of movement in the center of the palm trunks, down by the saw grass at their bases, a glimmer of shiny black like crow's wings. When his headlights hit it, the shape froze, then went to ground, a distinctly furtive move, like a black flag dropping down, a shimmery flutter into the grass, and then nothing at all.

Cat? Bat? Dog? Crow?

No. Too big. And the shape was wrong.

He rolled to a stop, lit up the scene with his high beams, and flicked on his dash-mounted video camera. Not a tremor in the tall grass around the tree trunks.

A feeling of . . . waiting.

Stillness but not emptiness.

Something is wrong here.

He was in a dark lane, an alley, all the streetlights behind him. If he got out of the car he'd be a silhouetted target against the glare coming off the Miracle Mile. The parkette was at the far end of the narrow lane, a good fifty feet away. Lot of ground to cover, and fences on both sides, like he was in a cattle chute. Two rutted tracks in the alley were full of black water. The rest was mud and gravel, palm leaves, trash and beer cans. Broken glass. Unsteady ground to walk on and not a place where you'd want to go down hard.

Be nice to have a partner.

He picked up the radio.

"Central, this is Nine Zulu."

"Nine Zulu."

"Central I'm gonna be ten-thirty-seven here at Scales and the Mile."

"Roger that, Frank. What's up?"

"Just a walkabout. Saw something weird in this parkette here, where Brodie's Gun Shop used to be. Got my dashboard video on."

"Got the Portable?"

"You bet."

"Scales is a bad sector, Frank. Lots of crank calls there all this week. Six Yankee is a couple blocks out. You want to wait?"

"What's their call?"

"A ten-ten."

Yuppie larvae fighting outside some bar.

Could be thirty minutes with that.

"No, Central, I'm good."

Barbetta keyed off, tugged at his Kevlar, and popped the door, thinking that the duty captain always told them *Be safe out there* and every time they heard that they all thought, *Horseshit, the only way to stay safe is never get out of the car.*

Coker and Twyla Disagree on a Question of Civic Virtue

Around the same time that Charlie Danziger was beginning to stitch himself back together in downtown Niceville (but technically an hour later—because of a difference in time zones), on a St. Augustine beach three hundred and fifty-nine miles southeast of the MountRoyal Hotel, the ex–Belfair and Cullen County staff sergeant—known as Coker to his friends, of which he had two if you counted Charlie Danziger—was sitting and listening to the Atlantic Ocean crash and boom in the dark under a sea of stars. Staring into the glowing embers of a fire, Coker was brooding a bit about Danziger and related recent events while drinking Laphroaig out of a sterling silver flask.

Next to him on the blanket was a young Cherokee woman named Twyla Littlebasket, lying on her back, mildly stoned, watching Orion move ponderously into the west. Twyla, who had once been described by a cop named Nick Kavanaugh as having "curves like a French staircase," was wearing the bottom half of a Tommy Bahama bikini in tourmaline and gold, and a sleepy, satisfied look. The night was sultry and smelled of sea salt and kelp and wisps of cedar smoke from the fire.

Behind them on a large dune was a glass-and-wood-beam

Frank Lloyd Wright beach house sheltered by a stand of palm trees and surrounded by pampas grass. A soft glow from the interior of the beach house lay on the sand around them like candlelight. In short, a lovely night, and it would have been perfect except for the house party five hundred yards down the shore, which was rapidly getting out of hand.

The shore was mostly dark, except for these two islands of light. It was lined with other homes every bit as expensive as theirs, but most of them were shuttered and empty on this Friday evening, the summer season drawing down.

But that thumping bass beat was getting louder by the minute. It was coming from the Kellerman place. The Kellermans, nice people—a tad vulpine and smug, but pleasant enough—were away on a Viking river cruise down the Rhine.

They had, however, left the keys to their beach house with their youngest son, Nathan, a second-string fullback at Notre Dame and a first-string pain in the ass. Nathan was now living up to his hard-earned reputation.

The bass beat from the Kellerman place was getting powerful enough to rattle Coker's windows, and in the middle of the blaring music and the drunken crowd noise Coker and Twyla could hear breaking glass and the sound of a girl screaming, cut off suddenly.

Twyla sat up, stared down the beach. "God, Coker. Should we do something?"

Coker leaned over, gave Twyla a gentle kiss on the cheekbone, and shook his head, the firelight glinting in his pale eyes.

"No, Twyla, we should definitely *not* do something."

More glass shattering and a burst of hooting male laughter, a dim-witted mass braying like a jackass choir. Twyla stood up, her hands on her hips—she was a pugnacious woman with a short fuse.

"I'm going to call the cops."

Coker got to his feet. He was about six-one, muscular and

lean, hard as a hickory cane, with short-cropped silver hair and a face that could be—and often was—considered flinty and intimidating.

"Twyla, you know the rules. We do *not* draw attention. We do *not* call the cops. You have to remember who we are."

"I know who we are, Coker."

"Okay. Let's review. Who are we?"

She simmered a bit, listening to the bass beat hammer the planet. She made an effort to shake it off. "We're the Sinclairs. You're Morgan and I'm Jocelyn. I'm your third wife. You made your money in currency trading, you're retired, and I'm—"

At that point there was a chorus of chanting, followed by a crescendo of bass that bordered on painful and the sound of expensive things breaking. And another piercing female shriek.

Twyla gave Coker her death-ray glare.

"Dammit, Twyla," he said, hesitating.

She kicked the death ray up to STUN. Coker knew the next level well. It was VAPORIZE, and you did not want to stand in front of that one.

"Okay. Okay, I'll call the cops."

Career Choices for Caligula

Nick Kavanaugh was a detective with the Belfair and Cullen County Criminal Investigation Division. Early thirties, maybe six feet, he was heavy-shouldered, flat-bellied, hard-boned, and quick, with gray eyes and close-cropped black hair going silver at the sides. He was wearing a navy blue suit, Italian cut, a white shirt, no tie. He had a blue steel Colt Python in a Bianchi holster on his right side. Nick was leaning, hip cocked and arms folded, on the edge of a beaten-down plywood desk in Lacy Steinert's office at the Probe—what Tin Town people called the Belfair and Cullen Counties Parole and Probation Service.

Lacy Steinert, a sport model with her motor running, had a secret thing for Nick but so far hadn't gotten a chance to show it to him, Nick being married and all that happy-sappy domestic horseshit. So the meet was all business and the business was a seventeen-year-old part-time car thief named Jordan Dutrow.

Nick was pretty sure that late last night Jordan Dutrow had dropped in on a couple by the name of Thorsson, who had a nice rancher in Long Reach, one of Niceville's more upscale neighborhoods.

While in attendance there, Nick believed that Jordan had officially graduated from the occasional impulsive car theft to Home Invasion, Unlawful Confinement, Aggravated Rape, two counts of Felony Homicide, and Grand Theft Auto. Jordan Dutrow was one of Lacy's juvenile clients, out on probation after getting popped in possession—while blind drunk—of a stolen Jaguar. Nick was reasonably sure that Lacy Steinert might have an idea where Jordan Dutrow could be on this rainy Friday night in Tin Town.

Lacy folded her arms, shook her head. "I'm gonna need some assurances from you."

"Like what?"

"Like if I help you find him you're not gonna just go Nick-olate the kid like you did Junior Wanless and Cory Frampton."

"Wanless resisted, and Frampton stuck his nose in."

"Which is now way off to one side and looks like an auber-gine."

"Aubergine?"

"Big ugly purple thing. Also known as an eggplant."

Nick had to smile.

"How about you stop calling these mutts kids, Lacy? Jor-dan Dutrow is one of the best middle linebackers Frederick Douglass Tech ever had. He's six-three, built like a Brahma bull, and if he had stayed out of trouble, he might have gone to Ole Miss or LSU on a football scholarship."

"He's still a juvie. And gentlemen never say the words *Ole Miss* around an LSU alumna."

"He's a client of yours. Which is why I'm here tugging on your sleeve at this unholy hour."

Lacy gave him a sideways look.

"You pretty sure he's the one who did the Thorssons?"

"I am."

"What have you got?"

"Thursday, around midnight, killer came up from a ravine over the fence, left prints on the wet grass—big running shoes, deep imprint, so a large guy. Entered through a breezeway door that had a faulty lock. Not obvious from the outside. Footprints show he went straight to it. Thorssons were at the back of the house, in the master. We figure he went right there, because the lawn had been cut and he got grass clippings on his shoes and they got tracked down the hall, all the way to the bedroom."

"Familiar with the house?"

"Looks like. The Thorssons had the house up for sale, and there was an Internet listing for it, had one of those digital photo tours of the house. It was all there, including the floor plan. People never think about that."

"How does that bring us to Jordan? Anybody could have seen that tour video."

"Video didn't feature the faulty breezeway lock. That was insider stuff."

"And . . ."

"Thorssons had a cleaning service—"

"Oh, jeez—"

"Yep."

"Jordan's aunt, LaReena Dawntay," said Lacy after a moment. "Crack addict. She's in Lady Grace, terminal cancer. She's one of mine. I see the daughter in the hallways sometimes. In a maid's uniform."

"Sweep No More. Her name is Cheryl Reid. She does the Thorsson house every second Thursday."

Lacy went quiet.

Rain hissed on the window glass and drummed on the roof. She could hear Nick's heart, or thought she could, or maybe it was her own. She really believed she had reached Jordan Dutrow.

"DNA or prints?"

"He wore gloves but no condom. Or it broke."

"So DNA?"

"Yes. At the lab now. Jordan was booked into Cullen County Detention for the Jaguar thing. They took a routine swab as part of the Intake."

"He's a juvenile. A school kid. They can't do that to a minor."

"But they did."

"Wouldn't be admissible."

"No, but it would sure as hell nail him," said Nick, with an edge.

Lacy cocked her head.

"You're pretty hot about this. What did he do? I mean, inside the home?"

Nick told her, sparing her nothing.

There was a long stunned silence between them.

"Christ," Lacy said once she had found her voice. "He's only *seventeen*."

"So was Caligula."

Lacy worked it through, went a bit green around her edges. "Dear God. That would have taken a while."

"Most of the night, if the ME is right about the time of death, which he puts at around two in the morning. The wife went first, finally; then he did the husband. No point keeping him around after that, we figure."

She looked at Nick for a while, processing it.

"Nick, that is *not* anything Jordan would do. The things you say he did, Jordan wouldn't even *think* of that. He'd have to be some kind of . . . monster. A demon. There would have been warning signs. I saw him on Monday afternoon. He had lost weight, said he was having headaches, but he was going to school every day, making every football practice. Played last Sunday, first string against Sacred Heart, made MVP in that game. Nick, really, we had a decent talk. There was . . . nothing like this. Nothing. In his childhood—"

"Lot of sadistic crap plays at your local multiplex. Video games are full of it."

"I've never bought the idea that slasher movies or violent video games make killers. Otherwise we'd have millions of kids butchering their families."

Nick shrugged.

"All I want is this one kid, Lacy."

Lacy went quiet.

Nick left it with her. He trusted her.

"Does he have anything to run on? Usually he's lucky to have five bucks in his pocket."

"Cleaned out the wall safe in the den—no idea what was there, but it's gone. Firearms says Todd Thorsson had a concealed carry permit for a Kimber .45. It's gone too."

"How'd he get away?"

"He stole the family ride. A red Mercedes SLS AMG."

"Good lord. That's a quarter-million-dollar car. He would have stood out like a . . ."

"Like a dumbass thug in a stolen red Benz."

"Any sign of it?"

"None at all. Disappeared off the face of the earth. He may have handed it off to some gangbangers. Beau Norlett is looking at security cameras along Bluebonnet as far north as South Gwinnett. So far nothing. It'll show. There's only two of them in this part of the state."

"How is Beau?"

"He's mending. Hates the desk, but he's lucky to be alive. So, any ideas?"

More silence, the rain drumming on the roof. Then Lacy said, "From what I know—or thought I knew—about Jordan, he'd go to family."

"We've tried them all. And the beat guys have been showing his photo to all the hotel and motel clerks in town. Nobody's seen him. Which is why I'm here. You're his PO.

You know the kid. You have to run him down. Got any suggestions, places where he'd go to coop up?"

Lacy thought about it.

"You know the Works Department toolshed under the Armory Bridge?"

"Yes. West end of the bridge, right next to the Tin Town Flats."

"Yeah. For a while there, Jordan had keys to it, from a summer job last year. One time he missed a meeting, and I found him there. Had a cookstove and a cooler and a cot. Very snug."

"What made you look there?"

Lacy tapped her nose.

"A tip."

"From who?"

"His mother. Celeste. She's a good lady, tries her best with him. Never quits."

Lacy stopped there, gave Nick a look over her half-glasses.

"Look, Nick—"

"You want to come with me?"

"Yeah."

"No."

"Nick . . . come on."

Silence.

"We find him there, you stay out of the way?"

"Promise."

"I've heard that before."

"This time I mean it."

Nick took a breath, let it out.

"Where's your piece?"

Lacy pulled open her desk drawer, lifted out a clip-on holster with a big fat Glock in it.

Nick sighed.

"Okay. Strap it on. Let's go."

Frank Barbetta Gets Out of the Car

Barbetta aimed his Maglite at the parkette. The saw-grass leaves were churning in the wind, wet and slick. They looked like knives. He stepped through the gate and moved into the shadows under the palms. About ten yards in, he found a manhole cover, which usually covered an old storm drain, flipped open and lying on the saw grass. Barbetta had been in this parkette a dozen times and never seen it open.

The manhole cover had writing on it—CITY OF NICEVILLE WATER AND POWER—and it dated from before the First World War. He always figured the storm drain had been welded shut, but now the cover lay on a stand of saw grass, flattening it down, and the opening to the drain was a wet black hole.

Something else. There was steam rising up from the surface of the manhole cover. He reached out, touched a finger to it, and jerked it back. The metal was as hot as a cookstove.

What the hell?

He stood over the opening, put his flash beam down the shaft. It went down a long way, farther than his flash could reach. There was a rusted iron ladder riveted into the concrete wall of the shaft, the steps receding into the deep, into the darkness at the bottom of the shaft.

Barbetta knelt down by the opening, avoiding contact with the rim, feeling the heat rising up from the shaft. He lowered the Maglite beam farther into the hole, trying to see how far down the bottom was, thinking, *There has to be a bottom, right?*

Well there was *something* down there. It looked like smoke, black smoke, a cloud of it, and inside the smoke there were golden sparks, glittering like cat's eyes. And there was a smell, a roasting meat smell, raw and acrid. Maybe some kind of animal? Raccoon or a possum.

Or rats.

Barbetta hated rats.

Could it be a fire down there?

The rain was running down the back of his neck and pattering on his flak vest.

There was no way anything could be burning at the bottom of a hundred-year-old storm drain on a night as rainy as this.

How about a power line shorting out?

Maybe the heat—the steam or something—had built up in the shaft until it popped the cover and now the rain was shorting out some old power line down at the bottom of the shaft?

Go down and check it?

Not on your life, my friend. I've seen that movie.

Barbetta sat back on his heels, wiped the rain off his face, pulled out his radio.

"Central."

"Nine Zulu."

"I'm at this parkette by Brodie's. I'm looking at what I think is some kind of electrical fire down at the bottom of this old drain shaft. I can see sparks and the shaft is real hot. I think we need to get some fire guys down here, and maybe some folks from Utilities."

"Roger, Frank. Lights and sirens?"

Barbetta considered the hole, watched the steam—the smoke, whatever—rising up. Under the pattering of the rain on the saw-grass blades he could hear a faint sound, rising and falling. It was some animal crying out, faint but full of pain and fear.

What in hell . . . ?

"Yeah. Lights and sirens."

High School Confidential

Nick and Lacy were in his navy blue Crown Vic rolling through heavy traffic about a quarter mile north of the on-ramp to the Armory Bridge when the cruiser got lit up with flashing red and blue lights, and then they heard the brass-throated bellow of the fire truck that was now filling up their rearview mirror.

Nick jerked the cruiser over to the right to let the truck pass, which it did, moving fast, weaving through the slowing cars. It disappeared into the mists and fogs of Tin Town, followed closely by a white panel van with *Niceville Utilities* painted on the side.

A minute later and Nick took a gap in the traffic to cut left across Riverside, killed the car's headlights, and pulled up to the gate in the chain-link fence that sealed off the Works area under the ancient iron bridge. The gate had a padlock on it, still in place.

The Works shack was a World War Two–era Quonset hut, a huge half cylinder of corrugated steel tucked in under the bridge pillars. It was streaked with rust and grime that had fallen through from the bridge deck. It looked squalid and beaten-down and depressed. Nick could see why. He would be too.

"Okay," she said. "We think he has a Kimber, right?"

Nick nodded, smiled across at her in the dark of the cruiser. "You want to call for backup?"

Lacy shook her head, smiled back at him. "You'll be okay, Nick. I'm right behind you."

"Yeah. How far behind?"

"Far enough not to get your icky bits all over me when he shoots you. Got Kevlar?"

"In the back," said Nick, killing the dome light. They climbed out of the cruiser into the rain, strapped on the Kevlar, and walked carefully through the pitted gravel to the gate.

They both had their weapons out, Nick's Colt Python and Lacy's Glock 17. Their shadows rippled ahead of them under the single sodium yard light. The bridge deck was streaming water down and thundering with the traffic twenty feet above them. Nick checked the padlock. It was in place, but it wasn't closed. He slipped it off the chain and pushed the gate open.

"This hut have another exit?"

Lacy shook her head.

"Nope," she said, in a hoarse whisper. "Just this one. Shed's used for gear storage, pumps, road salt, all that maintenance shit. Stacked up all over. Right inside this door there's a narrow aisle between rows of storage racks. They fill the hut and go all the way to the roof. At the end of the aisle is the room where he was cooping. Straight shot, and if he's in there, he's basically in a box. How do you want to do this?"

Nick was looking at the curved steel walls of the hut, thinking about that Kimber .45, about the power of that huge round.

"Nothing too complicated," he said, leveling his Colt at the door. "If he's in there, we light him up with the flash, and then it's up to him. If he goes for anything, make sure it's a gun and not a ham sandwich."

Lacy nodded. This wasn't her first dance.

The window in the door was a heavy pane of rippled glass reinforced with chicken wire. The glass was filthy, and no light was showing through it. Lacy took a breath and set herself to kick the door in. Nick stopped her.

"Try the handle," he said.

She did.

It turned and the door came open about an inch. Under the roar from the bridge and the pattering rain they could hear the rhythmic chug of some kind of machine.

"Sump pump," said Lacy. "The roof leaks."

A pause, a gut check, Nick nodded at Lacy, and in they went. Lacy kicked the door right beside the handle, a solid cop kick with all her muscle behind it. The metal door slammed against a post on the right—a huge clanging racket.

Nick was past her and in, gun up, flashlight on—Lacy checked their six and all the peripherals while Nick aimed straight ahead. The beam tunneled down a lane of storage racks and hit a rumpled cot about forty feet away, a pile of clothing on it, what looked like beer or soda cans littering the floor. An empty cot.

Lacy covered him as Nick edged sideways down one side of the aisle, gunning each rack as he passed it, and then right back to the ten ring, keeping his Colt fixed on the pile of clothing and bedding. Lacy held back, waiting for somebody to pop out from a hiding spot.

Nick got to the cot, booted it over, kicked the pile of clothing. Cans rolled and clattered away. Lacy came down the aisle, checking her six, but they both had that *nobody home* feeling all cops develop. Nick turned to her.

"Get the lights, okay?"

Lacy went back, pulled a cord, and a hard blue light filled the interior. The place smelled of grease and gasoline and rust. And something human. Sweat. Fear. Blood. Water was dripping down from a crack in the rounded metal roof onto a stack of Day-Glo orange plastic cones. The concrete floor was slick and streaked with mold.

She did a quick check of the rest of the hut, lane by lane. Found a bucket in the corner that had been used as a latrine, and recently.

She got back to Nick. He was down in a squat, using the muzzle of his Colt to poke through the tangle of bedding, pizza boxes, crushed cans of Miller Lite and Red Bull. Lacy looked at the pile of clothing, the boxes, and the cans. Little slivers of material, brownish-green, lay scattered around on the floor.

Nick picked one up, held it out to Lacy. "Grass clippings."

"Nick, we don't know this is Jordan. Could be a squatter, some homeless guy?"

Her voice trailed off as her eye fell on a scrap of material. "Can you hand me that black thingy there?"

Nick fished a shirt out of the pile with the Colt barrel. A football shirt. Frederick Douglass Panthers. Number 47.

"Jordan's number."

She turned the collar back, held it out for Nick to read the sewn-in label.

J. Dutrow #47

"His mother sewed that on so he wouldn't lose it," she said, her hope for the kid fading fast, getting replaced by a slow-burning anger.

Nick used the muzzle of the Colt to flip the mattress over. The cot was an old US Army issue, olive drab canvas, stained and threadbare, wooden bones showing through the cloth. There was a tattered spiral notebook shoved in under the mattress, the kind they hand out in high school. The cover was plain light brown, covered in illegible scrawls made with various colored pens and pencils—gang tags, cartoon figures, bits of rap lyrics, but the line for the owner's name was still visible, there in big blocky print:

Jordan Kyle Dutrow Room 11C

Nick holstered the Colt, reached into his suit jacket, pulled out a pair of latex gloves, worked them on, flipped the notebook open.

The date was a few weeks back, the start of the fall school year at Frederick Douglass Polytechnic. The first few pages looked like school notes, laborious lists of assignments, test dates, class times, football practices, a list of scheduled games for the fall season.

Jordan had started out writing things down carefully, complete sentences, staying mostly inside the lines, his printing childish and heavy—the pages were grooved with the weight of his pencil—but each page was full of information: class notes, test results, references to various school trips, hopeful beginning-of-the-school-year stuff. Lacy's name showed up a few times, along with the time and date of his appointments to see her at the Probe—a brief comment on the margin:

Do her do her do her in a heartbeat!!!

"Got a fan there," said Nick. Lacy just shook her head.

Nick went on, Lacy reading over his shoulder. In September Jordan's class had visited Charleston, another weekend trip to New Orleans. Another day trip three weeks back, the

entire class went underground to learn all about the power
and water systems beneath Niceville—*nasty* seemed to be Jordan's take on that; *nasty echoes nasty smells nasty whispers*—and
there had been an overnight bus trip to Pensacola ten days
ago to see the Naval Aviation Museum. Jordan had taped in
the bus ticket and some color pages ripped out of the museum
brochure; a note beside it read:

> recruiter see him maybe be a flier a fighter jock

The pages ran on until about halfway through the book,
and then, at what looked to be about midweek, any sign of
order and attention began to disintegrate. His writing ran all
over the place, a gouging scribble carved into the pages, harsh
scrawls and indecipherable images, snatches of song lyrics, a
lot of rap imagery—

> *so high nigga I could talk to rain—don't they know my
> nigga—gutter fuckin kidnap kids—no-torious biggie small—
> throw them in the river—skull fuck skull fuck skull fucked—*

Lacy shook her head.

"Jesus, Nick, what's going on with this kid?"

"Looks like his rivets are popping. When was the last time
you saw him?"

"Monday afternoon. He was late for the meeting. Said he
had a migraine. I made some notes, asked about school, football,
checked his attendance. Coaches were happy with him—like I
said, he was MVP last Sunday against Sacred Heart—and his
teachers were medium okay with his academic performance."

Nick flipped the pages. There was more and worse as
the pages went on, until the middle of the book, where there
wasn't one legible word, just page after page of dense manic

scrawls, swirls and loops and jagged thunderbolts—the paper ripped and shredded.

There was a small gap where pages had been torn out, just ripped apart and pulled loose, and then a final page where one phrase had been written over and over again, in a mad over-written tangle so dense the page was nearly solid black.

They stared at that last page for a full minute.

"Man," said Lacy, "Looks like an artist's impression of a brain aneurysm."

"It does," said Nick. "Game changer."

"Unless he's playing us."

"You really think he is?"

A pause.

"No. No way, Nick. He's not that clever. This shit is real."

"We'll need this," said Nick, folding the notebook in half, slipping it into his jacket pocket. He stood up, sighed, brushed the dirt off his cuffs.

"We'll put a surveillance car here, see if he comes back."

"What now?" said Lacy.

"Now we go—"

His pager buzzed at him. He pulled it off his belt, looked down at it.

TIG911

Tig was Lieutenant Tyree Sutter, CO of the Belfair and Cullen County Criminal Investigation Division. Nick's boss.

911 meant *Call me now!*

Nick did. He listened for a few moments, said, "Okay, we're moving," and clicked the phone off.

Lacy saw the look on his face.

"What?"

"Jordan Dutrow. They've got him."

"Where?"

"Niceville PD has him. Other end of the Mile."

"Where they taking him?"

"They're not. Tig didn't say why."

"But, he's *alive*, right?"

"That's what they're saying. You coming?"

"Yes," she said. "I'm coming."

The Vice Principle

Niceville PD had a cruiser parked sideways across the intersection of the Mile and Scales, its roof rack churning red and
blue and white, a blurry shimmer in the rain as Nick and Lacy
came down past the MountRoyal. Traffic was at a standstill,
jammed up like hogs in a pen, horns and angry voices. Despite
the rain, people were lining the sidewalks and staring out from
upper windows all along the street. There were a few lights on
in the MountRoyal. Nick could see the shadow of a tall man
standing in a third-floor window. From the angle of his head,
he was staring down at Nick's car—a big man, broad-
shouldered, with long hair. His face was in darkness.

Something about his shape went *click* in Nick's mind, as if
he might know the guy, but he had other things to think about
right then.

They rolled up with their own lights going, and a Niceville
harness cop wrapped in a big yellow rain slicker and wearing a
stupid rain hat like a clear plastic bonnet over his cap stepped
up and leaned down into the window. It was some new kid, big
as an RV, with a broad jovial face and small blue eyes. WOJECK,
from his name tag.

"Detective Kavanaugh?"

Nick had his badge out, although the car made that a tad redundant.

"Yeah."

"Staff Sergeant Crossfire said you'd be coming. She's at the scene."

Wojeck moved his cruiser and Nick pushed the unit slowly through a cordon of uniform cops, all in yellow slickers and those stupid rain bonnets, all of them staring at the unmarked Crown Vic as it made the corner at Scales and eased into the laneway.

Fire and the EMT guys had rigged a tent over the parkette at the far end of the lane, and they had arc lights set up all over the place. The big tent glowed like it was on fire. A flatbed truck with *Niceville Utilities Commission* on the side was parked at the fence, a big John Deere generator on the truck, rumbling and popping, bright blue power lines snaking out of it and running into the tent.

Nick parked as close as he could get and they got out, heads bent, running through the rain. A large figure, dark against the light from inside the tent, was filling the entrance: Mavis Crossfire, a red-headed pale-skinned Valkyrie, in a navy blue Niceville PD uniform with the gold chevrons of a staff sergeant on her sleeves. Nick could see her face as he came up. Mavis Crossfire usually radiated easy grace and a dry wit. Not tonight.

"Hey, Nick, Lacy. Get inside, we have coffee."

They came in out of the rain. The tent completely covered the parkette, strung from the tops of the palms, held down with ropes and pegs. The EMT and fire guys had set up a kind of field kitchen, and maybe three men and two women, all in heavy-duty rain gear and rubber boots, were standing around in the crowded space, drinking coffee and staring down at a video image on a screen. Mavis led them over, cleared a path around the laptop.

The closed circuit video feed was color, shaky, full of static lines. Nick assumed, correctly, that it was video of the scene down in the tunnels. There were people down there: a Niceville cop that Nick recognized as Frank Barbetta: two EMTs, a guy and a girl, backs turned but they looked familiar: and a firefighter with a breather tank. They were in some kind of cave area—dank, rough-cut stone walls, brick floor. The cave was full of steam and harsh white light from the arc lamps.

In the middle of the screen was a big blond kid, battered but conscious, staring out into the camera. His mouth was working but no sound was coming out. His teeth were red with blood and the tendons on his neck had popped out like wires.

Frank Barbetta was crouching next to him, looked like he was trying to comfort him. The video sound was full of beeping machinery, electric hum, and muted voices, and under it a kind of high-pitched sizzling whine—faint, but cutting, like a diamond drill.

When one of the EMT techs moved out of the way of the camera, they saw that the boy was literally trapped in some kind of fissure or rock seam. His upper body was free, but from his waist down he was buried in stone. Like the rock face had opened up its mouth and bitten down on him.

Lacy looked at him for a while, her face white and her lips blue.

"Jordan Dutrow," she whispered.

"That's him," said Mavis.

Nick looked across at the hole in the middle of the saw grass ten feet away, surrounded by tarps. Power cables were running down into the shaft, and noises were rising up, the tinny crackle of radios and the echo of voices from the bottom of the shaft. That diamond-drill buzzing noise, faint but everywhere.

"So that hole's where he got in?"

"They think so," said Mavis.

She led them over to the edge of the shaft. It was the mouth of an old storm drain, as far as Nick could make out. Steam was rising up from it in a wavering ghost shape.

"What the hell is this thing?" Nick asked.

Mavis glanced in the direction of one of the guys standing by the coffee table, caught his eye.

He came over, a seamed and weather-beaten older guy wearing a faded denim work shirt and hip waders. He had a thick neck and heavy shoulders, the build of a man who has worked against the weight of things all his life.

"Guys, this is Arnie Driscoll. Arnie, this is Detective Nick Kavanaugh, and Lacy Steinert here is Jordan Dutrow's probation officer. Nick's asking about the storm shaft here. Can you fill him in? Arnie's with Water and Power."

Arnie gave them a quick appraisal.

"Forty-eight years crawling around in Niceville's basement," he said, shaking hands. "By now I'm more cave troll than human. I know every bit of what lies down there. What can I tell you folks?"

Nick looked back at the video screen and then at Arnie.

"It looks like the wall just opened up on the kid and snapped down. Like a cave-in? Is that what happened?"

Arnie frowned, working out a reply. "Yeah, in a way, it sorta is. I went down there to check it out, see if the rock face was stable. I got a good look at his . . . situation."

"And . . ."

Arnie rubbed his cheeks with big blunt hands. His wrists were as thick as live oak branches and were coated in oily dirt. His pale gray eyes stood out against his oil-stained cheeks like quartz crystals in a mudbank.

"I can give you the four-hour lecture or the two-minute lecture."

"They'll take the two-minute version," said Mavis.

"Okay. Basically the whole valley of the Tulip River, from north of the Belfair Range on down to Cap City, is a few hundred feet of red dirt piled up on a geological formation known as karst. Kentucky is almost forty percent karst, why it has so many caves, and our state is maybe fifteen percent karst. Karst means the sublayers are water-soluble, either limestone or gypsum or dolomite. We've got a gigantic limestone shelf. Which means water can carve channels in the slope because limestone is softer than other rock and porous. Most of your big cave formations in the United States are limestone caverns, sinkholes, like Crater Sink, that kind of thing, and they happen because water makes holes and channels in the rock."

"Tallulah's Wall is limestone, isn't it?" said Mavis. Tallulah's Wall was the massive cliff that towered above the northeastern part of town. Crater Sink was the thousand-foot-deep well at the top of the cliff.

"Yep. Tallulah's Wall is now a limestone cliff, but it *used* to be a flat slab. Then some geological shit happened like a zillion years ago and it got tilted up straight, so it looks like it does now. But the rest of the Niceville valley is still more or less flat, sloping away to the southeast toward the sea. About two thousand feet under us right now is a big lake, more like an underground ocean, called the Sequoyah Aquifer. This aquifer is big, starts the other side of the Belfairs, and goes all the way down below Cap City. Cap City gets most of its water from the Sequoyah Aquifer. You good so far?"

"We are," said Nick. "So Crater Sink is part of this aquifer?"

"Not in the beginning. Crater Sink is what you call a limestone sinkhole. Softer than the stone around it. Long time passes, water working on it, it slowly sinks down. Sinkholes are usually circular, like Crater Sink. Ever wonder why the water in Crater Sink never drains away?"

"Yeah," said Nick. "I have."

"Couple hundred thousand years go by, Crater Sink finally works itself all the way down to the aquifer. Breaks through, taps into it. Boom. Maybe went up like an oil gusher, maybe just filled up slow over hundreds of years. Now it's stable. Pressure from the aquifer way up the valley keeps it that way. The Sequoyah Aquifer is why we have this shaft here."

It was obvious to them by now that Arnie really didn't have a two-minute version.

"The shaft is what's left of a public works operation. A hundred years ago the city decided to tap into the Sequoyah Aquifer, just like Cap City, and use the water pressure to generate hydroelectric power. Like they do at the Hoover Dam or up there in Niagara Falls. This here shaft was part of that construction. Only things didn't turn out so good."

"Which is why we've never heard of it?" said Mavis. Arnie nodded, his mood shifting, going dark.

"Yeah. My granddad worked on it. Saw some bad things. Wouldn't say much, but you could see it in his face. There were cave-ins, hot spots, gushers, explosions—all sorts of shit. Some unstable areas right down there where your guy is now. The limestone is fractured; huge slabs of it would just drop down, like a chop saw, like an ax. Shored-up sections would just crack and come down on a crew. Lotta workers died, a few went pit crazy—"

"Pit crazy?" asked Lacy.

"Happens to coal miners, tunnel crews, people who work deep down in the earth or inside those pressurized hulls they used to build the Brooklyn Bridge foundations. Maybe it's the atmospheric pressure, like the bends that divers get. On this job here, eleven different guys went pit crazy, went home after the shift and killed their families. Buncha other workers simply disappeared, like they just got swallowed up. After a while, end of the First World War, the city said hey, fuck this, too much grief and trouble. Everything got sealed up. Looks like your guy down there, Dutrow, he managed to get into the system somehow. Poor bastard, no way he should have known about this old shaft—"

"He was on a school tour," said Lacy. "Through the system. Maybe he learned about it then."

"I heard about that. Dumb-as-dirt idea. These old tunnels, the water mains, there's no way they should be dragging a bunch of high school kids through all that. Too damned dangerous."

"He didn't like it," said Lacy. "He thought it was nasty. Full of whispers."

Arnie gave her a sharp look. "He *said* that?"

"Wrote it, actually. In his school notebook."

"Well, there are places down there, you hear sounds, like whispering, hissing, and there's always this high-pitched whine, real faint. It was there when my granddad was working here. He said the trick was not to listen, because if you did you'd hear, like, words, voices and shit."

"Do you?" asked Nick. Arnie seemed to go inward, thinking about that.

"No. Crazy talk. People like to scare themselves with bullshit stories. Ghosts and crap like that. But the kid is right, about it being a nasty place to wander around in. Kid must have stepped into a fissure, a crack in the walls, some kind of weak spot ready to drop, a big slab of rock breaks away, comes down on him, and now you got what you got down there."

"Which is what?" asked Lacy.

Arnie's smile went away completely and he shook his head. "You got a big strong guy stuck under a sharp-edged slab of limestone. And it's slowly cutting him in half."

Nick and Lacy took that in.

"They going to get him out?"

"Oh, they'll get him out. Just not in one piece. That's why there's nobody down there with a jackhammer. Once he's gone, we'll shore up the cave and chip his body out of there, but there's no rush. What's keeping him alive is *the pinch*. Seen it before. Nothing to be done. Too bad, but there it is."

Arnie gave them each a significant look, his face solemn, and then he walked away. Mavis let the silence run, out of respect for the image they all had in their minds.

"Okay. Now, what do you want to do, Nick?"

"Can he talk?"

"Yeah. The thing he's caught in, like Arnie said, it's pinched him just below the waist. The EMTs have doped him up, but if they manage to get him out of that cleft—hole, gap, whatever—they're pretty sure that blood and viscera will pour out of him like from a tipped-over bait bucket. He'll be gone in a couple of heartbeats."

Nick had seen something like that with Special Forces in Basra, after an Iranian IED had flipped over an Abrams, trapping one of the tank crew halfway out of the turret.

He looked at Lacy. "I gotta go talk to him."

Lacy glanced at the shaft and then back at Nick. "You're gonna go down *there*?"

"Yeah. I am."

"Nick," said Mavis in a warning tone. "He's not gonna be up to answering any questions. And you heard Arnie. It's not safe down there. If you want to try to talk to him, Frank Barbetta has his radio. It's not working real good—some kind of radio interference; it's all buzz and static—but you could try."

Nick took that in, registered it, noted it, filed it, and shook his head.

"No. He's gonna die down there. I want to see him face-to-face."

Lacy saw that he was dead serious. She swore softly to herself. "Okay. Me too."

Mavis just shook her head and looked away.

Getting down there was ugly, even with the protective vests and boots the fire guys lent them. The rungs on the shaft ladder were slick and wet, and as they got farther down the shaft, the steam and the smells got worse. It was like crawling down the throat of a big carnivore.

By the time they reached the bottom of the shaft and stepped out onto a rocky shelf under an arch of stone like an underground cathedral, they were dripping with sweat and fighting claustrophobia.

They looked around, thinking that they had reached the belly of the beast. The air hissing down from the surface sounded like an animal breathing, and the pumps made a deep and steady heartbeat sound. The effect was . . . unsettling.

"Jeez," said Lacy. "Now I know how Jonah felt. They ought to set up tours, scare the hell out of a bunch of visiting Shriners. No wonder Jordan thought this place was nasty."

"He got that right. I had no idea this was all down here," said Nick, who was a newcomer to Niceville, having married into the town only a few years back. His hometown was Los Angeles.

"I did. The People knew about these caves back in the old days."

"They use them?"

"Hell no. We were Cherokee, Nick, not those knuckle-dragging Choctaw bozos. My people never came near this shit. Let's get this over with, okay."

At the far end of this cathedral space there was an entrance to a long tunnel that had been carved out of the limestone. A row of ancient bulbs inside wire cages led off into the dark, shedding a dim flickering glow, but they could see a cluster of halogen lamps about a hundred yards down the tunnel, and the yellow slicker of the firefighter and the blue jackets of the two EMT techs. Lacy looked at Nick, tilted her head, hesitating. Nick gave her a sideways grin.

"Hey," he said. "I'm right behind you."

Lacy shook her head, said something under her breath, and walked into the tunnel.

The roof was maybe two feet overhead, and the floor was lined with worn bricks slick with mold. The cutting was tall enough to stand up in, but for some reason they crouch-walked all the way down to the site, their boots echoing up and down the walls.

The crackle of radios got closer, and they could hear the murmur of voices, and that high-pitched buzzing whine was still there, faint but cutting, far out at the high end of hearing.

It sounded like a background radiation, the sound the universe makes, a continual stream of white noise and static and hiss. It worried Nick, but he didn't tell Lacy. Frank Barbetta saw them coming, pushed himself off the wall and came forward. He had taken his uniform shirt off and his white tee was soaked.

"Nick, Lacy. Hell of a thing."

"How'd you find him?" Nick asked.

Barbetta told them about the movement in the saw grass, coming in to look, finding the tunnel open. "I could hear something, sounded like an animal in pain, trapped down here. I called in Fire and the EMT truck. When they got here, I went down with them—"

"You *hate* tunnels," said Nick, who knew Barbetta pretty well. Barbetta flashed a brief grin, shrugged his shoulders.

"What're you gonna do? Everybody was standing around, staring at me, waiting for me to do something manly. I couldn't get out of it."

"Could have peed yourself and fainted."

"Nah, that might work for you Special Ops pussies. Us First Responders have to man up for real. Well, anyway," he said, cutting a quick glance over at the EMT team working on Dutrow, "I followed the noises he was making. And there he was, stuck halfway into the rock face. I had to go all the way back up to the surface to call it in on account of the radios don't work down here."

"Mavis said they were screwed up. What's wrong?"

Barbetta shrugged.

"I don't know. These new radios are supposed to work anywhere. Maybe some kinda low-level radioactive thing. You can get through, but the signal has a lot of . . . interference. Sounds like a dental drill or something. Hurts the ears. Anyway, I went back up and got onto Tig Sutter—we knew you'd wanna know."

"Is he conscious?"

"In and out. They've doped him up. He comes and goes. Right now he's gone."

"You find anything on him? Cash, maybe a big Kimber forty-five?"

Barbetta shook his head.

"Not on the part we can see. Maybe if it was in his pocket or something. It might be under that slab of rock sticking into him."

Nick looked over Barbetta's shoulder at the two EMTs tending to Dutrow. He knew them—Barb Fillion and her partner, Kikki . . . what? Something Hispanic. They worked a lot of the bad ones, and Nick was often there for the bad ones.

Dutrow's head and shoulders were all that was visible. The rest of his upper torso was covered up in red EMT blankets. There was an IV of blood running into the pile, and another of what looked like saline.

The fire guy, an older man with white hair and a grim expression, was standing clear, watching, nothing for him to do, but he was still there. He looked over at Nick, shook his head slowly. Nick knew him from around, remembered his name after a moment, Hennessey, Jack Hennessey, a captain in the NFD. Another Black Irish Mick just like him. Nick nodded, Hennessey gave him a WTF expression, lifting his shoulders, and Nick went back to the boy stuck into the wall.

Dutrow's eyes were closed, his lips blue and slack, his long blond hair streaked with blood and sweat. His breathing was a ragged rasping sound that they could hear over the beeping and thudding of the EMT gear. Now and then he'd arch and moan, his neck muscles popping up like cords, and then he'd subside again.

"Sweet Jesus," said Lacy, looking at him, the words echoing off the walls. At the sound of her voice Dutrow's eyes flickered open and he picked her out of the shadows. His lips moved.

Barb Fillion, the EMT tech, her young face bone white, leaned in, listened, and then she looked over at Lacy.

"He wants you," she said.

Lacy stepped in close, went down on one knee. Nick followed behind.

Fillion spoke to Lacy, a muted whisper.

"His signs are dropping. He's full of morphine so he's not suffering. Not too much, anyway. Are you his mom?"

Lacy shook her head, staring into Dutrow's eyes. They were packed with fear and pain. When he opened his mouth, a bubble of blood ran down his chin. The EMT wiped it off, touched his cheek, got out of Lacy's way.

Dutrow tried again.

"Miss Steinert . . . my mom."

"You want her to come, Jordan?"

He managed to shake his head.

"No . . . no. Please, no. You got to keep her away. You all got to keep away from me. Leave me alone down here."

"We can't do that, Jordan. We're gonna get you out of here—"

"No you're not. I know what's goin' on. These people think I'm out, but I can still hear what they're saying. I can't feel anything below my hips. I'm about chopped in two. I can feel the rock deep in my gut."

He closed his eyes, flinched, and gasped, reacting to something that seemed to go through him like an electric shock. His eyes filled up and tears started running. His voice was tight and choked.

"No mom. No Cheryl. And please tell them to shut that camera off. My mom sees this shit, she'll die. You gotta make sure Mom doesn't see no pictures, video, in the news, shit like that. Please, Miss Steinert. You got to promise me."

"I do," she said, her voice tight. "I do promise." She watched his eyes move up, widen, and saw the recognition in them.

He was looking at Nick.

"I know you," he said. "You're the guy who pulled that kid out of a grave couple years ago."

"Yeah," said Nick, who wasn't in a mood to reminisce about the Rainey Teague kidnapping. "I need to talk to you, Jordan."

Jordan closed his eyes again, seemed to go somewhere else. Lacy and Nick got the impression he was listening, but to what?

In the background the techs were silent. Barbetta's radio crackled—a burst of white noise so high-pitched it hurt—and he shut it off. Barb Fillion reached over and killed the camera. Kikki Something Hispanic flicked the monitor off and the beeping stopped. Hennessey shifted from one foot to another, made the sign of the cross. Quiet came down, the deathwatch.

You could feel it enter the cave and stand there, patient, silent, like a limo driver waiting for a passenger to come down the Arrivals staircase, he's holding a sign, says DUTROW.

The only sound was Dutrow's breathing, shallow and rapid, and under that, the high-pitched buzzing whine, right at the outer edge of hearing. It seemed to come right out of the rock face, out of the stone itself.

Dutrow opened his eyes, fixed on Nick. "I know why you're here. I know what I got to say. I got to confess. We did those people. Mr. and Mrs. Thorsson."

"We?" said Nick, sharp and edgy.

"Yeah . . . us. *Her. She* . . . It was *her* idea, but she needed me to do it."

"Who's *she*?" said Nick, closing in. "Your cousin? Your girlfriend? Who is *she*?"

Dutrow gave his head a shake, winced. "Not like that . . . She's in my head . . . and she can *sting* me. In the skull. In my brain. Like a wasp. Like a drill. *Hurts*."

He jerked, a spasm that was almost a convulsion, and that electric pain flashed across his features. He struggled against it, caught his breath, focused on Nick again. "She's doing it now. She doesn't want me . . . to be talking . . . but I still can . . . The morphine helps—she stings but it's . . . I can deal with it."

Lacy looked up at Nick.

"What's he *talking* about, Nick?"

"So it was *both* of you," said Nick, after giving her a warning glance. "The *two* of you did the Thorssons?"

A quick glance at Lacy—a law enforcement officer, a legal witness to a dying declaration. She got it at once, nodded, said nothing.

Dutrow nodded.

"We did them. I'm sorry . . . so sorry . . . Should have fought her . . . I tried, I'm sorry."

Nick was still, seeing the Thorsson crime scene in his head. There was only one killer, that much had been obvious.

"The *two* of you?"

"Yeah . . . She gets . . . she *needs* it. She'll *sting* you until you . . . give it to her . . ."

"And who is this *thing* in your head? A woman? Give me her name, Jordan."

Dutrow shook his head. "Not like that. No name. Not a woman. But a *she*. A bitch. The *bitch* in my skull," Dutrow said, and then he flinched, a flicker of agony arcing across his features. "There . . . she's stinging right now . . . She . . . *likes* it. What we did to those people. She tells you what she wants and then . . . she *feeds* on it . . . I came down here . . . to get her out of my head. She got in when we did the storm drain tour . . . with the school . . ."

Nick flashed back to Dutrow's notebook. "How did she get in?" he asked, in a softer voice. "Tell us how she gets in your head?"

"Starts with . . . *whispers* . . . You think it's just that noise . . . I hear it now . . . it's everywhere down here . . . just that buzzy sound . . . but then you hear the *words* in it . . . Soon as you start to hear the words . . . soon as you *listen* . . . you're done . . . She got into my head . . . She's talking to me . . . right now . . . You should all get out of here—all of you— she's . . . thinking about all of you right now . . ."

His voice faded, and a silent tremor ran through everyone there. They could all hear that electric buzz—*no, the kid was just crazy*. Dutrow's eyes stayed on Nick, and his expression changed. Shock. Surprise. A sudden realization.

"You know! You *know*. I can see it in your face. You know about *her*."

Nick shook his head, but Dutrow bored in, a sudden rush of power. Death was coming. He struggled with it, blood running over his lips, his red teeth showing, but the skull face was rising up out of the skin. His lips worked, a sound coming from his throat now, like gravel running down a tin pipe. His eyes stayed on Nick.

"She . . . she says she *knows* you. She says she *knows* your wife. She knows about that kid, got kidnapped—"

He went inward, seemed to listen, opened his mouth,

struggling for the words, fighting for them as if something was trying to choke them off.

"She knows about the *mirror* . . . in your house . . . she *knows*—"

Then he just . . . stopped, like a clock stops.

Nothing changed.

There was no sigh, no shudder, no last breath. His expression was the same, his mouth open, eyes focused on Nick, the next word right *there* . . . but he was dead.

Nick stepped away, put his back up against the wall. Lacy stood up, came over. He shifted his attention to her, an accusing glare. "Lacy, did you talk to this asshole about Rainey Teague? About the mirror?"

Lacy got pretty hot pretty fast. "Nick, *everybody* in Niceville knows that story! The mirror in Moochie's window. Rainey going missing. Where you found him. The coma. It was all over town. Jeez, Nick!"

"She's right, Nick," said Barbetta, shocked at his anger. "They're *still* talking about it. This sick little fuck was playing you. The voice in his head, that's complete *horseshit*. He went out lying and . . . and fuck him. It's FIDO, Nick. That's all this is."

Fuck It, Drive On.

But Nick wasn't hearing them.

Everybody knew about the *mirror*. But nobody other than Kate knew where it was *now*. In their house, locked away in an upstairs closet, wrapped in a blue blanket.

He was trying to work this out when Barbetta's radio crackled into life. It was Mavis Crossfire, up top, and although the static was brutal, what she was saying was clear enough.

"Frank, tell Nick to get back up here."

Barbetta keyed TALK. "What's up?"

"Got another ten-forty-three."

A ten-forty-three was a murder reported. Barbetta had everyone's full attention.

"Where?"

"One three two nine Palisade Drive. The Glades. Multiple vics. Tell Nick, Tig is saying it looks just like the Thorsson killings."

Barbetta turned to say something to Nick, but he was already moving. Lacy hesitated, caught up in the chase, but torn.

Nick stopped and looked at her, leaving it up to her.

Finally she shook her head. "No. I gotta stay with the body. He was my client. He went wrong, but he started out good. I owe it to his family."

Nick looked down at Dutrow's dead face, glanced across the stone slab that had cut him in half, came back to Lacy.

"You're a true heart, Lacy, and I admire that. But there's only one good thing you can say about Jordan Dutrow, and we all know what it is."

Charlie Danziger Fails to Sit
Quietly in His Room

More sirens, and flashing red and blue lights flickering all over his ceiling. Danziger sighed, swore, and got the hell out of bed. He reached the window in time to see a big black Chevy Suburban with Niceville PD markings racing north on the Mile, lights and sirens, followed closely by a navy blue Crown Vic with its strobes on. He looked at the clock on the bedside table: 2:17.

This now officially qualified as a lousy fucking night. He got up, looked at the bottle of pinot on the dresser, and decided that the last thing he needed right now was more wine.

What he needed was coffee—strong, black, and lots of it—and he was pretty sure the MountRoyal did not do room service.

He got dressed—the usual jeans, blue cowboy boots. As he was pulling the boots on something shimmered in his memory pool; he reached for it but it was gone like a fish in a stream. Got a fresh white shirt out of the closet, checked his face in the mirror while he was buttoning it up—yes, he was visible in the mirror, so there was that, anyway. He pulled his range jacket off the hanger, felt the weight of it, patted it, and pulled out a Colt Anaconda revolver.

It was fully loaded, and the sheen of rigorous maintenance rippled over the steel. It felt real fine in his hand, as familiar as his navy blue boots. As he hefted it another memory fish shimmered in that pool, but this one he caught.

An old barn deep in a forest, holes in the roof and sunlight streaming down sideways through a haze of straw dust . . . antique tin signs all over for White Rose Gasoline and Virginia Sweet Leaf Tobacco and a blue sign shaped like an owl that says Wise Potato Chips . . . the smell of bat shit and old wood and motor oil . . . he's sitting on an oil drum or something . . . there's another guy in the barn with him—hard-looking younger guy with a flame-scar on the side of his neck . . . it feels like they're waiting for something . . . then the cell phone rings and he picks it up . . . it's Coker on the other end . . . he listens to Coker talk for a while . . . hangs up, and says to the guy with him . . . go look outside, see if there's someone coming . . . the guy gets up and goes to look through the cracks in the barn board—Merle Zane, that's the guy's name—and while Merle Zane has his back turned, Danziger takes out a pistol and shoots him in the back . . . guy slams into the barn board—breaks through and goes down on his back . . . comes up with a nine-mill and starts firing back through the boarding . . . holes punching through . . . gunfire echoing all around . . . he's firing back at Merle . . . and he feels a round thump into his chest . . . last he sees is Merle Zane with a bullet hole in his back running off into a big pine forest . . . but the main thing here is there's a hole in his own chest and Jesus Christ, it stings like a bitch . . .

He touched the sore spot on his chest. Felt sort of like it could be from getting shot, but why did he have two of them?

Okay. Anyway, two clues here. Merle Zane and a barn in the woods, a really old barn that stinks of bat shit and motor oil.

So maybe a garage? Out in the country?

That would have to be the Belfair Pike General Store and Saddlery. Route 311, couple miles into the Belfair Range, down a rutted lane that leads into the forest, maybe a half mile in.

Was that where it happened?

Something to work with.

So why did Coker want me to shoot a guy in the back? That's not a Coker thing at all. Coker likes to kill people—I mean, who doesn't? But he likes to see the expression on their faces while he does it. That's why he was a good police sniper.

Questions are multiplying here.

So go out and get some answers.

Danziger gathered his stuff together and went out the door, feeling that maybe some progress was being made here, that he had a mission to accomplish, which was to stitch himself back into a complete person with all his memories intact, right up to how he ended up in the MountRoyal Hotel on a rainy night in Niceville with no idea who the hell he was. First thing to do, go find Coker and have a chat.

No, *first* thing, get a coffee.

When the Very First Swallow Came Back to Capistrano, Did Anybody Notice?

It wasn't hard to find 1329 Palisade Drive, because you could see the flashing lights of the emergency vehicles arcing across the low-lying cloud cover. Nick followed Mavis Crossfire's big black Suburban around a shady curve that ended in the intersection of Palisade and Flamingo Way. The Morrison house was right there, lit up by the strobes of six or seven Niceville black-and-whites. There was also an EMT ambulance parked a little way down, the techs sitting in the cab drinking coffee: nobody alive in the house, nothing to do but write it up and wait for another call. The rain had fallen away to a pale descending mist floating in the air. It gave everything a soft-focus look and bleached out all the colors, so the scene looked like an old black-and-white movie.

Harness cops were milling about, and they had set up a yellow-tape cordon to keep the neighbors—all of whom seemed to be up and watching from their lawns and porches—at a distance.

There was an old Mercedes-Benz 600, dark green and big as a tank, parked more or less in the middle of Palisade Drive, a huge black man in a long blue trench coat over a charcoal gray suit, pale gray shirt, and scarlet tie, standing by it and talking into his cell phone. They both pulled up, Mavis in the Suburban and Nick in his Crown Vic, and the big guy shut his phone down, scowling a bit as he waited for Mavis and Nick to get out of their rides.

"Nick, Mavis."

"Tig," said Mavis, snapping open an umbrella as big as a bivouac tent and holding it over them.

Tyree "Tig" Sutter, the CO of the Belfair and Cullen County Criminal Investigation Division, was a plus-size barrel of bone and muscle with a voice that should have been coming out of a pagan idol. He shook his head, drops of water running down his shaved skull, glancing at Nick, giving him a quick smile before his face went back to grim.

"I hear you two settled the Thorsson thing."

Mavis shook her head. "I was just a bystander. Lacy Steinert and Nick here ran it down."

"Kid's dead, right?" said Tig.

"Hard to get any deader," said Nick.

"I heard a cave-in?"

"Looks like," said Mavis.

"So what do we have? A dying declaration?"

Nick filled him in on the essentials, leaving out the bullshit about the voices in his head making him do it. Mavis, who hadn't heard any of that, agreed with the basics. Tig took it in.

"Man. Nothing on Dutrow's sheet adds up to that scene at the Thorssons. Lacy Steinert have anything to say about it?"

"Yeah. She saw him last Monday, said he was a bit ragged but seemed okay. His team played Sacred Heart on Sunday— beat them pretty soundly and he made MVP. He did complain about migraines."

Tig cocked his head. "Migraines? So maybe a head thing?"

"Maybe," said Nick. "We better get the ME to look for aneurysms, any kind of neural damage."

"Toxicology too," said Mavis. "He was a lifter, so maybe something steroidal?"

"I'll see they do that," said Tig. "Nice work, Nick."

"Trail was a mile wide," he said.

"Maybe. But good work anyway. Mavis, are you in on this thing here?"

"Up to you," she said. "CID ranks on multiple homicides, but I'd like to ride along for a while."

Tig looked at her. "You're not gonna enjoy it."

Mavis tilted her head, gave him a thin smile.

"You've been inside?" Tig's expression hardened. "Yeah, I have."

"You want us to take it from here?" Nick asked. Tig was a great CO, but he was closing in on retirement and had seen more crime scenes than both of them put together. Something vital had gone out of him with each one.

Tig looked at the house, sighed heavily. "Yeah. Fuck it. I'm out of here. Been one hell of a week. Yesterday morning Lucille Mills over in The Chase hears a noise on her front porch, goes to see what it is, finds her husband Barnaby asleep on the gliding rocker."

"Why's that weird?" said Mavis.

"Barnaby Mills went missing eleven years ago," said Nick. "One of the one hundred seventy-nine stranger abductions that Boonie Hackendorff is always banging the drum about."

That Mavis remembered.

Every law enforcement officer from Sallytown down to Cap City knew about Niceville's abnormally high rate of SAs—stranger abductions. A hundred and seventy-nine of them, and all of them still listed as unsolved. The name Barnaby Mills rang a bell, faint but clear—a *ping*.

Mavis shook her head. "I think I remember now. What'd the guy have to say for himself?"

"Said he could use some bacon and eggs," said Tig with a

weary smile. "Other than that, total amnesia, or so he's saying. Okay, I'm gonna leave this rat fuck with you two. I hate these things. I'm just . . . dog bone *tired* of them."

"We'll take it, Tig," said Mavis. "Go home, get some sleep. You look like hell."

Tig smiled at her. "Yeah, I saw myself in the bathroom mirror outside the girl's room. Nick, I'll give you anything you need. You called Kate yet?"

Tig had been the one who talked Nick into leaving Special Forces and coming on as a cop in Niceville, but Kate had been the one who talked Tig into doing it. Tig had never regretted it.

"No, I hope she's asleep. She was down in Cap City with Rainey."

"More tests?"

"Yeah. Neurology Wing at Sorrows. Dr. Lakshmi wanted a full rundown on him."

Tig left that alone.

An attendance officer from Rainey's school had gone into the Tulip River a while back. Tig was convinced that Rainey had put her there.

But hey, the kid had "medical issues."

"Okay. Give her my love. About this scene here, I called you in because it looked connected to the Thorsson killings. But the timeline . . . I don't know."

"Dutrow would have had to go straight from here to that storm drain," said Nick. "We'll get a time of death from the CSI boss—"

"She's in there now," said Tig.

"If it fits, maybe we can tie this to Dutrow."

"Jesus," said Tig. "I hope so. I don't want two of these assholes running around."

Is It Okay to Staple Bunny Ears
on Little Kids?

Florida State Highway Patrol had jurisdiction on the beaches this far south of St. Augustine, and they showed up about twenty minutes after Coker called 911: four cars, black under tan, flashers going, though no sirens, streaming past behind the house and going down the shore road.

No sirens because they liked to make an unexpected appearance at out-of-control beach parties. With the element of surprise, you saw a lot of interesting stuff, especially around the pool. Twyla stood at the kitchen window and watched them flashing by. The bass beat was still rattling the dishes in the cupboards, but that wouldn't go on a lot longer.

She smiled to herself—doing a good thing wasn't something she did often, so when she did, she savored it—poured two glasses of Barolo, and walked back out to the main room. Coker was sitting in the dark smoking a cigarette, staring out at the surf rolling in, the stars gliding above.

Twyla sat down next to him, handed him a glass. "You still mad, hon?"

Coker drank a bit of the wine, set it down on the coffee table. "No. Not mad. Worried. They'll stop in, after they've rousted the place, to give us a report. I'm not real happy about getting looked over by the Florida Highway Patrol."

"Coker, you've been Morgan Sinclair around here for ten years, coming out here every chance you got to build up that ID. And it worked. The cops already *know* who you are, a retired banker, so they're not suddenly going to start thinking differently about you. You've been a summer resident here for longer than most of these baby troopers have been on the job. Anyway, they're not going to drop by this late. And if they do, I'll talk to them. I'll say you're asleep. Okay?"

"Yeah, well, we'll see. Maybe we should go for a long run, just be out of here for a while. We could drive down to the Keys, maybe take the boat over to Freeport—"

Twyla was not fond of the boat. To her a long voyage across open water, even in a fifty-foot Hinckley Talaria, was your punishment for using a stapler to fasten bunny ears on little kids for the school's spring pageant.

"It would take us two days to get the boat ready, and Freeport is three hundred miles away. Couldn't we just get some scuba gear and hide out in the bottom of the swimming pool for a few days?"

That made Coker smile, which made her smile, because Coker wasn't himself these days, which was like saying that a wolf wasn't enjoying his kills, was just sort of picking at them and going all Hamlet about life in the wild.

"Coker, you're not you these days. Is it The Situation," she said, giving it the capitals.

The bass beat snapped off, and now there was only the boom of the surf and Dead Can Dance coming from the Bose, and far in the distance the stentorian crackle of a police bullhorn.

Peace had come back to the Atlantic shore.

"No, it's not 'The Situation,' Twyla. It's those assholes back in Cap City."

"You mean Boonie and the feds?"

"Hell no. Not Boonie. Not Nick or Mavis or Reed, either. They were just doing their jobs. I have no regrets, except for Charlie. I *like* my life. I don't do regrets, Twyla. Neither do you."

This was true. Charlie Danziger had once observed that Twyla Littlebasket had larceny in her the way alligators have teeth.

"Then what is this stuff about Cap City?"

Coker sighed, put his head back, closed his eyes. "It's what that Harvill Endicott mutt did to Charlie. And that Delores Maranzano broad, sitting there in her condo on Fountain Square, fat and happy—"

"We're fat and happy too," said Twyla. "Well, maybe not fat."

Coker was quiet.

Twyla could hear him brooding, though, and it worried her. Coker had a taste for random violence.

"Know what," she said, putting her glass down and slipping out of what little she had on, "you're right. We need a road trip. Let's do that. Let's go down to the Keys."

Coker moved to the left, giving her some room to maneuver. "You mean, like right now?"

Twyla smiled down at him. "No, Coker. Not right now."

If You Do Have to Get Out of the Car,
Then Don't Go Up the Stairs

First thing that hit Nick and Mavis when they came in the front door at 1329 Palisade was the smell. It wasn't meat or blood or fluids, although that was all there. It was the air in the house. It was *hot* and it smelled . . . baked.

There was a body in the front door, a round little guy, down on his back, his arms splayed out. His pants were down around his ankles. His legs were rubbery blue and covered in fine brown hairs. He had a black handle sticking out of his right eye socket. It took a second for Nick to get that it was the sort of handle you'd find on a round file or an ice pick. It was jammed up to the hilt in the victim's eye. There wasn't a lot of blood, so Nick figured it had gone all the way back to the guy's cortex and just shut him off like a switch. A hit like that wasn't an easy thing to do. It required arm strength and commitment. A whole lot of commitment.

There was a CSI tech in a white jumpsuit, a woman, she looked maybe twelve, doing something unseemly inside the guy's shorts and Mavis, who hated that sort of thing, looked away at the rest of the ground floor and then moved out into the main room, taking it in. Nick didn't know the tech's name and since she was wearing those all-white head-to-toe sperm suits the CSI people have to wear, all he had to go on was her face, a sort of cute cheerleader face, except for the sad eyes. She looked up at Nick, sat back on her heels, glanced at the readout on a digital thermometer. "Body temp is still too warm for a time of death, Detective."

Nick shrugged his suit jacket off, put it over his arm. "It's this heat. Maybe the killer ran the furnace setting way up to make the TOD impossible."

She shook her head. "Furnace wasn't on. This heat came in with the killer or killers. We have no idea how it was done, but for a while it was hot enough in here to melt the candles on their dining room table. And this handle, stuck in the vic's eye there, that grip isn't painted black, it's burnt black. It was red hot when it went into the guy's eye. Roasted his brain like a red-hot poker."

She said this with a degree of professional appreciation. Nick realized that CSI work could get pretty damn dull. At least this was . . . *interesting*.

"What have we got here, Miss . . ."

She stood up, a lithe lift only the young can pull off, removed her latex glove, offered Nick her hand. "I'm Sergeant Dakota Riley, Detective Kavanaugh. I've heard good things about you. Nice to finally meet you."

Nick shook her hand, thinking *Dear God, a sergeant at twelve years old.*

"Good to meet you, Sergeant. I'm surprised we haven't met before."

"I've only been on the force for six months."

"You made sergeant in six months?"

She smiled, shook her head. "I was with the state patrol in Alabama for ten years, based in Montgomery. I wanted to live in a sleepy southern town with live oaks and Spanish moss. Niceville offered me a job, said I could keep my rank, so here I am."

"What'd you do in Alabama?"

"Pretty much what I'm doing here. I trained at Quantico. Agency offered me a job, but I didn't want to be just another dweeb lawyer with a gun. I like forensic work."

"Even this?"

Something moved across her face, sadness, regret, and Nick got the idea that there had been some kind of loss, something bad had happened, and she had come to Niceville to forget it.

"It is what it is. Once guys like you catch the bastard, we can help you send him to hell."

"Lot of younger people think the death penalty is too harsh."

She got a flat-eyed look. "For what was done in this house, strapping the guy down on a board and slowly skinning him alive would not be harsh enough."

Nick could see she meant it. "I guess I'd better see it for myself. Can you lay this out for me?"

She stepped away from the corpse, led Nick into the living room, where Mavis was standing, looking hot and sick. The main floor was open plan. No vestibule. No foyer. If you were through the front door, you were in the house. A very nice house, with a big green leather sofa and love seat, a large oriental carpet in jewel tones, soft lighting, real oils on the walls, a huge Samsung flat-screen, the silky feel of ready money and lots of it.

Now all in ruins and everybody dead.

Mavis had loosened her coat, shrugged it off. She nodded as Sergeant Riley came up. The CSI tech pulled her hoodie back, showing a crown of golden curls, slick with sweat.

She took a breath, organizing. "Okay. We have four people in the house. Doug Morrison, the father, he's the guy in the hall, he went first, we're thinking, because from a tactical point of view in a home invasion—which this feels like—you take out the guy first. You're making a point, you're dominating the situation, showing you mean business. Next vic was the kid, Jared, he's over there by the wall. Every bone in his body has been broken. Not just broken. Crushed. Pulverized. When we rolled him it was like rolling a bag of jelly. I think he was just . . . thrown. You can see the impact where he hit the wall. Here, take a look."

She led them over to a corner of the living room. There was a little kid. His body was in a crumpled heap, back twisted into a sickeningly wrong angle. He might have been a cute kid. It was hard to tell without a face. A CSI tech was bagging the kid's hands. He looked up at them, sweat streaming down his forehead, his eyes buggy under his horn-rimmed specs. He pulled his mask down.

It was Dave Seth, a young Niceville patrol guy who'd gone over to Crime Scene after watching too many episodes of *CSI Miami*. It had come as a big shock to him when he found out that the CSI guys didn't even have guns and were generally considered hapless weenie losers by all the real cops.

"Hey, Sarge, you believe this shit?"

Mavis was trying to. "What happened to the kid?"

Seth looked at Sergeant Riley, who ranked him. This was her scene.

"Fill 'em in, Dave," she said.

Seth looked down at the body, still holding one of the kid's hands. He lifted the kid's arm and the way it hung there, limp, like a stuffed sock, told them a lot. "Whole body's like that. One way or the other, every bone in this boy's body has been broken."

He pointed to the wall above the kid. It was a hard corner, the wall made of brick, painted a soft creamy white. You could see the impact point where the kid had struck the wall, and the blood and tissue train as he slid down it, leaving a trail.

"He was thrown across the room, far as we can tell. Picked

up and hurled. By somebody so strong that if I ever meet him, I want to be in a Humvee when I do. The face hit first, which pretty much destroyed it. Some of his face is still on that wall. What's here, still in his skull, that's all orbital process, teeth, tongue, jawbone, what's left of it—"

Nick, sensing a lecture, cut in. "You figure the bones went then?"

Seth shook his head. "Nope." He touched the bloody ruin where the kid's face used to be. "See the way the blood spray works, on the floor here. Kid's heart was still going a mile a minute when he bounced off that wall. What I mean, he was still alive. Broken neck, maybe, but still alive."

"So . . . then what?" asked Mavis, trying to keep her last meal where it was. Seth deferred to Riley, who seemed to know her stuff.

She bent down, tapped the kid's bloody body. "See these indents? These impact points? There are literally hundreds of them, all over his body. Somebody stood over him and beat him into a pulp with some kind of tool. I'm thinking, from the rounded pattern of the impact, something like a ball peen hammer or the kind of tool you use on sheet metal—"

"Like car-body repair tools," said Nick.

"Yes. They would work. You can see the spatter pattern all over here, and up there." She stood up, pointed to the ceiling. There were long sweeping trails of blood spray in a feathery pattern radiating outward, maybe fifteen or twenty different streaks. The same blood-spray pattern was on the walls and on the carpeting. They could all see it in their minds, the hammer coming down, the frenzy of the attack, the hammer coming back up, soaked in blood, the spray flying off as the hammer came back down again . . . and again . . . and again.

"Jesus," said Mavis. "The guy must have got it all over himself. He would have looked like a Jackson Pollock painting."

Seth and Riley were looking at her. She looked back at them.

"Okay. *Insensitive*," she said, doing the ironic air-quote thing. Nick had to grin in spite of, maybe because of, the horror.

"You said four?"

"Yes. The mom, Ellen, she's down the hall."

They left Seth to his work and followed Riley out of the living room and down a short hallway lined with paintings—oils, the Southwest mainly, all of them well done, full of light and the sweep of desert and high plains.

At the end of the hall a female was lying faceup, fully clothed, in mom jeans and a blousy pink calico shirt. She was laid out on the terra-cotta tiles, her eyes black pools of bloody tissue. The skin of her face looked roasted. She lay at the entrance to a large well-appointed kitchen, stainless steel and copper and oak and brass, and beyond that a door into what might have been a sunroom or a lanai. It was dark, but they could see ferns and palms in the light from a backyard lamp.

Riley stopped at the woman's body, knelt down beside it, pointed to the knees of the woman's jeans, and then to a trail of bloody streaks that ran down the hallway from the living room. "She has blood in her hair, but it's not hers, I don't think. I think she came down the hall from the kitchen—the dishwasher is still open; maybe she was putting dishes away—when she heard what was going on in the living room. She came down the hall, saw what was happening. She turns, runs, but she only gets this far when whoever, whatever, came through that front door—it caught up to her, grabbed her by the hair. Fingers bloody from what he was doing to the kid, that's the blood in her hair, he brought her to her knees and then he . . . dragged her back out to the living room. There's fibers from the living room carpet embedded in the jean fabric here and on her shoe tips, her calves, and the blood trails out there back up this . . . scenario. We think the guy dragged her around to look at the bodies . . . and then he brought her back here."

"Her eyes?" said Mavis.

"Gone. No tool marks around the orbits. If I had to testify—and I sure hope I get to, 'cause this guy really needs to get caught and tried and executed—I'd say the guy used his thumbs. You can see bloody fingertip marks on her temples, so he would have held her head with his fingers and used his thumbs to—"

Mavis said, "Got it, okay?" and looked away, swallowing hard.

Riley watched her, cool but sympathetic. In a chilling way.

Nick got the feeling that *feeling* wasn't something Riley did too much of. Considering her work, that would be an asset.

"Her skin looks . . . burned," he said.

"Yes. You feel how hot the whole house is? Whatever was used to make it hot—maybe some kind of portable propane heater, maybe a really big ceramic coil—whatever it was, she was held up close enough to the heat source for her skin to start to fry. This was done before the eyes were taken out. We think the eyes would have popped, exploded, from the heat. There would have been a lot of pain. The eyes pop or melt, whatever, and then what was left in the socket was gouged out. I'm sorry to say she was probably still alive when this was done."

"So what killed her?" asked Mavis in a hoarse tone, wishing with all her heart that she had taken the vacation time that was due her—*overdue* to her—and gone up to her cabin in the Belfair Range to watch Turner Classic Movies and drink a case or two of Stella.

"Can't be sure without an autopsy," said Riley in that cool clinical tone, "but my money is on a heart attack. She's a bit overweight, a smoker, from the nicotine stains on her index and second fingers. Shock, terror, pain. Heart going like a hummingbird in a bell jar. Infarct of some sort, a defect, blows an artery or something. Or maybe we'll find an aneurysm."

A pause, while everybody absorbed that.

"Okay," said Nick. "The fourth?"

"Yes," said Riley, a different tone in her voice, less cool, more cold. She had turned up her chill. "The daughter, Ava. Fifteen. She's upstairs, in the back bedroom."

She stood up, walked to the bottom of the wide wooden staircase that curved up to the second-floor landing, stopped there, turned to look at them.

"You know, we're going to do a pretty thorough job here, all of us CSI people. Before we move anything, we'll do video, take shots, measure everything down to a micron, and it will all go on the computer, where you can see it all. See *everything*. I personally guarantee it, and I'm the best there is at this."

Mavis listened, getting a bit edgy. "Your point, Sergeant?"

"You don't really need to go up there."

"Yes we do," said Mavis, stiffening.

Riley shook her head, her sad eyes darkening. "No, you don't. And I really think you shouldn't. You just don't need to see it, have it in your heads forever. The pictures are enough for you to testify on. There's lots of precedent for this. We studied it at UV law. In *State vs.*—"

Nick cut her off.

"Enough. Let's go."

If You Can Keep Your Head When All About You Are Losing Theirs, Then You Obviously Don't Understand the Situation

Danziger hadn't found car keys or a parking chit in his pocket, so he didn't bother looking for a car. He came down the front steps of the MountRoyal, feeling the mist on his cheeks, cool and sort of nice. The rain had stopped, but there was a lot of water in the air and everything on the Mile was soft-focus. He stood at the bottom, patting his pockets out of habit, realized he was looking for his cigarettes, which he now remembered smoking all the time.

There was a magazine stand across the street, still open at this unholy hour. The traffic had died off and the night-life shut down. There were only a few people on the streets: a couple of shadows in the dark of an empty parking lot, a drug deal of some kind: an elderly hooker standing by a beat-up lime-green Camaro, cigarette hanging from her lips, eyes scanning the street, fumbling for her car keys with one hand, a chrome-plated Llama .32 in the other.

Music was coming from one of the biker bars—overamped headbanger howling with a crystal meth backbeat that made Danziger feel like going over that way and starting a fight.

But he didn't.

The news guy in the booth was asleep and Danziger woke him up with a tap-tap on a pile of *Vanity Fair*s. He was a tiny monkey-faced guy with no legs and thick-lensed glasses that made his eyes look like raw oysters. He was propped up on a high chair and had his hands folded on a stainless steel Colt .380.

"Smokes," said Danziger, looking right and left, feeling eyes on the back of his neck.

"Brand, sir?" said Monkey Guy.

Danziger had to think about that. "Camels," he said, and the guy flipped him a pack, along with a folder of matches with a logo on the front.

BLUE BIRD BUS LINES
IF YOU DON'T KNOW WHERE YOU'RE GOING
WE KNOW HOW TO GET YOU THERE

A phone number and an address: The Button Gwinnett Bus Terminal, 1745 Forsythia, at Tulip Landing. Danziger paid the guy, stripped the cellophane off the pack, extracted a Camel, lit it with ceremonial care, feeling a twinge in his chest as he pulled in the smoke, Monkey Guy watching him carefully all the while, as if he expected Danziger to burst into flames.

"Quieter now," said Danziger, making small talk.

Monkey Guy showed a set of teeth that would have looked right at home in a macaque. "Busy night," he said in a high thready hiss that had more air than voice in it. "Cave-in down in the sewers. Some guy got himself cut in half by a rockfall."

"I heard the sirens," said Danziger, aware of the two bulky shapes gliding down the Mile toward him and spreading out a bit to give themselves some room. Room for what?

Monkey Guy was nodding in jerky flinches. He held up a portable scanner. Danziger heard laconic cross talk coming from the speaker.

"I listen to the cops. They got a bad one up in The Glades. Four people killed. Makes six, on account of the two yesterday. Bad times in Niceville, sir, very bad times. Yes, sir."

Danziger was going to ask him some more questions but then he heard a voice coming out of the darkness between two streetlamps.

"Hey there, huckleberry." A young voice, but not a small one. Lot of cracks in it, like ice in the spring, and an undertone that sounded like fear mixed with anger.

Danziger turned and saw two large young men standing apart, maybe fifteen feet away. He turned back to Monkey Guy. "Better button up."

Monkey Guy nodded, reached for the steel shutter that protected his roost, saying, as it clattered down, "They're Dark Boys, mister. All wrong in the head. Not allowed in Tin Town. I'm calling the cops."

Danziger heard the lock click on from inside and Monkey Guy's reedy voice on a cell phone.

He stepped away from the booth, coming up the street toward the two men and stopping in front of a shuttered storefront, getting his back near it, feeling the weight of the Colt Anaconda in his jacket pocket.

The two guys moved in closer, each to a side, until they had Danziger in the pointy end of a triangle. They looked like Midwestern farm boys, big fat-faced pale-skinned kids with small stupid eyes and girly lips. Brothers, Danziger figured, sizing them up, maybe even twins, and a good illustration of what you end up with when your ancestors go to family reunions to pick up chicks. But big, damn big, and muscular, six feet four and better, round-shouldered, thick-necked, and long-armed. He didn't see a weapon but figured he would pretty soon.

"You a *real* cowboy?" said the one on Danziger's right. He was wearing a black basketball shirt with the number six on it. Lebron. His arms were bared, tattoos coating both of them from his biceps to his wrists. Danziger said nothing, just waited.

He knew where this was going. Everybody did. Talk just gave them a better idea of who he was.

The other one, wearing a stained tee and black jeans and shitkicker boots that were probably steel-toed, had full-arm tattoos as well, and Danziger remembered that they were called *sleeve tats*.

This one made a noise like a cross between a grunt and a cough, stepped in closer, stopping about eight feet away, and now there was something in his hand, a nasty curved blade that shimmered as the guy moved it back and forth.

"Give it up, huckleberry," said Basketball Boy, "and we'll go easy on you. Only fuck you up a little."

Danziger sighed and pulled out the Colt, cocking the hammer back as the revolver came on point, aimed it straight at Shitkicker's left eye.

There was a definite alteration in the general mood. Shitkicker opened his mouth, closed it again, and backed away quickly, shaking his head. "Don't, mister . . . don't," he said, in a higher voice than the one he'd been using a minute ago. "We were just kidding with you."

"Yeah," said the other one, Basketball Boy. "We didn't mean nothing. Look. We're just gonna walk away, okay? Just going to . . . walk away."

"Move an eyelash and I'll kill you both."

They didn't move an eyelash.

Danziger let the moment ride, feeling a strong urge to kill them where they stood, or should he just let them wander off to fuck up somebody else's life?

The *snickety-snick* sound of a shotgun being pumped and racked came as clear as castanets across the misty air. A spotlight hit them and the *blip-blip* of a siren, and then a hard-edged command in classic cop tones. "On the ground, assholes. *On. The. Ground.*"

Danziger didn't move, and he kept the Colt right on Shit-kicker's eye. A Niceville PD cruiser was stopped twenty yards away, and the cop was out, his shotgun braced on the roof of the cruiser. The cop was Frank Barbetta.

Basketball Boy and Shitkicker hesitated for just a moment, no longer—two heartbeats maybe. Shitkicker was about to drop his knife—Danziger saw the surrender, the defeat, the fear in his piggish eyes—but at that point Barbetta said, in a teasing singsong voice right out of the schoolyard, "Oh, Olll-iiieee, sweetheart, look at me, Ollie. Look at me."

Ollie turned enough to look at Barbetta, the cop rock steady, elbows braced on the roof of the cruiser, his shotgun centered on Ollie's head.

"What did I *say*, Ollie? What did I *specifically* say?"

"Sir," said Ollie, his voice trembling, "ahh, you said, ahh, we should . . . not come down . . . me and Gordon should not come down to the Mile."

"But here you are," said Barbetta.

"Yeah, Frank . . . well, yeah," said Ollie, his voice a chok-ing squeak. "We thought you went off duty at midnight. Me and Gordon, we were just—"

"Well, I *didn't* go off duty, did I? I'm right here, looking at you two pieces of shit. And I am . . . *disappointed.*"

Ollie dropped the knife and lifted his hands up, palms out. Maybe he heard something new in Barbetta's voice, the way he had drawn out the last word. Dis-*appoint*-ed.

"Frank, please—please don't—"

"Nighty-night, asshole," Barbetta said, and triggered the shotgun—a crack of sky-ripping thunder, short and deafen-ing, a sheet of blue flame flashing out of the muzzle, the recoil pushing Barbetta's shoulder back six inches.

Ollie's head disappeared with a thwacking sound and

turned into a cloud of pink mist. Danziger felt the pitter-patter of blood spray and bone bits hitting his jacket.

Ollie stood for a second or two longer, headless, pink rain drifting down in an arc around him. His legs buckled and he collapsed, hit on his knees, wavered there for a moment, and then toppled forward onto his belly.

Barbetta had already switched to Basketball Boy, Gordon, who was standing about ten feet away from what was left of his brother, dappled with blood and skull bits.

He was staring bug-eyed at Barbetta. "You can't—"

"I just did, Gordon" said Barbetta in a patient fatherly tone. "I *told* you, next time. Told you, and I told Ollie there. You didn't *listen*. You two never do. And now your poor brother Oliver is two hundred and fifty pounds of bad meat and it's your own damn fault. Get on your knees, Gordon."

Gordon got down on his knees.

He looked at his brother's body and started to cry, and got bigger at it and louder, accelerating into a chest-heaving, howling wail.

Barbetta walked over to him, smiled briefly at Danziger, and gun-butted Gordon in the temple, a quick snapping strike and Gordon went sideways and lay still. Barbetta turned to Danziger.

"Hey, Charlie, you good? Nice to see you. Put that fucking cannon away. This dance is over."

Danziger could feel something stuck into his cheek, a sliver of skull. He plucked it out with his left hand while he uncocked the Colt and put it away slowly, making an inner wish that Ollie didn't have anything communicable.

He was thinking *that was not a righteous kill* and in no way typical of Frank Barbetta, who, if he remembered correctly, had never fired his duty weapon—other than at the range—in over thirty years of hard service. And now, after thirty years, he does this?

Another silvery shimmer in Danziger's memory pool: a flash-
*ing image of a navy blue pursuit car in his side mirror—*OBJECTS
IN THE MIRROR ARE CLOSER THAN THEY APPEAR—*lights and*
sirens—the pursuit car is climbing right up his tailgate, so close
Danziger can see the cop's face . . . he looks over and the guy he shot,
Merle Zane, is at the wheel and Merle's talking into a cell phone or
a radio . . . the voice at the other end comes back—Merle is talking
to Coker . . . and now Charlie is shooting at the pursuit car . . . he's
shooting at a police car *. . .*

And the memory is gone.

That's it.

Like a video clip, a few seconds and then gone, and Danziger is back in the here and now, with Frank Barbetta kneeling by the corpse of the man he had just killed.

"Ollie, you dumb, stupid fuck," Barbetta said, picking
Ollie's knife up and slipping it into his jacket pocket. He was
patting the headless corpse on the shoulder. "How many times
have I told you, stay off my mile."

Danziger, shaking himself clear, looked around him and
realized that the Mile was now empty and dark from one end
to the other. The fog and mist hung in the air like shotgun
smoke.

He looked back at Barbetta, who was kneeling by Oliver's body, smiling down upon him like a new daddy at his
firstborn. Gordon, a few feet away, was snuffling and jerking,
coming around.

Barbetta stood up, his gun belt creaking. "Come on, Charlie. Help me get this sack of shit into the car."

"*Which* sack of shit?"

Barbetta laughed. "Yeah, I forgot. You state guys require
specific instructions for everything, probably need a laminated card with cartoon drawings on it shows you how to pee.
The live one goes in the back of the cruiser," said Barbetta, his
grin a bit wild. "Got a body bag for Ollie here. We'll get him

in the trunk, drive on over to the bridge and dump him into the Tulip. The rain will take care of all the blood and the rats will get the nibbly bits."

"It's not raining," Danziger said.

Barbetta looked up, then gave Danziger a Coker-like grin. "It will, Charlie. It will."

And What If the *Second* Swallow That Came Back to Capistrano Was Really a Crow?

It was after three in the morning when Nick and Mavis walked away from the Morrison house. The rain, which had been on and off most of the evening, was coming back on, veils of it shimmering down through the live oaks and palms and pattering on the asphalt drive.

All the cruisers were gone, Riley's CSI van, and Tig's green Benz too. The network satellite trucks and the print people from Cap City had come, pestered, pried, pontificated, and eventually pissed off after hitting a wall of No Comment at This Time from Mavis Crossfire.

There were street cops and detectives who liked to maintain civil relations with the local media. Nick was not one of those cops. His term for war reporters was "combat proctologists." His term for civilian media people wasn't actually a word.

There was a coroner's wagon parked up the block, sitting in a pool of light under a streetlamp, engine idling, smoke rising from the driver's window, a tiny red spark as the guy drew on his cigarette. The driver got out of his van as Nick and Mavis came down to the curb, his partner, a young woman in a black suit, following behind. Neither Nick nor Mavis knew the girl, but the driver was a Vietnam vet named Myron Silver.

Silver was old, easily into his seventies, and spoke in a slow hillbilly drawl, which was an accomplishment since he was born and raised in Baltimore. He flicked his cigarette into the night as he reached them. "We can bag 'em?" he said, speaking to Mavis.

"You can. We're through here."

"Four, right?"

"Yes. Four."

Silver looked at his assistant, back to the two cops. "Heavy?"

Mavis thought it over, looking at the girl. "The bodies?"

Silver tilted his head, waited.

"Not really. The dad ran one sixty. Woman maybe one thirty. The kid was small, and the girl . . . the girl . . . a lot of her is just not there. What is there is not all in one piece. You're going to have to use your judgment as to which piece is which. I think you and your assistant can handle it."

Silver nodded, made to turn away, and turned back to them. "One bag for the dismembered vic?"

Nick shook his head. "No. You'll need three. Tag each one."

"Tag them? Tag them how?"

"With tags," said Mavis.

"No, I mean, if we can't ID the pieces?"

"Improvise, Myron," said Nick. "Use your initiative."

Silver said he would, looked back at Mavis. "Mavis, no offense, you look like shit."

Mavis gave him a half-smile. "If I didn't, I wouldn't understand the situation."

Silver heard that. "Pretty bad?"

"Worst thing I've ever seen in my entire career."

Silver's eyebrow flicked up, his eyes widening. He looked

back at his assistant, who was standing a few feet back, watching and listening but saying nothing. "Well, I guess this'll break in Katie May."

"That's Katie May?"

"Just came on. This is her first night."

Mavis looked over at her. "Yes," she said. "It will."

Silver and the silent Katie May walked up the drive to see what had to be done and how to go about it. Nick watched them go, thinking about what was waiting for Katie May inside, then went back to his Crown Vic to get some wipes and wash his face. He worked at his hands and wrists a lot, feeling filthy inside and out.

He was watching Mavis at her Suburban, talking into the radio handset, her voice low and laconic. Nick heard her say "ten-seven" and something about the motor pool. She put the radio away as Nick came up to her.

"Something going on?"

"Yeah. Frank Barbetta never turned in his ride. His shift ended at midnight, but he never came back to the substation."

"They can't raise him?"

"No. He's ten-seven, and his GPS is turned off. Cell phone too. None of the units have seen him, but then, with this . . . thing . . . here, most of our guys are uptown looking for suspicious vehicles and doing random stops."

"Frank ever do this before?"

Mavis thought about it. "Yeah. Now and then. After Brenda flew the nest. No reason to go home, so he just . . . rides."

"Yeah? I can see that. Sometimes going home isn't all that appealing."

Mavis gave him a quick look, started to say something, but let it slide.

"Well, that was a hell of a thing down there in the tunnels. I'd want to drive around and clear my head after seeing something like that."

"Mavis, you *did* see something like that. You were there too."

"Not me," she said. "I was in the Rear with the Gear. Just one of those PUNTS."

Nick smiled. PUNTS was an Army term. It meant Persons of Utterly No Tactical Significance.

"So, Nick, would you like a cigarette?" she asked.

"I don't smoke," said Nick.

"Neither do I," she said, reaching into the truck and pulling a pack of Kools out of a side pocket. She offered one to Nick, who took it, and she used a brass Zippo with the crest of the NYPD Detectives' Endowment Association on the side to fire them both up. They stood there and drew in the smoke, let it go, watched it rise up.

"Well, that was real fucking unpleasant," said Mavis. "You think it was Dutrow?"

"No. Can't say for sure until we get the DNA and blood type. But that's my gut feeling. Timeline is too short. And the scene . . . what was done . . . it feels different. Less organized. More like the killer was in some kind of . . . what?"

"Frenzy?"

"Yes. A frenzy."

"That's what I was thinking. So we got *two* of these assholes? Exactly what Tig was afraid of."

"Yeah, it is."

Nick was scanning the block, looking at the houses, the cars in the driveways: a Benz, a BMW, two Caddys, and a Benz. A car thief's dream.

"This isn't a poor neighborhood. People around here would have security systems."

"Cameras?"

"Yes. Have we gone around and asked yet?"

"No," said Mavis. "The Morrisons only had a couple of motion detectors rigged to the yard floodlights. We did do a canvass to see if anybody saw anything, and nobody did. All shut in because of the rain, no one looking out at the street. I'll put some troops on the security camera thing in the morning. That's a good idea. Come to think of it, there's a red-light camera on the traffic mast where Lanai Lane crosses River Road. Maybe it caught something."

"Yes, do that. The girl, Ava," said Nick, "she was on Skype when her door came down. Did we get anything from that?"

Mavis flipped her notebook open, read it by the streetlamp.

"Classmate of hers. Julia Mauldar."

"Little Rock's kid?"

"Sister's kid. His niece. I sent a PW to talk to her. All the kid could say was that Ava was talking to her about another girl in the class—"

"What did the PW say? About this?"

"She woke the family up when she got there. So it was pretty obvious that something bad had happened. She basically said it was a home invasion that had gone badly. They took it . . . poorly. But Julia agreed to talk."

"Ava goes to Sacred Heart, doesn't she?"

"Yes. They both do. Did."

"The Frederick Douglass Panthers played Sacred Heart last Sunday."

"Yes . . . and?"

"Dutrow was a linebacker for the Panthers."

Mavis considered that. "You think that's a link?"

"I have no idea. Maybe. Ava was a cheerleader for the Sacred Heart Razorbacks. So Ava was talking to Julia . . . ?"

"According to the PW, they both had those earbud things on, so the noise downstairs, Ava might not have heard it, or maybe she thought it was something on the television. Julia told the PW that Ava's picture—her Skype video feed—just turned into static. Just went all hazy and crackly and turned into visual white noise. She heard Ava's voice under the static, said it sounded like she was talking to someone outside the room—"

"The door was shattered, you saw the boot mark where the guy kicked it in, so she had her bedroom door locked."

"Yeah. By then the Skype video was nothing but a field of haze and the audio was going nuts. Julia figured it was something with the Wi-Fi, but they were both on Ethernet cables."

"She make out anything useful?"

Mavis shook her head. "Just a noise at the end, Julia said it sounded like someone was shouting at her, at Ava, and then the Skype connection just . . . flicked off."

"What'd Julia do?"

"She phoned, a landline, it rang several times, and then the line picked up, but nobody answered . . . Julia thinks someone was there, not saying anything, just *listening*, and she asked for Ava a couple of times but got nothing. Then she got creeped out and hung up. She worried about it for a while, tried the number again an hour later. It rings and rings but no answer. Goes to voice mail, but Julia said she didn't want to leave a message—still creeped out—so she just hung up. Worried some more, sent an e-mail and texted her, Ava. Nothing back. Finally she went and got her mom to call the cops, see if they'd go around and check."

"And they did?"

"Well, Julia Mauldar's mom is Little Rock Mauldar's sister, and Little Rock's the mayor."

Nick looked back up at the house. Silver and Katie May were coming out the front door with a body bag on a gurney. All the lights in the house were blazing into the fog.

"Mavis, what do you think we're hunting here?"

"A sick fuck, Nick. A sadistic sick fuck. A very fucking *strong* sadistic sick fuck."

"Not what I meant. True and well said, but not what I meant."

"Then what *do* you mean?"

"The *buzzing* thing?"

"Yeah?"

"It interfered with the radios, down there in the shaft. You could almost hear it."

"Brownian motion," said Mavis after some thought. "It's always in your ears. Whenever things are real quiet, you can hear it. It's supposed to be atoms and molecules vibrating against your eardrum."

"Atoms and molecules aren't going to screw up radio transmissions."

Mavis shrugged.

"It's been my experience that radio transmissions can be screwed up by mouse farts. And that tunnel was three, four hundred feet into the bedrock. Any kind of mildly radioactive minerals—a seam of it buried in the limestone—that would be enough to do it."

Nick was unconvinced. "Rainey said he had buzzing in his head. He even used the same word as Dutrow. Like a wasp, he said, a wasp in his head. And Rainey called it a *she* too."

"Didn't Rainey get electroshock therapy?"

"Yeah."

"And that cured it, yes?"

Nick shook his head.

"Maybe. There are still some . . . Dr. Lakshmi calls them anomalies. They worry her. Us. Kate too. She took him down in Cap City—"

"You said. At the neuro clinic in Sorrows. So he's not . . . cured?"

"Kate thinks . . . maybe not."

"Rainey's been through a lot. The abduction, his mother and dad both dead, the whole grave thing, in a coma for a year. Now he's living with you and Kate."

Rainey Teague was a touchy subject between Mavis and

Nick. Mavis was on the kid's side, maybe just because she was a woman. Kate was totally committed to the boy. Nick was neither for nor against the kid.

He was just . . . extremely wary.

"Thing is, Mavis, when Rainey had this wasp noise in his head, at the same time, Hannah's hearing aids were all screwed up." Hannah, going on five, was Kate's niece.

"I remember. They had to be replaced."

"Yeah. At one point, when Hannah was complaining about them, the hearing aids, Kate listened to one, and she says it was exactly like a buzzing wasp."

"Like what we heard tonight, in the tunnel?"

"Yes. Exactly."

"And maybe like what screwed up the Skype feed here at the Morrison house?"

"Yes."

"So what you're saying here is that maybe some kind of horrible bad evil but totally invisible demonic wasp cloud of mind-warping free-floating crazy is flying around Niceville and it drills into people's skulls and turns them into sadistic psychokiller zombies?"

"No. I mean, it's more . . . complicated." Nick drew on the last of the cigarette, flicked it away, a tumbling firefly vanishing into the dark. Silver and Katie May were bringing out the dead again. There was something really *wrong* with Niceville, he knew that, and what was happening here was part of it.

Mavis said nothing for a while, sensing his mood, if not his thoughts, and then she patted Nick on the shoulder and said, "Nick, I'd love to stay and elaborate on your totally fucked-in-the-head theory, but I'm due back on the mother ship at dawn and if I'm late they'll give away my window seat."

Nick said nothing, smiled, shrugged it away. "Okay, you're right. Brownian motion?"

"Look it up."

"I will. Go home, Mavis, get some sleep—"

"Yeah, right," she said. "That'll happen."

"Have a shower, or three. And a bucket of martinis. Nothing more we can do tonight. The guy who did this is going to be a bloody mess—"

"Unless he wore a body suit."

"Yeah. So you've got units out right now—"

"Looking for anybody who is a bloody mess. So does County and State. Even the Parks Service."

"You give out a description?"

"Yeah," said Mavis. "I said the guy would look like Jackson Pollock."

One's Commitment to Slicing One's Head Off Tends to Taper Off Dramatically at Around the Halfway Point

Barbetta said it would rain, and it did.

Barbetta and Danziger got Gordon cuffed and Ollie bagged—not much fun because Gordon had puked and peed himself and they had to get a body tarp out of the trunk to put under him so he wouldn't leak all over the bench seat.

As for Newly Dead Ollie, he seemed to have gained weight just by getting himself decapitated, which made no sense, given that Ollie's head must have weighed in at around forty pounds, but it felt like it was true anyway.

They had just heaved the body bag containing Ollie's floppy carcass into the trunk of Barbetta's cruiser, the car shocks groaning, when the skies broke open and the rain came sheeting down, waving like silky drapes in a warm wind off the Tulip.

Danziger climbed into the shotgun seat as Barbetta started up the cruiser. In the back behind the security grid Gordon was sniveling and sobbing, nose running and his big body jerking and shaking, tears streaming down his fat cheeks. He looked like a big nine-year-old kid who wanted his mommy.

Barbetta twisted around in the driver's seat, banged the

grid with the palm of his hand. "Gordon," said Barbetta, "if you don't knock that crybaby shit off, I'm going to tase your fat ass right where you sit."

Gordon's sniveling stopped, or at least it slowed down and lost some of that glutinous boot-stuck-in-a-mudhole awfulness. He gulped down some air, swallowed hard. "Frank, you can't just shoot Ollie and dump him in the river, that's illegal—we got rights—"

"Jeez, Gordon," said Barbetta, shaking his head and putting the cruiser into drive, "give it a rest. You sound like fucking NPR. Write an op-ed for the *New York Times*. Okay?"

He looked over at Danziger, grinned at him. "Should have called in a ten-fifty-four and left him there."

A ten-fifty-four call was Dead Livestock Blocking Public Road. Danziger shook his head, offering Barbetta a smoke.

"We can have a beer, talk this over after you've got Gordon booked and bagged."

Gordon heard that, stopped sniveling just long enough to say, "You're so fucked, Frank. That was fucking cold-blooded murder and I'm telling everybody at the station—"

"Shut up, Gordon," said Barbetta, talking around his cigarette, this time with a lot more ice in it, "or you won't see the inside of a cell. I'll go down by the flats and leave you for the river carp."

"You can't . . . we got constitutional rights. This is so *fucking* illegal! Help me somebody! Help me!" Gordon started banging his head against the window beside him, banging it hard and often, screaming for help. While kicking the back of the front seat and making Danziger's chest hurt.

"Shit," said Barbetta, pulling over. "This'll just take a minute," he said, getting out of the car. He stepped back to the left-side door, jerked it open, and punched Gordon in the side of the temple, his meaty fist traveling no more than six inches, but it had all of Barbetta's weight and muscle behind it.

Gordon's fat face went all rubbery and he toppled over onto the bench seat. Barbetta slammed the door, got back in behind the wheel, his breathing slightly ragged, and they drove on in blessed silence for a while.

Danziger saw they were headed north through the Tin Town side roads toward the Armory Bridge and away from the South Sector Substation for the Niceville PD. There wasn't a soul on the streets, not even another squad car. And the radio was silent. No cross talk at all, and Barbetta hadn't called in to Central since the shooting. And the MDT, the mobile display terminal, was dark.

Not normal. Not normal at all.

Something wrong about this.

Not a righteous kill—the phrase ran through Danziger's mind. Frank Barbetta was a by-the-book street cop. He had a laminated card stuck in the visor over the passenger seat, with the cop's mantra printed on it:

> WALK THE LINE
> AND CUT NO SLACK
> HOOK 'EM AND BOOK 'EM
> AND DON'T LOOK BACK

Barbetta must have noticed Danziger looking at the card. "Okay. I can hear your brain moaning and bitching from all the way over here. Gordon's napping. You can tell me what's chewing on you."

Danziger drew on his cigarette, gave it a moment, and said, "Frank, my friend, that was not a righteous shoot."

Barbetta laughed, more of a snort, really. "Ya think? Ollie was coming at you with a fish knife. I'd say that made it pretty fucking righteous."

"Well, I had my Colt stuck up his nose and you had him

covered with your Defender and Gordon hadn't even shown a weapon yet—"

"Come on, Charlie. Ollie had a blade. I've seen what he can do with one. He may be a big guy, but he's quick and mean. I once had to take him out of a bar on my own and it was a near-run thing until I tased him. And you know a knife is ten times more dangerous than a gun. He was a few feet away from you, showing a blade, and even if you'd put one through his forehead, we've both seen guys get cut up by a charging felon. Lotta really important arteries and shit are maybe a millimeter below your skin, you can bleed out in three minutes."

Danziger considered this, with all of its carefully twisted evasions and half-truths. It was a plausible version of the events, as long as they were the only people telling it. Danziger reached out, tapped the dash cam on the cruiser's deck. "What about this?"

"I went off duty two hours ago. No dash cam after I booked off. No radio either. No MDT."

"We're still in your duty ride. It's got GPS. Central will know you're rolling."

Barbetta patted the wheel. "Yeah, we are. Love this car. Her name is Mariah. Got the high-power mill, racing suspension, beefed-up grill, bumper bars. Nobody else gets Mariah. She's all mine to do what I want. I always disable the GPS when I sign off. None of Central's fucking business what I do after hours, where I go, who I see. I want to see a CI, he's got to know I'm off the grid. It's called gathering intel, and you used to do it all the time."

Danziger had to admit this was true.

Part of being a good street cop was knowing who was doing what, and for that you needed snitches, and snitches needed to know you were being . . . discreet . . . when they met with you. Their lives depended on it.

"So you're just . . . freelancing?"

"Yeah. Didn't feel like going home. I like being in the car at night. Operating. Looking for pukes and assholes. I like the . . . jazz, the intensity down here. You know what I mean."

That was true. Being in a squad and rolling, ready for anything, knowing you were the meanest son of a bitch in the valley, and armed, with a badge—well, that feeling, once gone, could never be replaced.

Barbetta was nodding, feeling Danziger's connection. "Yeah. You get that. You know exactly what I'm talking about. I mean, fuck *home*. Feels like I'm already home, you know? Anyway, got a hell of a headache, some kinda migraine, and Brenda's long gone, nobody waiting up for me anymore, so there's no sleeping gonna happen at my place."

Witnesses. "That guy in the news booth," said Danziger, "looks like a monkey, I heard him calling the cops. Dispatch would have that 911 call tagged."

"The monkey-looking guy in the newsstand is Juko Aivazovzky. He's one of my CIs. He called me, not Dispatch. He works for *me*, not the city."

"Okay, another thing. You've got Ollie's fish knife in your pocket."

Barbetta went blank, patted his coat. "Jeez. I do. Thank you."

"You're welcome."

Danziger worked it through. He figured what was done was done. On the other hand, what had *not* been done yet required some thought. "You really are gonna toss Ollie in the Tulip, aren't you?"

Barbetta looked over at Danziger and then back at the street. The lights of the Armory Bridge were a string of yellow pearls stitched through the tree branches.

"Not us," said Barbetta. "Gordon back there."

Danziger took that in.

"Why he's along, right?"

Barbetta smiled, his heavy jaw and gloved hands lit up by the dashboard glow, the upper part of his face in darkness except for two small pinpricks of green light in his eyes.

"What'd Mommy always say? Many hands . . . ?"

"Make light the burden," Danziger said. "Frank, I'm okay with backing you up on the shooting, you know that, although I notice I now have Ollie bits all over my best range jacket—"

"I'll pay for the dry cleaning. And there's some Handi Wipes in the glove compartment, 'cause you've also got Ollie bits on your cheek there."

"Thank you," said Charlie, digging around for the Handi Wipes. "But now you want me to go along with dumping a headless corpse into the river."

"You afraid we'll get cited by the EPA? Ollie is completely biodegradable, fulla nutrients and shit, so he's good for the environment. Charlie, he's just another fucking suicidal ratbag from Tin Town. The world's a better place. Next objection?"

"A *headless* ratbag, Frank. Ollie is currently headless. Headless ratbags are not often considered suicides by the authorities, since one's commitment to slicing one's head off tends to taper off dramatically at around the halfway point. So the cops usually leap to that whole foul play thing."

"*One's?* You're using the word *one's?* Coker was here, he'd laugh his ass off, then probably shoot you. You sound like that dude in *Downton Abbey*. What the fuck gives with these *one's?*"

"Yeah. Good point. But you know what I'm getting at."

"He coulda done it with a shotgun."

"If you use a shotgun on yourself, it just sorta turns the entire skull into a big peeled-open banana skin. It doesn't *erase* it. Ollie got it from twenty feet. And how'd he get to the bridge?"

"So okay, it's not a suicide. Some gangbanger finally took Ollie out. Nobody in Tin Town is gonna be sorry to see the last of him. Jeez, Charlie, I'm beginning to think you just don't want to get involved?"

"I'd say I'm already involved. It's just that, I gotta say this, you're acting a bit weird."

Barbetta barked out a laugh, grinned at Danziger.

"I'm acting weird? *I'm* acting weird? That's fucking rich, coming from you. You have any fucking idea how *weird* it is, you sitting around in my cruiser giving me fucking grief about whether we dump a sack of dead meat into the fucking Tulip?"

"Why's that weird?"

"Because, Charlie, no offense or anything, not to put too fine a point on it, you're supposed to be dead."

Understandably, Danziger needed some time to process that. Barbetta let him. They were at the bridge now, and he pulled over next to the Works Department Quonset hut.

"Dead? What the fuck do you mean? How dead?"

"Dead enough to give you a funeral and everything. I went to it. In my dress blues. We all did. State, County, us guys. Mavis Crossfire gave a speech and we all got shitfaced afterward at the AmVets Hall. As Joe Biden says, it was a big fuckin' deal."

Danziger thought that over. Being dead would explain a lot—the whole memory-loss thing—but then it raised a lot more questions than it answered. Starting with "Was it an open casket?"

Barbetta's mind went back to look. "No, come to think of it. At least it was closed when I got there. Big US flag on it, honor guard all around it."

"If the casket was closed, how do you know I was inside it?"

"Christ, Charlie, who'd want it open? Look in the rearview mirror. You're ugly as a chewed boot right now. Think how much worse you'd look dead. Besides, I heard you were all shot to shit and like horribly mutilated and stuff. Nobody needs to see that."

"I was *mutilated*?" said Danziger, looking down at his crotch, which is the first thing guys check when they hear the word *mutilated*, his voice going a bit screechy. "Who the fuck mutilated me?"

Barbetta hunched his shoulders. "Okay, fuck, maybe not *mutilated*. I was just heating you up a little. Where's your sense of humor at, for fuck's sake? But shot, yeah, you were definitely shot. That much I do know."

"Who the fuck shot me?"

"Buncha mob pukes, I heard. Nick Kavanaugh was there, and Mavis Crossfire, paying you a visit, like, up in your ranch there. These mob guys show up, some kind of Sicilian vendetta thing over that Frankie Maranzano asshole Coker popped at the Galleria Mall. Five of them, suddenly it's like the OK Corral. You and Coker killed two, Reed Walker killed another, Nick Kavanaugh did a guy hand to hand right there in the sweet grass, and Mavis shot the last guy."

"Good for us. So how did I get shot?"

Barbetta laughed, shook his head. "Trying to be a fucking hero, Charlie. Story is a shooter was going for Mavis, you stepped into the line of fire, took two rounds meant for her."

"Where?"

"I think inna chest there. Pow, pow, and bingo, you're KIA."

Danziger touched the sore spots on his chest and felt the world slip sideways.

Barbetta was on a roll. "Yeah, you died a fucking hero. Which is why Mavis did the eulogy thing for you. Did a good job too. Had everybody all teared up. Pipe band played 'Danny Boy' and 'Amazing Grace.' Sun was shining. Cops in from all over the state, flasks of whiskey were going around the ranks. Icy cold beers in the trunks. Fuck, it was a terrific day . . . except for the you-being-dead part, I mean. No offense."

Danziger gave the whole concept some serious consideration. It sounded like he'd had one hell of a send-off and he sort of wished he could have been there. He decided he needed more data.

"You're gonna have to explain all this shit to me, Frank. You just don't tell a guy he's dead and get him to throw a stiff into the river for you and then we fuck off for donuts."

Barbetta thought that over. "Okay. Tell you what. We get this Ollie thing handled, you and me will go to Blue Eddie's, have some steak and eggs, some coffee—"

Danziger realized that he had come out for coffee, that coffee was how this all got started.

Shoulda sat quietly in your room, Charlie, like that Pascal guy was always saying.

"So, do we have a deal?" Barbetta asked.

Danziger thought it over, Barbetta tapping the wheel, Gordon wheezing in the back, rain drumming on the roof of the squad car. "Okay. What the hell. Deal."

Barbetta banged the steering wheel, reached over, shook Danziger's hand, grinning like a wolf. "Good man. I knew you'd back me up!"

"Yeah, yeah, okay. One last thing, Frank."

"Another fucking last thing?" Barbetta closed his eyes, dropped his head down. "Jesus wept. What is it now?"

"Is Gordon gonna go into the Tulip after Ollie?"

Barbetta glanced in his rearview, saw Gordon snorting and chuffing, still out cold.

"Well, he does look kinda . . . *depressed*."

There Is What We Know That We Know and There Is What We Know That We Do Not Know but the Real Danger Lies in Not Knowing What's on Top of the Fridge Hidden Behind the Tea Tray

It was almost four in the morning when Nick pulled up in front of their house on Beauregard, in the Garrison Hills section of Niceville.

Garrison Hills was a nice part of town, leafy blocks lined with Spanish and French Colonial houses, prewar houses with wrought iron galleries and curved staircases that led up from the street to the main doors, a holdover from when Niceville streets were simply dirt and stone and the dust kicked up by horses and wagons was always in the air. Live oaks that had shaded Beauregard Avenue from the sun when Confederate troops were passing through on their way north had now grown so large that their branches met in the air over the street, making it a kind of leafy green cave. Wisps of Spanish moss fluttered from the heavy oak branches, like the ghosts of hanged men.

The house had been in the Walker and Mercer family line

for a hundred and fifty years. Dillon Walker, Kate's father, a history professor at the Virginia Military Institute, had asked Kate to take over the house after the death of his wife Lenore seven years ago.

And it was a lovely house, a tall French town house with tall casement windows, a delicate black wrought iron staircase that rose up from the street level in a graceful curve, ending at a large double door, also black, shaped in an arch, with stained-glass window lights above and around it. The walls were a soft butternut stone that, in the late afternoon sun through the trees, made the house glow with an inner light.

Tonight, at four in the morning, the house was dark, except for a dim lantern shining above the door and a soft yellow glow from an upstairs bedroom. Their bedroom, which meant Kate was home after three days down at Our Lady of Sorrows Hospital in Cap City, home and awake and waiting up for him. She must have heard him at the door because she was coming down the staircase when he walked into the wood-lined front hall.

He watched her come down, feeling the weight coming off his heart. Kate was a beauty, full-bodied and elegant, fine-boned and long-necked, a Black Irish rose with green eyes and long black hair that was shining in a liquid fall around her shoulders as she passed by the landing light.

She was smiling, but he could see the worry lines around her mouth and eyes, the weariness in the way she was moving.

She reached him, gave him a full-body embrace and a kiss that radiated out from his lips and warmed him all the way down to his hips. She was naked under her white cotton nightgown. He could feel her hips and the muscles along her spine, her breasts and her slightly rounded belly against him.

She pulled away, looked up at him. "God, Nick, you look awful."

"Thank you. I've earned it."

"You've been smoking."

"Mavis held me down and forced one on me."

She laughed, pulled him through the hallway and into the kitchen at the back of the house. The kitchen, old-fashioned country style in pale yellow and creamy white, was lit only by a night-light in the stove hood.

Beyond the kitchen was a glass-walled solarium with wicker chairs, a huge yellow couch, bright blue pillows, and flowering plants, all in the dark now, with the pin lights in the backyard glimmering in the rain. He had a flash of the lanai at the Morrison house and pushed it down.

Kate was at the fridge, the door open, light pouring out around her, her body a pale pink vision through the paper-thin cotton.

Transparency, he thought. *It's not just for governments.*

"Eufaula made a pitcher of juleps," she said, pulling out a silver decanter, cold and dew-covered, and setting it down on the bar counter, along with two crystal glasses. "Sit." She indicated one of the leather-topped bar chairs next to the counter-top, and he sat while Kate poured out two mint juleps, adding a sprig of mint from a glass bowl. She put the pitcher back in the fridge, sat down opposite him, smiled at him.

They touched glasses, a tiny bell ringing.

"So," she said, putting the glass down carefully on the quartz counter, "I'm not going to ask you about your day."

"Tig called?"

"Yes. He gave me the basics. So we're not going there right now. Unless you want to?"

"No, babe, I don't."

"That bad?"

"That bad."

"Bad enough." She took that in. "Okay, *my* day then?"

"Is Rainey asleep?"

Rainey had a bedroom on the second floor, but he had

a tendency to wander, possibly sleepwalking, possibly something else. On the bad nights, they locked his door from the outside.

"I checked. He's out cold. They put him through a lot, and Dr. Lakshmi gave me some Ativans to see that he slept well. And I locked his door. So, do you want to hear?"

"What about Beth and the kids?"

Beth was Kate's older sister. Her husband, Byron Deitz, ex-FBI and a bad man, had been killed in a hostage taking at the Galleria Mall, along with mafia boss Frankie Maranzano.

Nick had done some of the shooting, and Staff Sergeant Coker, the best police sniper in the state, had done the rest. Part of the mayhem was caused by a boneheaded bystander with a Dan Wesson .44 Magnum, who inserted himself into the fire fight and got his ticket punched for his troubles.

The upshot of Byron Deitz's timely departure was that Beth and her two kids, Hannah, five, and Axel, nine, were now living in the Coach House at the back of the property.

"They're out back, sound asleep. But, Nick, it's not like Beth and I don't talk about all of this. Or with Eufaula, for that matter."

"I know. I just want some time alone with you. Hear about your week. You do look tired."

"I am. It was long. Three days and nights long. Sometimes I got to nap on a couch in the nurse's room while they were doing the prep stuff. And I was half asleep when I heard you come home."

Nick looked down at his glass, watching the light glimmer in the ice. Head still down, he said, "So, what's the word?"

"The word is . . . inconclusive."

"All the tests came back as . . . what's the word they had? Not *normal*?"

"Nominal?"

"That's it. Nominal. MRI, CAT, spinal tap, the whole calliope parade, pink elephants and all. The only thing they didn't do was a colonoscopy."

"So, if there's no . . ."

"Anomaly," said Kate.

"Yeah, no anomalies, then . . . what?"

"They're talking therapy."

"What, physio? Kid's as strong as I am."

"You know what I mean, and no, he's not."

"Not yet. But he's growing fast. He's going to be a real large boy by the time he gets to eighteen. What kind of psychotherapy?"

Kate took a sip of her julep. The way she did it told Nick that she had to tell him something that neither of them was going to be happy about.

"Okay, well, the way they're thinking now is that whatever Rainey's got, it might respond to a kind of psychological counseling called CBT."

"Which is?"

"Cognitive behavioral therapy. It's supposed to help a person focus on his problem patterns, on the way he thinks about what he's doing or saying, on the way he processes the world around him . . . You look skeptical."

"No. If I am, I don't mean to."

"So stop going all stony and coplike on me."

"Is that what I'm doing?" This was dangerous ground for them. Disagreeing about Rainey's destructive effect on their marriage a while back had ended up with Nick living in a hotel for a couple of weeks.

"Okay, to cut to the bottom line here, they think Rainey might have a form of . . ."

She sighed, and her lip trembled a bit. Nick reached out for her and put his hand on hers.

"Of schizophrenia. They think that's where these 'voices' are coming from—"

"Doesn't schizophrenia mean medication?"

"Yes . . . antipsychotic medications. They were talking about something called Risperdal, or Zyprexa—"

"Don't these medicines have a lot of weird side effects?"

"Yes. They do. Tremors, something called tardive dyskinesia, they're these uncontrollable facial tics. Weight gain. And they can also make the patient sleepy or depressed . . . Look, Nick, this isn't good, I know, but it's not the worst it could be. If we can get Rainey's . . . situation . . . under control, get him stabilized . . . he could have a normal life. Remember that man, John Nash—Russell Crowe played him in *A Beautiful Mind*?"

"I remember the movie, anyway. The guy was seeing people who weren't there, a roommate, a little girl."

"That's right. He was schizophrenic, so he was having these visions, these hallucinations—"

"Which never went away."

"Right, but with the help of some therapy and the right kind of medication, he learned how to cope with them, to live with them. So the thinking is that, with drugs and CBT, Rainey can be taught how to cope with . . . his condition."

"Kate—"

"He can have a normal life."

"Kate, his behavior when he's hearing this voice, the things the voice wanted him to do—"

"If you're talking about Alice Bayer—"

"I am sure as hell not talking about Alice Bayer. Or about Warren Smoles. That's in the past, and that's where it can stay. But you're the one who thought he had something . . . something very real—let's call it an *entity*—living in his head. In his mind. Lemon Featherlight saw those creatures on the front porch of Rainey's old house. I can understand Rainey having hallucinations, but Lemon? And didn't you see them too?"

Kate was closing down. "I was half crazy then. I don't know

what I saw. A couple of shadows, that's all. It had been a bad week, with Rainey sneaking off, going to Warren Smoles . . . I wasn't myself. Christ, maybe I'm the one with the condition."

"Honey, you're not crazy. Neither am I. We saw what we saw. It was real."

Kate shook her head, not in negation, but in confusion. She forced herself into the appearance of calm, and Nick realized how close she was to cracking wide open. So he kept his mouth shut.

"Nick . . . I'm not sure what we saw. Maybe we saw a cloud of dust or leaves, and maybe what we saw in that old mirror—Glynis Ruelle—maybe that was a trick of the light, like that camera obscura image you saw in Delia Cotton's basement. We were all exhausted . . . it was a terrible time, that awful bank robbery in Gracie, Dad going missing, Byron and Beth and the kids. Remember *that*? In the middle of all that, who knows what we saw?"

Denial, Nick was thinking. And *Be gentle here*. "And Lemon Featherlight?"

She looked down, which she tended to do when she was telling him something she was having trouble believing herself. "Lemon thinks he might have been mistaken."

Nick's reply was gentle, noncommittal. "He does? And when did he start thinking that?"

"He came to Sorrows two days ago. He was in Cap City to register his helicopter license with the FBI and then he was flying up to UV to see that Dr. Sigrid person about those bone-basket things you two found near . . . near where Alice was. He was on his way to the airport. He and Rainey used to be close. He looked in on Rainey, came and sat with me in the parent's lounge. We talked about everything, and he said maybe he might have been wrong too, that maybe he was just stressed out."

Nick worked that through. Lemon Featherlight was an ex-

Marine, a full-blood Mayaimi Indian, irritatingly handsome in a piratical sort of way, a condition made even more grating because all the women loved him, and made even more so because he was actually a decent guy, and nobody needed that.

He was one of the two people Nick knew who felt the way he did about "that wasp thing" in Rainey's head, because Lemon had seen it in action. Later, Lemon had talked about the "thing" being something called a Kalona Ayeliski, a Raven Mocker demon, something out of an old Cherokee legend. The folk who used to live around this part of the world believed the female demon lived in Crater Sink, on the crest of Tallulah's Wall.

If Lemon Featherlight was backing off in front of Kate, it was probably because he could see the effect all of this was having on her.

Kate was tight, but she was keeping it under control. "So you see, if even Lemon thinks Rainey can have a normal life . . ." She reached out and took his hand.

"Look, Nick, I've . . . I've decided that was all . . . mass hysteria. Fatigue. The power of suggestion. We all had it, one way or another, but now it's *over*."

She teared up here. "It has to be over. Because if it really was something . . ."

"From *outside*?"

"Yes. From *outside* . . . like that Raven Mocker demon that Lemon was talking about, then it cannot be fixed or figured out or defeated and we're all of us just . . . fucked. Totally and completely fucked, and we might as well just shoot ourselves now and get it over with. I think that's why I lost the baby. All that stress. And I am so *done* with it!"

Kate had suffered her third miscarriage a month ago, only eight weeks into her pregnancy. Nick didn't think it was just stress—perhaps the *thing*, whatever it was, that was "wrong" in Niceville, maybe it had caused it somehow. He had no idea how, but he knew that Kate was not a woman who needed a lecture about Niceville's insane history.

Kate gathered herself, took in a shuddering breath, dabbed at her eyes with a napkin. "So," she said, "if we follow through on this, help Rainey cope with his condition, with drugs and therapy—"

"I worry some about the drug thing."

"I don't like it either. But what else can we do? Call in an exorcist? Kill a white chicken by the light of a crescent moon?"

Nick smiled, tried for a lighter note. "Might be worth a try?"

Kate sat back, studied him, a warning sign. "You've got to try to . . . soften your heart about Rainey, Nick."

Nick had tried that and had been doing okay until Alice Bayer died. He refrained from saying this, which was just as well. Kate was as wary of another fight as he was. They were still hoping to have another shot at parenthood. Fighting over how to raise someone else's child had cracked open a lot of good marriages.

Time to shift the topic.

"Anyway . . ."

"Anyway?"

She gave him a wry smile, dried her eyes.

"Anyway, to take an off-ramp, Beth got some good news."

"Did she?" said Nick, happy to get away from the Rainey issue.

"Byron's estate cleared probate. She's getting most of it. It includes Byron's controlling shares in BD Securicom. She could get as much as seven million in stock and equities."

"Good for her. But I thought the feds were going after his assets for selling classified technology to a foreign government?"

Kate gave him a look. "Well, the case sort of fell apart after those Chinese spies died in the plane crash and then you and Coker shot Byron dead, didn't it? He had never even been formally charged, because he was still trying for a plea bargain when he escaped."

"So Beth is in the clear?"

"Yes. Finally."

"Any plans?"

"She's thinking of buying a house here in Garrison Hills. Or perhaps down in Cap City, to be near her work. She thinks she's crowding us."

Nick liked Beth, an older and less sunny version of Kate. Boonie Hackendorff had given her a job in his FBI office in Cap City. She was spending four nights a week down there and coming home on the weekends. Hannah was in the FBI day-care facility on Fountain Square, which left Axel and Rainey in Kate's care, and of course Eufaula's too.

Nick liked Beth's kids too, although he worried about Rainey's relationship with Axel. Axel looked up to Rainey like an older brother.

"Well, she's welcome to stay here as long as she wants. This was her house too, and Reed's. You guys all grew up here."

"We do have a full house, don't we?" said Kate. "You sure it doesn't bother you?"

"No. I like it. While I was growing up in Santa Monica, there was Nora and me, the only adults in the house, and two aging hippie wing-nut parents smoking weed and going to protest marches to save the Delta smelt."

"Of what?" she said.

"Pardon?"

"The Delta smelled of what?"

"It's a fish. The Delta—"

She laughed. "I know it's a fish. I was trying to make you smile."

"Anyway, I like having a family."

A pause. Kate gave him a tilted look. "Even a family with a schizophrenic kid?"

He smiled at her. "Long as I have you, we can handle anything."

He yawned, stretched, feeling suddenly bone weary. He looked at the kitchen clock, a replica of an old railway station clock. It was ten after five.

"Bedtime, babe?"

Kate nodded, picked up the glasses, went to the sink and then back to the fridge, opened the door, leaned in, poking around inside. "See anything you want before we go to bed?" she asked over her shoulder.

"Yes," he said, standing up and coming over to her. "And here it is."

She laughed softly, straightened up, moved back into him, pushing her hips into him, leaning her head on his chest as he moved his arms around to hold her waist and belly.

"You don't *feel* sleepy right now," she said.

"I don't feel Sneezy or Dopey either. What I *feel* is you."

She sighed, relaxed into him. "I was wondering how long it would take for this nightgown to get to you."

In Iceland All the Heat Is Below the Surface, Which Is Worth Remembering if You Ever Meet a Girl from Iceland

Around the same time that Kate and Nick were climbing the stairs in their house in Garrison Hills, Lemon Featherlight's bedside phone rang in the Charlottesville Hampton Inn. He caught it on the third ring, checked the clock—5:16 a.m.

"Lemon? Did I wake you?"

"Helga?"

"Yes. It is Helga, Lemon. You sound funny."

That made Lemon smile.

Helga Sigrid was born in Reykjavik, Iceland, and still had an accent right out of Wagner. She was almost as tall as he was, and as Nordic as it was possible to get without disappearing altogether whenever the sun came out. And he was as tanned and dark and angular as American Indians can get. When they were together they looked like photo negatives of each other. The only physical quality they shared was that they both had green eyes.

"Yes, sorry. I guess I was asleep."

A pause, during which she must have looked at a clock somewhere nearby. "Oh, *fjandinn! Skit og fjandinn!* It's only five in the morning. I am in my office, and I lost track. Look, I will call you back, yes?"

Lemon was sitting up, reaching for the glass of water he had on the sideboard. "No, no . . . I'm up—I was already up—"

"You are already up because you had to answer the phone. I am such an *hálfviti*—"

"Helga, stop it. You're not a half-wit. Why are you working so late?"

"Actually I am working so early. I have just worked through the report from Dr. Burnham at the University of Kansas—"

Lemon was trying to kick-start his brain.

"I'm sorry, Helga—Dr. Burnham?"

"He's the expert in vertebrate paleontology at the University of Kansas. We sent Freddy out to him?"

Freddy was her name for the sixth bone basket they had pulled out of the willow roots by the Tulip River. Like the other six—Adam, Billy, Charlie, Doug, Eric, and Gunther—Freddy was what looked like the fossilized remains of a human being, but subjected to some odd process that had turned it into a kind of delicate stone basket made of slender spokes that looked like ribs, curving up from a row of cylindrical objects that looked a lot like human vertebrae, but were not, or at least not exactly. Each "rib" tapered to a fine point as it arched upward and inward to create a closed arch over the interior, in the center of which was a single spherical object about the size of a five-pin bowling ball, covered in tiny seams that made the thing look like a model of the planet Mars, with those lines that everybody once took to be canals. The bone baskets varied in size, almost the way a child's skeleton would differ in size from that of an adult, and they varied in color as well, ranging from pale jade green to a deep ruby red.

No one in the forensic archaeology community had any idea how the hell they came to be, or exactly what they were made of, so Helga had sent four of them away to various other experts around the world, to see what they could make of them.

Apparently Helga had gotten her first answer tonight—this morning—from a paleontologist at the University of Kansas in Lawrence. That it was worth a call at five in the morning was clear in her voice, which was low and vibrating like an oboe.

"Yes, he is very excited too, Lemon. What he says is—"

"Helga, wait, hold on, I'm just going to put some clothes on."

"You are in the nude?"

"Yeah, well, pretty much."

"Too bad we do not have a videophone. I would like to see you in the nude."

Helga, being Icelandic, had no boundaries about sex, which to her was a cross between Pilates and judo.

"Yes, well, everyone needs a goal. Wait one."

He climbed out of the bed, padded across the thick carpet and slipped on the robe that came with the suite, flicked on the automatic coffee machine, sat down at the desk, picked up the extension.

"Okay. I'm good. Tell me."

"First exciting thing is that he says Freddy contains a high amount of a metal called actinium. Actinium is a radioactive metal formed during nuclear reactions. It is also rare and he says it is also quite valuable. They use it as a neutron source—"

"Helga, wait—these things are radioactive?"

"Yes, but do not worry. They are not harmful to us. Or maybe not too much harmful, anyway. He had Freddy tested in their metallurgical facility—"

"So Freddy's not made of bone?"

"You remember how fossils work? How they are made? Say, if a bone is buried inside a matrix, like limestone, then gradually the organic material of the bone dissolves over many years, and since it is buried inside a matrix, it leaves a hollow space, like a mold, and over many thousands of years the minerals from the matrix fill up the space—the mold—left by the bone. If it is then brought back to the surface, and found, what it looks like is something that was once alive, but what it really is just an exact three-dimensional copy of whatever creature—"

"Okay, yes, I understand that. So Freddy and all the other bone baskets, are they really copies of what was once a human skeleton? Human remains?"

"Dr. Burnham says very much so. But he is also quite puzzled, because as you know, this fossilizing process takes thousands of years."

"So these bones are seriously old?"

"He says some may be, and he is in touch with the others, the people who have Eric and Billy and Gunther, to see if there is an age difference. They are trying to carbon-date them. So here is the thing, Lemon, that is making for so much excitement. Dr. Burnham is absolutely convinced that Freddy was once a Native American Indian who died only maybe two hundred years ago."

"But how can that be possible?"

"It *cannot* be possible. The excitement is because we are all so wrong. We do not know what we are talking about. We must totally rethink our entire profession. It is all quite thrilling, to be involved in something this significant."

"Because Freddy is a fossil that's not old?"

"Yes, exactly. Because Freddy is a fossil of a Native American Indian just like you who was maybe twenty when he died and who is now radioactive because of the actinium in him. Somehow he got made into what he is all at once, in terms of paleontology, and not in a hundred thousand years."

"I'm not getting this. Help me out here?"

"So, silly, if Freddy is made all at once, we have a puzzle, and the puzzle is, what made him?"

"What do you mean, *what*?"

"Sorry? I do not understand?"

"By *what* do you mean a *process* or . . ."

"A person? No, of course not. Not a person, Lemon. A *process*. A natural phenomenon we know nothing about. This is so exciting, Lemon. Much work will have to be done. Grant money must—"

"But whatever *made* it, is Freddy now made of the thing that used up all of his organic stuff?"

"You are talking as if Freddy was eaten and then spit out. This is crazy talk, Lemon."

"But you said that whatever Freddy was in—"

"The matrix."

"That is what Freddy became. I mean, the stuff he's made of now—"

"Would be the stuff of the matrix he was in, yes. But Freddy was not *devoured*, Lemon. He was simply *processed*. By *nature*, not by some animal."

Lemon was thinking about the Kalona Ayeliski, the eater of souls. The Raven Mocker demon.

She needs to know about the "presence." The thing in Crater Sink. The Kalona Ayeliski. She needs to know now.

"Helga, we need to talk. There's something you've got to know about."

"You sound so serious, Lemon."

"I am, Helga. Deadly serious."

"Okay. I will be right over. Stay nude."

Blue Eddie Makes a Suggestion

Blue Eddie's restaurant, owned and operated by Blue Eddie Fessendein, had been designed to look like the bar in Edward Hopper's painting *Nighthawks*, complete with the white walls and the big curved mahogany bar and the overhead lights and the wraparound picture windows. The idea came from Blue Eddie's wife, Rosamunda, whose family had been "quality" and had, by some kind of osmosis, burdened Rosamunda with avant-garde pretensions.

Except that Blue Eddie's Diner wasn't in some nostalgic forties-era street corner in Chicago's South Side or Philly or Brooklyn, but at the intersection of Virtue Place and Atchafalaya Way, on the northern limits of Tin Town.

This was the kind of neighborhood where a wide-open wall of picture windows would have been stitched full of bullet holes or had an ash can tossed through it as soon as somebody could sober up enough to combine thinking about it with actually getting up and doing it.

This was a brutal fact of daily life in Tin Town that had, after fifteen years, persuaded Blue Eddie's wife Rosamunda to become Blue Eddie's ex-wife Rosamunda.

So Frank Barbetta and Charlie Danziger were sitting at a booth in the rear of a diner that looked exactly like the Hopper painting except all the windows were covered with chicken wire and steel bars, which made the place feel more like a dog pound than a diner.

It did, however, make beat cops feel safe, since there were only two ways in, the front door or through the kitchen, and the booth at the back had good lines of sight on either entrance, so there were usually uniform cops or detectives in or around the place, except for right now.

Tonight, this morning, whatever—it was still foggy and damp outside—Barbetta and Danziger had the place pretty much to themselves.

Blue Eddie was a fat man with long dirty blond hair and the general outlines of a walrus. A pale *blue* walrus, since some kind of blood condition had given his skin a vaguely bluish tint. Hence the name Blue Eddie.

He was sitting under a stopped wall clock on a badly overmatched swivel chair behind the antique cash register up front, listening to some kind of piano music, meticulously cleaning a .357 Llama Comanche revolver. He had recently taken this weapon away from a drunken Bandido biker who failed to anticipate that six feet and three hundred pounds of pale blue walrus might keep a baseball bat under the counter.

Blue Eddie had greeted them as they came in out of the rain with his usual witty banter—a guttural gargle in which the words *Hey dere Charlie Frankie how yoo doon* could be discerned by a practiced ear.

Barbetta ordered steak and eggs and a side of cornmeal muffins. Blue Eddie was an excellent cook and as long as you never, ever, under any circumstances, looked into the kitchen, you could enjoy almost everything that came out of it.

Danziger looked over the menu, Blue Eddie standing there staring down at him over the top of his half-glasses, breathing through his mouth and smelling of gun oil, cooked coffee, and bacon fat.

"Coffee, strong and black, three eggs over easy, bacon, sausage, side of pancakes with maple syrup—"

"Don god nun."

"Don god nun which?" said Danziger, who knew Blue Eddie of old.

"Mepple srup."

"God *ady* srup?"

"God anjamima."

"That'll do fine."

Blue Eddie oiled off to perpetrate their meals and left Barbetta and Danziger alone to contemplate the events of the night.

Which they did in silence, each man alone with his thoughts, until Blue Eddie came back with two cups and a carafe of strong black coffee. Danziger poured and Barbetta accepted a cigarette from Danziger's pack. Danziger lit them up with a match from the book with the ad for Blue Bird Bus Lines. They sat back into the battered green vinyl booth and looked out at the street, the rain pouring down, the fog shrouding the night, the streetlamps glowing through the mist like alien moons, both men feeling dead beat and vaguely blue.

"You think Gordon will talk?" asked Danziger.

Barbetta gave it a moment, sucking on his Camel. "Probably. Thing is, who's gonna believe him? And even if they do, it's gonna be 'Forget it, Jake, it's *Chinatown*.'"

"How come you didn't put him in the Tulip along with Ollie? I thought that was the plan."

Barbetta looked down at the coffee cup in his hands. "Maybe I shoulda. Just didn't . . . feel like it. Tell you the truth, Charlie, I don't feel like me tonight. I mighta caught something, like a bug."

"Like the flu?"

He shook his head. "No, not like the flu. Like a headache. A migraine . . . Listen, Charlie, where were you coming from when Ollie and Gordon took you on?"

"I was in the MountRoyal. Came out for a coffee, which I never got until just now."

"So you heard all the sirens and shit?"

"Your news guy, Juko the Monkey Boy?"

"Yeah?"

"He told me a guy was trapped in a cave-in, down in the sewers. That was what the sirens were all about, he said."

"Yeah. That was my call. I was on that."

"What happened?"

Blue Eddie was coming with trays.

"Tell you in a minute."

Barbetta waited until Blue Eddie had laid out their plates, set down a bottle of Aunt Jemima syrup, sides of toast, and strawberry jam.

Everything smelled wonderful and they spent some time digging into it. Danziger realized that he couldn't remember his last meal, and that made him think about this whole concept of being dead, but he pushed that down. Worry about that later.

They ate in silence, the only sound in the place the piano music Blue Eddie was listening to, something complex but soothing, slow but insistent. Classical, figured Danziger, and then he remembered that Blue Eddie was always playing classical music, that he would never play anything else, even when the beat cops were howling for *anything* else, please, for the love of Christ.

After a while Barbetta pushed his plate aside, wiped it with a piece of toast, popped the toast into his mouth, and wiped his hands on a napkin, looking out at the street.

A Niceville patrol car was gliding down the street, and the

cop at the wheel rolled his window down, raised his hand to them, then made the *call me* sign with his thumb and little finger. He cruised on down the line and was gone.

Barbetta picked up his cell, flicked it on, stared down at the screen. "Jeez. Fuckin' hysterics," he said. "Fifteen messages and a buncha texts—Mavis, the duty desk. You'd think I never went freelancing after hours."

"What's going on?"

He read down the screen, touching it with his thumb, frowning a bit as he read. "Busy night. No wonder we had Tin Town all to ourselves. All the squads are busy up north. All points out for a red Benz SLS coupe. Another from Mavis Crossfire for a guy wanted for a home invasion up in The Glades. Nasty—I was there when Nick got the call. Suspect may be driving a 1975 blue Caddy Fleetwood plate number Alpha Romeo 2987 Zebra registered to a Maris Yarvik—I *know* him, he owns Yarvik GM on Peachtree. Car ran a red-light camera near the Glades thing . . . That red Benz BOLO is connected to what happened in . . . what I was gonna say . . . in the cave."

He shut the phone off, set it aside.

"The cave-in?" Danziger said, prompting.

"Yeah. Jeez. Pretty fucking extreme."

Barbetta laid it out for Danziger, the whole thing, the Thorsson couple getting wiped out by this Jordan Dutrow kid, the kid's dying declaration to Lacy Steinert and Nick Kavanaugh.

Danziger heard him out while he finished his meal, pausing only when Blue Eddie came back to clear the table, after which he set down a Kool-Aid jug full of Chianti and two juice glasses with kittens and butterflies romping around the outside.

Barbetta and Danziger watched him lumber back to his swivel chair and pick up his Llama Comanche. The clock on the wall above him was eternally stopped at 3:48 in the morning. The rumor ran that it was 3:48 in the morning when Rosamunda had bailed out on Blue Eddie.

Barbetta seemed to be drifting, so Danziger brought him back. "So this kid, Dutrow, he said he had something in his head? Like he was hearing voices?"

"Not voices. A voice. Kinda like a whiny buzzing sound, it was in his head. Thing was, we could all sort of hear it: the EMT folks; Jack Hennessey the fire guy, he was there; I think also Lacy and Nick. Like in the air all around, faint, like it was a long way off, or real high up at the edge of what we can hear."

"And it was screwing up the radios?"

"Yeah, seemed to be anyway."

"Okay . . . and?"

"And, well, okay, don't laugh, but I think it's in my head now."

Danziger let that simmer for a bit. "*In* your head?"

"Yeah. I know. Crazy. But I can kinda feel it, right here—" He tapped the side of his left temple, where a vein was throbbing.

"It goes up and down, in and out, fades away and then gets stronger. The kid said you'd be okay if you didn't listen to it, if you didn't start hearing words. So far I'm doing okay, but . . ."

"But tonight?"

"Yeah. Might be affecting me, anyway. Thirty years, I never fired a shot in anger. Not one. And tonight, I take Ollie Kupferberg's head off for looking at me sideways."

Danziger kept his hands on the table, and said nothing, only nodded.

"And I do this after I start hearing this thing in my head. So, I'm wondering, you know . . . I'm *wondering*. About all of this. I'm just . . . trying to think it through."

He sat back, looked at Danziger. "And then there's *you*, Charlie."

"How come me?"

"Well, Charlie . . . you were saying, inna car there, that you were having trouble remembering shit. Recent shit, not way back stuff."

"Yeah. Some of it's coming back, bits and pieces."

"Like what?"

"Like I remember being in an old garage up in the Belfair Range—"

"The Belfair Pike Saddlery?"

"Yeah. And this matchbook here—"

He held it up.

"The Blue Bird Bus. Got this from your news guy when I bought the cigarettes. It means something, me getting it, like a clue, but I can't figure out what. Not yet, anyway."

Barbetta was nodding. "Yeah, right, all of a piece, this weird shit, it seems to be everywhere. All of a sudden, we got home invasions and crazy shit everywhere . . . including me and you . . . So here's the thing . . . gonna be blunt here."

"Always the best way."

"Yeah. Okay. Way I see this, either you've got amnesia or you're dead. One or the other. If you've got amnesia, it means you didn't really get shot and killed during a gunfight with some mobsters up at your ranch, and your whole cop funeral was faked for some conspiracy spy-shit federal dickhead reason we can't think of . . ."

"Personally, I'm leaning toward that."

"Because if we go the other way, you being actually dead, I think we're both fucked."

Danziger considered that. "You mean, if I'm dead, how can you see me?"

"Yeah, and Blue Eddie over there, and Gordon and Ollie and Juko. Everybody's seeing you, including me."

"Therefore I'm not dead."

Barbetta rubbed his temple, sipped at his juice glass of Chianti, grinned at Danziger. "Maybe not all the way dead."

"You're either dead or not dead, Frank. Like you can't be sort of pregnant. I don't *feel* dead, Frank, whatever that feels like."

"I'm being serious here, Charlie. If you're not all the way dead yet, maybe I'm not either. And that's why I can see you. Because of this thing that's moved into my head. There's another thing. Whatever's in my head, it doesn't like you."

Danziger sat back, his smile going away.

"Not *me*, you asshole," said Barbetta. "The *thing* in my head. It's gone all quiet, like it doesn't want to get noticed by you. I think it's . . . afraid of you. I can hardly hear it now. But before I got to you, down by the hotel, it was so loud it was like a dental drill going right through my skull."

"Migraine, that's all."

"No. Not a fucking migraine. Brenda had fucking migraines, so I know what they are. Compared to this thing in my head, a fucking migraine is—"

There was a burbling sound in the night air, and they both looked out the window. A sleek red blur, low and menacing, rolled out of the fogbank, shimmering in the light from the diner, gliding through the mist, headlights raking across the window, flaring into their eyes, moving on slowly. It was a scarlet Benz. It slithered through the light from Blue Eddie's and vanished into the fogbank again.

"Dammit," said Barbetta, standing up, flicking his cell phone back on, looking straight down at Danziger, throwing some money on the table. "Yeah, Central, this is Barbetta . . . yeah, I know I know. I was just cruisin' . . . Well, fuckin' sue me . . . Listen, willya, listen . . . I'm rolling at Blue Eddie's . . . I just saw that red Benz everybody is looking for . . . Christ, Billy, of course I'm fucking sure! It's a fucking SLS AMG, some piece of German steel like that, fucking quarter mill a pop, we only got two in the whole state . . . I'm rolling now! Like right fucking now! Get some cars on it . . . yeah, that's it, Blue Eddie's Diner!"

He put the phone in his pocket. He was up and moving fast down the aisle, looking back. "You coming, Charlie?"

"No. I can't. I gotta figure things out."

Barbetta stopped there, looking at Danziger.

"Hey, Charlie, I don't see you again, well, you were a great cop, and you died pretty good—"

"Yeah, well, I love you too. Now fuck off."

"Okay. You got my number. I gotta fly."

He was at the front now. Hand on the door, he paused, looked back again. "Charlie, one last thing. What about the buzzing in my head? If it's really afraid of you, got any idea what I should do?"

Danziger was thinking about it when Blue Eddie stood up, reached under the counter, and handed Barbetta something. Barbetta looked down at it. It was an iPod and a set of earphones.

"SHOW-pan," said Blue Eddie.

"Show pin?" said Barbetta, confused.

Blue Eddie shook his head, spoke more slowly. "Show-PAN. Freddie SHOW-pan. Piano music. Keeps yer head clear. Kills da buzzing."

"*You* have the buzzing," said Barbetta.

Blue Eddie moved his massive head forward and back and then showed his greenish teeth. "Fuggin' years. Goddid in Paddonz Ard. Onna pig-nig wid Rosamunda. Willa trees along da ribber dere. Fuggin willas are alwez buzzing. Godda nod lissen or words start coming. Den yer rilly fugged."

"And this works," said Barbetta, lifting the iPod up. "It keeps the words away? Chopin?"

"Yiz," said Blue Eddie. "Show-pan. Menly da NOG-turns. Nodda sonadas. Godda idee from Rosamunda. She hadda buzzin in her hed doo. Why she hadda ged oudda Nizeville. Da buzzin fuggin drove her crazy."

"Your wife thought of this?"

"Yiz," he said, in a solemn whisper. "Rosamunda did. She figgered id oud. Classigal musig. Didn't stop id, but id pushed id down. Keeps you from hearin da werds. You hear da werds, den yer . . ."

"Rilly fugged," said Barbetta.

"Yah. Rilly fugged. Rosamunda . . ." He stopped, gave a wistful smile, a heartache smile, his eyes moist and shining. "Rosamunda, she wuz . . . qualidy."

Barbetta was gone, followed shortly by a couple of other squads, their lights bouncing crazily off the windows and walls, sirens howling.

Danziger listened to the sirens fading slowly away. He lifted his juice glass, drained it, walked up front to Blue Eddie, who was back on his chair, cherishing the .357 with a fresh bar rag.

Danziger put the bill down on the counter, along with Barbetta's cash and another hundred of his own. Blue Eddie studied the pile over his half-glasses.

"Doo mudge, Charlie."

"How much was the iPod?"

Blue Eddie blinked at Danziger. "Free. Wuz Rosamunda's."

"What are you going to use now on the buzzing?"

He held up the Llama, grinned at Danziger. "Mebbe dis."

"Jeez, Eddie."

"Only kidding, Charlie. God Show-pan onna reddio right here. CD. God him alla time. Bud tings gedding strenge. Nizeville gedding priddy fuggin strenge."

"You mean Frank?"

"Nah. Keeps Show-pan on, heel be okay. Strenge izz yew."

"Me?"

Blue Eddie inclined his massive head. "Yew. Frank is ride.

You here, my buzzin backed off doo. Buzzin doesn't lige you. I tink yer here to fug with the buzzin. Boud fuggin dime doo."

"Maybe I should borrow the gun?"

Blue Eddie shook his head again, his cheeks glistening with sweat, his eyes clear and sharp. "No. Gun wod do id now. Wud yoo shud doo . . ."

"Yeah?"

"Tek da bus."

Twyla Discovers That an Apple
Can Bite Back

They came up the beach just before dawn, three strong young men. Five of them, the diehards, had been sitting around the Kellermans' pool after the patrol guys left, after *everybody* left, sitting around in the wreckage and litter, hungover, depressed, staring at the various citations the patrol guys had written them up for—*drunk and disorderly, underage drinking, supplying alcohol to minors, possession of cocaine for personal use, possession of Ecstasy for personal use* . . . the list went on for quite some distance, and they knew that there would be *repercussions*.

Serious fucking *repercussions*.

From the parental units certainly, possibly from the dean of students at Notre Dame, and from the coaching staff, perhaps even from John J. himself . . . At the very least, if all of this surfaced in the wrong places, they were off the squad and possibly suspended from the school. Expulsion was not out of the question.

To say nothing of the various criminal charges that were pending the further investigations of the FHP.

Unlike some other universities—say, Duke or UC Santa Cruz—Notre Dame did not look kindly upon the kind of butthead stunts these five young men and their minions had gotten up to last night.

And there was the cell-phone video some total moron had taken, which the cops had happily confiscated, because of the *other* pending charge, the *sex with minors* part.

The Kellerman kid, Nathan, was the first to come up with the notion of payback, but it caught on pretty quick with two other guys. Spencer Ramey was a second-string fullback and Anthony Torinetti Jr. was part of the practice squad; all three of them—Nate, Spence, Tony—were big, nimble, quick, long-armed, and rangy, and all of them were extremely happy to collide with things.

Blake Kellerman was Nathan's older brother, just turned twenty-one, almost as big and dark as Nate, but nowhere near as steroidal. His major was poly sci, his sport was lacrosse, and his participation in the evening had been restricted to the beer keg and the happy contemplation of all the naked girls in the pool.

The last kid was Louis T'Beau Barclay, a red-shirt freshman wide receiver, a rising star who was already being watched by the pros.

When Nate brought up the idea of payback, Louis Barclay, inevitably known as T-Bone, tried to shoot it dead right there. "No fucking way, Nate. We're already in the shit. Now you want to go harass some old retired guy? Waddya gonna do, take away his walker? Cut your losses. Start thinking about damage control—"

"It was none of that asshole's business," said Nate, flaring up. "He's five hundred fucking yards up the shore—"

"How do you even know it was that Sinclair guy?" Blake wanted to know. "You were making enough noise to wake people up in fucking Daytona."

Nate rounded on him. "I heard one of the state guys talking to that redneck sergeant who was running things. He wanted to know if somebody should drive up and interview Mr. Sinclair. The sergeant saw me looking at them, pulled the guy away. It was him. Sinclair. Who the fuck else could it have been? There's nobody else on the whole beach other than Sinclair and that skanky Puerto Rican punchboard he's shacked up with."

Blake shrugged it off, had some beer, and said, "You can go if you want to, Nate. But I'm sure as shit not dumb enough to go with you. We're already in deep shit with Mom and Dad—"

"They fucking got insurance, you dildo. You can pussy out if you want," he said, standing up, weaving a bit. "I'm going. Who's in?"

Spence Ramey got up, pulled at his beer. "I'm in. What the fuck. Let's go scare the shit out of the old fart."

Anthony Torinetti, Tony, was thinking about how being on the practice squad could help him get on the Irish full-time. He felt he needed to show some team spirit. He stood up, looked around at the rest of the guys. "Okay. Let's do it."

"Do what, Nate?" said T-Bone, not moving an inch. "Do *what*, exactly?"

Nate looked around, and then his face just went darker. "That man has just fucked my entire life. I'm gonna go fuck up his."

T-Bone shook his head, smiled up at Nate. "You go right ahead, Nate. You're the one who's fucked here, banging that tiny thing, letting Spence film it. Me? Hell, patrol ain't got shit on me, other than some dope, and even Barack smoked dope. I'm clean, I got people from the Rams, from the Saints, lookin' at my lovely black ass. I am not fucking that up so you and me and the guys can bond over some poor cracker's busted nose. The rest of you guys got any brains, you'll sit right back down here and we can co-*or*-din-ate some bullshit and get your asses out of trouble. Cool?"

"Cool with me," said Blake, leaning back in his lounge chair and popping another Stella.

Nate looked at them for a while, uncertainty in his eyes, but then he clouded up again, got red, turned without another word, and went down the wooden stairs that led to the shore.

Spence followed him, and after a second, so did Tony. They were in flip-flops, baggy plaid shorts, and tank tops. Blake and T-Bone Barclay watched them go, three pale figures against the sand, the wide ocean rolling and booming. Far away over the Atlantic a delicate pink glow was in the sky.

"Dumb fucks," said T-Bone.

"Should we call the Sinclairs, let them know? Warn them?"

Barclay though that over. *Get involved? Or stay off the radar?*

"We call, cops could say we should have done more to stop them. Other hand, if those folks know Nate's coming, they can button up and call patrol. Might keep those boys from doing something worse."

Blake thought about it. "Fuck it. I'm calling." And he did.

Coker said, "Thanks," and put the phone down. Twyla was standing beside him in the darkened kitchen.

"Who was that?"

"Blake Kellerman. He says that Nate and two of his friends are on the way up the beach to kick our asses. Says they're all big boys, football guys."

That did not please her. She turned without a word and headed for the rear hall deck. Coker knew she kept a security piece there, a small Colt Government Model .380 with a seven-round mag. It was a light piece, but he'd seen Twyla bounce a can of cream soda all over a sandlot with it, never missing, at a range of fifty feet.

He followed her down the hall, got a hand on her shoulder. "Honey, we can't be shooting the citizenry."

She had the gun out and turned under his hand, her muscular frame twisting away, her dark eyes hot. "I know what you're thinking, Coker. You're gonna go out there—"

"And reason with them," said Coker, and there was that smile, like moonlight on an ice field.

He pulled on a pair of white slacks and a black tee, walked across to the glass doors that led out to the beach, stopping as he got to the threshold. "No, babe. Stay inside. Please."

"Nate plays for the Irish," she said. "He's as big as a house, and so are the other two, I'll bet."

"We'll see, won't we? If it goes bad, don't be calling the cops again. Just scatter my ashes over the Bighorns, okay?"

She looked at him.

"Oh, don't worry. I won't be calling the cops. And fuck your scattered ashes."

"Too late now," said Coker, looking down the shore. In the growing light it was easy to see three large figures making their way north along the dunes. "Here they come."

Twyla stayed in the shadow of the deck awning, the Colt in her hand. As Coker went down the stairs and out onto the beach, she racked the slide and pumped a round into the chamber. The *snickety-snick* sound was faint in the roaring of the ocean, but Coker heard it and smiled to himself.

Twyla was a keeper, he thought, and then he stopped thinking, just came down to the hard sand by the water—the footing was better there—set himself, shook out his shoulders and his neck, and watched the three boys come up.

Nate was the guy in the middle, maybe a touch bigger than the other two. It was hard to make out faces in the half-light, but their general silhouette was informative. Broad-shouldered, narrow-hipped, long arms and big hands.

They stopped a few yards back and spread out a bit. Coker noticed they were all wearing flip-flops, the dumb fucks.

Coker was barefoot. Not even Bruce Lee could fight in flip-flops on beach sand.

"Sinclair, you fuckin' snitch," said Nate, his voice tight and slurred. In the shore breeze Coker could smell beer and dope coming off them. He figured that was good, because they'd still be drunk, or at worst badly hungover.

Coker didn't answer.

"You called the cops," said Nate.

"Yeah," said Spence. "You're gonna get beat, old man. Gonna get beat on like a bongo."

Coker sighed, remembering that he had promised Twyla he'd just reason with them. Not that she believed that for a second.

"Look, Nate, you were tearing the place apart. It sounded like people were getting hurt—"

"You're the fuckhead who's gonna get hurt," said one of the other two. Coker didn't know him. Coker kept his focus on Nate.

"You're a football player, Nate. You need your health. If you go ahead here, I promise you, your career ends tonight. You'll never play football again. You'll be lucky if you can walk."

All three of them laughed at that.

"You're a fucking *banker*," said Nate. "A wrinkly-ass old fuck getting his knob polished by some skanky Puerto Rican whore. So fuck you."

Coker ran right out of *reasonable* when they started talking about Twyla. He looked out at the ocean for a second, getting his focus, came back to the boys, and now his voice belonged to the lizard that lived deep down in his amygdala.

"Okay. Here's the deal. If you three have to talk until you grow some balls, I'll go back to bed and wait. Otherwise, shut the fuck up and let's get started."

This sent a ripple through the three boys, and they seemed

to fall back an inch or two. Then, with a bullish snort, Nate came at him, the other two going wide and trying to come in from his sides.

Coker turned slightly, braced, timed it, and kicked Nate Kellerman very hard in the left knee, just as Kellerman had planted his left foot in the sand, his right leg in the air, all of his body weight on that left knee. Coker caught him exactly right, putting all his power into it, a snaky scythelike sideways blow coming in fast and full of impact, and he felt Kellerman's knee snapping, a meaty wet pop as the sinews and cartilage gave away and the entire joint tore itself apart. He finished the follow-through and completed his pivot, seeing Nate going down, screaming, holding his knee, the angle sickeningly wrong. Coker came back to the ready, hands at his sides.

The other two kept coming, no hesitation, and Coker knew he was going to get hit, and he did. He felt a rocky fist bounce off his forehead, rode it back, felt strong arms on his neck, head-butted backward and felt someone's cheekbone crack, got punched hard in the left ear, and again felt the drum pop, pain bolting through his skull, and then the rage primeval came rushing in, a flow of streaming electrons, a bloodred tide.

He twisted away from an incoming punch, a straight left, felt it graze his right eye, caught the forearm of the guy connected to the punch—it was Spence—locked him there in a bar, stepped under and in and drove the butt of his open palm into Spence's upper lip, aiming for a place about a foot on the other side of the boy's skull.

Properly delivered, it's a strike that can drive the nasal bones right through the sinuses and into the brain. Coker didn't hold back, but he knew that he had come in a tad low.

He could feel the kid's front teeth crack and shatter under his palm, feel his own flesh shredding on the kid's broken stumps. The kid's head went flying back, blood spraying out in a fan, along with some of his teeth, and Coker pivoted, swept the boy's left leg out from under him, put a choke hold on his Adam's apple, squeezing it tight as he sent him to the ground, where Spence Ramey hit hard and lay flat, snorting, gagging, blowing blood and tissue out of his broken nose and his ruined upper lip.

There was a pause, a break, heavy breathing, and the third kid, Tony Torinetti, was moving back fast, holding something up in his hand, lifting it to his face. Nate was still shrieking and writhing on the ground. The kid, backing away, was saying *No, please no.* Coker thought *Gun, a gun? No, not a gun,* and then there was a flash and a dry click and another white flash and Coker realized it was a *camera,* a fucking cell-phone camera—the asshole was taking pictures. The kid snapped one more while backpedaling like crazy, turned and ran, ran fast and ran hard, his feet kicking up fan sprays of sugary sand.

Coker, his chest heaving, his ear on fire, and blood running down the side of his face, started off after the kid, but the kid was *fleet,* and there was something wrong with Coker's ankle. Twyla was there, with the Colt, breathing hard.

"Coker, are you okay?"

Nate Kellerman was out of it, crying and moaning, both hands wrapped around the pulped ruin of what used to be his left knee, his football days over forever. Spence Ramey was on his back, snorting like a hog, choking on his own blood.

Coker went over to Spence, flipped the kid onto his side so he wouldn't choke to death. Coker stayed there, checking his airway. Coker hadn't crushed his larynx. Too bad. His looks were fucked. Some reconstructive surgery, dental implants, he'd be almost new. Still be a world-class dumbass.

Coker walked away, bent over, put his hands on his knees, trying to catch his breath. Feeling his age. They both watched the third kid running, a black stick figure windmilling down the shoreline.

A camera. A fucking iPhone with a camera.

He looked up at Twyla, calmed himself. "The kid had an iPhone. He took pictures."

Twyla took that in, her expression calm. "Then I'll have to go get it, won't I?"

Coker shook his head. "Don't bother. Won't matter."

"Why not?"

"It was an iPhone, Twyla. Think about it."

She did. "Oh, shit. Photo Stream. Whatever shots you take, they go right into Photo Stream."

"And then into the fucking Cloud. And from there into every other Apple machine he's got."

Twyla stood up, watched the stick figure stumble up the steps of the Kellerman place. "There's more," she said, turning to him.

"More?" said Coker, straightening up.

"Yeah. It's called Photo Stream Sharing."

"Sharing? And that means?"

"That if he shares his Photo Stream with his friends, any shot that goes onto *his* Photo Stream will automatically turn up on everybody else's phone. Basically they'll go . . . everywhere."

Coker was looking down at the two boys, Nate still keening in pain, the other kid out cold.

"Define *everywhere*, Twyla."

"Social media. Facebook. Instagram."

"Fuck me," said Coker. "Fuck me blue."

Twyla started to laugh, a hard edge in it. "Do we have time?"

Saturday

———

Eufaula and Rainey Discuss Tea Trays

Nick had bloody awful dreams that he managed not to recall when he woke up to a Saturday morning in his own bed, sunlight streaming in through the gauzy bedroom drapes, the sound of swifts and skylarks in the branches of the live oaks outside his window, the dreams leaving only a low-level sense of crawling dread, which dissipated quickly as he came fully awake.

Kate was already up and gone to her office; she had a tricky custodial care hearing on Monday morning and had to prepare for it. He had been dimly aware of her moving around the room, getting dressed, trying not to disturb him.

He could smell breakfast cooking, coffee and bacon and eggs, and the sound of kids chattering came up the stairs, and Eufaula's voice carrying above the din, a calm competent woodwind tone in a Tidewater accent, something about not waking Nick.

Nick shaved, showered, did some push-ups off the end of the bed, making it a point not to think about the Thorssons or the Morrisons or anything work-related as he pumped out a quick one hundred, feeling his body moving, feeling a pleasant burn in his chest and shoulders.

When he got down to the kitchen he stood in the doorway, unnoticed, watching the kids around the big white table in the breakfast nook, part of him wondering where the word *nook* came from, the rest of him enjoying the domestic scene.

The kids were all gathered around the table, Rainey at his favorite spot on the end, a handsome kid—a lady-killer someday. Not so small anymore, he was filling out fast, losing the belly softness, getting shoulders and arms. He had silky blond hair that hung down to his shoulders, large expressive eyes of cornflower blue, a quick wit, maybe a touch sly, capable of cunning, but then, as Kate said, so were most kids.

Rainey didn't see Nick at the door and was gently teasing Hannah, a sweet-natured kid, white blond curls and huge blue eyes and a slightly demented sense of humor. Axel, looking on, was a thin wiry boy with shaggy brown hair that hung down in his eyes—long hair was the thing now for school-age boys.

Axel had big brown eyes that reminded Nick of a Disney rabbit—a sensitive kid, smart, but with a bruised quality that came from being the son of an abusive prick like Byron Deitz.

Nick liked the kid. If he'd been inclined to favorites, he'd have favored Axel, but he worked hard to resist that tendency. Axel had grace and style and a brave heart. Nick watched him watching Rainey wind Hannah up, thinking about older brothers and hero worship, and then about the social worker Alice Bayer, a thought he had pretty often when he looked at Rainey. So there was some ugly history between Nick and Rainey, and negotiating around it in a civil manner was a daily dance for both of them.

Eufaula saw him first and called out a cheerful good morning, and the kids, descending into mayhem, up to their ears in pancakes and maple syrup—not a pretty sight—chirped and hooted at him like a roost of brainless budgies.

Eufaula was their live-in housekeeper, a young woman training for dance, tall and graceful, a lithe and curvy body and the sculptural head of an Ibo River carving. Heart-attack beautiful, she was engaged to a cadet second class at the Virginia Military Institute, the same school where Kate's father Dillon had been a faculty member.

She was wearing a whole-body leotard in black, bright red ballet flats, a Liberty headscarf that Kate had given her, all reds and golds, and a scarlet apron. She was a pleasure to behold, as always. She came over. "Nick, how did you sleep?"

"Like a stone, thanks, Eufaula. And you?"

"Kate and I stayed up waiting for you. I went to bed at three. She says you didn't get in until four. You must be beat. I have coffee."

Nick took the coffee, served in a delicate bone china cup—Eufaula hated mugs—and he sipped at it as he leaned against the wall, waiting for the kids to finish their breakfast.

He tried never to sit down at a table where little kids were eating. It was like trying to eat beside a juice blender without the lid on. You came away stuccoed with sticky.

Eufaula was doing what Nick could only call a swirl: moving around the breakfast table, crossing the checkerboard kitchen floor, picking up this, moving that, setting other plates down, biscuits and jam, glasses of orange juice, floating over the chaos of the children, always moving, always in control, now and then sending him a flashing smile.

She had reacted with a cool and easygoing efficiency to the sudden arrival of three children and a newly made widow in a household that had been, up until recently, two adults who were hardly ever home. In short, Eufaula had become indispensable, and they paid her accordingly and treated her with respect. When she had slowed down enough to have a coffee of her own, Nick asked her where Beth was.

"Gone down to Cap City, to talk to Agent Hackendorff and the FBI lawyers about Mr. Deitz's estate."

"Kate was saying. Good news for her."

Eufaula sipped at her coffee and Nick got the impression she was framing a tactical answer. Nick noticed the quick glance at Rainey.

"It is. She's talking about buying something around here, but maybe she'll end up in Cap City, where her work is. Be easier for her, no commute."

Nick led her a bit. "Axel would miss Rainey. They're pretty tight."

"They'd still be family. See each other on holidays, like cousins do. Axel could use some friends his own age." She glanced up at Nick over her coffee cup. "Sometimes Rainey can lead Axel on some. Rainey has the devil in him, I think."

Somehow, over the din, Rainey heard his name and he looked up at them both, and that veiled look that he sometimes got flashed over his bright young face, as if he knew their thoughts and didn't like them, but then Hannah stole his pancake and he was all kid again.

Nick had long suspected that Eufaula wasn't a complete fan of Rainey's, but they had never talked about it, and they weren't going to right now either. It was forbidden ground in Kate's house, and they both knew it.

They exchanged a look that was full of tacit understanding, and Nick felt better knowing that there was someone else in the house who was keeping an eye on Rainey and on his influence with Axel.

They were schoolmates at Regiopolis, walked there and back every day, and were out and about the neighborhood on their bikes every weekend. Nick thought it was unusual for Rainey to spend most of his time with a boy almost four years younger.

Other than Axel, Rainey had not made friends at Regiopolis Prep, an ivy-covered Romanesque mansion on a huge forested estate in the heart of Old Niceville. It was a Roman Catholic school run with cheerful efficiency by the Jesuits, where the main events of the week were Punishment Parade on Monday morning, Benediction and Confession on Saturday afternoon, and High Mass on Sunday at eleven, followed by a football game at two.

Rainey was talking about trying out for the Bantam squad, and Nick hoped he'd make it. Playing football was good for the soul. Nick had been a pretty effective middle linebacker for the Citadel Bulldogs, and he felt that if Rainey could make the squad, it would give them something to bond over.

He was supposed to be running Rainey and Axel through some drills this afternoon, except that he wasn't going to be able to, thanks to whatever the hell had massacred the Morrison family last night. He went over to the table, ruffled some hair, kissed Hannah on top of her head, and told the boys he was sorry, but he wasn't going to be able to take them out for football practice today.

"We know," said Rainey, slurping his OJ. "Kate told us you were on this really bad case."

"Yeah," said Axel, savoring it. "We hear it was like this awful massacre, like the Indians did to General Custer."

"Custer?" said Nick. "Don't tell me you're studying the Battle of the Little Bighorn in grade four?"

"I'm in grade five, Uncle Nick!"

"You can't be. You're only nine."

"He's ten," Rainey said, smiling up at him. "He turned ten a month ago."

Axel was hot on the massacre theme. "So was it like awful and stuff?" he wanted to know. Rainey looked equally avid for details. Hannah was wiping her syrupy fingers on her dress and singing a song that could have been about polka dots and moonbeams.

"If you mean the Battle of the Little Bighorn, yes, it was."

"No," said Rainey. "We mean the case you're on. Was it real bad? Tell us something gross!"

Nick looked at both boys, wondering about them, what was in their heads, was this typical, or was he just an idiot, but Eufaula was right there.

"None of your business what it was like," she said, going to work on Hannah with a Handi Wipe. "Pay no attention to these horrible little boys, Nick. You have a call waiting in your office."

Nick checked his watch, five to ten. It should be Mavis Crossfire. It was. "We've got a line on a car—"

"From the red-light camera?"

"How'd you know?"

"I checked my computer before I went to bed. Beau posted it to the case file."

"What time was that?"

"Past five. Kate was up. She had mint juleps ready."

"At five in the morning? You do *not* deserve that woman."

"I know that. Where are you?"

"On my way to your house. About nine minutes away. Did you talk to Beau Norlett about the book, running all the case evidence?"

"Yeah. He's at the HQ with Tig right now, compiling all the notes, Riley's CSI report, getting it all into the computer, working out an assignment sheet. He says he's already heard from Chief Keebles about getting some of your NPD people on the case."

"We have five, pulled from Vice and Domestics, two from Bicycle Patrol—"

"Jeez, not those pathetic weenies in their latex bike shorts and those stupid helmets?"

"They're not going to wear their Bicycle Patrol outfits on this case, okay?"

"Good. I mean, what kind of loser cop lets himself get

assigned to *bicycles* anyway? Only thing weenier than that is a mall cop on a Segway."

"Thank you for the career advisory. I'll treasure it always. We did a canvass of the neighborhood again this morning—"

"The security cameras?"

"Yes. You were right. A whole bunch of cameras. It's going to take a while to go through them, and some of them store their video records in the Cloud, so that's gotta be pulled out."

"Warrants?"

"So far everybody's cooperating. They'd all like to see whatever got at the Morrisons get taken off the streets. Another thing. Frank Barbetta ran down that red Mercedes AMG coupe last night."

"Outstanding. Good for him."

"There was a bit of a chase. That's a damn fleet machine. It led our squad cars all the way past Mauldar Field. Guess who finally hooked it?"

"No idea."

"Your brother-in-law."

Reed Walker, Kate's younger brother, drove a high-speed Police Interceptor for the Highway Patrol. The muscled-up Ford cruiser looked like a Doberman on steroids.

But then so did Reed, so maybe he and his car belonged together.

"How did he get pulled in?"

"He was on the night shift. He heard it on the tactical channel, dropped down the side roads, and picked up the pursuit out by Charlie Danziger's place. Benz wasn't so fast on those gravel roads up there, and the driver was a chump. Reed got up close, they were doing one-twenty, Reed bumped it with his grill bars. The Benz went ballistic, rolled and tumbled and ended up in a culvert."

"Who was in it?"

"Two gangbangers, ZeeZee Boys. One male DATS, one female helivaced and critical at Sorrows."

"Conscious?"

"Not yet."

"I'm going to want to talk to her."

"Fifty-fifty. We'll see. Got Boots Jackson in the CCU with her. She comes around, we'll know."

"Yeah. Okay. Where do want to start this?"

"I thought you and me would go down to the Pavilion and talk to Glynda Yarvik."

"Polish babe, serious front porch on her, big blond hair looks like whipped cream, hips like a Cape buffalo, runs the Bar Belle?"

The Bar Belle was a high-end riverside bar and restaurant, part of a series of expensive shops and fern bars built on a quarter mile of cantilevered cedar-planked platform that jutted out over the west bank of the Tulip about a mile south of Patton's Hard.

"That's her. Remind me not to ask you to recap what I look like in a single sentence. That car that ran the red-light camera at Lanai Lane and River Road came back as a 1975 Cadillac Fleetwood, plate number Alpha Romeo 2987 Zebra, registered to a Maris Yarvik. He's the guy that owns Yarvik GM over on Powder Springs. Glynda called Central this morning, saying that he's been off the grid since Friday afternoon. So I think we—"

Nick heard a horn blasting and a soft curse from Mavis, and then she was back.

"Sorry, guy cut me off and then he gives the finger and points to my cell phone."

"You're not on the hands-free?"

"I'm in a 2010 GMC Suburban that is painted bright shiny black. It has *Niceville Police Department* painted in big gold let-

ters along the back and sides, and a big old roof rack loaded
with police lights."

"Civilians suck. How far away are you now?"

"Turning the corner by South Gwinnett and Beauregard."

"I'll be on the porch."

Eufaula was at the window in the living room when Mavis
Crossfire pulled up in her big black Suburban. Nick saw her
standing there as he climbed in, gave her a wave, and she waved
back. Sighing, she turned away from the window and went
back down the hallway, past the cedar-lined dining room with
the Gallé glass chandelier that Lenore Walker had brought
home from Paris the year before she died. Axel and Hannah
were scurrying around, putting dishes in the dishwasher, tidy-
ing up.

Rainey was sitting in his corner at the dining room table,
his back against the bow window, doing something with his
iPhone.

Eufaula pulled out a chair and sat down at the other end of
the table. Rainey didn't look up.

"Rainey, can we talk?"

Rainey looked up, glanced over at Axel and Hannah. Axel
was wiping down the kitchen counter and Hannah was standing at the door to the solarium, fiddling with her hearing aids.
He put the phone aside and sat back in the armchair, cocking
his head to one side, smiling brightly.

"Sure, Falla. What can we talk about?"

Eufaula reached into the pocket of her red apron and
brought out a Motorola walkie-talkie, bright blue plastic, a
solid well-made handset about as big as a cell phone. Rainey's eyes grew cloudy and that *veil* came down. The smile
remained.

"I found this on top of the fridge."

"Oh yeah? What is it?"

"It's a walkie-talkie. One of the walkie-talkies that you and Axel are always playing with."

"Oh yeah?"

"Yes. It was behind the tea tray. The *send* button was held down with an elastic so it would be on all the time. So you could hear what was being said."

"Yeah? Whoa. Who would, like, do that?"

She put her hand into the apron pocket again and pulled out a second handset, a blue Motorola. "I found this one under your pillow."

Rainey went a bit sleepy-eyed.

"Don't know as I like the colored help poking around in my stuff, Falla. I may have to talk to Kate about setting some boundaries for the staff."

Eufaula felt her skin get hot. Something harsh and acrid burned in her throat and she was forced to swallow. Words boiled up, but she kept her mouth shut tight, pushed that emotion down, not wanting Rainey to see how deeply he had cut into her. But now she knew what he was, and the look in her eyes should have warned him. When she spoke her voice was cold and clear and calm.

"I'd like to know why one of these was on top of the fridge, hidden behind the tea trays."

Rainey shrugged.

"I don't know. Maybe . . . Axel and me were playing Special Ops. Maybe he left it up there?"

"Maybe. But he doesn't remember doing it."

"You asked him?"

"Yes. This morning, after I found it."

Rainey looked thoughtful. "Axel is kinda . . . moony, you know. He probably forgot."

"Perhaps he did."

"Or maybe it was Hannah?"

"Hannah would need a ladder to reach the top of the fridge, and anyway she can't use these radios because they interfere with her hearing aids. You and Axel are the only ones who play with them. Axel says he hasn't seen these radios since last week. He saw them in your room. You told him they were broken and you were going to fix them."

"Yeah. They needed new batteries."

"And you replaced them?"

"Yes."

"So Axel was telling the truth?"

"About what, Falla?"

"That he hadn't seen them in a week, that the last time he saw them they were in your room?"

Rainey shrugged, picked up the iPhone, went back to poking at it.

"Rainey . . ."

He kept his head down.

"Yeah, what?"

"Rainey, I don't know what you were doing with these radios, but if it's what I think you were doing—"

He started to shake the iPhone up and down, poking at it. "Temple Run sucks," he said.

"Rainey. Put the phone down."

He didn't, but he looked up at her, a flat lidless stare through his silky blond hair.

"What? I'm trying to play a game here."

"Yes," she said. "You are." She got up, looked down at him, arms folded. "And I know what it is. If you don't stop it, I'll tell Nick and Kate where I found this radio."

The flat stare wavered for a second. Rainey felt that he had Kate under control, but Nick was another story.

"Do you understand me, Rainey?"

He was back to playing with his phone, head down, hair over his eyes, hiding his face.

"Rainey. I need an answer."

He looked up at her and there was nothing of the little boy in his face. Just that lidless stare. "Okay, Falla . . . what-*ever*."

Eufaula stared at him for another minute, but he kept his head down. Finally she walked away. She took the radios with her. Rainey watched her back as she went out into the sunroom. He could hear Axel and Hannah laughing, running around on the lawn in the backyard. They had a playhouse at the bottom of the yard, down near the pine and willow forest there, where the creek ran. Rainey listened hard, and after a while he heard Eufaula's voice mixed in with the kids' voices, some kind of stupid kiddie song about itsy-bitsy spiders.

The sound of the spider song got drowned out by the rising waspish buzzing in his skull.

she knows she knows she knows she knows

Rainey shook his head, making his hair fly, and then he went back to the iPhone game. The voice intensified, became shrill and sharp like a needle, like a rock saw, stinging, slicing, cutting.

she knows he knows they know they all know

"I know," said Rainey. "Don't. That hurts."

need to do something need to do something

"I *know*," he said, with heat. "I'll think about it. Now stop sticking me. Shut the fuck up."

Charlie Danziger Meets Albert Lee

Danziger found the Blue Bird Bus Line terminal right where Monkey Boy's matchbook cover said it would be, at the intersection of Forsythia and Peachtree, by the entrance to Tulip Landing Park. It was a small part of a much larger terminal called the Button Gwinnett Memorial Regional Bus Depot, right in the heart of downtown Niceville. It occurred to Danziger that although he had been into or had walked by the Button Gwinnett Bus Depot many times, he had never noticed the bay where Blue Bird lines carried on their business.

The Button Gwinnett depot was a huge barnlike structure with thirty-two sheltered bays where various bus lines operated—Greyhound, Stars and Bars, Old Dominion, Tres Estrellas, Happy Valley, Southern Cross, and apparently, Blue Bird Lines.

The rains from last night had stopped and the sky was blue, the day warming, but the whole station reeked of mold and diesel fumes. Steam was rising up from the cedar-shingle roof now that the sun had cleared the lip of Tallulah's Wall and was pouring heat and light down onto the center of Niceville.

Niceville downtown was a genteel Deep South shambles, an

old-fashioned city center netted over with a black tangle of telephone poles and power lines, most of it in the shade of a virtual
urban forest of live oaks, a random city full of lanes and alley-
ways, treed parks with fountains or statues of long-dead heroes,
streets laid out in a pinwheel pattern, like Paris or Washing-
ton. Needle-tipped church spires rose up over ragged roof
lines and wrought iron galleries fronted ancient redbrick store
fronts, creating shaded cloisters beneath that ran for blocks in
all directions. In the hazy fall light the town looked timeless and
old-fashioned, like a hand-tinted shot taken from an antique
calendar: *Niceville Seen from the Button Gwinnett Bus Terminal
Looking North Along Forsythia Avenue to Peachtree . . .*

Danziger stopped just inside the shadowy vault of the terminal, watching as a group of passengers filed one by one out
the front door of a very old Blue Bird school bus that had once,
a long while back, been painted a bright robin's-egg blue.

It had BLUE BIRD BUS LINES painted in faded black letters
on the back and sides, and, under the name, their slogan, in
the same Art Deco style:

IF YOU DON'T KNOW WHERE YOU'RE GOING
WE KNOW HOW TO GET YOU THERE.

Danziger approved of the slogan. It had a certain cheeky
style, but the people getting off the bus looked worn-down
and weary, like people seen at the side of a country road in pictures taken during the Great Depression. This Dirty Thirties
vibe was also in their trudging walk and the way they sagged
into themselves as they passed by him and went on out into
the sunlit streets of Niceville. Their faces were blank, expressionless, and there were no children.

After the people passed by, none of them looking his way,
he heard the bus brakes chuffing and sighing, and the rattling
old engine coughed, huffed, rattled, and died.

The bus springs creaked a bit as an old black man, soldier-straight and limber, but white-haired and lined with age, came down the stairs and stepped onto the oily pavement. He was wearing a crisp navy blue uniform. His boots were black and shiny. He was carrying a clipboard and a battered leather briefcase. He stopped by the bus, patted its side, and set the case down by the luggage doors.

He had not noticed Danziger watching him, or so it seemed, but after he had extracted a cigar from an inside pocket and fired it up, he looked at Danziger through the cloud of blue smoke. His eyes were yellow with age, but full of intelligence. He had good lines around his eyes, an open aura around him, a man who smiled often. "Good morning, sir. Might you be waiting for the two o'clock bus?"

Danziger wasn't sure what the hell he was waiting for, but he remembered what Blue Eddie had said to him. *Tek da bus*, and this was the only bus around that seemed to be waiting for him. Danziger came up to the man, who was shorter than he was, but he carried his own gravity with him.

"I'm not sure. I'm trying to get up to the Belfair Saddlery . . ."

"The Belfair Pike General Store and Saddlery? Would that be your destination?"

"Yes, sir, that's right."

"Well, sir, I can save you a trip. The Belfair Pike store got itself burned to the ground about six months back. Isn't nothing there now but a black patch of ground soaked in creosote and a bunch of goldenrod crowding the edges and a big old pine forest all around that."

Danziger's memory fish came shimmering back to his inner mind, Merle Zane firing at him, the bullet holes punching through the old barn boards, spears of sunlight cutting through the haze inside the barn, the smell of gunpowder and kerosene. Then the image flickered away again.

"I didn't know. What happened?"

"Well, sir, the stories vary, but it seems that a couple of bank robbers had a gunfight in it, and that old barn was full of grain dust and gas fumes, so it just caught fire and went up like a bonfire."

"Bank robbers?"

The old man looked at Danziger for a moment. "You don't know the story, sir?"

"Can't say that I do."

"You must be new to Niceville, then."

Danziger hesitated, and the old man noticed that. He checked his watch, an old Hamilton on a leather strap. "It's only the biggest bank robbery ever to happen in this part of the state. If you have a mind to hear it, I'm going across to the Sunrise Grill there to have a bite of lunch. If you'd like to join me, I'd be happy to tell you all about it."

Danziger said he'd be pleased, and they crossed the busy street together, dodging the streaming traffic running up and down Forsythia, stepping quickly out of the path of one of Niceville's famous old trolleys, painted blue and gold, heavy as an Abrams tank. The driver clanged his bell at them as the trolley car rumbled past, shaking the ground; the old man waved back.

The Sunrise Grill was an old-fashioned shotgun-shack diner, fifty feet long and about twelve feet wide, with one long battered wooden bar and a row of stools running the length. The ceiling was covered in stamped tin tiles painted white, the board-and-batten walls were decorated with prints of Civil War scenes taken from calendars, and the lighting came from a line of fifteen green-shaded cones hanging on black wires, each with a dim yellow bulb flickering inside it.

The diner smelled of Dustbane and cigarettes and grilled cheese sandwiches. It was filled with noise and smoke and people, but the old man found a couple of stools down near the back and they bellied up to the counter, where a round damp woman wearing black slacks and a crisp white shirt and a hard-boiled expression was right there, tapping a pencil on her order book. They ordered lunch, grilled cheese and coffee for Danziger, a chicken-fried steak and a pint of ale for the driver, and when she was gone he turned to Danziger and offered his hand.

"I'm Albert Lee, sir. Lee as in the general, not Lea as in the Minnesota. And you are?"

"Charlie Danziger," he answered, shaking the man's hand, a strong dry grip, a leathery pink palm.

Albert Lee seemed to react to the name, and a shadow of some emotion passed quickly over his face and was gone. They made some small talk about Niceville, about the weather, the rains last night and now this mini-heat-wave, and after their meals came, they set about them efficiently, Danziger realizing that although there was a lot wrong with his memory, his appetite was working just fine.

After the plates were cleaned and gone, Albert Lee leaned back, patted his uniform tunic, and took out an old and shiny flat gold case with the initials *JR* engraved on the cover. He flipped it open and offered Danziger a slender cheroot, and lit them both from a brass Zippo with a medallion on the side, a green shield trimmed in white with a red number one in the middle of the green. Danziger recognized the unit patch of the 1st Infantry Division, known as the Big Red One.

"You were in the service, Mr. Lee?"

"I'm Albert, if you will."

"I'm Charlie to my friends, then."

"Charlie it is. 'In the service,' as in the Big Red One? No, sir. This case and lighter came from a dear friend of mine. His widow gave them to me, and I keep them to remember him by. He was killed in the war, and his younger brother maimed in the same battle. A bad war, and we had no business getting into it, and it's all on that grinning fool of a president we had back then. From your ring I'd guess you were a Marine."

"Yes, a long time back."

"I myself was not allowed to serve in a combat unit, the Jim Crow laws being what they were back then, and I wasn't about to spend the war years cooking grits and cleaning out latrines. But I was going to tell you about this robbery, took place up north of here, in a town called Gracie."

Gracie. The name struck Danziger with a tiny crystalline chime. But Albert Lee charged on, leaning into the story. By the time he had finished it all up, Charlie Danziger was all the way back.

The Wind in the Willows

Now that the sun had cleared Tallulah's Wall, a convection wind had come up, and as they cruised down Riverside past the willows along Patton's Hard they could see branches flying and tossing in what looked to become a pretty brisk gale.

Nick, watching them from the shotgun seat in Mavis Crossfire's Suburban, felt the same shiver of dislike that he always felt for that mile-long stretch of old-growth forest that ran along the west bank of the Tulip, from Garrison Hills south to within a half mile of the Pavilion. The willows were abnormally huge, almost grotesque, and according to an arborist from Portland, Maine, who had made a study of such things, they were easily the oldest willows in America.

There was a map of Niceville, engraved around 1820, that clearly showed a large willow forest in this location at that time, and the same trees were still here, towering, thick, with twisted trunks and spreading branches. Which, according to the arborist, was unheard of. The average life span of a weeping willow was around a hundred years. Yet his examination of their trunks confirmed that the willows of Patton's Hard were easily twice that age.

Stepping through the hanging curtain of leaves and into the interior of one was like entering a gigantic green cave that swayed and whispered and creaked over your head, making you feel trapped, almost claustrophobic, or at least that's how these trees made Nick feel.

Nick and Tig and Lemon Featherlight—with the help of a portable crane and five divers from the Sandhaven Shoals Coast Guard station—had pulled Alice Bayer's car and later on Alice Bayer's body out of the river next to one of those towering old willows, and Lemon Featherlight's bone baskets had been ripped out from the tangled netting of willow roots that ran for a mile up the banks.

It was a matted weblike wall of roots that had seemed to fight hard to hold on to those bone baskets, as hard as it fought to hang on to Alice Bayer's body. Seven bone baskets were all they were able to wrench free, although the Coast Guard divers had seen hundreds, perhaps thousands, more of them embedded deep inside the root mass.

Mavis had been looking at the willows as well, and when they cleared the edge of them and were back into main streets, she glanced over at Nick. "Place still gets to you, doesn't it? I've been living near or walking through or driving by those damned willows most of my young life, and they still creep me out."

Nick looked at her and then back out at the traffic streaming all around them. Away in the northeast the ancient trees along the rim of Tallulah's Wall were touched by fire and he could see a tiny cloud of black specks whirling above the trees, right around where Crater Sink was located. A flock of crows, thousands of them, infested the trees around that bottomless black pool, and they had probably been there as long as the willows on Patton's Hard.

Right now it wasn't just Patton's Hard that was getting on his nerves. Or even Tallulah's Wall and Crater Sink. It was

Niceville itself. "Frankly, Mavis, the whole damn town is getting on my nerves."

"I can see that. Maybe you and Kate should take off for a while, let Eufaula and Beth see to the kids. Go to Savannah or even Paris."

"I can maybe afford a weekend in Cleveland."

"Kate's got family money. Don't be such a stiff neck about it."

"Kate's money is Walker family money. It belongs to Beth and Reed and Kate. I don't have a share in it and I don't want one."

"And your money is Kate's money too?"

"Yeah. Of course. We're married."

"So it's also Walker family money?"

"Mavis . . ."

"So why isn't her money *your* money?"

"That's not how it works. I'm her husband. She's my wife. It's my job to take care of her. Why are you riding me about this?"

"Honest?"

"No, lie to me."

"Because I think you two really should get out of Niceville for a while. Kate's half crazy over losing the baby and then all this stuff about Rainey. And if she's half crazy, you're three gallons of crazy in a two-gallon bucket. Tell you the truth, I worry about you."

Nick had something sharp to say but he didn't, but Mavis knew how far to push him and changed the subject. "More weird shit: You remember the two EMT techs yesterday, they attended at that scene down in the tunnel, with Dutrow?"

"Sure. Barb Fillion and Kikki . . . something."

"Kikki Matamoros. Well, middle of the night, outside the Lady Grace ER, right at the end of his shift, somebody mugged Matamoros in the parking lot. Cracked his skull. It's not looking good for him. He's a Catholic and they've given him Last Rites."

"What about his partner, Barb Fillion?"

"She'd already left. They called her to let her know, went to her voice mail. So far she hasn't called back."

"That's not like her. They're a tight pair. They still trying to reach her?"

"Text and e-mail and voice mail. But then she was look-ing at ten days off, so maybe she's gone on a trip or some-thing. She lives alone, so . . . well, anyway, there you go. I have something else if you're game?"

"Let's hear it."

"That 1975 Fleetwood we're looking for seems to have dropped off the planet."

"I was wondering about that. How many 1975 Fleetwoods can there be in this state?"

"According to Motor Vehicles, three hundred and four with active plates."

"Really? That's a lot of old Caddies."

"Yes. It was a tank, and a lot of older people like that. They were built to last. And the South is kinder to old metal than the northern states. So they tend to . . . endure. County and State Patrol guys have stopped close to a hundred of them since last night—no Maris Yarvik yet—and they're running down the rest, but it'll take a few days. They've even got the choppers out, looking at country roads, wood lots, backyards . . . any-where you could stick a car that size. So far, zip."

Nick thought about it. "He's gone to ground."

Mavis nodded. "Yeah. Parking garage or even some rental storage place. If he has, then we're not going to luck out and stumble across it. He's going to have to move."

"Any way we can *make* him move?"

"We'll see what Glynda has to say. Wanna hear some more weird shit?"

"How weird?"

"Oh, you'll love this one. You know the Dark Boys—"

"Ollie and Gordon Kupferberg. They still around? I thought Frank Barbetta warned them off, said if they ever showed up on the Mile again he'd disappear them both."

"Yeah, well, that's the point. Ollie Kupferberg has actually disappeared—"

"Finally, some good news."

"Agreed, long overdue, and praise the Lord, but now Gordon is going around telling anyone who'll listen that Frank Barbetta is the one who disappeared him, right outside the MountRoyal, blew his head off with a shotgun, and then he dumped Ollie's body off the Armory Bridge. At least this is the story he's retailing to the South Sector Duty Desk."

"Good for Frank. I favor proactive policing."

"Yeah, me too. And if he did, and he had a good reason, I'm okay with it, but being as I'm nominally his CO, I'd have appreciated it if he'd sort of mentioned this shooting to me when he debriefed us on the Mercedes-Benz chase this morning. I'm supposed to know who is shooting whom in my sector. I don't, I feel a tad disrespected."

"Well said, especially the 'whom' part. Have you talked to Frank about this?"

"Called him soon as I heard, got him out of bed, I think. He seemed to get a kick out of the whole thing, asked me to tell it twice, and then he said that if he was going to take Ollie's head off with a shotgun he wouldn't leave Gordon around to talk about it, would he?"

"How about that news guy, works the all-night stand right across from the MountRoyal? Juko something."

"Juko Aivazovzky. The duty sergeant talked to him. He says nothing happened anywhere near him other than a fight in some yuppie bar, and of course all the emergency vehicles down around Scales and the Lower Mile."

"Any bloodstains, tissue traces?"

"Desk sergeant sent a squad to look. Nothing. It did rain hard all night. But no ejected shotgun shells, no bits of bone or brain. Might have been at some point, but the rats down there are very efficient street cleaners."

"So, on the evidence, it's bullshit."

"Yeah, although Juko works for Frank, really, not for us, but yes, I'd have to agree."

"Did anything Kupferberg-ish turn up on the shoals down by Tin Town Flats?"

"Not yet, and I had a squad go check."

"There you go. The Tin Town Flats catch all the floaters. Gordon's not the most reliable witness. He's snorted his way through more cocaine than Tony Montana. Ask him his name, he has to check his driver's license."

"Yeah, I agree, but here's the truly weird part. Gordon says that Frank had help doing it."

"Okay. Interesting. We get a description?"

"He said the other guy was dressed like a cowboy, wore boot-cut jeans, cowboy boots, a range jacket. An older guy, looked like a hardcase, with a big white cowboy mustache and long silver hair down to his shoulders."

There was an understandable silence.

"Did he have a name?"

"Gordon didn't hear one, but he said the guy was real close with Frank, like they were old friends. He said the other guy was a cop, had that cop attitude, and that he had a gun on him."

"Gordon say what kind?"

"Not a pistol. A revolver, a big one. A Colt or a Smith. Probably a Colt."

The silence came back again. The wind rocked the Suburban and Mavis watched the road.

"That," said Nick after a time, "is just plain nuts."

"I agree, and it undercuts Gordon's credibility, not that he had any in the first place."

They drove on a while in silence, watching the sunlight glimmer on the wind-whipped surface of the Tulip, bikers and joggers and dog walkers along the riverbanks in Boudreau Park, all braced against the wind, a big brown barge butting north against the flow, bow waves curling white under its hull.

"Charlie Danziger is dead, Mavis."

"Tell me about it. I gave the eulogy."

Nick was thinking about the shadow he had seen standing in the window of the MountRoyal Hotel last night, about how the shape had seemed familiar.

They were coming up on the Pavilion. They could see the deck of the Bar Belle, the usual Saturday crowd under the café umbrellas—upscale, shiny, loud, like Armani geese and Gucci parakeets. There was music playing, ragged, staccato, irritating, like a jazz quartet falling down a fire escape. Mavis parked the truck, killed the engine, looked at Nick, who looked back at her, and said, "Mavis, my dove, I got *nothing*."

"Neither do I, honey pie," said Mavis, "So it goes in the FIDO file. Let's go see Glynda."

Glynda Yarvik had seen them arrive. She met them on the steps of the restaurant, a large broad-shouldered woman with Chinese eyes and Slavic cheekbones and whipped-cream hair. Her gray eyes were smeared and teary and either she had no makeup on or none of it had survived the morning.

She got a hug from Mavis and shook Nick's hand, her palm cold and damp, and then she walked them through the indoor section to her office at the back, a large room lined in bamboo and hung with red plastic lobsters caught in blue plastic nets. Her desk was set in front of a picture window that looked out on the Tulip River and the industrial buildings, the wharfs and warehouses and lumberyards that lined the eastern bank.

Nick looked up at the ridge along the top of Tallulah's Wall, far away in the northeast, rising up over the town. The crows were still wheeling around up there, a black cloud with reddish sparks inside it, sunlight glinting off their wings. Something was going on at Crater Sink and the crows didn't like it.

Glynda was crying now, sobbing, coming apart, and Mavis was standing over her, patting her shoulder while Glynda shredded a blue handkerchief covered in pink polka dots. After a minute or two Glynda managed to subside. Mavis asked her when she had last seen her husband Maris.

"Yesterday, Friday, around two. He . . . he came home for lunch, from the car lot, a late lunch . . . I made pierogies and he kissed me and took some with him . . . He went back to the dealership . . . and he never came home again."

She went off again for a while, looking out the window but seeing something else entirely. They let her go for a time, and then she took a deep shuddering breath that made her front porch heave, swiveled around in the chair, and put her hands on the desk. The polka-dot hankie was a goner.

"And you haven't seen or heard from him since?" asked Nick in a soft voice.

She shook her head, wiped her nose. "No. I'm calling his cell and it always goes to voice mail. It's an iPhone, so I go on the computer—Find My iPhone, you know this app?"

They did.

"And it's not showing. He has it turned off, I think. But isn't it true you can't turn an iPhone off, not really?"

"No, that's not true," said Mavis. "If you power it off, the phone is dead, and the Find My iPhone won't work. Motorola phones are the only ones that shut right down if you take the battery out. Have you tried the carrier to see if there's a GPS signal?"

"I have," she said. "Verizon says no."

"Okay, Glynda," said Nick, "is there any reason your husband would be visiting anyone up in The Glades?"

She gave it some thought. "Why there?"

Mavis explained about the red-light camera, tracing the tag on the Cadillac.

"Yes, that's his car. He was driving it . . . I don't know anybody in The Glades. We don't know anybody."

"Maybe a client, something to do with the dealership?"

"Yes, that could be . . . Are you looking for his car? The police?"

"Yes, we are. Everybody in this part of the state is looking for it. County, Highway Patrol, all of us. Can you tell us if your husband has a garage or a storage unit? Someplace big enough to park the Caddy inside it."

Glynda thought about it. "Well, he has the dealership, but nobody there has seen the car around."

"No storage unit somewhere?"

"Not that I know of, and I do the books, so I would have seen the bills."

She was quiet for a moment. "I don't know why he would do this, but we have this other business . . . we buy houses and fix them up? Sell them, we make a little money, so . . ."

Nick was right on that.

"Do you have any houses like that now?"

"Actually, yes, we have three. One is—"

"Any with garages or covered parking?"

She thought about that. "I think they all do . . . Men like to store things in garages, so we always—"

Mavis had her book out. "Can you give us the addresses?"

"You think he might be in one of those? They are all being worked on, so there would be no—"

"We understand, Glynda," said Mavis, staying calm. "But if you could just tell us where they are so we can follow up?"

She looked flustered for a moment, but then she pulled open a drawer in her desk, dragged out a fat file folder, opened it up on her desk, ran a finger down a list of addresses. "Okay, here are the ones we are working on right now—"

"May I have a copy of that, Mrs. Yarvik?"

She looked unhappy, but then she had every reason. "Of course," she said, handing Nick the sheet. "I have another copy right under—"

"I'm seeing nine houses here, Mrs. Yarvik. But you're working on only three?"

"Yes, three we are renovating—I mean, our contractors— and there are two that we have rented out—"

Nick set the paper down. "Can you just put a check beside all the houses that are empty right now?"

She scanned the list, took a pen, and put a check mark beside seven addresses. Two of the houses up for rent but empty were on the northern edge of Tin Town. The three houses being renovated were all over town, and the final two vacant rentals were in Garrison Hills and Lower Chase Run.

Lower Chase Run was part of The Chase, Niceville's most exclusive neighborhood—gated mansions and treed deer parks and wrought iron fencing, old-money mansions and rolling lawns and ornate gates and cobbled driveways, all of this riding up the slopes at the base of Tallulah's Wall.

Nick looked out the window and he could see The Chase neighborhood on the eastern edge of Niceville, just emerging from the shadow of Tallulah's Wall. The cedar shake roof of Delia Cotton's mansion, known as Temple Hill, was partly visible through a forest of ancient live oaks.

Garrison Hills was Nick's home neighborhood. The rental in Garrison Hills was on Sable Basilisk Lane, on the far side of the Confederate Graveyard from Nick's own home on Beauregard.

Nick gathered the sheet up, folded it once. "Mrs. Yarvik,

can we have your permission to send some police officers to these places, and if we have to, if there's no one home or no answer, can we open them up and go inside?"

"Go inside? You mean, like, you need my permission?"

"It would make things easier," said Mavis, who didn't want to blow the rest of the afternoon setting up seven different search warrants. "You're the legal owner, right?"

"Well, our corporation is."

"But you're an officer of the corporation?"

"Yes. I am the CFO."

"Can you just write out a quick note then, saying that we have your permission to enter these properties? I mean, if Maris is inside one, he might be sick and need help, perhaps urgently, and we wouldn't want to waste any time with papers."

Glynda got Mavis's point and went a whiter shade of pale. Mavis felt guilty as sin, or at least she tried to.

"Of course . . . just a handwritten note?"

"That would be great. And then sign it?"

Glynda wrote fast, leaning over the paper, her pen flying, and then a scrawled signature, and as an afterthought, the time and date. She handed the note to Mavis, who gave it a quick look. It would hold up.

"Thank you, Glynda. This will help so much."

"So *everyone* is looking for Maris? The county people and the Highway Patrol too?"

"Yes," said Nick, wary now.

Glynda looked grateful, then less so. "So much people. Is this . . . *normal*?"

A good question, and Mavis let Nick answer it. "No, actually, it isn't. Maris has only been missing for a few hours. With an adult, a male, we don't pull out all the stops until forty-eight hours."

"Then why so many . . . I do not want to look ungrateful . . ."

Mavis could see that Nick, who was not a gifted liar, was trying to find a way to answer that wouldn't blow Glynda's mind, so she tried to distract the woman before she could zero in on exactly why Maris was getting all this official attention. "Tell me, Glynda," said Mavis, radiating sweetness and light, "when you saw Maris, was there anything about him that was different? Was he worried, maybe some trouble with the business?"

"No, the business is fine, no trouble there. And no trouble between us, Detective Kavanaugh. We have a good marriage . . ."

And she was gone again. And she wasn't coming back any time soon. Mavis looked across her bowed head at Nick and gave him a silent *Don't tell her.*

Nick got up, and Mavis came around to the front of Glynda's desk. Glynda looked up from her hankie, her face a red blotch, her eyes streaming.

"We have everyone looking," said Mavis in a soothing tone. "If you think of anything . . . anything at all . . . that might help us figure this out, here's my card."

Glynda took her card, set it down on her desk, wiped her nose. "There was . . . have you checked the hospitals?"

"Yes. There was no accident report involving a 1975 blue Fleetwood, and your husband hasn't checked into any clinic or ER in a two-hundred-mile radius. Why a hospital?"

Glynda looked back and forth between the two of them. "He had a terrible headache. Why he came home at two. Like a migraine. He *never* gets them. I said go to the doctor, but Maris never goes to doctors. He says doctors just make you sick."

Nick registered the migraine element, but he said nothing. Didn't want to deflect Glynda's train of thought. Mavis promised that they'd keep checking the hospitals, asked her if she had thought to phone her husband's doctor herself.

"Yes, I did. To see if maybe Maris had some problem he didn't want to tell me. But the doctor said he hadn't seen

Maris for a month, since his last checkup for . . . for you know, the . . . the glove thing they do? To men?"

"Tell me, Mrs. Yarvik, did either of you happen to know a young man named Jordan Dutrow?"

Mavis held her breath, but Nick was right. They weren't from Social Services. Glynda went inward, and came back with a smile. "Yes, I think Maris knows him. Maris goes to all the Sunday high school games. I think Jordan Dutrow is this football player. A kickbacker?"

"A linebacker?"

"Yes. Maris thinks much of him. Says he will go to Ole Miss one day. Maris plays rugby for fun, and sometimes they play against the young men in Boudreau Park. I know once Jordan was there, because Maris said he was a big tough boy. He give him a drive the other night too."

"A *drive*?"

"Yes, was on Thursday, I think. Maris was coming home late, way after midnight, because of his poker playing, and he saw Jordan walking by the road, so he gave him a lift."

"This was *Thursday*?" asked Mavis.

"Yes, but late, more like into early Friday morning, I think. It was maybe four, but Maris didn't like to see the boy walking alone so late. He told Maris his car had broken down."

"Jordan had a car?"

"Yes. A nice red sports car. Shiny red. He told Maris it had broken down and he was just walking away to get help. Maris said the boy looked tired. So he helped him. Maris is . . . such a good man."

Nick and Mavis exchanged looks.

Glynda missed that, went back to thinking about Maris. And then she was gone again. Mavis patted her shoulder, and they got the hell out.

Back in the Suburban, Mavis fired it up, but before she put it in gear, she called up the CID desk and got Beau Norlett.

"Beau, Mavis . . . Yeah, he's right here . . . Nick, Beau says hello."

"Hello back."

"Nick says hello back . . . okay . . . He did? When? Okay . . . okay . . . I'll tell him."

"Tell me what?"

"Lemon Featherlight called, asking for you, said it was real urgent. Something about those bone thingies you guys fished out of the river, and some stuff about the Raven Mocker demon?"

"That's the Cherokee story . . . she's the eater of souls. Lemon had a theory about what was wrong with Crater Sink, had something to do with that old legend."

"The Raven Mocker? *Really?*"

"I'm just saying, Mavis. He leave a number?"

"He leave a number, Beau? Yeah, okay, no, text it to Nick, otherwise we'll both forget it. Look, Beau, we think we might have a lead on a suspect in the Morrison case. Name Maris Yarvik . . . Yeah, the 1975 Fleetwood we're looking for . . . You've got his driver's license shot, get it onto everybody's MDT—okay, already done . . . good. Anyway, we need to have some people go out right now, like right this minute, go check a bunch of different addresses, 'cause Yarvik might be cooped up in one of them."

There was some back and forth while she and Beau worked out who could do what and when and how long it would take them to do it.

"Okay, yeah, thanks, Beau. Thing is, tell these folks to take care. No saying what they're going to run into, so go in with their heads up . . . Yeah, very funny, Beau, heads up as in eyes open, not as in heads up their butts . . . and this Maris Yarvik guy, plays rugby, weighs in at two forty, he's six-three, built like a grizzly, has a head like an anvil, so warn our people, if he

wants to rock and roll, they better get on top of him quick . . .
Yeah, good . . . one last thing. That gangbanger chick, one
of the ZeeZee Boys. Did she ever surface? Yeah, okay . . .
yeah . . . okay good, I'll tell Nick. Thanks for this, Beau."

She clicked off, looked over at Nick, who was reading a
text from Lemon:

Left Charlottesville this morning driving down with Helga Sigrid filled her in on Nothing—maybe she's the Raven Mocker—
and she has a wild theory about Nothing that you're going to
want to hear we'll be in Niceville by this evening really want
to meet ASAP text me back at this number we're just passing
through Raleigh hope all is okay L

"What's he saying?"

After some hesitation, Nick read it to her.

"She has a wild theory about *nothing*?"

"Not *nothing*. With a capital *N*, as if it were a name. Like
Odysseus used on the Cyclops."

"And what is it? This Nothing thing?"

"To be honest, Mavis, I think it's what's wrong with Niceville."

"And so does Lemon? And this Helga chick?"

"I don't know what she thinks, but Lemon, yes, we're on
the same page about it."

"Okay . . . demons, soul-eaters, obviously this is too complicated to get into here—"

"Absolutely."

"But we *will* get into it, you and me, okay?"

"Okay."

"Scout's honor?"

"Mavis . . ."

"Okay . . . this is me dropping it. Back to the case. They're
rolling some people now, cover the house list Glynda gave us.

I said we'd take the Garrison Hills one, okay? I figured we should cover that. Too close to home, right?"

"I was thinking that."

"That girl, the ZeeZee Boys girl, she woke up this morning. Still critical, but they say she'll probably pull through. I had Boots Jackson with her, in case she woke up."

"I remember you saying."

"She told Boots they found the car by the side of the road. Just sitting there, keys inside. From the way she was doped up, Boots figured she was probably telling the truth."

"So maybe Dutrow just walked away from it?"

"Well, getting caught with it would be pretty damned incriminating, wouldn't it? I guess, when he cooled down after the Thorssons, he sorta came to his senses and dumped the Benz."

"And Maris Yarvik just . . . happened along?"

Mavis shook her head. "I don't know. We're going to have to find him and ask him a whole lot of questions."

She put the truck in gear, started to roll, stopped at the curb and looked at Nick. "Didn't Jordan Dutrow . . ."

"Yes," said Nick. "He had migraines too."

Kate and Eufaula Have Tea

What Rainey had said—and what he had not said—stayed with Eufaula all the rest of the morning. She set it aside for now, did what needed to be done, the daily Saturday routine, packed some box lunches for Rainey and Axel, saw them out the door and onto their bikes—they were going to ride down to the riverside park near the Pavilion and have a picnic—and Hannah had something called a playdate with Chloe, a little girl from down the street.

Chloe's mom showed up in a tan Maserati Quattroporte and it took the two of them to get the girls safely tucked inside. Eufaula watched the cruiser power away, making a sound like a tiger purring, and thought about what it would be like to have money, but not for long.

She climbed back up the curving staircase to the front door, stood there for a time on the landing, and looked across the street at the park with the live oaks and the marble fountain. Sunlight was sparkling in the fountain spray, making rainbows dance in the air.

Eufaula had once seen a woman there, surrounded by a cloud of green dragonflies. The woman looked like Kate but she was too thin and all she was wearing was an antique-looking cotton nightgown. The woman had waved to her, and then the light had changed and she was gone, and Eufaula, who was a practical woman and knew something about Niceville, understood that she had seen a ghost.

But then ghosts were as much a part of Niceville as the Spanish moss on the live oaks. They could be seen everywhere, depending on the light, if you had the gift, and her family had always had the gift.

She went back inside, looked at the clock, saw that Kate would be home soon, so she put on the kettle and laid out the silver tea set. The tea tray on top of the fridge she left alone.

She was sitting in the conservatory watching the light change in the forest at the bottom of the lawn when she heard the silver bell tinkle as Kate came in the front door.

"Kate?"

"Eufaula . . . where are you?"

"In the garden room."

Kate came down the hall and through the kitchen, looking rumpled and weary, her long black hair tousled, her cheeks pink. She was wearing a pale green dress with something gold at her neck and golden earrings that caught the light and put teardrops of fire on her neck.

She kicked off her pale green ballet flats and sat down with a sigh on the end of the large yellow sofa that ran the length of the inside wall.

Eufaula had the tea ready—this was a Saturday ritual for the women of the house—and she poured Kate a cup, handed her a small saucer with three mint wafers on it.

"How did it go?"

Kate sighed, had a mint. She had a custody fight set for Monday and they always depressed her. "We're as ready as we can be . . . but the courts still favor the moms, and Judge Broom is one of the worst. Especially with little girls. I'm hoping . . . well, the best I can hope for is that Ryan will have regular access."

"Maybe he shouldn't have been running around on his wife in the first place."

"Eufaula, normally I'd say yes. But his wife is as mean as January rain. If she's the only influence on that poor little girl, the world will have *another* calculating coldhearted bitch to deal with in ten years. If Perdita Burke were my wife, I'd have poisoned her years ago."

"Not the usual feminist position, Kate."

"No. But I'm not a usual feminist, Eufaula. Neither are you. How are the boys?"

"On the way to Boudreau Park, with enough food to feed the multitudes. Hannah's with Chloe, and I haven't heard from Nick yet."

"I have," Kate said. "He texted me. He's with Mavis Crossfire. They're on that . . . investigation . . . from last night."

Eufaula sipped her tea and asked no questions. Everyone in Niceville had a rough idea of what had happened to the Morrisons and the Thorssons and few of the sane ones wanted to know anymore. It did seem to Eufaula that Niceville was showing some cracks—more so than usual, at any rate.

They sat together in silence, looking out at the sunlight dappling the lawn, watching the leaves change color. Although the day was warm, fall was in the air, that slanting light, and the slightest chill in the shadows.

Winter is coming, thought Kate, and that made her think of Rainey Teague again. She put her cup down on the glass tabletop, sat back, curling her legs up under her and hugging one of the bright blue feather pillows.

"Eufaula, you remember what we talked about, last night, before Nick came home?"

"I do, Kate," Eufaula said, sitting back.

"I told Nick, about the cognitive behavioral therapy idea . . ."

"And about the schizophrenia diagnosis?"

Kate nodded.

"How did he take it?"

She looked at her hands. "To be honest, Eufaula, I think he pretended to believe it because he thinks I'm cracking up."

Eufaula reached over, touched Kate's hand, let her fingers rest lightly on it. "It's a very . . . plausible . . . diagnosis, Kate. Dr. Lakshmi is . . . I have a lot of respect for her. She helped my brother with Jeremy, and you know how hard it is to deal with autism. And they haven't *confirmed* schizophrenia yet, have they?"

"No. Not yet. They're consulting with some people at Vanderbilt in Nashville, and we're waiting for that . . . but I really need something to hope for, Eufaula. I *need* this to be the answer. I really do."

Eufaula left her hand where it was and waited to see if tears came, but Kate held them down, smiled at Eufaula.

"You spend a lot of time with Rainey, Eufaula. What do you think?"

This was a question Eufaula had been afraid to hear, and she had not yet decided how to answer it. Her talk with Rainey, about the two-way radios, had left her deeply shaken.

"Kate . . . we've never talked about last spring. About how Mr. Dillon disappeared, about that whole awful time."

"No," said Kate simply. "We haven't."

"And we haven't said too much about Rainey going to see that lawyer a couple of months ago."

"No, I guess I'm not . . . I don't see how it can change anything."

"Can I ask what Beth thinks?"

"Beth," Kate said with a weak laugh. "Beth thinks Rainey

is a wild child . . . and Axel adores him. But then Beth wasn't around for what happened last spring, and even during the Warren Smoles affair . . . Byron had just been killed . . . I don't like to trouble her with . . . my fears."

She stopped, studied Eufaula for a time. "Eufaula, do you have something you're trying to tell me? Something about Rainey?"

Eufaula tried not to look away but she did.

"You do, don't you?"

"I do, Kate, but I don't want . . . I hate you losing that baby. And I'm . . . scared for you."

"Scared? Why are you scared?"

Eufaula looked down at her hands, realized she was mistreating a fine linen napkin.

Kate leaned over and put her hand on Eufaula's arm. "Eufaula, I'm not made of glass. Tell me what's on your mind? Is it to do with Rainey?"

"Yes, Kate. It's about Rainey."

"Then please, Eufaula, we're friends. You can tell me anything. Is it so terrible?"

Eufaula looked at Kate then, and Kate felt the chill gather around her again, the way it had weeks before, the sense of oncoming grief, the loss of a child, the death of her happy life, a dread of the winter and what it might bring.

"Then tell me, sweet. Just . . . tell me."

Eufaula sighed, gathered herself, and then told it simply, but then it was the kind of story that needed no drama added.

Kate, the lawyer in her, listened carefully and asked only one or two clarifying questions. Eufaula got to the end of it, the part where she had confronted Rainey with the two radios, and what he had said to her in reply.

"He actually *said* that?"

"Yes, he did. I'm sorry to—"

"He actually said, '*I don't know as I like the colored help pok-*

ing around in my stuff . . . I may have to talk to Kate about setting some boundaries for the staff.' . . . He *actually* said that? To your face?"

"I'm afraid so, Kate. I hated to—"

Kate's anger was right there.

Eufaula could see it in her face, and she tried to calm her. "Kate, he's just a kid. They lash out, especially when they get cornered. They don't—"

"Eufaula, first of all, I apologize to you, for what was said, and how it was said. You know what you mean to this family, don't you? You've been in it far longer than Rainey Teague has."

"I do, Kate, and you mean as much to me. All of you. It's not what he said to me—I'm not made of glass either, and I've heard a lot worse—it's what he *did* that really worries me. Do you remember everything you talked about when Nick came home? Because you said you were sitting in the kitchen there, so if Rainey was listening . . . what would he have heard that maybe you wouldn't want him to?"

Kate went back to that moment and got much angrier, a bright flush of blood rising into her cheeks, her forehead hot, her throat tight . . .

"You don't feel sleepy right now."

"What I feel is you."

"I was wondering how long it would take for this nightgown to get to you."

Eufaula watched as Kate's anger went from red-hot to blue-white cold.

"Kate . . . try not to—"

"Does Rainey have his cell phone with him?"

"I . . . yes. I put it in his pack, with his sandwiches and stuff. But Kate, I think you should take a moment to think—"

There was a phone by the sofa and Kate was already dialing it. Eufaula sat and watched her and waited. And worried. Worried for *all* of them.

Under a Harvest Moon

The Blue Bird bus was filling up for the two o'clock run up-country. The crowd was the same weary threadbare folks, all of uncertain race and age, so average they stood out, tired spiritless people who never spoke, who didn't make eye contact, and who just shuffled glumly past Danziger and Albert Lee as the two of them sat there on a bench by the ticket booth, smoking. Now and then Albert Lee would cast a quick worried glance across at Danziger, who was leaning forward, his forearms on his knees, staring at the pitted grease-stained concrete floor of the Button Gwinnett Bus Depot, his long hair hanging down, Danziger saying nothing at all. Albert Lee, a good soul, was concerned about him.

"Look, Charlie, there's got to be a rational explanation for all this."

"I'd be happy to hear one," said Danziger without looking up. He took a last pull on his cigarette, crushed it out on his boot heel, and flicked it into a nearby ash can.

Albert Lee worried about that too, since the ash can was half full of shredded bus tickets. However, fires had started in it before and he knew where the fire extinguisher was.

"Well, you're no more dead than I am," said Albert Lee. "In my opinion, you're having some kind of nervous conniption."

That made Danziger look up. "A *conniption*? Albert, I think I may have taken part in a bank robbery where four cops got shot, and later that day I shot a guy in the back, and farther down the same year I get involved in a shootout with some mob people and take two rounds in the chest. I don't think *conniption* quite covers all that."

"Yes it does. If it happened at all, I mean, you being a part of it all. What you're thinking is exactly what a nervous conniption fit is like—"

"Have you ever had one like this?"

"Why, yes," he said, pleased to be able to add something to the discussion. "Last spring I was involved in a shooting of my own, up in Sallytown. I myself was shot in that encounter."

This brought Danziger all the way upright. "You were?"

"I was," said Albert Lee. He tapped the left side of his uniform jacket, just above the waistline. "Right here, in the side of my belly. And it stung something ferocious too. But now and then I'm pretty sure it never happened. That it was just a bad dream. A conniption."

"Do you have a scar?"

"No. And neither do you, I'll bet."

This was true, and it gave Danziger something to hold on to.

"How'd you come to be in a fire fight up in Sallytown? I mean, in your dream?"

"That is a long story, and I'd love to regale you with the whole lunatic adventure, but I have to get these here people back up-country . . ."

He paused, thought about it. "Look, Charlie . . . what are your plans, anyhow? What you figuring to do about . . ."

"Being dead?"

"You're not *dead*, Charlie. But you're troubled. I'd say you need to get out of town for a while, calm down, think this thing through."

Danziger had to admit the idea had some appeal. "You have a suggestion, Albert?"

"Well, you look like a cowboy. A real one. You ever worked with horses, with livestock?"

"Yeah, I have. I was born in Bozeman, my folks ran cattle, and I used to have a ranch in the foothills north of Niceville, up at the edge of the Belfair Range. I raised Tennessee Walkers and Morgans."

"I know those horses. Pretty black horses, long manes, high-curved necks, Arab noses, have a way of stepping high and a nice easy canter."

"That's the breed."

"Ever worked with heavy horses?"

"How heavy?"

"Percherons or Clydes?"

"I've worked around them. Draft horses. They're a steady beast, damn big, but you don't want to have one step on your foot. Average full-grown Clydesdale will weigh in at two thousand pounds. They run bay or golden, with white chests and big white fetlocks. Good-natured. Smart."

"You know 'em, I guess."

"Horses are horses, Albert. Only kind of horse I won't work with is a pony. Why are you asking?"

"Well, a lady I know has a sort of plantation up in the Belfairs. She could use someone who's good with horses. She has a few big old Clydes; one of them, his name is Jupiter—Charlie, you'll have to see him to believe him. I think you'd like the lady. She's a born farm girl, tough boss, but fair, and she has a true heart."

"What's her name?"

"Glynis Ruelle. Place is called the Ruelle Plantation. Been

in the Ruelle family for years, after Miss Glynis and her husband John bought the farm from Lorelei and Albemarle—"

"John Ruelle? As in *JR*, the initials on that cigarette case?
Served in the Big Red One?"

Albert Lee gave him a sideways look. "I surely can believe
you're a police officer, Charlie. You got an eye for details. Yes,
it was her husband was killed in the war, and his brother Ethan
maimed for life. Ethan's gone too. Why she's all alone now, with
that big farm to run. And now, with the Harvest coming on,
she'll need the help pretty bad. Does this interest you, Charlie?"

What Albert Lee had just said gave Danziger a lot to think
about. Danziger remembered a couple of things pretty clearly,
and one of them was that the search for Rainey Teague after
his disappearance two years ago had ended up at a barrow grave in the old Confederate graveyard, and the grave
belonged to a man named Ethan Ruelle, who had been shot
dead in a duel on December 24, 1921. And the name Glynis
Ruelle was familiar as well, from a story Nick Kavanaugh had
told him a few weeks after the Rainey Teague abduction case.

So something pretty complicated was going on in his life,
and he needed to think about it, and he had a feeling that some
of the answers could be found at Glynis Ruelle's plantation.

Danziger looked out at the streets of Niceville, the people
and the cars streaming back and forth out there under the soft
autumn light, the trolley cars clanging and rumbling, a line of
crows stretched out on a net of wires across Forsythia, all in a
row, staring back at him, flat-eyed and still, like black beads on
a wire. Danziger had a strange feeling that they were waiting
for him to decide what he was going to do so they could all fly
off and report.

To whom he had no idea.

"So," said Albert Lee, "does this work for you, Charlie? I
do think it's for the best."

"Yes, it does. How do I get there?"

"Well, I drive right by it, don't I? Blue Bird stops right at the bottom of her lane. Some of these here folks, they're going back up there for the Harvest. You can be there by evening, time for a late supper, talk it over with the lady."

"What's the crop?"

"The crop?"

"Yes, the crop she's harvesting."

Albert Lee got busy lighting another cigar, his head down, watching his own hands. He got the cheroot lit, puffed out a cloud of blue smoke that had a strong scent of eucalyptus.

"It's an odd thing, the Harvest, Charlie. I think you'll need to see it to understand it. It's not about a *crop*, although it takes place out in the fields, down there by the piney woods. It's more a kind of family ceremony. Happens twice a year, spring is *the Planting* and fall is *the Harvest*. They are both surely something to see."

"Maybe we should call, see what she thinks?"

Albert Lee shook his head. "Miss Glynis, she doesn't hold with phones too much. She's got one, of course, but she'll never answer it. But you needn't worry, Charlie. I think she'll like you. And I think you'll like her right back. I know I do. What do you say?"

Danziger stood up, straightened his range coat, smiled down at Albert Lee. "You know Eddie Fessendein, Albert?"

"I do. Runs the diner, Blue Eddie's, down there near Tin Town. Sort of an odd dude."

"He is an odd dude. He's why I'm here."

Albert Lee gave Danziger an appraising look. "Blue Eddie sent you here?"

"Yes. He said I should take the bus."

Albert Lee got up, his face serious, and his manner suddenly solemn. "Blue Eddie said that?"

"I think so. You know his accent. It came out like *tek da bus, Charlie.*"

Albert Lee took that in, his expression grave. "Then you should take the bus, Charlie."

Danziger took the bus.

Rainey Does Something for Nothing

Rainey and Axel were sitting on the bank of the Tulip River tossing crusts of bread into the water to feed the ducks that lived along the edge of Boudreau Park. The wind was still blowing and the river glittered with sunlit chop. Behind them on the bike path a pack of skinny guys in those geeky biker outfits were streaming by, hogging the lanes, farting and grunting, their bikes making a swish-swish-swoosh sound as they hissed by in a snaky chain. Down the riverbank a bunch of girls were having a picnic and playing badminton and squealing like piglets in a pen. Rainey and Axel were enjoying disapproving of the girls, who were happy to disapprove right back at them.

Axel looked away to the northeast, where the cliff loomed up over the town. Axel had never been up on top of Tallulah's Wall.

The closest he'd ever come had been a trip on the Peachtree trolley line to the top of Upper Chase Run, where there was a trolley loop right at the bottom of a set of rickety wooden stairs that went all the way up to the top.

Rainey and he had gone there one night, and Rainey had

left him alone at the loop while he climbed up the stairs. Something bad had happened to Rainey up there, on the path that led to Crater Sink. Ever since then Rainey had not been the same.

Right now he was still not the same, and Axel decided to ask him what was bugging him.

At first Rainey didn't answer, just sat there, slouching down, his hair in his eyes, tossing crusts to the ducks. He balled up the rest of the lunch, stuffed it into a paper bag, and tossed the bag into the river, where the fast-moving current ran away with it like a dog with a bone.

"Axel, did Eufaula ask you about the radios?"

Axel was a skinny little guy with big Disney-rabbit eyes and a mop of long curly hair, but he wasn't a little guy inside, and lately he'd been doing a lot of thinking about Rainey.

"Yeah, she did."

"What did she want to know?"

"When was the last time we'd played with them. I told her last week, and then you said they had to be fixed. New batteries and stuff."

"You did, huh?"

"Yeah. Shouldn't I?"

Rainey studied Axel for a time, and that look was in his eyes, the look Axel was beginning to think was pushing out the part of Rainey that Axel liked. His father used to have that same look when he was deciding to get really mad about something and thinking about who was going to get smacked around first.

"You shouldn't be a snitch to her, Axe. We gotta stick together. She's just the help. Haven't you ever had help?"

"Help with what?"

"No, I mean, haven't you ever had servants? Colored people, doing stuff, cooking and cleaning, picking up after you?"

"No. Once we had a nanny, but Daddy scared her away. So it was always just us."

"Well, with people like Eufaula, you gotta understand, she's not like family—"

"She feels like family," he said, his tone stiffening. "She's always doing special stuff for us, and Kate and Nick, and Mom. And you."

Rainey laughed, picked up a small stone, threw it hard at a misinformed duck who had stayed behind, thinking maybe another crust was on the way. Instead she got a rock on the beak. She took off across the water, orange feet pattering along the waves, wings laboring, and then went airborne.

Rainey aimed another rock at her but missed by yards. Down the line one of the girls called up to him to stop throwing rocks at the ducks. Rainey gave her the finger and turned back to Axel.

"Look, Axe, Eufaula's *not* family. You gotta keep your distance. Those people don't really like us. They're always thinking about slavery and shit and how evil bad white people are. You can't let them get over on us. Eufaula and her kind, they aren't like us, and they hate us for it."

Axel had heard this kind of talk before, and not only from his father. He was just a kid, but he didn't buy it. It wasn't money or family that made you a good person. It was how you treated other people. It was beginning to dawn on Axel that maybe Rainey wasn't a very nice person and that he might grow up to be just like Axel's father, mean and greedy and dangerous.

"Rain, you're just pissed because she found out about the radio on top of the fridge."

"Yeah," said Rainey, and that *look* was there again. "And how'd she find out about that?"

Axel moved back a bit, but not too far. "Not from me, Rain. It was your own stupid idea to put it there. And I warned you. She cleans the kitchen. You think she was never going to clean the top of the fridge? Get real."

Rainey got colder. "Axe, you don't *ever* want me to get real with you. Not ever."

Axel looked at him for a short time. "Rain, sometimes I don't like you."

"Like when?"

Since you pushed that old lady into the Tulip, he was thinking, but he was too smart to say that, with the river only six feet away.

"Like right now . . . since you been doing all that sneaky spy stuff."

"Not just me. We were playing detective, that's all."

"What about running the spy car into Eufaula's room?"

Rainey lost some color. "What are you talking about?"

"My Spy Gear Spy Video Car VX6 that mom bought me from Toys "R" Us. I saw you. You ran it into Eufaula's room while she was in the shower and you were looking at her on the remote screen. When she was in the shower. I saw you doing it."

"I was not. It's a remote car, you dumbass, you run it all over with the wireless remote. That's what it's for. *You* play with it too."

"It's a remote-controlled car with a camera in it and it sends pictures back to the screen on the controller when you run it around so you can see what it sees and you ran it into Eufaula's bathroom when she was in the shower so you could see her naked."

Rainey put a smiley face on. "I was just playing with it. Besides, she had the shower door closed and the glass was all steamy, so I didn't see—"

"It wasn't right. You gotta stop doing stuff like this. We'll get caught, like you did with the radios, and if Kate ever finds out—"

"Who's gonna tell her? You?"

"No. But I'll bet Eufaula will."

"She better not, if she wants to keep—"

And because Fate takes an interest, pays attention, and likes to move things along at a brisk pace, his cell phone rang.

And rang, a shrill beeping that riveted their attention. Axel stared at him as Rainey rattled through his backpack until he found the phone. He looked at the screen.

KATE KAVANAUGH

He let it ring while they both sat there and stared at each other. It went to voice mail, and Rainey keyed the button to hear the message. It was from Kate, and her voice was cold and tight, not all warm and oozy the way it usually was when she was talking to him.

Rainey, I want you and Axel to come home right now. I mean right this minute, whatever you're doing. If you're at Boudreau Park you can be home in half an hour. Call me when you get this message. If you don't call me back in five minutes I'll come looking for you, so don't play any games with me.

The message ended just like that. No *bye, babe* and no *love you.* Rainey had never heard that tone in Kate's voice before. Neither had Axel.

"Jeez, Rain. She's really pissed."

Rainey didn't answer. Axel thought he looked like he was listening to something in his head.

Axel was right.

need to do something about these people need to do something now right now if you won't I will

Rainey was looking at Axel as if he didn't know him, and Axel felt a cold thing grow in his belly and spread up into his chest and then into his throat. He tried to speak and only got out a croak because his mouth was dry. Rainey was looking at him like he was something dead by the side of the road. Finally Axel got some words out.

"Rainey . . . what are you thinking?"

Rainey didn't answer. He seemed to be listening to something Axel couldn't hear.

Then when he finally answered, he didn't make any sense at all. "Maris Yarvik," he said. "Maris will fix it."

"Maris Yarvik? Who is Maris Yarvik, Rainey?"

Rainey seemed to surface.

He smiled at Axel, his first really friendly smile in a long time, and the cold thing in Axel's chest backed off a touch and he forgot to worry about the river being so close.

It was good to see Rainey smile like that.

"A guy we know, Axel. He does favors for us."

The View Across Fountain Square
Came at a Price

The recently widowed wife of Frankie Maranzano was a ripe Latina number by the name of Delores, sleek as a seal pup, sexy as a pair of Louboutin stilettos, as deep down cold as glacier ice. Although she was sitting in Frankie's Eames chair behind Frankie's huge desk—a slab of black granite held up by two Lions of Saint Mark acquired illegally from a church in Venice—and all the splendor of Fountain Square lay spread out before her through the plate glass windows of her ten-thousand-square-foot penthouse suite in the Memphis, a glittering obelisk visible to all of Cap City—in spite of all this material splendor, Delores Maranzano was not a happy woman.

She absently stroked the silky pelt of an emaciated Chihuahua named Frankie Twice—a typical Chihuahua, fifty percent hate and fifty percent tremble—but since she had arranged for his vocal cords to be sliced, Frankie Twice was now a mute Chihuahua. Both she and Frankie Twice were staring out through a glass wall at the main living area of her suite, and not with loving affection.

The reason for their dissatisfaction—the reasons in plural, in *triplicate*—were out there in the open-concept living room of her penthouse in all their greasy-assed cigar-chomping glory, three syndicated thugs by the name of Desi Munoz, Mario La Motta, and Julie Spahn.

They were all recent graduates of Leavenworth Prison, courtesy of the late Byron Deitz, and now they were slouching about in various states of undress and inebriation on her previously pristine white sectional couches, scattering beer cans and pizza crumbs and cigar ashes all over her snow-white wall-to-wall carpeting, and talking in aggrieved tones about some fucking crisis that had come upon them and what they should do about it.

Circumstances—namely the fear of sudden death—had forced her to accept Mario and his two business partners as the inheritors of all of Frankie's business concerns, with the full and forceful agreement of Frankie's former associates around the country, an agreement worked out between Julie Spahn and Anthony Torinetti Sr., known as Tony Tee, who operated a waste management business out of Miami.

Although Delores was born in Guayaquil, she had always been attracted to Italian men, starting with Al Pacino in *Scent of a Woman*. She was ruefully aware, watching Mario La Motta through the wall of glass that separated Frankie's office from the living area, that although he was Italian, he looked nothing like Al Pacino.

Mario's head was perfectly round, perfectly bald, except for his thick black eyebrows, which he grew long and brushed upward, giving him a permanently surprised look.

His body, overrevealed in his wifebeater, was apelike in shape, as cold and white as sour milk, and covered in thick black hair.

Seated at an angle to Mario were his—her—other two business partners: Desi Munoz, not quite as pretty as Mario but hacked from the same slab of rancid fat, and on the other side of the triangle, Julie Spahn, spindly and birdlike, with a chicken-skin neck made for wringing and the sharp flinty eyes of a raptor. Spahn was the guy currently holding the floor, an iPhone clutched in one of his claws.

"So was the kid hurt?" La Motta wanted to know. Spahn shook his head.

"Not Little Anthony," he said, holding up the iPhone, the display showing a lean hard-looking older white guy, barefoot, in a black tee and white slacks. It was taken on a beach somewhere, a flash shot, taken at night, and the man was staring—no, *burning*—into the camera.

The image was shaky and it was hard to make out the details—the shooter, Tony Torinetti, was backpedaling and peeing himself at the time it was taken, although the three Mafia guys didn't know that. But you could see the glint of serious and very effective hate in the man's eyes, a killing hate. It scorched through the camera lens and sort of sizzled there on the screen.

Munoz shook his head, blowing smoke from his cigar and littering the couch with ashes.

"Tony Tee says his son's okay. Shook up pretty good, but not hurt. But the other two, they're fucked. One a the kids, this Nate Kellerman mutt, his knee's like totally whacked. That guy—the dude in the picture—did some sorta karate thing and blew the kid's knee apart. I mean, it was like ripping the leg out of a roasted turkey. He's never gonna play ball again. He'll be in a fucking wheelchair for weeks."

"That's the Notre Dame guy?" asked Munoz.

"Not anymore," said Julie Spahn. "And he was second string with the Fighting Irish."

"Fuck the Fighting Irish," said La Motta. "What about the other kid? Ramey whatever?"

"Don't know about him," said Munoz. "Anthony Junior was saying the Ramey kid basically got his teeth rammed halfway up the front of his face. Nose is all busted up, upper jaw shattered, all his upper teeth knocked out. Head went back so sharp he got nerve damage in the back of his neck. Lucky he didn't lose an eye. They're both inna private clinic down in Daytona right now."

"Fuck me," said La Motta. "That's one hell of a shot to the mouth. Banker guy's got skills."

"A private clinic?" asked Munoz. "How'd they get there?"

"The banker guy," said Spahn. "The dude in the picture here, he called some kinda private service, they scooped the kids up right off the beach into an ambulance. Daytona's only fifty miles from St. Augustine. Banker paid the whole thing too. Including the emergency stuff at the clinic."

"What about the cops?"

"That's the thing, Mario," said Spahn, looking at the phone screen. "No cops involved. No charges either way. Everybody involved wanted it kept under the rose. The Kellerman kid, his folks are away in Europe, and there had already been a beef with the cops on account of some house party they were having, and his older brother didn't want the cops there again, because it was like an unprovoked assault on the old guy—"

"Some fucking old guy," said Munoz, spluttering out pulpy cigar bits, laughing, making a sound like a toilet backing up.

"Anyway," said Spahn, going back to La Motta, who was the muscle in the room, "the upshot is no cops, all hushed up pretty good, no charges or lawsuits, and the banker is picking up all the—"

"What's his fucking name again?" asked La Motta. Spahn thought about it.

"Sinclair, I think. Morgan Sinclair. Looked him up, retired guy, used to be a money changer—"

"What," said Munoz, "like money laundry?"

"No. Currency and shit. Buy Euros and sell deutsche marks and pocket the vig," said Spahn, who understood these things pretty well.

Munoz and La Motta mulled that over.

"Okay," said La Motta. "If Tony Tee's kid is okay, other than being scared shitless, and the other two assholes aren't squat to us, why are we even hearing about it?"

Spahn put the phone down, picked up his G and T, swirled it around, making the ice clink, taking his time to get his answer right. "Well, what Tony Tee is saying is, he wants this Sinclair guy . . . chastised."

"Why?" asked Munoz. "I mean, why go looking for more shit to step in?"

La Motta was in line with the sentiment. "Yeah, and if Tony Tee wants the old fuck . . . what was it?"

"Chastised," said Munoz, who liked the word.

"Yeah, *chastised*, then he's got people down there. Miami's got more zipperheads than fucking Palermo, send a couple of them up to this beach place, take care of it. Nothing to do with us."

"Tony Tee is asking it as . . . a favor."

The word *favor* had a certain vibration as it floated there in the middle of the room. La Motta glanced over in the direction of Frankie's office, saw Delores and Frankie Twice sitting there, staring back at them.

"Hey, Delores, whyn't you take that rat dog and go do some shopping, do lunch or something like that. Okay?"

"We're happy here," she said with a thin smile. La Motta considered her for a moment, thinking *Gonna have to deal with her soon*.

"Yeah, well go anyway, willya, buy some jewelry or something. We gotta do some business here, you follow?"

Delores sighed, stood up, gathered Frankie Twice and stuffed him into her purse, got her car keys, checked the mirror in the hall, and left without saying good-bye, closing the door behind her gently. The three men watched her go, and after a moment Spahn said, "Mario, I don't think Delores is all that fucking happy here."

"Fuck Delores," said La Motta, "and fuck Frankie Twice too. Only dog puts out more fumes than that rug rat is a greyhound."

"You need to think about her," said Spahn.

"I am. I am, Julie. So what about this *favor* for Tony Tee. What exactly is it?"

"This Sinclair guy, he's got some serious fucking skills, like karate and all that Chink shit, he kicked the crap out of Little Anthony's buddies, crippled them, and, according to Tony Tee, he scared the living *fuck* out of Little Anthony. Kid was crying on the phone. Tony Tee, he don't like to hear his kid crying like a fucking pussy. So he figures he's gonna blood the kid, let him dip his beak inna blood, make an example."

"I can see that," said La Motta. "But why us? Why this *fucking* favor?"

"Tony Tee wants to make this . . . memorable. For Little Anthony. To make the point with the kid, stiffen his dick, make a man out of him."

"Yeah? So?"

"So he wants to borrow one of our guys."

"Yeah? One of our guys? Who?"

"Tito."

There followed a shocked silence, broken only by the sound of Mario La Motta trying to breathe and Julie Spahn swirling the ice in his G and T.

"Tito Smeraglia? The *Istriano*? No fucking way," said La Motta after a couple of minutes. "Anyway, he's not even in the country. He's . . . where the fuck, Desi?"

"In Trieste," said Munoz, still trying to breathe. "Seeing his mother, she's got the cancer up her ass. How'd Tony Tee even *hear* about Tito?"

"My bet?" said Spahn. "Fucking Delores."

"Delores?" said La Motta. "How would she even know

about a guy like Tito? We brought him into the operation, recruited him off those fucking Slovenians, Croats, whatever the fuck country over there. He wasn't even one of Frankie's people."

"Delores *listens*," said Spahn. "We were talking about Tito a coupla weeks back at the table, you know, that thing he did for us in Montreal, that Frog lawyer and his wife?"

La Motta brought it back, and considered it. "The correction thing? Jeez, she'd sure as shit remember that. Was she around?"

"Delores is *always* around," said Spahn, who didn't like women. Or men either.

"Why would Delores tell Tony Tee that story?"

"Tony Tee was sweet on Delores, Mario, even when Frankie was alive. I figure she's keeping him on the simmer, thinking maybe she can use him someday. So she feeds him this Tito story—you know, information is coin, like—and of course he's gonna remember what Tito can do if you let him loose."

"Tito's . . . too fucking extreme," said Munoz, "especially for this Sinclair guy. All that's needed here is a good professional beating. Break the guy up. Let Anthony get in a few hits, get his balls back. Tito's too . . . too much for this job."

"We can't afford *not* to do a favor for Tony Tee neither," said Spahn. "We're still figuring how things work down here and we need him on our side, need him to owe us something. So we make a decision. We tell him no, he'll want to hear that fast. Miami guys always like to get their bad news fast."

"Tito's too valuable," said Munoz. "He's a specialized weapon. We use Tito to send messages, to let people know the cost of fucking us over. We use him too much . . . no. I say no fucking way."

Spahn took that in, turned to La Motta. "I'm saying we gotta do this," Spahn said. "We gotta keep Tony Tee happy, show him some respect. He went to bat for us on this deal, brought the other guys around. Now he's asking for some payback. So, Mario, one for and one against. It's up to you."

La Motta sucked on his cigar. It had gone out but he hadn't noticed until just now. "Fuck it," he said, pulling out a matchbook. "Tony Tee wants Tito, give him Tito. Give him the whole Tito Smeraglia Experience. That's one fucking favor he'll never forget. We're showing him respect, show we're stand-up guys, onna team like. Plus we'll have something on Tony Tee, on all the Miami people—leverage or whatever. They'll owe us."

The other two were nodding at this. It never hurt to do a friend a favor, especially if it gave you a fishhook in his balls for later.

La Motta put the match to his soaking wet cigar, sucked on the end. It smoldered and fell apart. He brushed it off his lap, looked around the apartment.

"Fucking Delores. Look at this rug. The sofa here. Shit everywhere. Place useta have some class. Now it looks like a Dumpster. What does that lazy bitch do all day?"

"She listens, Mario," said Spahn. "She listens."

The Difference Between Purgatory and Limbo

Three thirty-four Sable Basilisk Street turned out to be a Federal-style townhouse in a row of similar houses built along a shady street across from the southwestern border of the Confederate Graveyard.

The graveyard, a former battlefield, was a hilly grass-covered triangular field fenced off by an undulating ribbon of black wrought iron spears surrounding acres of the Civil War dead, its crosses and barrows and tombs rising up and falling away into the autumn mists. This was a grim rock-filled terrain studded with live oaks and Georgia pines, each man's grave a white cross or a Star of David marked by a small Confederate flag fluttering on a black spear. There were also hundreds of low barrows, redbrick mounds half buried in the earth, tightly sealed and barred and covered with mold.

Looking at them, Nick remembered the night almost two years ago that Rainey Teague had been extracted alive from one of them, a barrow containing the body of a man named Ethan Ruelle, who had been killed in a duel on Christmas Eve in 1921. Whatever was going on in Niceville, for Nick at least, it had all started that god-awful night.

Beyond the barrows there were a few whited sepulchers made to look like Grecian temples or Roman tombs. Each one was a dim cold crypt populated by the glorious dead, and on each lintel was the carved name of a Niceville family—the Haggards, the Teagues, the Mercers, the Ruelles, the Cottons, and the Walkers—the founding families who had made Niceville what it was on this golden afternoon.

They pulled up in front of 334 and Mavis worked the Suburban into a space that should have been too damned small for a Prius; Nick was duly impressed. Mavis shut the truck down and they looked up at the yellow limestone townhouse for a moment. The dusty sash windows were shuttered and the front yard was running to weeds. A litter of faded circulars lay scattered across the stone porch in front of a heavy wooden door painted a dark English green. It had shining brass fittings that looked new and a stained-glass fan window that matched the stone arch that sheltered the porch.

A discreet FOR RENT sign on the lawn carried a number and the name *www.YarvikProperties.com*. The place had that tired look that a lot of rentals get. Too many people coming and going, no one really giving a damn. There was an attached garage in the same yellow limestone, with two wooden gates painted the same deep green as the front door. The brass handles on the gates looked brand-new, but the chain holding them shut was a rusted wreck and the padlock hanging from it looked like it should have gone to the home for retired padlocks back in the Eisenhower years.

"Looks empty," said Mavis.

"It does. Let's check it out."

They got out and walked up the pathway to the front door, stopping there to let their instincts work on the place. What their instincts got was *silence*. The house was calm, still, radiating nothing back, a house with a clear conscience.

Sunlight filtered down through the trees lining the street.

A dog was barking in the distance. Across the street in the graveyard a worker was cutting the grass with a riding mower, the sound a distant purring murmur.

Nick moved across the lawn and examined the garage lock. Although the chain was new, the padlock was still firmly locked in.

He tugged hard at the chain and the doors creaked, but they stayed shut.

He looked at the gravel drive in front of the doors. A litter of dry leaves and dust coated the drive. Nothing larger than a dog or a possum had disturbed it in weeks. If there was a gigantic navy blue Cadillac Fleetwood inside this garage, somebody had slipped it in under the door.

Yarvik isn't here, he thought. *The place just feels . . . empty.*

"I'll find the back," said Nick, looking up at Mavis. "I'll click the radio when I'm in position. Then you knock on the front door. Knock hard. Remember to stand aside, Mavis."

"Remind me again why we're not just using the key and walking in?"

"Because neither of us is alone and there may be neighbors watching us right now, so we have to follow the rules for legal entry, especially if Yarvik is in there and we end up shooting him dead. I'm not perjuring either of us in a courtroom when a little due process makes it all legal."

"What if I just close my eyes?"

"Mavis, just bang on the door when I click you, okay?"

"I will. If there's no answer?"

"I'll hear you. If you get nothing, I'll bang on the back door. If we both get nothing I'll come around and we can use the master key."

And that's what they did.

It took Nick a while to squeeze down the narrow space between 334 and the next townhouse, stepping carefully over a tangle of old wooden fence slats and piled-up leaves.

He came through a rusty gate that groaned when he pushed it open. There was a tiny backyard, no grass, just cobblestones surrounded by a rickety slat fence. There was nothing in the yard but dead leaves and an ancient gliding rocker made of brown wicker, sagging into twigs and rusted iron.

He came around and stood in the middle of the yard, looking up at a narrow wooden porch; a tattered screen door; a second door behind that, wooden, painted a faded yellow; and beside the porch a large picture window staring blankly out at the yard, covered with a Venetian blind, twisted and filthy. What little he could see through the slats was all dust and darkness, a dim suggestion of bare rooms and gloomy interior halls.

There was a coating of dust on the steps and on the floor of the porch itself. It looked untouched, except for some small scrapes in the dust that could have been made by a possum or a skunk. The house gave off nothing, an inert hulk. No subtle hum that houses seemed to give off if there were people inside, even people trying hard to be quiet.

He pulled out his radio, double-clicked the send button, and got a double click back. He took out his Colt, cocking the hammer back as he did so, and put a foot on the back stairs, lightly, no weight at all, waiting for . . . waiting for *anything*.

Less than three feet away from Nick, on the other side of the door, in the gloomy kitchen of the townhouse, a naked blood-stained man the size and build of a Kodiak bear was breathing softly through his half-open mouth and aiming a heavy Kimber .45 pistol at the middle of the door, waiting for the cop out there to step up onto the porch, which would bring his chest into the line of fire. The man's name was Maris Yarvik, but he wasn't Maris Yarvik anymore.

————

Mavis had stepped back and away from the line of the front door. She had her Beretta out, the safety off, and all her attention focused on the house. She was imaging the interior, trying to get a sense of it, trying to *feel* her way into it.

And she was now getting . . . something. It was in the air, a muted high-pitched whine, coming from nowhere and everywhere, like cicadas in summer, that continuous electrical hum.

Then it came to her that perhaps what she was hearing actually *were* cicadas humming, and she smiled to herself and got ready to pound on the front door hard enough to shake the hinges of Hell.

Sixty seconds had ticked past since Nick had first taken a position at the bottom of the back porch steps. On the sixty-first second he heard the forceful thudding of Mavis Crossfire's heavy fist on the front door.

The house was vibrating from the force of her blows. He could feel the vibrations coming up through the wooden step under his right foot. He could hear her saying *Police department, open up. Police, open up.*

They both waited.

No response.

Mavis went through it again—pounding on the door, *Police, this is the police, open the door*—and she got the same result.

Nothing.

Now it was his turn.

He carefully put his weight on his forward foot, tense and ready, and he came up onto the first step.

And then one more.

His attention was fixed on that faded door panel. He reached the porch floor, stepped off to the left to get his body out of the line of fire—

———

For the thing that lived inside Maris Yarvik, everything was illuminated and clear. The biological on the other side of the door was level with the pistol, but had moved off to one side, as if it could read her thoughts. She moved the pistol to compensate for this action and felt sure that she had reacquired the correct aim point.

Nick raised a hand to knock on the door, and when he did he felt a kind of magnetic radiation coming off the wooden panel. He moved his hand closer to the door and he felt a tingle in his palm. The hairs along his forearm began to rise.

He held his hand a few inches off the panel, thinking *There is something waiting on the other side of this door*—

Nick leveled the Colt at the door, steadied his grip, reached out with his left hand, palm open, to slam it against the door, and his cell phone rang. The sound made him jerk and he almost squeezed the trigger of the Colt, so tightly had he been holding it, already fully committed to firing. He swore, swore again even more creatively, and pulled the phone from his jacket pocket.

"What? What the *fuck* what?"

"*Nick?*" It was Beau. "*Nick, you okay?*"

Nick took a breath, trying to counter the adrenaline surge, backing away from the door, getting off the porch— going down a step, but keeping his eye and his gun on the door—*Something is in there, something is waiting.* His heart was hammering against his ribs, his throat felt tight—was he *afraid*?

"Beau, look, sorry—caught me at a bad moment—"

His radio came to life. Mavis calling. "Nick, what's up?"

"Beau, wait one—" He keyed the radio. "Nick, I heard your cell. Are we going in?"

"I have a call from Beau—"

"What's he want?"

"I don't know yet—wait one, Mavis."

He came back to the cell. "Beau, what is it?"

"They think they've got Maris Yarvik."

"What? In custody?"

"Not yet. But they located his Caddy and they're pretty sure he's in it. Air Unit spotted it in the trolley switching yards off Long Reach Boulevard. It was partially under the round-about roof, but Air was able to get enough of a sideways look to make the plate. I have units there now, perimeter sealed and secure, but they're hanging back—"

"Why?"

"Air has a thermal sensor and it's telling them that there's someone inside. Big hot return, but no definition. And there's a heartbeat, but it's real odd, real rapid—"

"So it's a medical emergency. Go in."

"Well, Tig is thinking maybe we need the BDU people. A stressed-out heart rate might mean that Yarvik is sitting in there with a bomb in his lap. They can't get a visual because the windows are all tinted. What do you think?"

"Tig's the CO."

"He says this is on you. Your case."

Yellow rat bastard.

"Okay. Hold off. Call up the BDU, but have them stand off. We'll be there in ten minutes."

"Where are you?"

"At 334 Sable Basilisk. We're moving now."

He came back around the side of the house at a run, leaping over the pile of fence slats, coming back to the front yard. Mavis was on the lawn, her Beretta still in her hand.

"What's happening?"

Nick told her as they headed for the Suburban. She got in behind the wheel and started it up, but she didn't get rolling immediately because Nick was still staring up at the townhouse.

"What is it?"

"I'd like to put a squad here. Right away."

"Okay. I'll get Central on it. Can I ask why?"

"Yeah. There's something in that house, Mavis. I could feel it."

"You think Yarvik is in there?"

Nick shook his head. "No. I don't know. But *something* is."

"You want the squad guys to go in?"

He thought about it for a second. "No. But I want them to seal it up front and back. Fast as they can. Nothing goes in and nothing comes out. Front and back, sides and roof. Windows, doors, chimneys, mailboxes. Seal it all up. Make sure they stay right here until we tell them to stand down. No pee breaks or going for donuts."

"Okay. Done."

She put the truck in gear, worked it out of the parking spot, hit the lights and siren, and got onto Central, calling it in. Nick's cell beeped, an incoming text. It was from Kate:

> Nick I know you're busy Rainey is at it again and now
> we can't find him or axel phones dead no GPS either
> they were at boudreau park can you send someone to
> check love K

Nick braced himself against the door, managed to text Kate back:

> Yes will send squad to look right now mavis is with me
> going to the trolley yards may have found our guy will
> call you when things calm down

"What was that," asked Mavis. Nick told her and she got on to Dispatch, spoke for a moment, clicked off. "They've got a squad a block away. Rolling on it now. They'll report in."

"Thanks, Mavis."

"Kid's a hat-full, isn't he?"

The question was rhetorical. Nick looked at his watch, thinking he had told Beau ten minutes.

It took them seven.

The Niceville trolleys operated out of a big railyard center that had once served the Atchison, Topeka and Santa Fe line. Now it was the repair center and switchyard for the twenty-seven navy blue and gold trolleys that formed the main public transit system for Niceville.

When Nick and Mavis powered into the yard, bouncing over the track lines and scattering gravel as Mavis braked to a stop, there were nine cop cars, black-and-whites and a couple of unmarked Caprices, set up in a containment arc around the south rim of the big circular storage shed that housed the trolleys when they weren't in service.

Nick and Mavis could see the tail end of a big blue Caddy sticking out a few feet from the shadow of the roundhouse roof. Everybody was keeping a careful distance and everybody who had an M4 rifle was leaning on the roof of his squad car and pointing it at the rear window of the caddy.

There was also a large blue panel van with State Police markings, and under that BOMB DISPOSAL UNIT in big gold letters. Harness cops were keeping the gawkers at a safe distance, and two short bullet-shaped guys wearing half of their BDU gear were standing talking to a large Niceville police sergeant with his back turned to Nick and Mavis. He heard the Suburban doors slam and turned around. It was Frank Barbetta.

He gave them both a huge smile. He had earbuds in his ears and dark blue wires running down to his uniform pocket. He plucked the buds out of his ears as they came up to him. "Nick, Mavis."

"What's with the ear thingies?" asked Mavis.

"Chopin," he said, apparently enjoying the effect this comment had on them both.

"Chopin? As in *Frédéric*, the piano guy?"

"That's right, Mavis. I'm totally about art and culture and antithetics and all that artsy-fartsy shit. And it's FREE-drick, not FRED-a-rick."

"I think you mean *aesthetics*, Frank," said Nick, thinking about Charlie Danziger.

"Yeah, whatever," he said, turning to introduce the two Bomb Disposal guys from State. "This is Pete Dorn—"

Dorn, a lean young guy with a worried expression that looked like it was going to become permanent, smiled and nodded.

"And this ugly mook here is Lou Zitto."

"I'm his cousin," said Zitto. "You're Nick Kavanaugh, right? I heard about you. Special Forces and all that?"

"All lies," said Barbetta. "Nick spent his war years collecting urine samples at Walter Reed. So tell Nick and Mavis what you were telling me."

Zitto, who was wearing a T-shirt with a picture of a leaping gazelle on it—under the antelope were the words *BOMB DISPOSAL TECH: If You See Me Running, Try to Keep Up!*—glanced across the yard at the tail of the caddy and then came back to Nick and Mavis.

"We put the thermals on it and there's *definitely* somebody in there. A big return but diffused, which makes sense, since it's kind of a warm day and he's sitting inside there with all the windows rolled up and the engine shut down, so no air conditioning. Got to be ninety inside that car. Which could also explain the heartbeat thing."

Mavis picked up on that. "You said it was irregular?"

"No," said Zitto. "Not irregular. It's steady okay, it's just way too fast. Like a mile a minute and staying there. That's why they called us in. Most guys who are strapped to an IED, they get nervous. Israelis use long-range mikes to pick up on stuff like that, suicide bombers—"

"Guys who suffer from premature detonation," said Barbetta.

"Yeah, like that," said Zitto, "so we were waiting for you, Nick. What do you want us to do?"

Nick looked at the caddy and said nothing for a minute. He'd come to hate IEDs more than anything else in the combat zone. "Have you got a robot?"

"We do," said Dorn. "You want to send it across?"

"Can it sniff?"

"It can."

"Okay then. Go sniff."

Dorn looked happy and he and Zitto bopped around inside the van for a bit, emerging with a kind of steel wagon the size of a large microwave, with big fat rubber wheels, an articulated arm ending in a complicated pincer device, another short blunt tube alongside the arm, and a stalklike neck with a pair of cameras right about where the eyes should be.

"This is Lonesome Leroy," said Dorn, looking down on the device with affection.

"On account of nobody wants to go anywhere with him," explained Zitto.

"What's the tube?" asked Mavis.

"Shotgun. Semiauto. It's loaded with deer slugs. We use it to stimulate suspicious packages."

"That'll do it," she said.

Dorn had a handset with a TV screen in the middle and two joystick controls. He did something nimble and Leroy took off across the gravel at a brisk pace, watched by about twenty cops and maybe a hundred civilians and a camera guy from Live Eye Seven. As the robot got closer to the tail of the caddy, Dorn concentrated on the screen.

In the picture the rear end of the car loomed up like the Hoover Dam. Dorn was biting his upper lip while he worked the machine and looking worried.

"Run it alongside the passenger door," said Zitto. Dorn maneuvered Leroy around the end of the car and trundled it slowly up the right side of the passenger door. He stopped it there and adjusted the camera stalk, raising it up until the camera eyes were level with the passenger window.

Then he raised the remote arm and brought it into close contact—very lightly—with the rubber edge at the bottom of the window.

He left it there for a few seconds, studying a readout screen on the remote.

"No explosives," he said after a minute.

"You sure," asked Nick. "It's safe?"

"I'm sure there are no explosives," said Dorn. "But I'm not sure it's safe. There's a heartbeat, okay, and a thermal mass. I'm also getting carbon dioxide . . . and something else. Like an acid . . . I don't know. Never seen this signature before."

"Get Leroy to knock on the window," said Mavis. They all looked at her.

"Well, maybe he's asleep?"

Zitto nodded at Dorn, who raised the remote arm, extended one of the pincer claws, and tapped gently on the glass. The robot had a mike so they could all hear the metal ticking against the glass. Leroy tapped about five times and they all saw what happened next.

Something big slammed into the inside of the window, a

blur of fangs and claws and wild yellow eyes, and it howled at Leroy through the glass and now something wet was running down the inside of the window, and then the *thing* came back again, screaming, clawing at the glass, and they all drew back from the picture, as if whatever it was could come straight through the camera at them.

"What the *fuck* is that thing?" said Barbetta.

"Okay," said Dorn, still watching his chemical readouts, "now I'm getting mercapto-methylbutan—"

"And what the fuck is *that*?" Barbetta asked, still staring at the TV screen.

Dorn took a second. "I think it's cat piss."

Nick was staring across the yard at the caddy. "Oh crap," he said, and took off running. Everybody tracked him, a lone man in a pricey suit and expensive loafers pelting across the gravel toward the rear end of the caddy.

After a short hesitation, Mavis followed him, not quite so fleet, but she caught up to him as he got to the passenger door. "Nick, are you fucking nuts?"

Nick had his hand on the door and was nudging Leroy away with his foot. He looked at Mavis, his eyes wild, and said, "Mildred Pierce, Mavis," and then worked the latch and tugged the door open. Mavis braced herself for an explosion, but it didn't happen. A large and unhappy Maine Coon cat recoiled from Nick as he stood in the door, hissing and spitting and showing its fangs. The interior of the car reeked of cat shit and cat piss and something much worse, the stench of human decay.

"Oh, Christ," said Mavis. Nick, moving fast, reached in and pinned the frantic cat down, getting a hand firmly wrapped in its ruff. The cat literally screamed at Nick; it was soaking wet and Nick could feel the cat's heart hammering against its ribs, Nick plucked it off the seat, stepping back as he did so, and holding it away from his body, trapped its rear legs in his other hand, immobilizing it.

He held it up to Mavis, who was dabbing some Vicks VapoRub on her upper lip. "Mildred Pierce," said Nick, holding the cat as gently as he could, but firmly. "The Morrisons had a cat, remember? Mildred Pierce. A big Maine Coon. Used to belong to Delia Cotton. Doug Morrison was a forensic guy for us, remember? Beau and I took the cat to him for blood work when Delia Cotton went missing."

"Dammit," said Mavis. "I totally forgot."

"So did I. Hold her, will you?"

"Not a *fucking* chance," said Mavis, backing away from the cat's murderous glare. "That thing is half sabertooth."

"I have to check the car, Mavis. There's something dead in here."

"*I'll* check the car. *You* hold the tiger."

At this point Barbetta and Dorn and Zitto had come up. Barbetta took one look and one whiff and turned around to wave off the cops who were still pointing their shotguns and M4s at them.

"Guns down, people. Guns down!"

Nick tried to hand the struggling cat to Barbetta, but he backed off fast, saying "Whoa, dude, I'm like allergic—"

Mavis had jerked open the rear door. "Oh, hell," she said.

"What is it?" asked Barbetta.

Mavis stepped back from the car, breathing through her mouth, looking paper white. "Ah Jeez, I think it's what's left of Ava Morrison."

Nick stepped up, still stuck with the damned cat, and they all looked in at the backseat and the footwells. Nobody said anything for a while until Pete Dorn said, "Excuse me," in a hoarse tight voice and walked off about twenty feet and sat down on a concrete block and put his head in his hands.

Nick went around to the driver's side, opened the door, popped the trunk hatch, went back and made sure the trunk

was empty, placed the cat into it and gently—but quickly—closed the lid.

They heard footsteps, somebody running toward them. Barbetta turned and saw the Live Eye cameraman trying to close in for a shot. Barbetta went out to welcome him. His encounter with the camera guy got on quite a few cell-phone cameras and went viral on YouTube shortly afterward.

Nick pulled out his radio. "Central, this is Detective Kavanaugh."

"Roger that."

"I want to get in touch with the squad covering that house on Sable Basilisk."

"Wait one, I'll patch you through."

Nick waited, watching what was going on between Frank Barbetta and the camera guy. Apparently Frank Barbetta shared Nick's strong views on the proper relationship between the media and law enforcement. Central came back. "Detective Kavanaugh?"

"Here."

"Well, sir, we can't raise that unit, sir."

"What do you mean?"

"Nine Charlie isn't responding, sir."

Nick felt his chest get tight. "Central, get some cars up there! Roll on it! Get some fucking units up there right now! Tell them to go in hot, with guns! Now move!"

His voice was flat and hard as slate and it carried across the whole yard. People stood in stunned silence, staring at Nick. For a second, anyway. And then everybody was moving. Thirty seconds later Nick and Mavis were in the Suburban and headed north at speed. Lights and sirens.

Axel Goes with the Flow

Axel was in the river. That was all he knew. He had no idea how he got there or what he was going to do about it, but he remembered from Safety Swimmers that the dog paddle was just going to wear you out and you had to get rid of your shoes, so Axel did that, all the while feeling the Tulip racing away with him like . . . like a dog with a ball. Now and then he could get his head above the waves and catch a glimpse of the grassy banks of Boudreau Park and he could see those girls who were playing jump rope down the way from them.

They were shouting at him and running along the bank and he tried to shout back, but then he went under again. The water was warm and brown and moving real quick, but now that he had kicked his sneakers off he wasn't going down as fast.

He looked up and saw the sunlight doing flickery light things on the waves and he felt his heart slamming around inside his chest and then he figured *I'm going to drown and be dead and they'll stick me in the ground and worms will crawl inside my mouth and nose and eat my brain and lay worm eggs in my eyes,* so he started to fight again and his head popped up and he was still only a few yards off the bank and now a whole lot of people were running and screaming and pointing at him.

The girls with the rope were screaming words at him in really high shrieky voices and one of them was tossing the rope at him.

It landed close and he made a grab at it and he almost had the handle and then he was pulled away from the shore and he went under again, started to spin sideways like the river was a spider rolling him up in a web to save him for later and a voice in his head was saying *don't fight it just go with the flow let go let go* and his arms were getting heavy and his chest was on fire but all he could say to the voice was *worms will eat me* so he kept fighting and now and then he could claw his way back to the surface and take some air in.

Now he was racing by the Pavilion and he could see people sitting at tables with glasses of beer and all the colored umbrellas with COORS and HEINEKEN and MILLER TIME on them and nobody ever looked at him as he went flying past them and he felt a stab of anger at all the stupid people having stupid beers while a little kid was being carried away to drown in the stupid river.

And then the water took him for a while and it dragged him deeper than before so that when he looked up the yellow dancing lights on the waves seemed a long way away and then a huge dark shadow came across the waves and the sunlight went away and he was in a dark gloomy water world and he saw a wall of concrete sliding past him and he knew he was going under the Armory Bridge.

The voice was right there in his head saying *stop fighting go with the flow* and all the fight that was in his wiry body was slipping away from him and then he slammed into something big and sort of soft and it came away with him and got swept along with him.

It felt like some kind of rubbery raft and as it raced along with the current it rose up toward the light and Axel got on top of it and let it carry him upward and in a moment he had his face in the sun again and he stayed there, gripping the raft and floating on the surface of the river.

His heart was still slamming in his chest and he was choking on river water, but after he threw up again he felt his chest clear and he could breathe and breathe so that's what he did, he just lay there holding on to the raft as the river carried them away, and he closed his eyes, and he breathed in that wonderful air for a long time, just floating and drifting, and breathing and drifting.

Axel went with the flow.

Delores Maranzano Chooses to Be Proactive

Delores Maranzano had a thing for shoes—more of an addiction, truth be told, especially the stiletto kind with the scarlet soles. She had eleven different shades of the same shoe, and right now she was thinking about making it a perfect dozen. She shopped for shoes every other day, and always at Neiman Marcus in Fountain Square.

She was sitting on a butternut leather banquette in the butternut-and-auburn-walled and dimly lit Private Client lounge at Neiman Marcus, sipping a crystal flute of Veuve Clicquot, twiddling her naked toes in the halogen downlights.

She liked the muted bustle of all the wealthy young concubines just like her as they went back and forth between the cases, waited upon by willowy clerks, all male, all pretty, all sexually adaptable, all fluttering around them like a sparkly flock of cinnamon-scented Tinkerbells.

Frankie Twice was nested up in a corner of her Venezia bag, nothing but his nose showing, and she took a second to make sure he wasn't peeing on her stuff, which he was entirely capable of doing.

As she was leaning over the bag, the clerk—sorry, the sales

associate—came back, her favorite new shoe clerk at N and M, a muscular young man so sinfully gorgeous he made Ryan Gosling look like a box of stale macaroons.

His name was Raylon Grande—pronounced *gran-day*—and he had only been at Neiman Marcus for two weeks. He had quickly become her favorite because, although he tried hard to fake it, Delores was convinced that Raylon was, against all the odds, not even slightly gay.

There was another reason as well. Delores was always interested in new people who came into her life, especially new people who showed an interest back. Delores had looked into Raylon Grande's background—she had her sources—and found out a few intriguing facts, other than the gay-faking thing. Which was crazy obvious on the face of it.

No seriously gay guy would have the trouble Raylon Grande was having whenever she gave him the Full Delores, and she was letting him have it right now as he stood there with the shoe box in his hand, staring down the front of her blouse as she leaned over to ruffle Frankie Twice's nerves.

She let him enjoy that for a while, until Frankie Twice, sensing her insincerity, nipped her on the thumb. She fake-yelped, sat back, and gave Raylon Grande an up-from-under smile as she licked the tip of her thumb with her pointy pink tongue.

Raylon, his skin flushed, kneeled down at her feet, patted Frankie Twice's head, got a snarl and a tremble for a reply.

Now Raylon was in a position to give *her* an up-from-under through a lock of his shiny blond hair that always managed to fall just so over his left eye. Part of his gay act. Not even slightly persuasive. More like a parody, how a straight guy would think a gay guy would act.

Raylon was slipping a jade-green stiletto onto her left foot, slowly, gently, and with feeling, and she encouraged him by letting her thighs wander just enough to make him get even pinker. She had undressed carefully for this part.

Gay, my sweet dimpled ass, she thought, wondering how to go about what she had decided to go about today. And then Raylon asked her a very convenient question, and she was on her way.

"I know this is a personal question, Miz Maranzano—"

"Please, call me Delores."

"Thank you, Miz Mara—thank you, Delores. I was just going to ask you if you're feeling any better now? I mean, after your tragic loss?"

She put a faraway glaze in her eyes and then smiled bravely. "Oh, Raylon. How *kind* of you to ask. Honestly, I do find the nights are the worst. That big empty bed. I *cannot* sleep in an empty bed."

Raylon gave her a shy smile. "Then you should find a way to fill it," he said. "You're a beautiful woman."

"Dear *darling* Raylon. No. I couldn't. It's much too soon," she said, her voice breaking ever so slightly. "The wound is simply too . . . too deep. Frankie . . . was the one true love of my life. My shining star. I need time for my heart to *heal*."

She managed a plausible lip tremble while lifting her right foot to receive the other stiletto. She watched him struggle to maintain meaningful eye contact as her knees parted company.

He finally gave up on that, and let his eyes wander slowly over her body in a way that heated her up wonderfully. "But you're not *alone*, I hope. You have family?"

Curious guy, isn't he?

"Oh my yes. I have houseguests. Actually, I wish they'd go away."

"Relatives?"

"No, not really, although they are *family*, if you know what I mean?"

Raylon's expression remained blank. She decided to follow through a bit more.

"I mean, they're all business associates. Of Frankie's, really.

They're staying with me while I sort out the estate, the business complications. That sort of thing."

She stood up and walked across to check out the Louboutins in a mirror. Very nice. She pivoted to check the other angle, aware that Raylon was watching her ass with more than a professional interest. She *owned* this guy.

"I love them, Raylon. I'll take these and the black ones."

"You already have three pair of Louboutins . . . Delores."

"I know. But I hate it when the red gets all scratched up. I like my soles pure."

Raylon smiled as she came over and sat down again. "I like my souls marked up some," he said, slipping the shoes off her feet and putting them back in the tissue paper. She crossed her legs again, watching him watch.

"Well, aren't you a *bad* boy. Can you *deliver*?"

"I beg your pardon?"

"The shoes, Raylon. Can you take them over? I mean, up to the suite? I hate to leave packages with the concierges. They're nosy and careless."

"Oh. Of course. Will someone be there?"

"Yes. Unfortunately. They never go out. They just sit around and stink up the place. I'll be happy when they're gone. Ask for Mr. La Motta."

"You want me to take them *personally*? We have a messenger service? I mean, of course, I'd be delighted."

"If you would, Raylon? I'd love it."

"Of course . . . right now, then?"

"Please. I'm taking Frankie Twice to the vet. Just ring through and one of them will buzz you up."

Raylon said he'd be happy, and Delores signed the account slip, saying as she did, "Raylon, don't be too upset by the way they talk."

"I'm sorry?"

She leaned in to whisper at his cheek, making sure he

breathed her in. "Mario and Desi and that nasty Jew. They're sort of rough people. The things they say, it would curl your toes to hear."

"Yes?" he said, his smile faltering, staying with her whisper, leaning in close enough for her to smell his skin, which reminded her of fresh-cut hay. "What kind of things?"

"Oh, you know. Business stuff. I never knew what Frankie did for a living—"

As if.

"But he certainly seems to have kept some rough company. Oh my yes. Well, tah for now. You will do the shoe thing?"

"I will," said Raylon, and his eyes stayed on her until she was out the door with a backward finger-twizzle.

A dangerous little bitch, he was thinking.

The security guards at the Memphis phoned up to the Maranzano suite and got an okay to send Raylon Grande up with the shoes. On the penthouse floor the double doors got jerked open by a fat sweaty man with a face like a baboon's butt who gave Raylon a once-over—Raylon could see the thought bubble appear over his bald skull: *faggot*—and took the packages with a guttural grunt. He was about to slam the double doors in Raylon's face when Raylon held up the receipt form.

"I'm sorry, sir, you'll have to sign?"

"Fuck me," said La Motta, and walked off, presumably to find a pen. He left the door open wide enough for Raylon to get a look at the main room and the other two guys in it, both of whom were staring back at him, a thick-bodied guy with a brush cut and a birdlike freak with a bony skull and sharp black eyes. The room was clouded with cigar smoke and beer smell and stale pizza fumes and the reeking haze of tough talk and bad intentions. La Motta found his pen, waddled back, and scratched an indecipherable signature on the clipboard.

Raylon got to say most of his *Thank you, sir* to a hard-slammed door. "I guess that means no tip, then?" he said.

Fifteen minutes later he was in the Starbucks in the lobby of the Bucky Cullen Federal Building. Sitting in the booth across from him was a large barrel-bodied guy with a round beef-steak face and a ratty beard. He was wearing a rumpled blue suit, a crisp white shirt open at the collar, and a badly knotted red silk tie. His name was Benjamin Hackendorff, but he was generally known as Boonie, and he was the special agent in charge of the Cap City FBI office.

"She did that?"

"She did," said Raylon. "It was her idea."

Boonie shook his head, sipped at his mocha latte. Raylon had some of his espresso while Boonie thought it over.

"And you saw them?"

"I did."

"La Motta, Munoz, and Spahn. All three of them? You made that ID? Solid? It was them?"

"It was sure as hell Mario La Motta. I remember his intake shots from Leavenworth, after Deitz threw them all under the bus. I'd need to see the best shots we have of Munoz and Spahn. But . . . yeah, I'm pretty sure it's them."

He placed the clipboard on the table, handling it carefully. "And I got this. I asked La Motta to sign. And he did."

Boonie looked down at the clipboard.

"Fingerprints?"

"Pretty sure," he said, smiling like a Velociraptor. Raylon Grande was a happy man.

"How the fuck did they get past our watchers?" Boonie was wondering. "And why didn't Leavenworth let my office know these mutts were headed my way? Who the fuck's their parole officer? This is exactly the kind of intel we're supposed to get from DC. Useless dickheads."

"It happens, Boonie. It's the frontline guys out here in the wilderness who actually get stuff done. Guys like you."

"You can knock off kissing my ass, kid, although I admit I'm enjoying it. What I don't get is why she's so *careless*. She's been a mobster's *goo-mai* for years. And here she is talking loose and ditsy with a shoe clerk—"

"Hey. A *sales associate*, if you please."

"Bite me. I still don't get it. Jeez, you think she's onto you? That she *knows* you're a Fed? You think maybe she *wants* these guys busted out?"

Raylon considered it. "I don't know. I doubt it. Maybe she just hates them. I mean, from what I saw, having those three mutts for houseguests would be like raising warthogs in your living room."

"Well, we gotta think about what that might mean. I mean, she pisses them off, she's not gonna want to lose her end of Frankie's business."

"Maybe she already has. Or she's afraid she's about to. I can't see those guys being too fair-minded about the Maranzano operation."

"So . . . right now she's vulnerable. We could bring her in, lay some bullshit on her, you know, aiding and abetting a criminal conspiracy, that sort of thing. Scare her a bit and see if she wants to cut some kind of deal?"

Raylon shook his head.

"No. What's in it for her? And scaring that broad is easier said than done. She's a rock-hard little diamond, Boonie. And I just don't buy that she thinks I'm a Fed. I mean, she knows *you*. You've questioned her yourself, after that fire fight at Charlie Danziger's place. Why not just make an anonymous call to you? No. Tell you the truth, I think she's just looking for some male companionship. From a guy who doesn't stink of cigars and pizza and isn't uglier than Barney Frank. She's a hot number and she knows it. She's got her motor running, that's for sure. Just to let you know, I might have to . . . *fraternize* . . . You know, sacrifice my virginal body on the sacred altar of justice?"

"Virginal? And anyway, you're a married man."

Raylon looked prim. "It's not infidelity if you're more than five hundred miles from home. Anyway, May and I have an open marriage."

"May fucks around too?"

Raylon was scandalized. "Fuck, no. She's a good Catholic girl."

"Then what's all this bullshit about an open marriage."

"It's a compromise. She's married and—"

"You're open. What if May hears about that?" Raylon's leer went away fast. "Christ, Boonie, don't even *say* that. She's Irish. She'd fucking *assassinate* me."

Boonie shook his head in rueful . . . rue. "Anyway, sleeping with a target is against agency policy."

"Only if *you* find out about it."

"Well, I might let it slide if you got pictures. She really coming on to you?"

"Like a vampire bat on a big toe. I can see why shoe salesmen have to be gay. She gave me the complete guided tour up the Vale of Cashmere while I was slipping on her Louboutins."

Boonie visualized that for a while. "Man, I wish I could go undercover."

Raylon laughed. "Maybe at a Pep Boys, Boonie."

"Yeah, well, looks aren't everything."

"Lucky for you. So. What do you want to do?"

Boonie gave it a moment.

"You know we've got a line-of-sight angle on the Maranzano suite right from my office?"

"Yeah. I've seen it."

"We could put a laser mike on their windows right from the lunchroom. Wouldn't even have to find a place to set up."

"That's right."

"And we've got paroled felons who're under a federal court order not to associate with each other or they get their early outs revoked and they're on their way back to Leavenworth. And they're all sitting around Delores Maranzano's apartment right now. Three mob mutts in a suite owned by another dead mob guy with links to Tony Tee and his Miami machine? Any judge in town would give us a warrant in a heartbeat."

Boonie looked out the Starbucks window.

He could see the glittering tip of the Memphis pinnacle. There were lights on in the penthouse suite.

"Jeez," he said, looking predatory. "You can put all three of them right up there right now?"

"Yep. Two warthogs and a buzzard."

"What?"

"I was being colorful."

Boonie was gazing hungrily up at the Memphis. "Well, don't."

Raylon Grande—whose real name was Special Agent Kurt Pall—went back to his undercover role as a shoe clerk at Neiman Marcus. From the interior of the Fountain Square First Third Bank about fifty feet away, Delores Maranzano watched him cross the cobblestones, noticing that his walk was getting more and more theatrical the closer he got to the Neiman Marcus store.

She looked back at the Starbucks, where Special Agent Benjamin Hackendorff, who had been all over her after Frankie's death, was just coming out the door, talking into his cell, looking urgent.

She smiled down at Frankie Twice, who was also staring out at the square. "Told you," she said. "Didn't I?"

Frankie Twice trembled and then he licked his lips, staring back at her with his big buggy eyes. He trembled some more and then farted.

"I'll take that as a yes."

Shall We Gather at the River

There being no other useful course of action, Kate and Eufaula sat in the conservatory in silence and stared out at the flowers in the garden and the sunlight shimmering on the lawn, and they waited for the phone to ring.

They had waited about fifteen minutes when Beth came home. She walked through the living room and down the hall, sensing something wrong in the house, something pending and heavy. She found Kate and Eufaula in the sunroom, surrounded by flowers and ferns, looking like women at a wake.

"Hello—oh dear, what's up with you two?"

They both looked up at her and Beth caught her breath. She was an older and less sunny version of Kate—living with Byron Deitz takes a toll—but she was every bit as quick.

"Oh, Christ. It's the boys again, isn't it?"

Kate stood up, took her purse and coat, got her to sit down on the couch. Beth, a fully crisis-conditioned woman, started to vibrate. Kate put her hands over Beth's, knelt down and looked up at her.

"Calm down, Beth. Yes it's the boys, but they've just done another scamper."

"They're missing?"

"Not *missing*, Beth. Just avoiding some well-earned consequences."

Beth looked slightly less frantic. "Wait. Where's Hannah?"

"She's still at her playdate," said Eufaula. "Remember? She won't be back until eight."

"Of course. Sorry. Thank you, Eufaula. I am not myself. The boys? What have they done now?"

"Not *they*, Beth. Just Rainey."

"What did he do?"

Kate told her, the walkie-talkies, and what Rainey had said to Eufaula. When Kate was finished, Beth looked down at the tea set, shook her head. "Fuck tea. This calls for booze."

Eufaula cocked her head at Beth. "You really want a drink, Beth?"

"What Rainey said, Eufaula, I think that's perfectly vile. I hope you can find a way to . . . put it out of your mind."

"I already have. Do you really want a scotch? You never drink before five."

"It's five somewhere, and it's either booze or heroin. Get one for yourself too."

Eufaula laughed. "I would, but I'm supposed to drive up to VMI tonight to see Bradley. But I'll get some for you? Heroin or scotch."

"Do we *have* any heroin?"

"No. I could go across and borrow a cup from the Sheridans."

"I'll have a scotch," said Beth.

"Straight up or rocks?"

"Rocks. And maybe some branch?"

"Right back with branch," said Eufaula.

Beth turned to Kate. "You have the police looking?"

"I do. I made the mistake of calling Rainey and telling him

to come home at once. With Axel. I should have just waited and let him walk into it."

"When he does get back, what are you going to do?" She put a hand to her throat. "Oh my, does Nick know about this?"

"Not yet."

"Are you going to tell him?"

"I haven't decided yet."

"Kate, you can't go on keeping things from Nick. He's part of this family and you're shutting him out. That's not good."

"You know how he feels about Rainey?"

Beth paused, framing an answer. "Well, he's not all that wrong, is he? And you and he are letting your marriage suffer over this. And you have a terrific marriage. Trust me, I know about bad marriages. As much as you want to help Rainey, you cannot sink your relationship with Nick trying to help a young boy who may not want to be helped. Nick's already moved out once. Next time he might not come back. It happens."

Eufaula was back with Beth's scotch and a glass of white wine for herself. Beth sipped at hers while Eufaula took a chair by the window

There was a silence.

Consequences, thought Eufaula, looking at the sisters. *There have to be consequences.*

"There have to be consequences," said Beth.

Kate was nodding.

"I know. I'm just not sure what they should be. Dr. Lakshmi thinks—"

"Kate, this doesn't feel like schizophrenia," said Beth. "This is just too . . . organized. Too calculated. And now he's off again, and Axel is with him. Have you heard from the police yet?"

Kate shook her head. "No. And that means they haven't found them."

"Do they have any money?" asked Beth.

"I gave them both ten dollars," said Eufaula. "And I think Rainey has money in his bank card."

"So they might be hiding out at the Thalia, watching movies and munching popcorn."

"With their phones off," said Eufaula.

"Consequences," said Kate in a whisper.

"I agree," said Beth. "And this time they have to count. You need to read Rainey the riot act. Rainey's running off the rails and if we don't get him under control . . . I'm afraid he'll take Axel with him."

"Axel's no fool," said Eufaula. "He looks up to Rainey, but he wasn't taking any of the blame for the radio thing. That was all Rainey, and I could see that Axel didn't approve of it."

"Yes," said Beth. "Don't worry, Kate. Axel can take care of himself."

They heard the front door open, the silver doorbell tinkling.

"They're here," said Kate, looking at once relieved and angry.

"Remember, *consequences*," said Beth.

"Oh, trust me," said Kate. "I will."

But it wasn't the boys.

It was Nick and Mavis.

When they got down to Boudreau Park there was a huge crowd of people stretched out along the riverbank, all of them silent, everyone watching the police boats: big white Boston Whalers with light bars and NICEVILLE MARINE PATROL in large blue letters along the hulls—five of them in a ragged line, backing water, going slowly down the Tulip, officers with long poles in the bows, looking down into the churning water, their faces set and grim.

Farther down the river, officers were walking the banks, looking into every tangle of weed or branch or vine. On the decks of the Pavilion the crowds stood silent along the rail-

ings, every face turned to the river, the music shut off, the
day turning slowly colder as the sun moved down in the west
and long violet shadows began to creep out from the trees and
grasses along the river.

The only sounds were the muted burble of the patrol boats
out on the river, the rumble of the current, the wind hissing in
the trees, and the flap and flutter of bar umbrellas.

Mavis parked the Suburban next to a row of squad cars and
they all got out, Kate and Beth and Eufaula, the women looking scalded, shocked and silent and frightened, Nick pale and
white with anger, worried sick, holding it all in.

They all walked down to the riverbank, where a patrol
supervisor named Bob Mullryne was talking to a small group of
girls, maybe twelve or thirteen years old, all of them wrapped
in towels or blankets, all of them looking up at Mullryne.

Mullryne turned as they reached him, looked back at the
girls. "You were very brave, all of you. Thank you for being so
observant too. There's some hot chocolate in that truck over
there."

He nodded to a PW standing nearby, a muscular blond
with her hair in a ponytail, and she gathered the girls up,
herded them toward a large red van with NICEVILLE FIRE in
gold letters.

Nick noticed one of the fire captains standing talking to a
patrol cop. It was Jack Hennessey. Hennessey saw Nick, lifted
a hand. He had something in his ears. They looked like earphones.

What's with this earphone thing? he wondered, and he made
a note to ask Hennessey about it when he got a chance. Mullryne came back to them, and Nick introduced Kate and Beth
and Eufaula. Mullryne, a big pale expat Brit with careful eyes,
tried for a hopeful smile and fell a bit short.

"Look, the good news is there's no sign of him along the
river—"

"That's *good* news?" said Beth in a tight voice, her face white and her eyes shining with tears. Mullryne stayed with positive.

"Well, it means there's still hope."

"How far down have you looked?" said Nick.

"We've got boats and people as far down as the Armory Bridge. We have to go slow because there's lots of places where . . ."

"A body can get snagged?" said Beth. Mullryne winced and then nodded.

"Yes, ma'am, but if we haven't found one . . . that's not a bad thing—"

"How'd he get in the river?" asked Kate.

"Nobody saw him go in," said Mullryne. "It was the girls who spotted him going by. They started yelling, got everybody's attention. They even threw him a line, but the current took him—"

"Was it Axel?" said Beth.

"Well, it was a little boy with long brown hair and big eyes. He was fighting hard, ma'am."

Beth lost it there and went to her knees in the grass. Kate and Eufaula knelt down beside her, holding her. There wasn't much to say.

Nick came back to Mullryne. "Was there another kid with him?"

Mullryne nodded.

"Yes. An older boy, thirteen or fourteen, long blond hair down to his shoulders. The girls noticed him because he was throwing rocks at the ducks and they told him to stop."

"That's Rainey," said Nick. "Anybody holding him? Any of the squads here?"

"No. And they've been looking. But it was the young lad who was getting most of the attention, you see, so the other boy could have gotten lost in the crowds. Everybody was shouting and pointing, everybody was looking at the river, trying to see the boy—"

"The boys rode bikes down here," said Eufaula. "I'm looking at Axel's right over there. I'm not seeing Rainey's."

"What sort of bike was it?"

"A Gary Fisher mountain bike. Red and gold, with those big fat tires," said Kate. "Cost a fortune. He loves it. If it's gone, he's on it."

Mullryne had his note pad out. "What was he wearing?"

Eufaula said, "Navy blue sweatshirt with a gold crest on the right side and *Regiopolis Prep* under it, blue jeans with the left knee torn, black high-top sneakers with red laces, a North Face backpack, navy blue with gold straps, and Ray-Ban sunglasses on a gold braid keeper."

Mullryne's pen was flying. Kate and Beth were staring at Eufaula, who shrugged and said, "I notice things. What can I say?"

"His name is Rainey Teague," said Nick, now in full cop mode. "DOB January 17, 2000. He's five-seven, weighs one forty, blue eyes, blond hair shoulder-length. On the muscular side. I want that kid found," said Nick with an edge they all caught. Kate looked at him, but she said nothing.

Mullryne looked uneasy. "Jesus. You don't think he—"

"I have no idea. It's possible. I really want him found. Found soon."

Mavis said, "I'll get some squads in from Tin Town and down from North Station. These units here," she said, taking in the cars and the cops who were standing around, "can we spare some of them?"

"We can," said Mullryne, and he went off to make things happen. Nick turned, got down on his knees beside Beth, put his hand on her chin and turned her gently so that he could look into her eyes. She looked like hell, but she was listening.

"Beth, that sergeant was right. Until we find him, you don't have to go all the way down."

"This is bad, Nick, it's so *bad*—"

"Yes. This is bad. But something's telling me that Axel is okay. He's had two years of Safety Swimmers. He's a wiry little guy in terrific shape. He doesn't panic. He's been through a lot and he's a real tough fighter. You know that. Everybody said he was keeping his cool in the water. He wasn't screaming. He wasn't thrashing around. Everybody said he was—"

"Going with the flow?" said Beth, tears streaming down her cheeks, her lips blue.

Nick kissed her on the cheek, tasted salt, looked at Kate, who got his message.

"Come on, Beth," she said. "Let's go to the van, get some hot chocolate, let these people do their job. Okay, hon?"

Beth got to her feet, shivering, unsteady. Kate and Eufaula led her across to the fire truck, got her a folding chair, and wrapped a red blanket around her. Kate looked back at Nick and her message was clear. *Find him, Nick. Find him.*

If You Can't Get There from Here Then They Can't Get Here from There

As a precaution, in the wake of what Twyla was calling the Bloody Beach Smackdown, she and Coker had pulled out of the shore house and checked into the Casa Monica Hotel in downtown St. Augustine.

The hotel, built in 1888, looked like a film set for a thirties musical with Fred Astaire and Ginger Rogers, a sprawling, block-long, vaguely Moorish-looking Spanish Baroque mansion in gleaming white stucco with ornate terra-cotta towers and carved Juliet balconies, stained glass and flowers and ferns everywhere, a massive vaulted lobby walled with polished mahogany and studded with original art, and an Old Hollywood courtyard pool surrounded by medjool date palms.

They checked into the Flagler Suite under one of Coker's alternate IDs, Mr. and Mrs. R. J. Quirk from Atlanta, Georgia, made it a point to decline the turndown service each night, and let it be known to all parties that they were there for *privacy*, not *attention*, which they were promised they would get, or not get, or . . . well, yes, sir, and you have a real nice stay.

The Flagler Suite took up an entire tower of the hotel, with three separate floors, the bedroom being on the highest level, two kings, and a wraparound view of the town, even a sliver-glimpse of the sapphire-blue Atlantic.

Twyla, a dedicated sybarite, found her jagged nerves soothed by the old-world luxury. She was feeling pretty tentative right now, having been the Predicate Cause of the Bloody Beach Smackdown, although Coker wasn't the kind of guy to blame others for his own excesses.

And they both agreed that beating the living daylights out of those two dim-witted college boys had been in retrospect a tad excessive.

Not to mention *expensive*.

So they settled in to await events, should there be any events to develop, having decided that when there was nothing to be done but wait and see, it was best to do that in comfortable seclusion.

Right now they were down in the main floor living room, both in their bathrobes, Coker sipping a single malt with a bandaged right hand—punching a guy in the teeth has consequences—and Twyla with her glass of Santa Margherita Pinot Grigio, a habit she had picked up from Charlie Danziger, who drank enough of it every year to warrant a personal thank-you note from the mayor of Valdadige.

A moment of relative peace after a hectic interlude, and a time for quiet reflection on the future. Until Coker turned on the big flat-screen.

The news was on, but the sound was muted, apparently a taped repeat of a news story broadcast earlier on Fox, and what was filling up the screen was Mavis Crossfire, looking splendidly Wagnerian in her harness blues, talking to a reporter from Cap City CNN, a stainless-steel blond with bee-stung lips and gunfighter eyes. Under the video a news feed was spooling across the screen:

. . . serial killer stalks southern town . . . police baffled . . .
two officers down . . . officials struggle to cope . . . citizens
arm themselves and barricade their homes . . .

The reporter was holding a mike up to Mavis Crossfire's face while Mavis, clearly working hard to hold her temper, was talking down to her.

Literally. Mavis was a tall girl.

In the background was a Federal-style stone townhouse with yellow crime-scene tapes strung all over it and two plain-clothes cops standing in the doorway, a big black man in a dark brown suit and a shorter white guy with a hard face and salt-and-pepper hair.

"That's Tig and Nick," said Coker, turning off the mute button. Mavis's voice—a Virginia-tinted baritone—filled the room. ". . . not a fair description—"

"But there are two officers down, Sergeant Crossfire, in the house behind us, both shot—"

"Lady I have already told you twice that they were *not* shot—"

"Is it true they were answering a call and were ambushed by persons unknown?"

"They were on duty, yes, and answering a call, but so far—"

"We understand you have a suspect at-large?"

"We do, and we'll be putting out a description of him in a few minutes."

"One white male?"

"That's our assumption, but we are not limiting it to that."

The interviewer pounced on that like a chicken on a bug. "Are you saying there may be other killers loose? What steps are you taking to protect the citizens while these serial killers remain at—"

Mavis got a lot chillier and even the stainless-steel news chick got the message. "It's irresponsible of you to put out that kind of misinformation. We have only one suspect, we have a clear ID of him, we have been looking for him, and we have at this time no reason to believe that he's being assisted by anyone else."

"Is this the same suspect as in the Thorsson killings?"

"No. That's a different case."

"Any connection to the Morrison family?"

"It's too early to say."

"But you're not ruling it out?"

"I'm not ruling it *in*, either, you follow?"

"But two fatal home invasions in two days and in both cases we understand there was—"

"Look and listen. I just told you these are *two different cases*. If it will help you to comprehend this, I can go get a whiteboard and some colored Sharpies. Now you can go ahead and make up stupid crap if you want to, kid. I have to get back to work. You have a nice day now."

The reporter had more questions and she tried shouting them at Mavis Crossfire's back, getting nothing, so she turned back to do the direct-to-camera wrap. She was trying to do *solemn and portentous*, but all she was getting was *vampire in a blood bank*.

"This sleepy southern town of Niceville is locked in fear and horror today after the tragic events of the past few days as a suspected serial killer or killers stalk the streets and a total of six innocent citizens including two young children lie brutally slaughtered in their own homes. As you have just seen, these small-town police officers are baffled and confused, and they admit they have little to go on—only one unnamed suspect— while two of their own patrol officers were found inside this house behind me, the apparent victims of a savage attack by person or persons unknown. This is Sarah Band for—"

Coker flicked the mute back on as Twyla reached for her iPhone.

"Twyla, wait—"

"I've got to call Bluebell!"

Bluebell was Twyla's sister, the only family she had left after her father flew his Cessna into the side of Tallulah's Wall last spring. Bluebell lived in Niceville and worked as a psychiatric nurse at Our Lady of Sorrows hospital in Cap City.

"Yeah, but not on that phone, remember? Use the Motorola. And switch out the SIM card."

"Oh, Jesus. I can never keep that stuff straight. Where's the SIM card holder?"

"In your purse, last time I looked."

Twyla, flustered, disorganized, bustled around until she found her purse on the hall table by the suite door. She ruffled through it, pulled out a flat sterling silver card case, and came back to the couch, sighing theatrically.

"Now what do I do?"

"Pick a SIM card, put it in the cell."

"I *hate* these things," she said, fumbling at the lid lock. "I *never* remember to change them, or I forget which one I was supposed to use, and I can never get them in right. And why do they have to be so fucking *tiny*?"

"Just slow down, Twyla. Take a breath."

Coker handed her the Motorola, an older model flip phone but unlocked and equipped for quad-band. She stripped out the battery pack and looked down at the SIM card holder, biting her upper lip.

There were fifteen different SIM cards in it, each one registered to a different user, all of them valid accounts. She pulled Chicago out of its case and, after dropping it a couple of times and getting it in backward once, and cursing all the while, she finally eased it into the SIM card slot, inserted the battery, flipped the phone over.

Coker stopped her there. "Before you call, what are you going to say?"

"I want to know if she's okay, Coker."

"Yeah, I know, but get yourself under control before you call her. The way you are now, you'll just spook her. So be calm."

Twyla gave him a modified death glare, but Coker had his reading glasses on, so it didn't fry his retinas. She was tapping keys and vibrating like a Cherokee Chihuahua.

"Hello! Hello, Bluebell, it's me!"

"Twyla. Thank God. Where are you?"

Twyla hit speakerphone and Bluebell's whiskey tenor came on against a background of murmuring voices, bells, and beeps, and someone talking over a PS system. Hospital sounds.

"Never mind me. Where are *you*?"

"I'm at work. The ward is going crazy. We're overrun. Are you okay? Is . . . can you tell me *anything*? I wish you could come home. I miss you!"

"I miss you too, honey. We're watching the TV. What's going on there?"

"We don't know. The whole state is going nuts. We've had five people admitted to the secure ward today. All of them are people who went missing—you know, the Niceville Missing that guy did the *60 Minutes* thing on—"

"The ones who got abducted?"

"Yeah. I'm hearing the total is up to twelve of them so far, and some of them are supposed to come here for evaluation. None of them have any memory of where they've been. The cops are still trying to figure it all out. We have one guy here, an old man named Barnaby Mills, he turned up on his wife's porch the other day and now he's like totally losing it . . ." A clatter of steel as somebody dropped a tray, and voices raised, female, edgy, and contentious . . .

"Damn, going nuts here. Can I call you back?"

"No, honey, you can't. Can you get to a quiet place?"

"Hold on . . . hold on . . ."

The background noise got muted, muffled, the sound of a

door closing. "There . . . I'm in a supply closet. Can you still hear me?"

"I can . . . Bluebell, calm down. I can practically hear your heart racing . . . just tell me what's happening."

"What's happening is Niceville is coming apart at the seams. This old guy here, you want to know what he's babbling about—and this is from an old *white* guy—he's talking about the Kalona Ayeliski—"

Twyla went silent, looked over at Coker, got her voice back. "A *white guy* said this?"

"Yes . . . this Mills person . . . we have his file here. Dr. Lakshmi has her staff doing a complete work-up on all these people. The FBI is on the way. Mills was an *insurance adjuster*, for Christ's sake—he was born in fucking *Newark*. What would a seventy-nine-year-old white insurance adjuster from Newark know about the Kalona Ayeliski? Nobody knows about the Raven Mocker anymore. Not even our own kids get told *that* story any—"

"Bluebell, you sound pretty shaky."

"I *am* pretty shaky—there's just no place to hide from a Raven Mocker."

"Bluebell, you've never even believed in one yourself."

"Daddy did. Remember he used to talk about the Kalona Ayeliski that was feeding on our people up at Blue Stones? How they had to call on a spirit singer to hunt it?"

"He was telling us ghost stories around a fire, honey. There is no such thing as a—"

"There was a cop down here from Niceville. He was one of the guys who brought Mr. Mills down, and I heard him telling one of the Cap City cops that six people had been killed over the last two days and that all six of them had been—his exact words—*made to suffer*, like the killer wanted it to last as long as possible. What does *that* sound like? That's what a Raven Mocker demon does, she feeds on—"

"Honey, what about the ravens that are supposed to travel with her? There are no—"

"There are sure as hell *crows*. A flock of crows from Crater Sink *killed* Daddy last spring. Made him fly into Tallulah's Wall. They said the flock was huge, thousands of—"

"Honey, listen, you have to calm—"

"No! I'm not going to calm down. Look, wherever you are, can I come and stay with you? I mean it, I have to get out of here . . . These *yonega* morons—these *Europeans*—they have no fucking *idea* what they're dealing with and they never—"

"Honey—"

"Please! Let me come to you."

"Look, have you got any money?"

"What . . . yes . . . well, not a lot."

"Credit cards?"

"One. It's all maxed out."

"Can you get online?"

"Online? Yes. I can."

"Then I can e-transfer you some cash."

Coker stepped up. "Honey, put her on mute for a second."

Twyla gave him a crazed look.

"Bluebell, honey. Can you just hang up for a minute—"

Bluebell's voice was getting higher. "Will you call me right back? I can't see your number—wait, what's three one two? Is that Chicago—are you in Chicago?"

"Honey, I'll call you right back, okay? I promise . . . honey, just one minute."

Nothing but Bluebell hyperventilating.

"Okay . . . one minute . . . don't forget."

"I won't. One minute."

She clicked off and turned on Coker, ready to fight. Coker backed away, lifted his hands.

"Relax, Twyla."

"*Relax!* How the FUCK am I supposed to—"

"We can help her. We just can't send her any money. It's too traceable."

"Fine. Then I'm going to go and get her."

"Twyla—"

"Coker, I am *not* leaving her there. You heard her! She's falling apart. She's never been strong and after Daddy killed himself and then we . . . we left town . . . every time I talk to her she's getting . . . worse. She's coming apart. I can hear it in her voice. I *cannot* leave her there. She's all the family I have now. There's nobody else, Coker, nobody but you and Bluebell!"

"You *can't* go get her, Twyla—"

She lit up like a road flare. "Fuck you, Coker, I sure as hell can do whatever I damn well—"

"*You* can't. But I will."

That damped the blaze. "But, Coker, if you go back, if anybody recognizes you . . ."

"They won't. It's a quick extraction. I can be in and out in thirty-six hours."

"But . . . what if . . ."

"Fuck *what if*. This is what it is."

"You'll come back? With Bluebell? Jesus, Coker . . . you're not seeing her as a threat, are you? I mean, you wouldn't just go there and—"

Coker got a touch steely. "You really thinking like that?"

She caught the warning. They had a good relationship, but a careful one.

"No, Coker . . . I'm sorry. You can be . . . harsh . . . but I know you better than that, and I wish I hadn't said that."

"So do I . . . but I guess I've earned it."

"We've both earned it, I'd say. I guess we belong together, like a pair of . . ."

"Handcuffs?"

"I was going to say wolves."

Coker smiled, not always a heartwarming thing to look at. This one was pretty good.

"I'll go get her, bring her back safe. You have my word. We'll figure out what to do with her afterward. Now you call her back, calm her down. Tell her to book some time off and go back to her house. She's still in your dad's home, up by Mauldar Field, right?"

"Yes. But you always said they'd have somebody watching it in case I ever came back."

"Sounds to me like there's a lot more pressing stuff going on in Niceville right now than keeping a surveillance team on your daddy's rancher. Call Bluebell, tell her to go lock herself down at home. Tell her you've got something set up. Don't tell her it's me. Then we'll have some dinner. I'll figure out how to do this, get on the road before midnight. I can be in Niceville by midmorning. Okay? Does that work for you?"

She gave him an odd look. Suddenly wary. "This isn't like you, Coker."

"What isn't?"

"You doing this . . . Lancelot thing. You know. Riding to the rescue."

"Yeah? Well, you know, maybe I'm not Lancelot. Maybe I'm just . . . bored."

"With me?"

"No. You're a lot of things. Boring is not on that list. Maybe I'd just like a road trip."

Her look slipped sideways some more. "This wouldn't have anything to do with Delores Maranzano and that Harvill Endicott guy, would it?"

Coker gave her a wide-eyed stare, put a hand over his heart. "Twyla, you *doubt* me?"

She had to smile at his expression. He looked like a wolf with a mouth full of bunny rabbit, trying to explain why Easter got canceled.

"All the time, Coker."

"Probably a good policy."

"Going after Delores Maranzano is stupid and risky. And if you get killed, what happens to me?"

"You'll be a rich young widow. And you'll meet a decent young guy who might live long enough to give you some babies and a normal life."

"I don't want to be a rich young widow. And I sure as hell don't want *children*. They're sticky and they're smelly and they leak. I just want *you*. So do NOT get killed. And you *will* get Bluebell? You'll see her safe *first*?"

"On my sainted mother's head."

"Your mother was an alcoholic hooker. What about me? Do I stay here?"

"No. Too exposed. Go back to the beach house. Lock it down. Turn on the alarms. Gun up. Don't answer the door."

"The beach house . . ."

"Yeah. You'll be safe there."

In a stuffy back room on the seventeenth floor of the Bucky Cullen Memorial Federal Building on the west side of Fountain Square an FBI civilian intern named Esmé Phuong was sitting at a computer console with her earbuds in listening to a Malaysian boy band named NeetDaScreet bludgeon their way through a medley of Nine Inch Nails tunes. She was also reading *Wolf Hall* on her iPad, so she was not immediately aware of the pop-up message that had just now appeared on her monitor:

FILE 23901 POSITIVE HIT

It was accompanied by a soft-spoken computer-generated female voice with a Mid-Atlantic accent saying *attention please a key word has been detected in an active file please notify case manager attention please a key word has been detected in an active file please notify case manager attention please* . . . the Mid-Atlantic voice, being a matrix of electrons arranged into an MPEG loop by an IT subsidiary of Samsung, was quite willing to go on in this vein until Jesus Christ got a decent haircut, but she was no sort of competition for a Malaysian boy band with the volume set to stun, so it was fortunate that Esmé Phuong's immediate supervisor happened to be passing by the door to the Collections room and he overheard the warning message.

He stepped into the office without first tapping on the doorjamb—a serious breach of HR's boundaries policy right there—and stood for a moment taking in the scene. A seasoned bureaucrat, the supervisor had only recently rememorized the departmental mission statement and he was mindful of its soul-stirring exhortation that *promotable agents will proactively exhibit leadership initiative in all eventualities where precipitate action may be required, bearing in mind all situational factors and probable outcomes, and will by example optimally enhance and support dynamic interactivity within an achievement culture that incentivizes our excellence mission* . . .

Anyway, he got her attention and a couple of hours later—operational procedures had to be followed to the letter—a fax—yes, a fax—was sitting one floor up on the desk of Boonie Hackendorff, the SAIC of the Cap City office:

NSA subscription link to FBI HQ DC
Forward to FBI CAP CITY RE CASE FILE 23901
LITTLEBASKET, Twyla—Non Warrant Intel Only
KEYWORD INTERCEPT—>> Twyla <<
INTERCEPT TIME: 1339 Hours EST
INTERCEPT LOCATION: Chicago Illinois

Partial Transcript:

BL: (Bluebell Littlebasket) (Agitated)

Hello . . . hello?

UNSUB: Honey, it's me again.

BL: Oh, God >> Twyla << I'm so scared.

UNSUB: I know, honey.

BL: Can I come to you?

UNSUB: Here's what I want you to do. Just go back home right now.

BL: I can't. I have to work. The whole ward is going nuts and these disappeared people—

UNSUB: You're going to come down with a migraine right now and go home, okay?

BL: I'll get suspended—fired—

UNSUB: So what? Just go home and lock the doors and get Daddy's gun and wait there.

BL: How long? Why? What are you gonna do?

UNSUB: Just do what I said. Do it now.

BL: But how long? I can't just—

UNSUB: Soon. Very soon. Now go.

DISCONNECTS: NEGATIVE GPS fix timed out.

Five thousand miles north and east of Boonie Hackendorff's corner office in Cap City—where Boonie Hackendorff was currently *not*, since he was out petitioning a local judge for a surveillance warrant for Delores Maranzano's penthouse suite in the Memphis—and far around the curve of the slowly turning earth, a white Fiat cab pulled up at the departure gates of the Friuli Venezia Giulia airport outside Trieste, Italy.

It was raining, around one in the morning, but the airport was still busy with travelers from Venice and Pordenone, Padua and Udine and Ljubljana across the border in Slovenia.

It was a warm night, almost sultry. Low clouds and a drifting mist blurred the constellation of radar and microwave tower lights that studded the peaks of the Tyrolean Alps in the far north.

The airport, set down on a broad alluvial plain that had seen a thousand invading armies pour across it, from Hannibal to Napoleon to the Wehrmacht, was grim and nondescript and run with Teutonic efficiency. There was a distinct Austrian bite in the accents of the people milling about in the concourses and walkways.

On the far side of the Tyrol lay the land of the Tedeschi— the Bavarians and the Prussians and the Austrians. Their intermittent visits had left an indelible impression on the region. Even the Italian spoken here had a Germanic edge, and the local dialects were almost incomprehensible to people from the south of Italy.

Harsh sodium arc lights burned away the surrounding night, making the airport feel like an outpost on a distant planet. It had none of the disheveled amiability that makes the rest of Italy so appealing.

The man getting out of the Fiat suited the airport and the region. He was Istrian, almost a separate race from the Italians. His ancestors were pirates and raiders. It took the Roman empire two separate campaigns to hunt them down in their mountains and cliffs and put them under the sword. Although his name was Tito Smeraglia—an Italian name—his high cheekbones and heavy jaw and his pale gray eyes came straight from the Caucasus.

His skin was as pale as parchment and his age was hard to determine, but the Croatian passport he handed to the Dogana e Immigrazione official listed his DOB as the fifteenth day of March, 1954, his place of birth the village of Piran, a desolate salted plain in the north of ancient Istria, a grim and ill-favored moor swept by rain and war and successive waves of conquerors for over two thousand years. It was a good place to raise up killers, and Tito Smeraglia was a killer.

He was not showy or flashy or in any way striking. He left no particular mark on anyone unless he was killing them, and they were never around to file a report on his true nature.

Tito Smeraglia's central gift was that he simply did not care. To a certain degree his work bored him. He found it tedious, but it paid well. It supported his hobby, which was collecting antique dental tools.

His purpose, in the words of his employers, was *"fare un'impressione durevole"*—"make a lasting impression"—and he did this with the bloodless and meticulous detachment of an auditor of banks, which was his traveling cover, and it suited him perfectly.

The passport official compared the photograph on the document with the squat, blunt-faced man standing silently in front of him. He felt no pulse off the man at all. It was as if the man was made of salted mud.

The official noted that he was Croatian but with an Italian name. He contemplated a friendly comment but decided against it. He noticed that Smeraglia's passport showed many visits to America, and that he had only returned to Istria a few days ago, and now he was going away again. He was professionally moved to inquire.

"Ciò che le imprese che hanno riportato in Croazia, Signore Smeraglia?"

What brings you back to Croatia?

Smeraglia blinked at the man for a while, and then said in English, "My mother is dead of the cancer two days ago. We put her in the ground."

"Mi dispiace . . . le mie condoglianze."

The man shrugged, looked down at his shoes. *"E qual è la sua destinazione finale?"*

And what is your final destination?

Smeraglia seemed to stir, he lifted his eyes, focused on the official. The official looked back without pleasure. Smeraglia was not a joy to look upon. One's heart did not rise up with the larks. His lips looked dry. Everything about the man looked dry. If you cut him, would red dust pour out of him like salt from a box?

"Jacksonville, Florida," said Smeraglia in a thick Croatian accent.

"Jacksonville," said the official, who had been to the area on his honeymoon, although his wife was now dead. *"Vi è una graziosa cittadina nei presse di li. Si chiama sant'Agostino. Si consiglia di visitare esso."*

There is a pretty little town near there. St. Augustine. You should visit it.

Smeraglia blinked at the man and said nothing. The official shrugged, thought *uomo fango—a mud man*, and stamped his passport. Smeraglia took it and walked away, wondering if this had been a message, a sign of which he should take note.

And then he dismissed the notion. There are no secret messages, there is no hidden world.

He had cut living men open and he knew that the distance from the breastbone to the spine was about six inches. That was how deep the world was. Six inches of quivering bloody pulp and then you hit the table they were lying on.

He walked through the concourse, a squat, blunt meaningless man in a long cloth coat the color of mud, with short heavy legs and long-fingered hands and an air of dull-witted perseverance that trailed him like a miasma, and his hardshelled rolling bag following along behind him across the terrazzo like a mud-colored tortoise.

In a way they were much alike, Smeraglia and his suitcase. Hard-shelled, vacant, crawling over the surface of the world like a tortoise. He turned the officer's words around in his head.

"There is a pretty little town . . . St. Augustine . . . you should see it."

Perhaps.

When his work was done.

At the beach house.

It was a poor heart that never rejoiced, his mother used to say. But then, she was in the ground.

Danziger Orbits Jupiter

It was early in the evening when the Blue Bird bus came to a clattering, chuffing stop on a dusty gravel road that climbed up into the shaded valleys and grass-covered hills of the Belfair Range. The setting sun had turned the landscape into shining gold and even the pines and pampas grass seemed painted with fire.

Albert Lee brought the bus to a halt at the entrance to a tree-lined road that curved up a long grassy slope toward a large and very old country house set in a stand of willows and live oaks. Weathered and worn, a rectangular and symmetrical facade in the Federal style, badly in need of paint, it retained an air of self-contained simplicity that reminded Danziger of a Shaker church he had seen up in eastern Canada.

It had a cedar shake roof, silver gray with age, two huge yellow limestone chimneys on either side of the house, a wide veranda with a few plain hardwood chairs and one wicker couch. The glass in the tall sash windows was rippled with age.

There were outbuildings farther back, chicken coops and possibly a workshop, a fenced-in pasture, what looked like a summer kitchen, and one ancient wooden barn, charcoal gray trimmed in navy blue.

Lights were on inside the house and in some of the outbuildings, and from a distance came a low muttering sound that Danziger was able to identify as a generator. He saw no power lines. The Ruelle Plantation seemed to be a long way off the grid.

There were about fifteen people left in the bus, not counting Danziger and Albert Lee, the last of the careworn and silent travelers who had set out from Niceville in the midafternoon. The others had been dropped off in ones and twos at crossroads or the ends of narrow lanes that led off into the pine forest, or sometimes just at the side of the gravel road. None of them had been met; none of them said good-bye.

But all of them stood for a while and watched as the Blue Bird trundled off up the country road, Albert Lee working it through the gears, the engine straining, the exhaust muttering and popping.

Now the last of them were stirring.

Albert Lee turned and smiled at them. "Second-last stop, ladies and gentlemen. The Ruelle Plantation. Next stop is Sallytown."

They all rose, in that scattered, stiff-necked way that people have when they come to the end of a journey. They did not speak to each other and they had not spoken to either Danziger or Albert Lee at any time during the trip. They were a silent and glum and timeworn lot as they gathered up their bags and cases. Danziger wondered who they were and how they got that way as they slowly shuffled past him and went down the stairs, assisted with amiable grace by Albert Lee. They seemed to have no extra luggage stowed below.

The last passenger edged by him, a middle-aged woman who might once have been pretty. Some of her beauty remained, hazel eyes and long white hair as fine as corn silk, and a sweetly rounded figure under the thin fabric of her cotton-print dress.

Danziger caught her downcast eye as she slid by him and she gave him a thin fleeting smile.

"Are you here for the Harvest?" she asked him, in a voice that had a smoky southern lilt.

"I believe I am," said Danziger.

She stopped to consider him. "I don't know you. Are you for the Harvest or the Reckoning?"

Danziger, puzzled, said, "I have no idea, miss. I suppose that will be up to Miz Ruelle. Will I see you there?"

"Oh yes," she said, her smile going away. "We will all be present in the morning, one way or another. If you wish to take part, we are having a fellowship sing tonight, down in the Annex by Little Cut Creek. That's where we all stay, in the cabins down there. It's a ways back, on the far side of the wheat field, hard by the pine forest."

"Thank you," said Danziger. "I'll try to attend. It depends on Miz Ruelle."

"Yes, of course. Well, good evening to you."

And she left him there with her scent, which was a candle-wax smell, and under that something soft and floral. He watched her go down the stairs, and then stood up as Albert Lee came back and sat down behind the wheel, sighing.

He reached into his jacket, came out with a silver flask, unscrewed the cap and offered it to Danziger. "Cognac," he said, "not that god-awful corn liquor. If you like?"

Danziger did, and it was splendid.

He handed it back and Albert Lee took a sip, savored it, offered Danziger a cigarette.

"Well, Charlie, have you decided to go see Miz Ruelle? If not, the end of the line is up ahead in Sallytown. Expect you could get a room and a meal at the Lucille House."

Danziger took the cigarette, leaned over as Albert Lee lit it up, and then sat down in the seat opposite Albert Lee, watching the passengers file slowly up the lane toward the big house on the hill.

"I think I'll probably go see Miz Ruelle. Tell me something, Albert Lee, if you will?"

"If I can, I gladly will."

"Who the hell were all those people?"

Albert Lee puffed on his cheroot and watched the last of the stragglers as they disappeared into the twilight woods surrounding the farmhouse. "They were my passengers, Charlie."

Danziger sat back, gave him a big cowboy grin, put his boots up on the rail, hooked his thumbs into his belt, and spoke around his cigarette. "Don't go all cryptic on me now, Albert Lee."

Albert Lee didn't smile. "Well, I think you're sort of working it out a bit, aren't you, Charlie?"

Danziger took the cigarette out of his mouth, but the grin stayed. "I'm thinking they're all ghosts. And I'm wondering about you and me and Miz Ruelle and what sort of things go on up here in the Belfairs."

From a long way away came the trumpeting sound of a horse, a damn big horse, and then the earth-pounding thump and jingle of it galloping across a field.

"That'd be Jupiter?" said Danziger.

"Yes. Miz Ruelle lets him run free. He comes and goes pretty much as he pleases. Would you care to meet him?"

"I would. So can you help me out here, Albert Lee?"

Albert Lee was quiet for a moment. He sipped at his flask, handed it over to Danziger. "Well, they're not ghosts, exactly. They're kind of stuck in between two worlds."

"Do they know that?"

"They may suspect it, the ones who've been here longest. To most of them I think it's like being in a dream."

"Are we 'in between' too, Albert Lee?"

The old man shook his head, looked down at his cheroot, looked back up at Danziger. Here he paused, considering what to say. "I have come to sort of a . . . position . . . on the issue, if you'd care to hear it?"

"I surely would."

"Well, ever see that trick done with the two big magnets? Where they get placed just exactly so far apart, one I saw it was about a foot, and then the science fellow, he places a hollow copper ball just exactly right in between the two magnets?"

"I remember. The ball just floats there, held up by the magnets. Doesn't go either way. Just hangs there in midair."

Albert Lee nodded. "That's right. So I'm thinking maybe that's where we are. In between two big old magnets, and we're just sort of floating there, spinning a bit, vibrating back and forth, not going either way."

Danziger gave it some thought. "So what are we being held up by?"

"You mean, like where are the magnets?"

"Yeah."

He looked up the slope, at the lights of the big house glimmering through the trees. "I figure she's one."

"Miz Ruelle?"

"Yes. I believe she is."

"And the other magnet?"

Albert Lee frowned, pulled on his cheroot. "Something not so nice. The opposite to her."

"You mean, like the devil?"

"No. It's not like that at all. It's not about God and Satan or Heaven and Hell. That's all too far away. This is *local*. It's about something real bad that lives right around here, in the Belfairs, in Gracie and Sallytown and Niceville."

"Like the Cherokee myth about Crater Sink? That demon supposed to live there?"

Albert Lee nodded, butted out his cheroot.

"The soul-eater. I believe that Crater Sink is the center of it, yes. But it spreads out from there. Like a shortwave radio signal. Radio waves are real, but we can't see them. It's like that. You can't see it, but if you listen hard, you can almost hear it. Sort of a high-pitched buzzing that seems to come from everywhere. Like cicadas in a tree line."

Danziger was thinking about Frank Barbetta. "I talked to a man last night, said the same thing. Said there were words in it."

"Haven't heard words," said Albert Lee. "And you don't hear it so much up here at the plantation. But down in Niceville, it's in the air everywhere. And the closer you get to Crater Sink, the worse it gets. That's why everybody stays away from there. Even if they can't say why."

"And what can we do about this?"

Albert Lee gave him an up-from-under look as he lit another cheroot, puffed out a cloud of blue smoke, grinned at Danziger through the cloud.

"A man came up here last spring. He was a man a lot like you. What we used to call a gunhand. His name was Merle Zane. He had a bullet in him and Miz Ruelle took it out for him. I guess the bullet was the one you put into him. Would you agree?"

Danziger took that in. "I'd have to say yes. What happened to him?"

"Well, he went to work for Miz Ruelle."

"What kind of work?"

"He fought that duel I was telling you about. Up at the Gates of Gilead in Sallytown. It was Merle Zane who killed the bad man. Merle Zane was a good brave man and I liked him, Charlie."

"So did I," said Danziger. "And I regret shooting him. And where is he now? Is he here at the plantation? Maybe waiting for me?"

"No. He too was killed in the duel. Both shots were mortal. Both men died. It happens sometimes."

"Who was the bad man?"

Albert Lee went quiet, thinking what to say. The heavy beat of hooves sounded on the lawn, and the stamp and rumble got louder. Now they could hear the snuffle and chuff of a horse breathing. The dark was coming down all around, and the house lights glimmered through the trees like fireflies.

"I think I have to leave that part to Miz Ruelle. But you might want to think on this. You ever hear of a man named Fernand Desnoyers? Was a Frenchmen—a painter, I think?"

Danziger finished the cigarette, stubbed it out on his boot heel, and tossed it out the door onto the gravel. "You're back to being cryptic, Albert Lee."

They heard a loud snort and a trumpeting whinny and they both looked up the lane as a massive horse came out of the shadows and stood in the glow of the interior lights of the Blue Bird bus. A Clyde, but bigger than any that Danziger had ever seen, a war-horse from the Dark Ages, easily twenty-five hundred pounds, a white blaze on his muzzle, his ears forward, a magnificent head, alert brown eyes rimmed in white, a curved muscular neck, a chest as broad as a river barge. He had a long white mane, four white fetlocks, and a golden brown coat that in the dim light seemed to shimmer.

He stopped at the bottom of the drive and stamped and snorted, stared at them for a moment, huffed once more, and then dipped his head and started cropping at weeds by the side of the road.

"Damn," said Danziger, getting up and going down the bus steps to take him in, "that's a magnificent animal."

The horse looked up at the sound of his voice, shook its massive head, blew out a hot breath, and pounded a hoof into the earth so hard Danziger could feel it in his boots. He turned around and looked up at Albert Lee. "Well, I guess I'm invited."

"Don't feel too special, Charlie," said Albert Lee. He reached under the driver's seat and pulled out a burlap bag, handed it to Danziger. "Apples, Charlie. I always give him apples. That's what he's here for. Go make a friend."

Danziger hefted the bag, smiled at Albert Lee. "I guess I will."

He picked up his range jacket, slipped it on, feeling the heft of the Colt in the pocket. He started to walk away, stopped, turned back.

"You were gonna tell me about the French guy?"

"Yes. He lived in Paris in the 1850s. He once said, 'Among the dead there are those who still have to be killed.'"

He started up the engine, put his hand on the door lever. Danziger looked up at him and he felt the big horse's muzzle and his hot breath as he pushed it against Danziger's back.

"Is that what I'm going to do? Kill somebody who's already dead?"

"That depends on the Harvest. Miz Ruelle is up at the big house. She'll have some supper waiting. Mind you listen to what she has to say. Like I said, she's sort of a power in these parts."

He closed the door and put the bus in gear, and the Blue Bird rattled off up the long grade, taillights burning hellfire red in the velvet dark.

Danziger turned around, ran a hand down the horse's muzzle, felt the heat in the silky hide, stroked his neck, and fed him an apple. The horse snapped it once and it was gone and then he looked at the bag in Danziger's hand and then into Danziger's eyes, nuzzled the bag and stamped a hoof, and Danziger gave him another apple.

He took the horse's halter and turned him around—it was like turning a cruise liner around in a canal—and they went back up the long dark lane toward the lights that shone through the trees.

The wind carried the scent of horse sweat and sweet grass and fresh-cut earth and cowboy coffee and pine smoke from a fire and Danziger knew that he had been called here for some purpose.

And he was fine with that.

When Death Loses a Bet
Death Will Double Down

When the news got out, everybody met at the Walker house. Reed Walker arrived in his pursuit car just as Mavis and Nick were leaning on the Suburban and smoking cigarettes in the street outside Kate's house. Yes, they were smoking again, but only when they were stressed, which lately was always, so yes, they were smoking again.

They waited while Reed shut the engine down, popped the door, and came over. He was still in his Highway Patrol uniform, charcoal gray, crisp and military, with a gold six-pointed star on his Kevlar that glittered in the lamplight.

"Where is he?"

"Inside," said Nick.

"And he's *okay*?"

"He's shaken up, but he's fine," said Mavis.

"No shock?"

"Nope. Not even that. He's one hard-core young guy. ER docs did the whole nine yards. Axel said there was no way he was going to stay in a hospital, so in the end they decided to bring him home. He's in there now and Beth is holding him so tight I think his eyes are gonna pop out."

Reed, a hard-faced muscular cop with his black hair in a Marine cut, managed to look almost sunny as he took this in. Almost. "Jeez. I can't believe it."

"Believe it," said Nick.

"Anybody figure out how he fell in?"

Mavis and Nick looked at each other.

"We've got a theory," said Mavis.

Reed went back and forth between them and got it in one. "Shit. They're buddies. Why would Rainey push his buddy in the river?"

"Rainey has a history of shoving people into the Tulip," said Mavis, who was no longer in the Rainey Teague Fan Club.

"Alice Bayer. That was never laid on him," said Reed.

"Tig and the ADA figured they'd never make the case," said Nick. "Psychological issues. A minor. His personal history. The abduction. Any decent defense counsel could kick the case to splinters."

"What does Axel say?"

"He says Rainey told him to rinse their picnic stuff in the river. Next thing Axel knew, he was going in. When he got back to the surface, Rainey was nowhere around."

"And he's still gone," said Mavis. "We've had squads out looking for him. Not a sign."

"No way a fourteen-year-old kid can stay gone that long. We've taken the town apart. Kid's gone to ground. Only possibility."

Mavis shook her head. "Gone to ground *how*? He's a kid. Who's gonna help him? Who's gonna hide him from the police?"

Nick had no answer.

"Or he's in the river himself," said Reed.

Nick shook his head. "Not *that* kid. People saw him running away on his bicycle. He was going south. Rainey's no suicide, Reed. He's fourteen going on forty."

A matte-black Ford F-150 came around the corner, engine burbling. It came to a stop behind Reed's pursuit car.

"That's Lemon," said Nick.

Lemon Featherlight stepped out of the truck, and a pale and beautiful blond woman got out of the passenger side. In the amber half-light of the evening she looked like she was made out of spun gold.

"That's Helga Sigrid, the forensic chick," said Reed in a reverent whisper.

He had made a heated run on her a few weeks back. They'd had one spectacular evening, after which she'd kissed him and told him that *while she would love to have play sex with him anytime, she was thinking maybe she was wanting to have the sex also with Lemon Featherlight.*

"I hear she been doing a number on those bone baskets, according to Lemon," said Nick, cutting into Reed's thoughts.

"Oh, my. Oh, my. She's so fine," said Mavis in an appreciative whisper as Lemon and Helga Sigrid came up. Mavis, whose sexual inclinations were flexible, was struck by how different they looked, Helga pale and Nordic, Lemon as dark as mahogany, with long shiny black hair. After some reintroductions, Mavis couldn't help saying "You two have eyes exactly the same color."

"We do," said Helga with a wide smile. "The green eyes come from Alexander the Great's soldiers. Maybe Lemon and I, we are related."

Lemon was looking at all the cars parked every which way. "Something's going on here?"

"Oh yeah," said Nick.

"Can I hear about it?"

So they told him. When they were finished, Mavis and Nick taking turns with it, Reed and Lemon and Helga Sigrid were silent for a few moments, and then Helga said, "He floated on a *dead body*?"

"Yes," said Mavis. "A headless dead body. We ID'd him from his tats—"

"What are these tats, sorry to ask?"

"Tattoos. The body had tattoos all over both arms. We were able to ID him from those tats."

"Who was he?" asked Lemon.

"Guy named Ollie Kupferberg," said Mavis. "A local thug. Looks like he was killed some time Friday night."

"How he was killed?" asked Helga, who had a professional interest in such things.

"Shotgun blast, from medium range. Took his head clean off. Body might have gone into the river from the Armory Bridge."

Reed was ahead of the game. "Where it gets caught up on rebar or something on the bridge footings—"

"And stays there decomposing and generating gases," said Nick. "Until Axel comes along and bumps him free—"

Mavis just had to finish it. "And Ollie Kupferberg turns into a raft and he floats Axel all the way down to the Tin Town Flats, where he comes ashore in the weeds and gets spotted by one of our Tin Town units."

Helga and Lemon shook their heads.

"Man," said Lemon. "That's just so freaking . . ."

"Niceville," said Nick.

In spite of the grim times that had come upon them, the fact that Axel had survived the Tulip River—few creatures that went into that river ever came out alive—made a kind of impromptu party out of Saturday evening.

Eufaula stayed to say hello to Lemon and met Helga, told Lemon she approved of her in a whispered aside, suggested he keep an eye on Reed in that connection, and then left for the long night's drive up to VMI to see her cadet.

They all had a barbecue out in the backyard and a lot of wine and beer was taken on, and after Axel and Hannah got put to bed in the Carriage House, the rest of them—Nick and Kate and Beth, Mavis and Reed and Lemon and Helga—sat around on lawn chairs and talked in soft voices about all manner of things.

Out of regard for the civilians, nobody asked too many specific questions about what had happened to those two cops who had gone into the house on Sable Basilisk. They were in the ICU at Sorrows, physically unharmed, completely out of it, dazed and sedated, the neurologists clustering around.

There was still no word on Rainey, or for that matter, on Maris Yarvik, who was now the subject of an ever-expanding search, since the guys on the scene had figured out that Yarvik was actually inside the Sable Basilisk townhouse when Nick and Mavis had gone to check it.

A search of the Garrison Hills area had offered up nothing useful, and seven hours later the search perimeter had been expanded to include just about all of Niceville west of the Tulip River.

Combined NPD and County patrol crews were going house to house, everybody in town had been asked to check on neighbors and relatives to see if they were being held hostage, and an Air Unit chopper from State equipped with infrared and thermal sensors had flown over every playground, park, and green space in the entire city, including four random sweeps over the Confederate Graveyard.

Results so far: dick all, other than a couple of thousand freaked-out raccoons and possums and an elderly couple in the midst of a complicated carnal encounter in their own backyard who had gotten themselves lit up by the Air Unit hovering at a hundred feet above them.

The subsequent sincere apology offered to the couple by the chopper pilot was not entirely helpful, since it was delivered through a bullhorn and was loud enough to rattle windows and raise eyebrows in all the neighboring houses

Yarvik's wife Glynda was offering a reward of $10,000 for *any* information, but so far nothing. Crime scene specialist Dakota Riley's report from the Morrison killings had come through, and its basic message was that Maris Yarvik's DNA was everywhere it had no reason to be.

Around eleven Frank Barbetta showed up with a supersized cat carrier containing Mildred Pierce, the Maine Coon cat who was the only survivor of the Morrison killings. The cat had been cleaned up and medicated by some guys from the Canine Unit, and Frank Barbetta had decided to adopt her. He was her third owner.

The first was Delia Cotton, now either missing or dead or living like a recluse in Temple Hill, her mansion up in The Chase. The second was Doug Morrison, who had adopted her when Delia Cotton went missing. With Morrison now dead, along with the rest of his family, Frank Barbetta had taken her on.

It did not occur to him that Mildred Pierce was not a harbinger of good fortune.

Barbetta stayed for a couple of beers and they told him the Ollie Kupferberg story and Barbetta sat there with the Chopin nocturnes turned down low and took it all in with a quiet smile, thinking his own thoughts.

Nick, who'd had a couple of G and Ts, was feeling loose and getting ready to take Frank aside and ask him about Frédéric Chopin when Beth came back out of the Carriage House, where she had gone to check on the kids. She sat down in her chair, looking distracted, picked up her glass.

"Axel just said something odd," she said.

"I'll alert the media," said Lemon, who, unless Helga could drive a truck, was definitely going home in a cab. He'd been up since five in the morning and had driven all the way down from Charlottesville. Helga looked over at Reed, who mouthed the words *hammered to the gills* with a wolfish smile and got a sideways look back. *Never say die*, Reed was thinking.

"What'd Axel say?" asked Kate.

"This man you're looking for, the suspect in the Morrison case. Have you released his name yet?"

"Beau put out a press release at five."

"And what was his name?"

"Maris Yarvik," said Mavis.

Now everyone was picking up Beth's tone.

"Beth? What is it?" asked Kate.

"And this was at *five*?" asked Beth.

"Yes," said Nick. "Right around there. It went out to all the stations, the papers, the wire services."

"But before that, nobody knew it?"

"Nobody outside the investigation," said Nick. "What's bothering you, Beth?"

"Axel got shoved into the Tulip at three, right?"

"Yes, best guess, according to Bob Mullryne."

"Okay . . . I went in to check on Axel and he was awake, so I asked him how he was, and he asked me who Maris Yarvik was."

"Okay," said Kate. "He was in the ER around five, and they had a television in the waiting room."

"No. What he said was that *Rainey* had told him about a Maris Yarvik."

"Rainey?" said Barbetta. "There's no way he could have known about Maris Yarvik. Not at three."

"Nobody knew," said Nick. "Nobody who wasn't a cop. Is Axel sure?"

"He's sure. He repeated the name. He said that Rainey was upset about Kate and me being mad at him—they were right by the river there—and Rainey got a funny look—Axel said it was like Rainey was listening to something—and then he got real happy and smiled at Axel and he said something like Maris Yarvik was some kind of handyman or servant and he did favors for Rainey."

That sent a ripple through the cops. "*Rainey* said that?" asked Barbetta.

"At *three*?" asked Reed.

"Is this so strange?" asked Helga. "Forgive me for asking this."

"It is certainly passing strange," said Lemon, enunciating carefully, fooling no one.

"Too damn strange," said Nick.

"What does it mean?" asked Beth.

"It means we need to find Rainey," said Mavis.

The evening, like the fire, was winding down. Barbetta had gotten the impression that Lemon and the Valkyrie had driven all the way down from Charlottesville with something important to talk about with Nick, but given Lemon's current condition, it had been decided that Reed was going to drive them to the Marriott in Lemon's pickup and come back in a cab for his Interceptor.

So, time to say good night, Gracie.

He picked up his cat carrier, said his good-byes to everyone, gave Reed a cautionary look that Reed was delighted to completely ignore, and headed around the house to the driveway.

Nick caught up with him at the gate.

Barbetta heard him coming, figured he knew what Nick wanted to talk about, so he waited, thinking that whatever happened, he wasn't going to lie about any of it. What he had done was done.

"Frank, I wanted to ask you about those earplug things. About Frédéric Chopin."

That surprised Barbetta. "Not about Ollie Kupferberg?"

Nick looked out at the street, watched some guy ambling along in the dark about two hundred yards up the street, walking a dog, maybe.

Nick let out a sigh, fumbled for his cigarettes, offered one to Barbetta.

They lit up and Barbetta waited.

"To be honest, Frank, I don't want to hear one more fucking thing about Ollie Kupferberg. He's dead and Axel's not. Kupferberg was no earthly use while he was alive, but he was exactly the right guy in exactly the right place when he was dead."

Barbetta considered that. "Okay. If you and Tig and Mavis are good with that, so am I."

"Good," said Nick, smiling at him through the smoke cloud. "So, the Frédéric thing?"

"It's FREE-drick, not Frederick."

"Right. Freed-rick. I'll try to remember. You've been wearing them how long?"

Barbetta gave him a look. "Well, since we did that tunnel thing with the Dutrow kid."

"Okay . . . this is going to sound strange—"

"Jeez. Something strange in Niceville?"

"Are you wearing those earphones because you're hearing something?"

Mildred Pierce was starting to pace her cage and growl. Barbetta set the cage down. "Yeah. You could say that."

"You picked up something when we were down there, didn't you? Something got into your head."

Barbetta looked out into the night. He saw what looked like a blue shadow far away up the block, passing in and out of the streetlamps.

Somebody walking his dog? Nope. No dog.

Looked like a big guy, sorta bulky. Bulky and Dogless. Sounded like a law firm.

"Well, I did come away with something."

"Like a buzzing?"

"Yeah. Like bees."

"And the Chopin makes it go away?"

"Keeps it under control. Although Chopin wears you down after a while. I'm thinking of trying some John Coltrane instead. Blue Eddie gave me the idea. He has the buzzing too."

That surprised Nick, and he showed it.

"Didn't know that. How long?"

"Years, he said. He thinks the buzzing is what drove Rosamunda out of town."

"And he uses Chopin?"

"Says he does."

"You know Jack Hennessey?"

"Of course. He was down there too."

"He's wearing headphones now."

"I know. I ran into him at the Bar Belle and he said he was hearing something weird. I told him about the headphone thing and he went straight off to Best Buy. I been wondering, who were the medics who were there? Barb and Kikki?"

"Barb Fillion and Kikki Matamoros. Barb's dropped off the map and Kikki Matamoros is in the ICU with a fractured skull. Same night. Would have been on your MDT."

"I'd booked off. What happened to him?"

"Mugged in the Lady Grace parking lot as he was going off shift. Security camera missed it. So far no arrests."

"Anybody trying to find Barb Fillion?"

"They've e-mailed and texted her and left messages on her voice mail, but she had ten days coming, and she's a camper, a trekker, so nobody official is looking. Yet anyway."

"But *you're* thinking of it, aren't you, Nick?"

"Yeah. I am. Everybody who went down into that tunnel is . . . Jesus, Lacy."

"What?"

"Lacy Steinert. She was there too. I haven't heard from her since."

"I have. I saw her at the morgue after they pulled Dutrow out. Which was ugly, by the way."

"When was that?"

"Late Friday night."

"Nothing since then?"

"No."

"Hold on a second."

He pulled out his cell, hit a contacts number. Nick smoked a bit, looking tight.

So did Frank.

Tick. Tick.

"Lacy, this is Nick. Gimme a call as soon as you get this, Okay? No matter when. I really need you to check in ASAP. Okay?"

"Too late for her to be at the Probe, Nick."

Mildred Pierce started to hiss, a low snaky sound, building in volume, shifting into a growl.

Barbetta kneeled down, looked into the bars. The cat was curled up tight against the back of the carrier, her eyes wild, her ears flat against her skull. When Barbetta got in her line of sight, she bared her fangs and hissed at him so intensely that he felt the heat of cat breath on his face. He stood up, shook his head. "Something's really bothering this animal."

"You think?" said Nick absently. He was looking up the street. "You see a guy up there?"

"I did," said Barbetta. "While ago. Big guy. Bulky and dog-less."

"He's gone now," said Nick.

A pause. They looked at each other.

"Fuck me," said Barbetta, reaching for his Beretta. Both men hit the deck. The shot exploding out of the dark blew the night to pieces, a huge shattering blast and a blossom of blue flame.

They both felt a big fat round sizzle over their heads, a humming burr and a hot wind on the back of their necks. The round smashed into the wall of the Carriage House garage at the bottom of the drive, spraying brick chips and shattering the mullioned windows. Someone—Beth or Helga or everybody—screamed.

Reed and Mavis came running up the lane just as another explosion came from the park—a different spot, off to the left; the shooter was moving—and a skittering hail of steel balls ricocheted across the driveway—low, a grazing shot. Mavis yelped and went down.

Reed had his service piece out, a Smith & Wesson .45 with an eleven-round mag. Barbetta had his Beretta 92 with fifteen rounds, and he and Reed poured concentrated semi-auto fire on the general area in the park where the shots had come from. Nick's big Colt Python punctuated the fight with methodical single-shot blasts, Nick counting out his rounds—got to six, dumped the brass, heard it clanging and tinkling away, dumped in six from an autoloader, fired again. They heard Mavis on the radio calling it in.

"Ten 78, shots fired, shots fired—officer down, need immediate backup—three one four Beauregard Lane, require immediate ambulance and backup—"

And the instant reply: *"Roger that, bravo six, rolling now!"*

Reed and Barbetta stepped over Mavis, got down in front of her, shielding her. She was on the ground, holding her right ankle, blood running out between her fingers.

"Fuck that, I'm fine," she said, "Move out! Go engage. Move it."

Lemon was there, cold sober.

He got it in one, reached down, checked her wounds—multiple punctures from the shotgun pellets, felt like a broken ankle, but no arterial pumping—and then, without a word, pulled Mavis back down the drive and out of the line of fire.

Reed and Barbetta went left and right down to the curbline, putting fire on that parkette, trying to keep the shooter off balance. The sounds of the shots—the deep, heavy-cadenced *boom* of Nick's Colt, the sharper air-splitting crack of Reed's Smith .45, and Barbetta's lighter nine-mill—racketed around the streets and houses. Their muzzle flashes lit up the drive and the parked cars.

Nick put two final rounds out—one on either side of the spot where the shots had come from in case the target was doing a shoot and scoot. Now he was out and he had only one more autoloader. He pulled it out of his belt. More huge percussive booms erupted from the park, and blue fire flared out, blinding them.

Nick recognized it, twelve-gauge semiauto, a police duty weapon, a deer slug already in the chamber—a classic entry round, big as a lipstick tube; that was what had hummed by inches from his skull—and then six shells of double-ought steel balls in the magazine. Exactly the load-up sequence an entry team would use. Exactly the weapon taken from those two cops at Sable Basilisk.

Maris Yarvik. Had to be.

The shotgun kept pumping fire at them—one, two, three, four, deafening blasts that rocked around the street. What the hell were the neighbors doing?

He loaded up his last spare, slammed the cylinder shut, picked up his aim point again, steadied, fired . . . slow and calm . . . counting his rounds, aiming at the muzzle flashes across the street. Steel balls were in the air like killer bees, car windows shattering, ricochet rounds skittering off the walls of the townhouse, window glass blowing in.

Nick clicked empty, swore, ejected his brass; it scattered across the pavement—he was empty and out of the fight. Another blast and a thudding impact and Barbetta went down hard beside his squad car, crawling now, silent and grim, holding his left thigh, getting behind a tire rim.

Then a halt.

No more fire from the park.

Exactly, thought Nick.

Seven shells, one deer slug and six double-ought. They triggered up, everybody checked their mags . . . a pause . . .

The silence came down heavy and sudden. Nick's ears were ringing.

"Reed, you hit?"

"No," came the voice, slightly shaken, from a shadow by Lemon's Ford truck.

"Frank?"

"I got a burst in the thigh. I think it's not too bad."

They watched him moving in the dim light from the streetlamp, doing something with his wound. Reed got into a low crouch, set himself, and dashed across the open space and came down on a knee beside Barbetta, pulled his hands away, checked the wound. Barbetta's upper thigh looked like a pit bull had been chewing on it, and in the middle of the shredded mess bright arterial blood was pumping out in rapid bursts.

"Shit, Frank," he said, "that's femoral."

Barbetta looked up at him, his face white and wet. He opened his vest, started fumbling at his equipment belt. Reed was ahead of him, found his plastic cuff case, ripped two out, linked them—his fingers a blur—and got the extended cuff around Barbetta's upper thigh. He cinched the cord cuff tight and the blood flow slowed down.

Barbetta looked up the drive. "Somebody move my cat, will you!"

Nick had forgotten about Mildred Pierce.

He jerked the carrier up, heard the cat snarling, an oddly wolflike sound; checked her briefly; got a faceful of cat hiss for his troubles—no blood visible; and shoved her out of the line of fire.

He ran down to the sidewalk, took a knee beside Reed and Barbetta.

Barbetta's face was white, his lips blue, his breathing shallow.

"Shock," said Nick to Barbetta, Reed staring down at him.

"Where the fuck is the cavalry?" said Reed.

They heard footsteps, turned to see Lemon coming down the lane in a crouch. He looked at Barbetta's wound pumping out blood and his face went stony. "We gotta move him now," he said in a flat calm voice. "Gotta get him to an ER. Gotta do it right away."

They were on the curb right next to Barbetta's squad, staying out of the line of fire. Reed jerked the rear passenger door open, picked Barbetta up bodily and threw him inside. Lemon chuffed a breath, did a gut check, was about to move when Reed handed him Barbetta's service piece.

Lemon took it, got back to the tailgate of the cruiser, was about to go around into the open and try to get behind the wheel when the shooter opened up again, this time with a pistol, a fucking *big* pistol, muzzle flaring out of the dark. A huge round shattered the streetside passenger window.

Reed and Lemon fired back at the flash and Nick reached into the squad and jerked Barbetta's duty shotgun out of the rack between the two front seats, worked the slide as he pulled back out and moved over to the hood. He pumped two quick rounds into the park and Lemon, covered, started moving.

Nick put out two more rounds, feeling the big gun kick back and buck like a horse, saw a flash and a round hummed by his left ear, and then came the heavy thudding crack of the pistol. Nick fired again, thought he heard a cry, a shout, maybe pain, maybe he had hit the guy—

Lemon was at the door of the squad car. He was in the seat, his hands on the wheel, reaching for the keys, when another heavy blast from across the street carved a glancing furrow across Lemon's left shoulder. He bellowed in rage and pain.

Reed leaned in through the open passenger door, fired two

rounds through the open driver's door, the muzzle flare lighting up Lemon's face, his black hair wet with blood spatter. He was conscious, he blinked, shook his head as if to clear it, spat out some blood, started the squad car with his right hand, looked across at Reed, his eyes wide, blood on his chin and cheekbones, slammed the driver's door.

"Get clear," he said, working inside the pain.

Reed started to shake his head.

Another shot from across the street, not from the same place. The shooter was moving, but he sure as fuck wasn't going away. The round blew the front windshield out and Reed and Nick hit the sidewalk and Lemon put it in gear and punched the accelerator and the tires smoked and the engine roared. The squad jackrabbited out of the slot, fishtailed wildly—Lemon corrected—and it was gone into the night. They saw the brake lights flash on and heard the siren start to howl just as the squad car reached the cross street and squealed around the corner.

Reed and Nick scuttled back to the cover of Lemon's Ford F-150. They got there, backs against the tires. The shooter opened up on Lemon's truck, blowing out both left side tires. Now he was methodically shredding the Ford—the air was alive with glass bits flying and ricochets zinging around and the heavy chunk-chunk of rounds punching through metal. The truck's right-side window blew out and shards of safety glass showered down on them. Reed and Nick looked at each other.

"This what a war is like?" said Reed.

"Close enough," said Nick, grinning.

"Waddya want to do?"

A pause—*the asshole must be reloading*—Nick figured it was the Kimber .45 from the Thorsson murders. This shooter wasn't going to quit.

"Fuck this," said Nick.

"You think?" said Reed, changing out his magazine, a crazy light in his pale blue eyes.

"I do," said Nick, reloading Barbetta's shotgun. "Let's go take him."

"On three?"

They heard a pistol slide being racked—

"Fuck three," said Nick and they went left and right around the truck—Nick with his shotgun braced, pumping out rounds and Reed on his feet, firing, both of them walking across the street, firing, their muzzle flashes strobing on the trees and the park and lighting up a big blue figure by the fountain, his gun arm extended.

Reed centered the pistol, fired. The shooter fired back, blue light sparkling. Two more flares from Nick's shotgun— he saw the blue man rock back—he'd hit him square in the chest . . . *fuck he's got Kevlar.* Another blast and Nick felt something slam into his ribs, like getting hit with a baseball bat, and down he went—hit the pavement, rolled onto his back. Heard Reed's pistol, three quick sharp rounds—a grunt from across the street, a heavy body thumping into earth . . . a long pause . . . He heard Reed say, slowly and clearly and in a hard flat voice like steel on flint, "Fuck you, asshole."

And then three shots from Reed's pistol, slow, aimed, no hurry . . . *crack* . . . *crack* . . . *crack* . . . insurance shots into Maris Yarvik's skull.

Silence. Wind in the trees.

Nick, spitting blood, looked up at the lamplight in the branches, the Spanish moss drifting in the night wind . . . someone running. Now Reed was there, floating above him, his face white and shocked, his lips moving. Nick couldn't hear him . . .

Then Reed was away and he was looking up at the trees and the Spanish moss and the patches of night sky showing through the branches . . . *this fucking town,* he was thinking . . .

I really hate this fucking town . . . Kate . . . I really do . . . eight years of combat . . . not a fucking paper cut . . . I come to Niceville . . . and I get my ticket punched . . . it's fucking embarrassing . . . Kate . . . maybe she'd come . . . maybe Reed had gone to get her . . . he'd like to see her again . . .

Kate . . .

Kate . . .

. . . and then he was gone.

She looked like the forties, Danziger thought, thinking of calendar art that he had seen in garages and poolrooms out west, or old sepia photographs of prairie women in the thirties.

"Miz Ruelle?"

"Yes, and you must be Mr. Danziger," she said in a throaty tenor voice with a lot of Old Virginia in it.

Danziger stopped in front of her and she looked up at him and offered her hand.

"Welcome to the Ruelle Plantation, Mister Danziger. Albert Lee told me you might be coming." She stepped back and held the door wide for him as he came across the threshold, smelling pine smoke from a fire, saddle soap, and from the kitchen behind the parlor, the scent of cowboy coffee.

Danziger paused in the doorway, taking the house in while Miz Ruelle closed the front door. It looked as if nothing had been done to it since the Depression. The front hall was bare boards, oak, worn but well cared for, covered with an oval hooked rug, and off to the side, by a broad wooden staircase that led up to a landing, an antique wardrobe, open, with field coats and boots and scarves hanging on plain brass hooks. Beyond the front hall was the main room, a huge parlor that ran the width of the house, full of windows, lit from two overhead bulbs, clear glass, large and old-fashioned, hanging from thin black wires, the bulbs pulsing in time to the sound of the generator in one of the outbuildings. What looked like a kitchen through a double door on the far wall.

Although sparsely furnished, it was a pleasing homespun room, furnished with bare wood chairs, oval hooked rugs here and there in rust and green and gold, one large brown leather couch set in front of a big stone fireplace, a pine wood fire blazing in the hearth, a few framed photos, sepia-tinted portraits carefully laid out on the mantel.

There was a four-slot gun rack above the fireplace, with

What Happens Between the Night Before
and the Morning After

As Danziger came up the steps, the front door opened, and the lady standing in the open doorway was truly worth the bus ride. She was some way past her middle years, but well-shaped, on the lean side, full-breasted, good hips, sensual- and strong-looking, her home fires still burning, her green eyes bright against the rough tan of her skin, long shiny black hair pulled back.

No makeup at all and she showed signs of a life lived mainly out-of-doors, but she was, in the warm light of the veranda lantern, perfectly beautiful, in an unadorned and countrified way. Her expression was thoughtful and remote, as if she hadn't quite decided what to do with him yet.

She smiled as he came up to the door, showing strong white teeth, slightly uneven, with a gap between the two front ones, full lips and a handsome but hard-cut face, an uncompromising careworn face that had seen hard times and beaten them.

She wore a simple cotton dress in a flower print, green leaves and white flowers on vines—jasmine? It buttoned down the front, an old-fashioned cut, falling well below the knee thin green leather pumps with ankle straps.

two Winchesters, one carbine, and a long rifle with a tubular brass scope, both rifles browned, with octagonal barrels, he noticed.

Antiques, but in mint condition. Under that one old Springfield, a cap-and-ball gun, resting on the bars. And on the top a long angular and mean-looking weapon that Danziger recognized as a BAR, a Browning Automatic Rifle, a .30-06 full-auto monster that hadn't been used in the field for decades.

Miz Ruelle led him on into the parlor, asked him to take a seat on the couch, stood before him, gave him a formal smile. "I have a cold collation laid out in the kitchen, just some boiled eggs and corn bread and a jeroboam of chilled sillery, but perhaps you'd like something stronger to drink. The Blue Bird is a bumpy old machine, and it's all gravel road this side of the Belfair Saddlery, isn't it?"

"A drink would be very welcome," said Danziger.

She nodded, went to a sideboard, opened the cupboard, and considered the interior.

"My husband liked his bourbon, Mr. Danziger. We have Southern Dew or Old Charter. Would either please you? I may also have some lime cordial."

"Old Charter would be great," said Danziger, thinking that the last time he'd seen a bottle of Old Charter or Southern Dew was at an estate sale in Baton Rouge.

She came back with two crystal tumblers, each with about three fingers of straight-up bourbon in it, handed one to Danziger, and sat down on a hardwood chair beside the fire. It was burning low and cast a warm glow over the right side of her face and put yellow sparks deep in her green eyes.

Danziger lifted his tumbler, said, "Your good health, Miz Ruelle." She raised hers and said, "May we drink down all unkindness," and they sipped quietly for a moment.

Miz Ruelle set her glass down on a side table, crossed her

legs at the ankle, folded her hands in her lap, and said, "Mr. Danziger—"

"I wonder, ma'am, if you would call me Charlie?"

"If it would please you, I will call you Charlie. You may call me Glynis." She seemed to note his reaction. "My name is familiar to you?"

"Yes, it is, ma'am," he said with a tight throat. He took a sip of bourbon to ease it.

"Please, Charlie. It's Glynis. May I ask in what connection? I imagine Albert Lee has talked about our plantation?"

"He has, Glynis. But I know you in another way as well."

"Do you?"

"Yes, I do. I saw a mirror once, an antique mirror in a golden frame. There was a card on the back of the mirror, with a signature. The name was Glynis Ruelle."

She looked at him for a time.

"I know the mirror, Charlie. Its twin is on the wall in my sister Clara's quarters, the Jasmine Rooms, on the second floor. They've been in my family for generations. They came from Paris—an unhappy time for my family. It was the Revolution there, and many of our people went under the guillotine. How odd that you should know of them. There was more on the card than just my signature. Can you tell me what else was on that card?"

"'With Long Regard,'" he said.

"Yes," she said, looking pleased. "The mirror you describe was given as a gift to a young lady named Delia Cotton, on the occasion of her tenth birthday, at a family reunion in Savannah, a long while ago. The Niceville Families Reunion. It was held at John Mullryne's plantation there. Perhaps you know Mr. Mullryne? The mirror was part of a set, as I have said. The other one is upstairs. They were made in London, England, by an Italian artisan—I used to know his name, perhaps I can look it up—and they were brought to Anjou, which is in France, around 1750, by a distant relative of mine, Thierry Sébastien Mercier. Delia so loved the mirrors. Was it in her house that you saw it?"

Danziger didn't have the heart to tell her it was in a pawnshop called Uncle Moochie's on North Gwinnett Street in downtown Niceville. "No, actually, it's now with a lady named Kate Kavanaugh."

"Kate? A Walker, wasn't she? One of Lenore's daughters. Do you know Lenore?"

"No, I'm afraid I don't." *Other than watching her die in my arms after her truck rolled over the I-50 twelve years ago.*

"She stayed with us for a while, but now she's gone up to Sallytown, to live with relatives up there. I was sorry to hear that her husband is dead? Dillon Walker?"

"Well, he disappeared, they're saying. He was up at VMI at the time. Last spring. Hasn't been seen since."

Glynis took that in, and Danziger had the idea that she had chosen to say nothing on that subject. She asked about Kate. "Are you a friend of her daughter?"

"Yes," he said after a pause. "I know the family well."

"Kate's a lovely young girl. Married now, I believe. Someone from away, a man named Nick?"

"Yes. From California. Los Angeles."

"Oh, dear. Not an actor, I hope?"

"No. Nick was a soldier. Now he's a detective."

She looked disappointed. "Not a Pinkerton man, surely?"

"No ma'am. Not a Pinkerton man."

"Good. They are a bad lot, every one of them. Albert Lee tells me you were a police officer yourself?"

"Yes, I was."

"No longer?"

"No. Retired."

"He also tells me you are familiar with livestock, with horses?"

"I am. My family had a ranch out in Montana."

"You mean the Territories?"

"No, the state, Glynis."

"Of course. They joined the Union just before the war. I keep forgetting."

She paused here, looked into the fire, took a sip, sighed, and came back to him, it seemed to Danziger from some distance.

"Well, it's late, and tomorrow we have the Harvest. We should go and have some of that collation before the sillery gets warm. I approve of you, Charlie Danziger. Would you consider taking work here?"

"Certainly. I'd be delighted."

"We can't pay much. It would be room and board and a few dollars a week?"

"Fine with me. You want me to go out, see to the horses tonight?"

"No. I've changed the straw, cleaned their harnesses, and set out their mash. We have only six, five of them Clydes, one of them a colt. We keep them for the plow and the wagons. I have a Hanoverian mare for riding—her name is Virago—and Jupiter is more or less a pet. You've met him?"

"Oh yes. Hell of—a magnificent animal."

"He is."

"And the generator? Do you leave it running?"

A troubled look flashed across her face. "Generally no. But for this night, I think we'll leave it on. For the lights."

She stood up, and so did Danziger.

"May I ask you a question, Charlie."

"Surely can."

"Would you be a gunhand, at all?"

"A gunhand? Yes, I guess you could say that. Do you *need* a gunhand, Glynis?"

She looked a little sad.

"I hope not. It depends on the Harvest."

"Albert Lee says you had a gunhand here a while back. A Merle Zane."

"Yes. Did you know him?"

"Well, in a way."

"Was he a friend?"

"More of a business partner, I'd say."

"You thought well of him?"

"We sorta parted on bad terms."

"A business disagreement?"

"Yes, but I respected him up to the end."

"I see. I am grieved to tell you that Merle was killed last spring. I was sorry to lose him."

"I guess you were. Am I here to replace him?"

She considered him. "We'll see. Let us go and have some sillery."

Danziger, who had no idea what the hell *sillery* was, followed her out to the kitchen, where he was pleased to find out that *sillery* was champagne.

And they had a pleasant hour together, sitting on lyre-back chairs around the bare-board trestle table, passing the plates back and forth, savoring the champagne, smelling the sweet grass and the hay, hearing the wind in the pines.

It was a still and silent night, oddly so for the country. The cicadas were quiet, and the frogs and nightjars, even the owls. Jupiter, wherever he was, wasn't making a sound.

They shared Danziger's cigarettes and talked of horses and stock and crops and the weather until the kitchen clock began to chime midnight.

Glynis cocked her head, listening to its soft musical chime.

She sat back in her chair and looked at Danziger for a while. Danziger looked back, feeling a strong carnal tug as he considered her.

Somewhere in the house a radio was playing, a Big Band tune, maybe Vaughn Monroe, the one about racing with the moon. There was no other sound in the house, and although Glynis had mentioned her sister Clara and the Jasmine Rooms, Danziger was pretty sure they were alone this evening.

The people from the Blue Bird bus were somewhere else on the plantation. Earlier in the evening he had heard the sound of a choir singing far in the distance, faint across the fields, "Shall We Gather at the River" and, later, "Bringing in the Sheaves."

But now there was only the sound of the outer silence all around, and the darkness pressing up against the window glass, the yellow flicker of a few yard lights out by the barn, and inside the house Glenn Miller's band, playing "In the Mood."

"You're wondering about the people from the bus," said Glynis.

Danziger was getting used to her ability to track a man's thoughts. He hoped she wasn't tracking all of his right now, since he was acutely aware of what she was wearing and what she wasn't wearing. He shifted in his chair—he had to—and leaned forward to put his cigarette out.

"Yes, tell the truth, I was. I spoke with a lady on the bus. She invited me to a fellowship meeting. I think I heard them singing a while ago."

"Yes. They stay in the Annex, down by Little Cut Creek. They seem to prefer it down there."

"The lady mentioned the Harvest."

"I suppose you are curious about it?"

"I am. Very. I get the idea it's not about bringing in the sheaves, is it?"

She smiled, but sadness seemed to rise up in her. "No. It's

not at all like a hymn. I think I have to prepare you for what may be a difficult afternoon. Have you ever heard of a place called Candleford House?"

"Yes, I have. It's a deserted sanatorium in Gracie, I think. Grim old pile, boarded up and fenced in. Had an ugly reputation."

"Yes. Hard-earned and terrible. It was actually a kind of hell house, a brutal prison where quack doctors and outright charlatans, aided by sadistic guards and so-called nurses, tormented thousands of supposed mental patients over a hundred years. They used shock therapy, cocaine, opium, solitary confinement, starvation, beatings, every kind of horror. Rape was common, a public entertainment for the staff and the guards. Unmanageable patients or people whose families could no longer afford the fees were routinely suffocated, their bodies burned in a crematorium in the basement. The state finally closed it down, but not before my sister Clara was imprisoned there by the man whose family money sustained Candleford House. She was wrested free of him and now she lives with us here, but she is terribly shattered and I keep her sheltered from most people. As I may have said, she lives in the Jasmine Rooms upstairs."

"What happened to the man who ran the place?"

"He lived a long time, unnaturally long. He was shot and killed in the spring of this year."

Danziger took this in, sat back and looked at her, and she looked back, no tears now.

"Up in Sallytown?" he said. "At a place called the Gates of Gideon?"

"Yes. A palliative-care hospice. He lived in that place, in a closed-off suite of windowless rooms, aided only by his . . . creatures. His *guardians*. They served him in every way. He never went out-of-doors, not once in all the years he lived there. I tried many times to reach him, but he was . . . protected. Finally I found someone who could reach him and who was brave enough to try."

"Merle Zane."

"Yes. Merle went to Sallytown and fought his way past the man's guardians. Albert Lee was there and he was wounded in that fight. But they persevered and they confronted this man in his chambers."

"His name, was it Abel Teague?"

"You know him?"

"I sure know the Teague line."

"I am not surprised. Abel Teague lived as long as he did with the help of this power I spoke of. After Merle killed him in that duel, his spirit, his shade, somehow came to us, and I have decided he must face the Reckoning he has so long evaded. For six months we have kept his *shadow* here, in confinement, because he remains in every way a Teague."

She smiled at him. "I see this puzzles you, Charlie. Do not mind that this is difficult to understand. I have had a long time to accept that it is true, and I no longer look for understanding."

"But that's not the end of Teague's story. That's why you need me, isn't it?"

She looked at him. "Yes. The power that helped Abel is trying to free him. There may be violence, I believe it is inevitable, and all my fighting men are dead. I *hoped* for you, I admit, but I did not *bring* you."

"What is the Harvest, Glynis?"

She was quiet for so long that Danziger thought she wasn't going to answer.

But she did. "I can't remember when the Harvest ceremony began. It may have been with Lorelei and Albemarle, my parents. But now it is in my hands, and I keep it going, since it serves the people around here. Each season some of our people choose to come and look in the mirror—the mir-

ror up in the Jasmine Rooms—and see what they have sown
and what they must reap. Most do it happily, looking for an
end to what they call their *dreaming*."

"Is that what they're doing, Glynis? Dreaming?"

"They think so."

"And what do you think?"

She went inward, looked for the words. "I believe they're
lost, caught between the two mirrors, the one down in Niceville and the one in this house, and they want to find a way
out."

"Lost?"

"Yes. They've gotten caught up between life and death,
and this state feels like dreaming to them."

"How did they get to this . . . state?"

Again she smiled at him. "Many people believe that when
a person is dying, unless all the mirrors in the house are covered, the dying person's spirit can pass into the mirror and live
in that world, not knowing how to leave it. In France, during
the Terror, the executioners used the mirrors from our house
to show my family their own severed heads, taken from the
basket while life was still in them, and they looked at the mirrors and sent their souls into them, and there they all stay. My
great-grandfather, John Gwinnett Mercer, said that the mirrors had been 'opened' by these dying souls. I believe there is
something in what he said."

She finished her drink, set it down. "So we have the Harvest, Charlie, and the people, if they are ready, use the mirrors
to try to put an end to their dreaming."

"Are you dreaming too?"

She looked thoughtful. "I don't question my life, Charlie.
I feel very *present*, and I have good work and my plantation
and the animals and Clara, and I have the care of these people
until they find their way. That is what the Harvest is for."

"Like Judgment Day?"

"No. I never believed in that kind of a god. That god wouldn't be much different from the *thing* that lives in Candleford House. The Harvest is simply for waking up and crossing over. And tomorrow is Abel Teague's time to do that. But he always looks for a way out."

"And he has these *guardians* to help him?"

"He does. They may already be here. Have you noticed? The horses are quiet. All the animals are quiet. The cicadas and the owls too. They are never quiet. And now, as you can see, the dragonflies have appeared, as they always do in troubled times. They are waiting for the morning."

He sighed, took a deep breath, sat back in his chair, stubbed out his cigarette. "Then let us, you and me, see to the dishes and lock up the locks, and then we will go do the same."

She pulled her shawl around her shoulders. "I'm so afraid of this night, Charlie."

"So am I," he said, giving her a wolfish smile. "Terrified down to my boots. Shaking in my socks. Shame to have to fight through this night all alone."

She looked up at him and read his mind. She found a sideways smile to give him back. "You are not a very *good* man, are you Charlie Danziger?"

Danziger put on his innocent face, which was even less convincing than Coker's innocent face. "Mrs. Ruelle. I am the *soul* of virtue."

"Well, we'll see about that, won't we?"

Sunday Morning

Boonie Found the Fax

They got set up and ready long before dawn. Seven men and two women, all geared up, wired and rolling, two cover trucks, one a Niceville Utilities truck, the other a ten-year-old junker minivan, and three nondescript beige-mobiles, Toyotas and Hondas from a government-approved used-car dealership. This involved almost the entire operational wing of the Cap City FBI crew—two of them had been left behind to cover the surveillance taps on the Maranzano apartment and answer the office phones, which, because of all the shit that was happening in Niceville, were ringing pretty much nonstop. They had a couple of fly-ins from Atlanta to assist, and so far it was by-the-book boring. They had all done this before, in training at Quantico and on the streets for real, and being FBI, they knew how to do this pretty well.

They were setting up a box lift, an invisible surveillance square around the subject—in this case, Bluebell Littlebasket's ranch house on Skyway Road, a short block away from Mauldar Field.

The dawn was just a milky tint in the sky above the black bulk of Tallulah's Wall. Sunday morning in Niceville, and nobody out on the streets, no cars, and only the red strobes of the Mauldar Field landing lights off to the northwest.

A building wind, and maybe storms later, but right now, quiet and cool.

Boonie Hackendorff was staying well back, a half mile away in the Mauldar Field parking lot, in his own ride, a vintage Shelby Cobra Mustang in racing green, an exact clone of Steve McQueen's ride in *Bullitt*, and only slightly less conspicuous than a circus wagon.

Boonie didn't care. He loved it, and he wasn't planning on getting anywhere close to the action. If there was any, which he sincerely doubted. It seemed highly unlikely that a street operator as smart as Coker would let himself get taken down on a residential block in suburban Niceville, certainly not while trying to extract one of his girlfriend's relations.

Coker had never been a guy for the Grand Sentimental Gesture. He was as cold as ditch water and he always had been.

It was more likely that he had sent some kind of intermediary, a person with no wants and no warrants, who would come by either to transport Bluebell or to deliver the route docs and let her get on with it by herself. Either way they were going to stay on it until the trail led to Twyla or a dead end, or just maybe possibly to Coker himself.

The tricky part here was that, technically, Bluebell Littlebasket hadn't actually *done* anything illegal, other than take a call from her sister, who wasn't on a wanted list either.

Judge Stonehouse, a bit of a stickler for due process, had—grudgingly—given them a warrant loaded with restrictions, but it was enough to get the thing rolling.

All Twyla Littlebasket had against her was that she was a person of interest in the search for Coker, who was wanted on several federal warrants, including interstate flight, armed robbery, four counts of felony murder of police officers, and two counts of manslaughter one in the matter of a downed news chopper.

Tell the truth, Boonie's mind was really on the Delores Maranzano file, and those three Mafia goombahs she had holed up in her suite at the Memphis.

Acting on Kurt Pall's affidavit, Boonie had gotten a surveillance and intercept warrant on the apartment, and right now taps were on the phones and the Internet connection and a laser mike was trained on the living room window of the Maranzano suite, recording everything that was being said and done inside the place.

The results of which so far had been pretty much dick, mostly increasingly unpleasant exchanges between Delores and Mario La Motta—no love lost there—and a lot of back and forth between the goombahs about everything from business deals to Chihuahua farts to the World Cup of soccer and who was going to win it this year. Nothing bored Boonie Hackendorff more than soccer, a game that seemed to turn on who could trip over his own shadow and fall down writhing more convincingly than the other guy.

The one good hit they got was a short telephone exchange between Julie Spahn and a guy named Chi-Chi Pentangeli in Miami, who might or might not be connected to Tony Tee's organization. In the call, which sounded like it was about truck parts, Pentangeli had made one slip—if that's what it was—when he said something about the package coming in from Istria.

Spahn had changed the subject so fast that it stood out, and Pentangeli had picked up on it as well, so there was a lot of meaningless babble that went nowhere, much of it in Calabrian.

But Boonie knew that Istria wasn't even a place anymore, that it was part of Yugoslavia or maybe Croatia now, and the

Istria connection just might mean a reference to a double homicide up in Quebec a year ago, a French-Canadian lawyer and his wife, who had been tortured and killed in a truly spectacular way.

The lawyer had been part of the Commisso-Racco network and the hit—there was no other word for it—had been so mind-blowingly gruesome that even some of the button guys around Montreal had been talking about it too much, and once in front of an RCMP snitch. The snitch picked up one useful bit of information—namely, that the hit was a "demonstration" done to make a point with the Commisso-Racco crowd, and that the rumor was running around that it had been done by *L'Istriano*, whoever the hell he was.

The RCMP Organized Crime guys had brought it to DC and asked the FBI for a data-mining search through the NSA, the results of which were three brief mentions of the Istriano, and one linked name, Tito. So they had Tito who maybe was a hired assassin called the Istriano and maybe was just some low-level mob guy named after the thug who used to run Yugoslavia.

Intel, they called it, probably because *irrelevant crapola* was already taken.

"Six Actual?"

Boonie, who was Six Actual, picked up the radio and keyed it. "Six. Go."

"Six, this is Blue Three." Blue Three was the Niceville Utilities truck.

"Go, Blue Three."

"Six, I have the Eye on the subject and she's just turned on the lights in the living room. She's moving around, still in her robe."

"Roger that, Blue Three. Everybody else hold tight. No radio checks. Just sit on it."

A series of double clicks as the other Blue Team units acknowledged the transmission. The Eye was the name given to any member of the Box Team who actually had the subject in sight.

The rest of the units were set up in a roughly rectangular grid on the side streets east and west and south, and north on the perimeter fence that ran along the southern edge of Mauldar Field. No matter which way Bluebell moved, if she did, and no matter which way someone might approach the house, they'd be seen by one or more of the surveillance units.

The only thing that could screw it up was some civilian phoning in a suspicious vehicle parked outside her house at four in the morning.

And that could be tricky, because Boonie had made the operational decision not to inform the Niceville PD about the surveillance op this morning.

That was because the Niceville PD was thoroughly rattled by the totally crazy shit that had gone down over the last few days and in their current state could not be depended upon to shut the fuck up about what the Cap City feds were doing.

Boonie had gone down to see the cops last night and he'd found a pack of state and county and city cops crowding the halls of Lady Grace, all of them looking for payback, blood, anybody's blood.

A State Patrol captain named Martin Coors—Reed Walker's boss—had told him that Reed was with the Walker family and friends in a private waiting room down the hall from the critical care unit, and that's where Boonie found them all: Kate Kavanaugh and her sister Beth; Reed, a block of ice with an inward stare, looking down at his hands; Tig Sutter, looming large and weary in a corner; Beau Norlett, Nick's old partner, in a wheelchair; Lacy Steinert, a PO with the Probe, sick with shock; a Nordic-looking blond he didn't know who was introduced to him as Helga; and a gorgeous young woman in a Niceville Transit uniform who said she was Doris Godwin, apparently a special friend of Lemon Featherlight's. Godwin was a Cherokee, had that aristocratic look, dark shining hair, and a strong face, and there seemed to be some tension between her and the Nordic woman.

Boonie went straight to Kate, who was a wreck. He hugged her, hugged Beth, shook hands with Reed; asked about Nick and Lemon and Frank Barbetta—didn't like what he heard, not at all; spoke quietly in a corner to Tig, who smelled of cigars and looked like hell; hugged Lacy Steinert; patted Beau Norlett on the shoulder and got a weak grin back; looked around the room—*grief and fear and pain and anger*—and then, sensing that he was one visitor too many, got the fuck out of their way.

Out in the hall, in a tangle of cops and a few media types, he pulled Marty Coors and Jimmy Candles off in a corner. Jimmy Candles was a staff sergeant with the Belfair and Cullen County Sheriffs, and they were all old friends.

Boonie got the details, and the prognosis.

Lemon Featherlight, now a certified hero, was probably going to live, but he might have some nerve damage from the bullet track across his left shoulder. Mavis Crossfire was down in the bone clinic, getting fitted for a cast, and she'd be back on the job in the morning. Frank Barbetta had lost a lot of blood and the wound was septic and he was fighting shock and there could be blood clots, so who knew.

And then there was Nick Kavanaugh, who, by the faces these two cops were wearing and the mood in the halls, and from what Boonie had heard in the private waiting room, and from what he had seen in the CCU—Nick surrounded by machines and LED displays and sensor readouts and wires and harried nurses and doctors trying to get his heart rate stabilized—had them all running scared.

"Six Actual, Blue Three."

"Blue Three."

"I have a Cap City cab pulling up."

"Roger that. Everybody, ready to roll?" Multiple clicks.

"Blue Three, still got the Eye, subject is in the living room now, she's dressed, got a coffee, talking on her cell, looking out the window. Cab is at the curb. I can see a driver—"

They had no warrant to tap Bluebell's phones, which was a serious pain in the—

"Subject is moving to the hall. Got her coat on now—"

"Can you ID the cabdriver?"

"Female. Black. Not Coker."

"Roger that. Everybody hold."

A minute passed.

"Six, she's still inside. Not coming out yet."

"Six, this is Blue Four."

"Go."

"We've got a cab rolling south here. Looks like he's hunting a street address."

"What company?"

"Ace Cabs. Don't know them. He's turning onto Skyway now, a black Crown Vic."

"Four, this is Six. Can you see the driver?"

"No. Tinted windows."

"Six, this is Blue Two. We've got a cab rolling north on Carrier Drive—just went by us, a Windstar minivan, Peachtree Cabs. He's turning left onto the service road."

"This is Six. Can you ID the driver?"

"No. Tinted windows."

"This is Blue Five. We've got him. He's rolling past us right now. There's some light from the streetlamp here . . . Wait one . . . a woman, white."

"Okay. Everybody hold."

"*Six, this is Blue Four. Ace Cabs is rolling up to subject's house. How many cabs is that?*"

"Cap City, Ace, Peachtree—this is a stunt."

"*Six, this is Blue Two. We have another fucking cab coming toward us—Airport Limo!*"

"Everybody shut up and hold. Don't get rattled just hold your positions."

"*Six, this is Blue Three. We have four cabs all pulled up in front of subject's house. No drivers out. Subject still in house.*"

"Blue Three, this is Six. Do you have the Eye?"

A moment. "*Six, we haven't seen her leave.*"

"But do you have the Eye on her?"

"*Negative that. You want us to move in?*"

"With what? Our dicks in our hands. We got no warrant to contact her. All we can do is follow."

"*Roger that.*"

"I want the rest of you to acknowledge."

"*Blue Two, roger that.*"

"*Blue One, copy.*"

"*Blue Four, copy.*"

"*Blue Five, copy.*"

"Blue Three, what's going on?"

"*Garage door coming up. No lights. Someone's moving. Dome light in the Airport Limo just came on. Now off. Airport is rolling. Repeat, Airport is rolling. Fuck. All cabs are rolling now. Peachtree, Ace, Cap City, all rolling out. Six, do we follow?*"

Shit. What now?

"Anybody got the Eye?"

"*Six, this is Blue Three. She's in the Airport Limo.*"

"Have you got the Eye?"

Hesitation. Doubt. "*Windows are all tinted.*"

"*Six, this is Blue Four. These cabs are going in different directions. They're scattering like bugs. We should stop them all.*"

"On what grounds? And if we do, then what? We have no warrant for interception until she's in contact with our target. Judge Stonehouse made that crystal clear. We stop her now, and even if she's got Coker stuffed into her panties, it's all fruit of the poisoned tree—"

"*Six, she's scampering. We gotta—*"

"Look. Everybody pick one and—"

Boonie's cell phone rang. Boonie grabbed it up. "What the fuck?"

"*Tell them to sit tight.*"

That voice. Holy shit. "Coker?"

"*Tell them to hold their positions.*"

"Why the fuck would I do that?"

"*Because I have a hostage.*"

"Coker, who the fuck have you got?"

"*You.*"

Boonie looked around his position. He was in the airport parking lot. Wide open. In a pool of white light under a streetlamp.

"Coker—"

"*Tell them.*"

"Hey, Coker, fuck you!"

Boonie's driver's side mirror blew into a thousand pieces. Bits of plastic and glass showered across his windshield. Boonie heard no shot, saw no muzzle flash. He just got the thunk-smack of Coker's round coming in and the shattered mirror at his left elbow, hanging from the mount.

"*Tell them.*"

Boonie got on the radio. "All units, this is Six. Hold your positions. Repeat, do not engage—"

"*Boonie, she's getting away. Call for Air!*"

"Repeat, hold your positions."

"*Six, this is—*"

"Everybody shut the fuck up."

They did.

"Coker, what the fuck good did this do you?"

"It got Bluebell out of Niceville."

"And now we got you, which was the point."

"Haven't got me yet."

"You're in the tower, Coker. Line of sight."

"Sorry about your side mirror. I know you love that Bullitt car."

"You killed four cops, Coker. We're not buddies anymore."

"Sorry to hear that. It was just business. So is this. And stay off that radio."

Boonie was already moving toward the broadcast button. He stopped six inches away. "You got a scope on me?"

"Yeah. Wide-angle, Boonie. You need to lose some weight."

"Six, this is Blue Three. What do you want—"

"I want you all to observe total radio silence. Do. You. Follow?"

A pause.

An eloquent pause.

Boonie could feel the disapproval radiating out of the car speakers.

Finally, "Roger that." The *asshole* part was left unspoken, but everybody heard it.

"Coker? You there?" Silence. "Coker?"

"I'm here. Answer me a question, Boonie?"

Boonie tried to get his temper under control. "Yeah. Be my fucking guest. I got all the time in the world."

"What the fuck is going on in Niceville?"

"Waddya mean?"

"I mean, six dead civilians, two serial killers running loose—"

"You been traveling, haven't you?"

"Why?"

"Haven't been following the news?"

"Not close. I saw Mavis on CNN yesterday."

"Then you don't know?"

"Know what?"

"About Nick?"

"No. What about him?"

Boonie told him, about Lemon and Frank Barbetta. And Nick. There was a long silence.

"Nick's down?"

"Yeah. He's the worst. Lemon, he'll have nerve damage, need a bunch of surgeries. Barbetta's sixty-forty to make it through. But Nick . . ."

"How bad?"

Boonie thought about it. "They don't get his heartbeat steadied, he could be dead by sunset. Or not. He could be up and around or he could be down in the morgue. Could go either way. "

A long silence.

"Who was the shooter?"

"Maris Yarvik."

"The GM guy? Owns the dealership? I've played rugby with that guy. What the fuck he do that for?"

"Still trying to figure that out."

"What's his status now?"

"Buck naked on his back on a tin tray."

"Who did him?"

"Reed Walker."

"Jesus. Any idea what was going on?"

"What the fuck do you care?"

"You're still breathing, aren't you? What was it all about?"

Boonie thought about everything he'd heard. "Looks like some of our regular citizens are going nuts on a random basis. Seriously psycho nuts. People with no history. People just like you. Nick was working on a lead, but it was all fucked up."

"What was it?"

"Coker, this is crazy. Come on in and we'll have a beer and I'll explain it all to you while they're strapping you down on the death gurney."

"*I repeat. What was Nick's lead?*"

"He thought it had something to do with Crater Sink. The whole Niceville thing. We talked about it coupla months ago, over drinks at the Bar Belle. I had a dead guy I couldn't figure out—"

"*Merle Zane?*"

"Yeah. Him."

"*Died twice, right?*"

"Yeah. That's what it looked like. Nick was onto that. So was Featherlight. They had a theory."

"*And now they're both down. Tell you anything? 'Cause it fucking well should.*"

"I'm working on it."

"*If you're working on it, why the fuck are you dicking around trying to catch me?*"

"What? You're a fucking fugitive!"

"*Ever hear of allocating limited resources?*"

"I don't get it."

"*You're the goddamned FBI, Boonie. Go find out what the fuck is wrong with Niceville.*"

"And then what?"

"*Fix it, Boonie. Fix it.*"

"Yeah, well, thanks a heap, Coker. A lot of our people around here think that *you* are one of the things that's wrong with Niceville. Is that your excuse, Coker. The demons made you do it?"

"*What, the bank? The cops? Fuck that, Boonie. I don't do excuses. That was all me.*"

"Charlie Danziger said it was all him. He said you had nothing to do with it."

"*Charlie Danziger couldn't shoot the balls off a Brahma bull if it was standing on him. He was just trying to take the heat off.*"

"He died a good man, Coker."

"*Yeah, I was there. You ever find that Endicott asshole? The one who killed Luckinbaugh and sent those shooters up to Charlie's ranch?*"

"We found most of him. In a Dumpster behind the Marriott. He was missing a head."

"*Delores Maranzano did that?*"

"No way. She's just a *pass-around broad*. Not a player. That was all coming from those three mob mutts up in Leaven—"

Boonie realized he was about to fill Coker in on the three goombahs squatting in Delores Maranzano's suite at the Memphis. And then he remembered that Coker wasn't on the side of the angels anymore and he slammed the lid on it.

He suddenly felt sad, tired, sick. "You know, all in all, I really wish you hadn't done it, Coker. I really do. It just fucked up . . . everything."

"*Jeez, Boonie, man the fuck up, will ya? What's next, snow-flakes and mittens and whiskers on kittens?*"

"Yeah, well, fuck you and enjoy your day, Coker. I'll be seeing you soon. Real soon."

"*Sooner than you think, Boonie.*"

Present Malice

The Lady Grace ICU, just before daybreak, when all the family members have finally passed out on the couches in the private waiting rooms and the bone-weary nurses are getting ready for the shift change and out in the dark halls an old man is pushing an electric scrubber over the terrazzo tiles and the entire floor smells of bleach and blood and death. Joan Styles, the duty nurse for the ICU, is sitting at the center station, head down, dog-tired, working on patient reports for the shift-change briefing coming up in two hours.

"Joan?"

She looked up from her work, saw a pretty young blond woman standing there looking back at her. She was wearing a navy blue paramedic uniform and a careful smile. Her name tag read FILLION.

Joan shook her head. "Barb, where the heck have you been?"

"I know. I just got back from Marietta. I was out on the trail and there was no coverage."

Joan's expression changed. "You're here to see Kikki?"

"Yes. I heard it was bad?"

Joan got up and came around the desk, stood in front of Barb. "Honey, he's gone. He died. Kikki died."

It seemed that Barb Fillion didn't register that at first. She tilted her head to one side. "No, wait. I heard he was . . . I heard he—"

"He never came out of it. He had a No Code DNR note in his Living Will. Two hours ago the RTs took him off the tube to see if he could breathe on his own. He crashed and they had to let him go."

Fillion took one step backward, and then another. She turned and put her hands on the counter, bent her head. Her shoulders started to heave and a thin keening sound came out of her tight lips.

Joan put a hand on her shoulder, said nothing for a while, just let her go.

After a bit, Fillion straightened, sighed. "Where is he now?"

"Downstairs. Do you want to see him?"

Fillion shook her head. "No. Not yet. Did they ever find out who attacked him?"

"Not yet, honey."

"I heard it happened right after I said good night to him. Right there in the lot. Didn't the cameras catch anything?"

"Nothing useful. Somebody in a dark jacket and pants. Came out of nowhere and hit him with some kind of steel canister. They found a fire extinguisher in the bushes. It was taken from the ambulance."

"No prints?"

"No nothing, Barb. Honey, I'm so sorry."

Fillion nodded, made an effort to pull herself together. She looked around the ward. There was a wall of windows along one side, and beyond the windows there were ten ICU bays, separated by hanging curtains. Seven of them were occupied: four elderly men, already skeletal; a young girl with yellow skin and a shaved head; a black man with a neck brace and skull wrappings; and a younger white male, his hard face pale, his black hair brushed back. He was surrounded by LED readouts and machines, was on intravenous drip. A young black-haired woman was curled up in a chair next to the bed, wrapped in a pale blue blanket, her head back, sound asleep.

"You're busy tonight," she said in a whisper.

"Yes," said Joan, relieved to be on more neutral ground, one medic to another.

"Is that Nick Kavanaugh?"

"It is," said Joan. "They just brought him back from Cardio."

"Who was the doc?"

"Ginsberg."

"Ginsberg's good."

Joan nodded, her face solemn.

"He is. Ginsberg said it was an odd case. In a way this man was very lucky. The bullet was a forty-five hollow point. You've seen what they can do, I know. This one came in at a slight angle—they think Nick was turning as he got shot. Broke some ribs and ripped a big trench along his right side, but because the slug was a hollow point it flattened out and didn't penetrate the peritoneal cavity. It did transfer a lot of kinetic energy, so there was hydrostatic shock. The shock wave affected his heart somehow. They've stitched him up and wrapped his torso, but his heart rate is all over the place. We're just trying to stabilize it. That's his wife with him. Kate. A lovely woman. She's not supposed to be in there, but . . . how could we say no?"

Fillion walked over to the glass, put out her right hand, laid her palm against it. She inhaled through her mouth and closed her eyes, seemed to go down inside herself. *As if she were trying to feel them through the glass*, Joan thought.

the female is in anguish, but the male is dormant—go wake them

Fillion shook her head several times, opened her eyes, quickly backed away from the window. There was something in her expression that Joan had never seen there before. Barb Fillion was a marathon runner, an outdoor girl, vibrant and funny, a bit wild off duty. None of this was there in her face. She looked . . . absent.

"There were three others, I heard?"

"Yes. Mr. Featherlight is down in ICU. He's got nerve damage. He'll need a lot of physio."

"Mavis and Frank? What about them?"

Joan hesitated, something crossing her face, a dark feeling, there and gone. She brightened. "Well, you know Mavis. She's indestructible. They put a cast on her and tried to admit her, but she told them all to go bugger themselves. She came up here on crutches and looked at Nick through the glass. Then she spoke to Kate and gave her a bear hug and then I heard she drove herself home in a big black police truck."

"That's Mavis. What about Frank?"

Joan went sideways, looked at her watch. "Honey . . . I'm not at liberty to comment. About Staff Sergeant Barbetta, I mean. His condition. There's not a lot we're allowed to say at this point. Not even to an EMT. You follow?"

No, Barb Fillion did not follow.

Barb Fillion took the elevator down to the main lobby, which was still packed with cops and firefighters and plain-clothes cops from the CID. She walked through them, saying hello to people she knew, and came out into the half-light of dawn.

There were several satellite trucks scattered around the parking lot, their dishes extended, people milling around a catering van. The air smelled of gasoline fumes, cigarette smoke, and burned coffee. Nobody noticed her and she moved quickly into the shadowy walk that ran around to the auxiliary parking lot.

Her EMT truck was sitting there, engine idling. She beeped it open and got into the driver's side, slipped her belt on, and looked into the back, where there was a stretcher braced against the side wall. Rainey Teague was strapped down on the stretcher, covered in a red blanket.

An IV drip ran into the elbow of his right arm. His long blond hair was matted and dirty and tied back with an elastic. His skin was dry, his breathing deep and rhythmic, his eyes half open, a thin slice of pale blue glittering between the lids. He was heavily sedated. A monitor glowed overhead, showing his vital signs.

She looked at him for a while, feeling nothing, and then she put the truck in gear and rolled slowly out of the parking lot, sliding past the media vans and the news people clustered around the catering truck, chattering like parakeets.

The EMT truck reached the exit, turned west onto Peachtree, made a right at Bluebonnet and then another right onto North Gwinnett.

Up on the sixth floor, at the window down the hall from the ICU, Kate stood and watched the ambulance roll away, wondering about it and about the woman who was driving it. She went back down the hall.

Joan Styles was standing there, a worried expression on her face, her hands together. "Are you all right, Kate?"

Kate said nothing for a moment. "No, I guess not. Who was that woman, Joan?"

"Her name's Barb Fillion. She's a paramedic."

"Is she?" said Kate in an abstracted way.

"You look . . . worried."

Kate smiled at her, a thin wry smile that emphasized her fatigue and her fear. Joan shook her head. "I didn't mean about Nick. Of course you are. I was thinking about Barb Fillion. Did you know her or her partner Kikki?"

"No. It's just that . . . a while back, when she came to the window and touched it, Nick's heart rate went up. The beeping started again. I was going to call you, but as soon as that woman took her hand away, he went right back to normal. Well, normal for now."

Joan didn't know what to say to that. "Kate, why don't you go home, have a shower, get some rest. I have to do some things for Nick anyway . . ."

Kate's whole body seemed to falter, and she began to cry, cry hard, deep wrenching sobs, and all in silence, her tears streaming down.

Joan took her in her arms, held her.

"He's going to die, Joan," Kate said, burying her face in Joan's shoulder. "I can *feel* him going. He's just . . . fading."

"Honey, he's not fading. He's not going to die. He's basically pretty tough. Yes his heart rate is irregular. We're dealing with it."

Kate held on to Joan for a time. Joan could feel her body trembling, feel the sobs go through her, shaking her to her core.

Time passed.

Finally Kate pulled back, took a tissue from her pocket, wiped her eyes, looked up at Joan. "I'm sorry . . . that was—"

"Long overdue," said Joan. "And I'm telling you the truth. He's going to be fine. The operation went well, and we don't see any sign of internal bleeding in that lung. His vitals are—"

"A roller coaster. I sit there and I can't take my eyes off those monitors, and then I look at him and then back at the monitors . . . back and forth, back and forth, I can't seem to stop. I am afraid that if I stop, then he'll die, but if I just keep going back and forth I can keep him alive. I think I'm going crazy, Joan. I really do."

"You need to go home, get some sleep."

"But what if . . . if I'm not here, won't he know? What if he's waiting until I leave so then he can . . . he can leave too.

And if he leaves, I don't know what I'll do. And he'll be dead because I took Rainey Teague into our house, and that boy is . . . evil. That boy sent Maris Yarvik to kill us all and he did a pretty good job and it's all my fault . . . it's all my fault."

Joan studied her. This was borderline hysteria, she recognized the symptoms. "Look, Kate, first of all, it's Maris Yarvik's fault. He's the one who did the shooting. I don't know what to think about Rainey Teague. I do know that you've been tough enough for three wives. And you need to stand down. I have to see to Nick's dressings and change his IV. It'll take a while. You really need to go home now. He'll be right here when you get back."

Kate was looking at her but not hearing.

The mirror.

If he does die, he could go into the mirror, like Anora and Clara and Glynis and Mom.

He could go to that farm he saw on the wall in Delia Cotton's basement.

Then I'd always know where he was.

And one day maybe I could go into the mirror too, and then we could be together there.

I have to go home and get the mirror.

She kissed Joan on the cheek, said she would do that, she'd go home and have a shower, but she was coming right back.

"Kate, really—"

"No," Kate said with heat. "I'll be right back. An hour. No more. Whatever you do, don't you let him go. Promise me? No matter what, you keep him *alive*. One hour. Promise me."

Her eyes were green fire, her skin as pale as chalk. Joan was going to say something vague and comforting, but she felt the intensity.

"Yes," she said, stiffening, rising up to it. "I promise. I will not let him go."

"Your word? One hour?"

"One hour. My word."

Barb Fillion was rolling northeast, heading for Route 311. Route 311 led to Gracie. Candleford House was in Gracie. That was where she was supposed to take the kid. She had no idea why.

Fillion had the EMT com set off and her cell phone too, but she had some music playing on the EMT truck's FM radio, a slow jazzy number. It helped to keep the *thing* in her head quiet. She found it almost bearable to be alive if the voice could *just be quiet*. She would do what it wanted.

She had to. If she didn't, she got *stung*.

But if the voice stayed quiet, Fillion could go a while longer without trying to kill herself. The voice had promised her that she would be released as soon as she had done what was required.

The streets of Niceville were deserted, the lights glimmering amber under the canopy of live oaks and the crosshatched netting of the streetcar wires and telephone lines that stitched downtown Niceville together. All the storefronts were dark, their windows reflecting the image of the ambulance as it went north along the main street, heavy tires rumbling over the streetcar tracks.

A mile up it drifted past the darkened storefront of Uncle Moochie's Pawnshop, where Rainey Teague had first looked into Glynis Ruelle's mirror three years ago. Where it had all begun.

A light was burning in the upstairs window above the store. Uncle Moochie, a morose Lebanese, was sitting in a battered leather chair in a parlor cluttered with antiques, listening to zither music, *The Third Man* theme by Anton Karas.

He was reading by the light of a stained-glass lamp, smoking a long curved pipe. The smoke was rising up into the still air in a single column until it reached the yellow tin ceiling, where it flattened out and coiled into itself like a snake.

Uncle Moochie heard the sound of a truck going by, looked out the window, and saw the ambulance roll slowly past, no lights and no sirens, its interior dark, the driver's hands visible on the wheel, pale and slender, a woman's hands.

Like they're transporting a dead man, he thought. *No point in rushing things*.

He wished them well and went back to his book, *The Shining* by Stephen King. Uncle Moochie enjoyed tales of horror and the supernatural. They were a wonderful distraction from the deadly dullness of everyday life in Niceville.

Over his head the smoke snake coiled and twisted against the tin tiles. The sound of the ambulance faded away. Far off to the east, beyond the black shoulder of Tallulah's Wall, the sun was a crescent of fire on the rim of the Atlantic Ocean.

The crows who lived on top of the wall were waking, puffing their feathers, clacking their beaks, spreading their wings, scuffling and squabbling in the branches of the old forest that grew along the spiny crest. In the heart of the old forest, Crater Sink looked like a black hole in the middle of the world.

It was time for the Harvest.

Since the gunfight had scared the hell out of Axel and Hannah, Beth had taken them to a hotel. There was a squad car parked outside the house, guarding the scene, roof rack slowly turning, sending red and blue light arcing all around the neighborhood. The parkette across the street was wreathed with crime-scene tape, but Yarvik's body had been taken away hours ago. Even the spent brass had been policed up, and Reed's shot-to-bits pickup had been hauled away by a wrecker.

Kate spoke to the two young patrol cops, both of whom wanted to know how Nick and Frank were doing. Kate gave them the best news she could manage, and they took it as if it were totally true, which everyone knew it wasn't.

The main floor lights were on when she stepped into the front hall, broken stained-glass cracking and sliding under her feet, the reek of gunpowder residue hanging in the air like stale cigarette smoke. She looked around at the damage.

Amazingly, other than the front-door glass and one of the sash windows, and the chalky footprints of patrol cops all over the main floor, the place wasn't in terrible shape. She sighed, as people do when they are trying to keep themselves together but what they'd really like to do is fall to their knees, curl up, and fade out.

She took a deep breath, turned away from the mess, and went up the stairs. The mirror should still be where they kept it, in an upstairs hall closet, wrapped in a blue blanket. Climbing the stairs, fatigue rolled over her like a black wave and she stopped on the landing to get her breath back and her courage up. The landing on the second floor was dark, so she hit the switch and got nothing.

No light.

Just dark shadow at the top of the stairs.

She stood there on the landing, looking up into the darkness. A cold tremor rippled through her chest and an artery in her neck began to thump. "Hello," she called, first in a small voice, and then again with more force, "Hello? Is there someone up there?"

Maybe a cop, still looking around?

Something was there. She could feel it.

"Hello?"

Nothing?

Was Nothing there?

She tried the switch again, and this time the upstairs hall light came on, but low, a dull green glimmer. The bulb looked as if a firefly had been caught inside it.

No. Not a firefly.

A dragonfly.

A glowing green dragonfly.

The light in the bulb began to grow stronger, slowly filling the upper landing with an emerald-green fire. Her fear subsided slightly, for reasons she couldn't explain. She climbed the second flight of stairs slowly, her senses straining, and the green light grew brighter all around her. She reached the top of the stairs, stepped into the upper hall. It was filled with emerald-green dragonflies, each one a tiny spark of green fire, a cloud of them hovering in the hall, dazzling and hypnotic.

There was a shape inside the glowing cloud of dragonflies. A woman.

Kate knew her.

"Hello, Kate," the woman said, coming forward, growing more solid and clear, surrounded by that dazzling emerald light.

"Glynis?"

"Yes," the woman replied.

"Why are you here?"

Glynis Ruelle smiled at Kate, but it was a troubled smile, something else underneath it. Concern? Fear?

"I need to be," she said.

Delores Maranzano Moves Things Right Along

Delores, a nimble little thing and a skilled multitasker, was whipping Raylon Grande around the clubhouse turn to a standing ovation from the choir invisible, while at the same time keeping an eye on the clock on the bedside table.

It was almost six-thirty in the morning, a Sunday—the Lord's day—and they had been at it most of the night. Raylon Grande had tremendous staying power, but she could tell he was beginning to falter, and it was long past time to transition to stage two of the master plan.

So she dug down deep within herself and came up with one of her most convincing fake orgasms. Later she looked back on it as one of the best of her fall season. It started out with a kind of steam-whistle puffing, her head thrown back wild-eyed—*oh my, popcorn stucco on the ceiling, how awful*—her gasping rapidly escalated into a cross between a coyote yodeling at the moon and Inva Mula Tchako's aria from *Lucia di Lammermoor*.

She cut it off before somebody started pounding on the hotel wall and collapsed across Raylon's muscular chest, burying her face in his neck. She could feel his carotid thrumming like a trapped bat, and his chest was heaving so hard that she thought he might buck her right off.

She pulled back, letting her hair fall just so across his face, creating a curtain of intimacy around them, stared down into his slightly buggy eyeballs. "Raylon sweetie. Can I tell you a secret?"

Raylon swallowed and got his breath and looked up at her like a big old puppy dog in a basket full of daisies, licked his lips. "Please, honey. Anything."

She kissed his wet nose. "I know you're a fucking fed."

His color changed. "What?"

She smiled down upon him. "You're a fucking fed. Actually, to be precise, you're a fed, fucking."

Raylon started to unspool a string of lying lies. She stopped him with a warm wet kiss. "Wait," she said. "There's more."

"Delores, I have no idea what the—"

What she said next chilled him to the core. "Raylon, we have to talk."

"Delores—"

She climbed off, leaned down and gently patted his rapidly receding courting tackle. "Come on, sweetie. Get dressed. You're not going to want to hear this while your little turtle-head thingy is going all pinkly-wrinkly."

He was still goggling at her amazing butt, but now with mixed emotions, as she wriggled into the en suite and gently closed the door.

He stared at it for a while, his mind racing, and then, feeling unfriendly eyes upon him, looked across the room to the credenza, where her mammoth braided leather Bottega Veneta bag was propped up against the flat-screen. A pair of buggy eyes were glaring back at him.

Frankie Twice, her goddamned Chihuahua.

Raylon had made several attempts to go through that bag while Delores was in the bath, but every time he went near it that fucking dog would start snapping and snarling. Dog had teeth like a piranha.

The dog had stayed there the entire night—maybe he had diapers on; he wouldn't put that past Delores—and now he was regarding Raylon Grande with a censorious frown.

"What the fuck are *you* looking at?" said Raylon. Frankie Twice licked his lips, twitched, blinked, farted, but otherwise declined to comment.

They reconvened in the living room of their suite at the Quantum Park Marriott Hotel and Convention Center—"*Conveniently Located Just a Hop and a Skip from Mauldar Field*"—and sat down on opposite sides of an ottoman as big as a dead buffalo and sipped at their drinks, in her case a champagne and orange juice mimosa, and for Raylon two Excedrins washed down with black coffee.

The residue of last night's dinner lay scattered all over the top of the ottoman, along with a silver tray streaked with cocaine and a number of squished-up spliffs jammed into an empty jar of Dijon mustard. The unmistakable scent of stale weed and crazed sex floated in the still air.

They had taken the Temple Hill Suite, the largest and most luxurious suite in the place and the only suite in the Marriott where smoking was allowed. The rules were not specific about what could or could not be smoked, but the management was probably going to draw the line at goat.

"Okay," said Raylon, sitting back into the couch and adjusting his trousers. "Say what you gotta say."

Delores made a pouty face. "Why, Raylon, aren't we friends anymore?"

"Not when you start accusing me of being some kind of government snitch."

"I'm not accusing you of being a snitch, Raylon. That would be offensive. I am merely stating that you are an agent of the Federal Bureau of Investigation who has been assigned to an undercover role as a sales associate at Neiman Marcus in order to establish contact with the widow of an Italian businessman named Frankie Maranzano. Unless you are ashamed of your job, you shouldn't feel offended at all. You should be proud."

Raylon looked up at the ceiling and then across the room to the window wall, where the sun was just clearing the edge of the world. "You know, Delores, you can be sort of a trial sometimes. I have no idea—"

"Oh, but I do, and guess where I got it?"

"Do I have to?"

"The Starbucks at Fountain Square, where I saw you having a coffee with Special Agent Hackendorff of the FBI."

Raylon tried not to look ashen and failed.

"Yes," she said with a sympathetic smile. "Just the other day."

"I have no idea—"

"Sweetie, this isn't *Oprah*. I'm not trying to wring a tearful confession out of you so I can give you a Prius. I'm just trying to establish the terms of our new relationship."

Raylon got to his feet and started to hunt for the rest of his clothes, talking at her over his shoulder as he stumbled around the suite. "I said this is nuts and I don't know what the fuck is going on, but you know, Delores, I am outta here anyway and I hope we can still be—"

Delores had turned on the flat-screen television while Raylon was bustling about trying to create a diversion. When he came back out into the main room the flat-screen was showing a video of Raylon and Delores working their way through a small mountain of cocaine set out on a silver tray. Seeing this video was sufficient to get all of Raylon's attention. "You . . . evil . . . bitch," he said rather predictably.

"No, sweetie, the evil part comes later."

Raylon sat down and watched the video for a while. It was

grainy and flickery and dim, but he was pretty certain that if it were to be run in the office of the director of the FBI, the man would find it endlessly fascinating. He leaned back into the couch and smiled at Delores.

"Honey, about undercover ops, you need to know that FBI policy allows for UC operators to engage in some light drug activity and even some sexual contact if it helps to establish their—"

Delores reached over and retrieved her MacBook Air, talking while she hit a few keys. "But, honey, I'm not thinking about the FBI people in DC. I'm thinking about the person whose e-mail address is *'maypallcutie@gmail.com.'*"

Raylon went all the way to puce. "How the *fuck*—"

"Never leave your iPhone in the bedroom while you're in the bathroom admiring your abs."

He took that in. "Horseshit. That phone's got an encrypted password. There's no way you'd ever be able to—"

"Didn't need it. You left the phone on. All I had to do was go look at your contacts."

"You'd have no way of knowing—"

"I know your real name is Kurt Pall, and that you've been with the agency for sixteen years."

Puce intensified, verging on russet. "How could you know that?"

She shook her head teasingly. "I'm always interested in people who take an interest in me. So when you showed up at the store and started to work your way into my panties—"

"Not a lot of work."

"And I've enjoyed every minute you've spent there. But you got my attention. So I took a picture of you with my iPhone and sent it to one of Frankie's associates who collects photographs of federal law enforcement people. He did something called Facial Recog—I have no idea—but a guy who looked exactly like you had been working as a pool boy at the

Delano in South Beach last spring. And you were playing the same game, getting close to the wife of a made guy. You rolled up three of Tony Torinetti's guys on an extortion beef. They finked out, and now here you are, following up."

"No way they'd get my fucking name."

"You were on the DA's list of witnesses for that case."

"That list is sealed."

She blinked at him. "Not for people inside the DA's office."

Raylon sagged into himself. "You got people in the Miami DA's office?"

"Tit for tat, in a way. Seems only fair."

Raylon took a belt of his coffee. "What are you doing with the laptop?"

She looked over at the flat-screen, where clothes were coming off at a frantic pace and various body parts were jiggling and throbbing. "I have a copy of this MPEG attached to your wife's e-mail. If I hit the SEND key it will ruin her Sunday afternoon. And probably yours too."

"How did you get the . . . of course. That goddamn purse. You never leave it."

"I never leave Frankie Twice either."

"Yeah, right. So now the fucking dog makes porn films?"

"No. But he keeps you out of my purse. I hear him snapping at you whenever you try to get into it. Oh, Raylon, don't look so glum."

"Why the fuck not?"

"Because I have no intention of sending this silly video to your wife."

A ray of hope for Raylon. "What, then?"

"You're watching my condo right now, aren't you?"

Raylon struggled with it, but in the end he just nodded and looked at his hands. Over on the flat-screen, things had gotten pretty graphic, so he wasn't looking there anymore. He was glad the sound was off. Nobody wants to hear himself doing what he was doing. Seeing it was bad enough.

"I thought you might be. Frankie Twice keeps snapping and staring and moaning at the windows that look out on Fountain Square. Your offices are right across the square. So you have some kind of listening thingy set up."

"Yeah, we do. You want it shut down? Because there's no way I could get Boonie to do that."

Delores stood up and came over and kneeled down at his feet and gave him an up-from-under that, in spite of himself, he could feel in his hip pocket. "No, I don't want it shut down, honey-booboo. I want you to keep listening. Is there any way you can make it more irritating to Frankie Twice?"

"Maybe. Probably. But why?"

"Just do it. Also, do you have any bugs inside the apartment?"

"No. Those assholes never go out. As soon as they do, we'll be all over it."

"But right now, nothing?"

"Contact mike under the suite number plate on the front door. But we're not getting anything off it."

"Can you lend me one? Like for a phone?"

"What? I guess so. Why?"

She ran her hands up his thighs. It was a cheap trick, a really shopworn move, almost a cliché. There's a reason why things get to be clichés. Because they're true *all* of the time. Long story short, Delores got everything she wanted.

Tito Detects Stuff

Tito Smeraglia was finding this assignment vexing. After driving down from Jacksonville in a rented panel van, he had located the Sinclair beach house easily. It was right out on the shoreline, one of a long chain of elaborate homes that seemed to run down the coast and on into a misty infinity.

Most of the homes were shuttered and barred. Tito figured they were seasonal homes and this was an inconvenient season for these pampered parasites.

The wealth of America had always vaguely offended him. These people had no . . . restraint. Everything was always too much and too much of too much. They were a vulgar people, unlike his own people back in Istria, who were all modest, hardworking, humble, and pure of heart, at least, the holy few who weren't thieves and thugs and killers.

The beach house was a big angular structure, all wood beams and glass and offset grids and elevated decks sticking out here and there. Handsome in a masculine way, not like some of the other houses along the shore, many of which looked like pink-stucco wedding cakes or exploding car parts held in place with stainless steel rods.

But he had passed by the Sinclair house slowly enough to get a thorough look at it, and one thing it was *not* was easy to break into.

There was an outer fence made of cedar planking, with cameras and sensors and perimeter lights all over. As he sat in his van looking at the pictures on his digital camera he knew in his heart that getting inside it was going to take patience and finesse.

Well, Tito had patience and he could approach finesse, and he started by going to a local store—called, for reasons he didn't give a damn about, Alvin's Island. He had noticed there were Alvin's Islands all over this part of Florida and they were all chock-full of bloody awful beach crap and bloody awful-er souvenirs, all of them made in China, probably by political prisoners in a slave-labor camp.

He bought a huge straw hat with corks hanging off the brim and a pair of rubber sandals and a baggy shirt with hula dancers on it in hues and tints that even God had never seen coming, and baggy shorts in a riotous plaid and a pair of those wraparound bug-eyed sunglasses with the mirrored lenses and a pink plastic backpack with a picture of someone named Hannah Montana on the flap.

And he bought a metal detector.

He parked the van at a public lot a half mile up the shore from the Sinclair house, changed into his beach gear in a public washroom that smelled of pee and marijuana and mold.

Then he headed out, his backpack loaded with his trade tools, feeling like a circus clown, to do what even he had to admit was best described as a reconnaissance in farce.

The sun had wrested its big round glowing butt free of the Atlantic long before, and now it was floating in the middle of the sky like a hot air balloon as he made his slow shuffling way down the beach, the waves booming and crashing in.

He kept dutifully sweeping the metal detector back and

forth as he went, and he could feel the heat building on his skin. Sunscreen. Next time, may the Merciful God forbid there should ever be one, get sunscreen.

An hour later Twyla Littlebasket was standing in the living room of the beach house, holding a cell phone and idly wondering about the short, squat old man with the metal detector who was making his crablike progress down the beach. Not that old men dressed like circus wagons were a rare sight along this shore. In the high season they outnumbered the pelicans. But this was not the high season, and she was thinking that there was something odd about him and she had almost but not quite figured out what it was when her call got picked up.

"It's me."

"How are you?"

"I'm not supposed to say names."

"I asked *how*, not who."

Bluebell felt the need to whisper, as if there were a law that required all fugitives to whisper into cheap cell phones. "I'm tired. But I'm almost . . . there."

"Good. How long?"

"I don't know for sure. Maybe two hours? They keep stopping by the side of the highway to let people off. All you have to do is stand there and the bus stops and people get on and off. I had no idea people still traveled like this. It's like the Great Depression never ended. Except people don't dress as well. And they stink. Will you be there?"

"I'll leave now."

"Have you heard from . . ."

"No. I don't expect to. We worked that all out. He'll be here when he can."

"Okay. I guess I better go. My battery is getting low. These phones don't last long."

"That's why they call them throwaways. Okay I love you and I'll see you soon."

"I love you too. I can't wait."

"Neither can I," she said, watching the absurd old man work his way down toward the Kellerman place, sweeping that metal thing back and forth. *God, how dull that must be*, she was thinking

How deadly dull.

Then she walked away from the window and locked up the place and set the alarm and went out to the garage and got into her scarlet Jaguar and skimmed off up Beach Front Road to the highway.

She planned to be in Jacksonville a good two hours before Bluebell's bus pulled into the terminal. She wanted to see if anybody else was waiting, because if anybody was, then as much as she loved Bluebell, she was going to leave her standing by the side of the road and execute Plan CUL8R, which Coker liked to call Operation Bug Out.

Tito Smeraglia was a good judge of empty houses—they just *felt* different—and as he stood on the beach in front of the Sinclair home staring at the tinted window wall, he had that sense right now. Earlier there had been a young dark-haired woman standing at the window, watching him as he went down the shore with this ridiculous machine.

She had seemed alert and attentive, as someone might well be who sees a stranger wandering down the beach in the off-season. So, being a smart girl, she paid attention to what was going on outside. But there was no one at the window now.

And the house felt empty.

It had been Tito's experience that a job either just broke open and went smoothly or became a dreary slog that took days to accomplish.

The difference was *audacity*.

A risk-averse man was never going to rise to Tito's level

of perfection and dedication. To the timid, every opportunity was a veiled threat.

Yes, there was security. He could see it everywhere. He was certain he was being monitored by a camera right now, but these days, who wasn't? And the woman was gone, he was certain of it.

And beach homes all over the world were like turtles. All their armor was on one side. They were closed off to the land, but wide open to the sea. That was the whole idea. So he took the opportunity to do a walkabout and see if the house had any vulnerabilities. It took him the better part of an hour before he found it. A small one, but enough.

The garage door was automatic and it had closed after the woman had presumably driven off, to be gone how long, Tito had no idea.

That was the part that required nerve, to go about the work in spite of that uncertainty.

The garage door had not closed properly. There was a slight gap between the bottom of the door and the surface of the drive, which was made of interlocking stones set into sand. There was a motion detector on the eave, but it was aimed out toward the beach road. Time to be *audacious*.

It took a few minutes to get under the garage door, and one minute later he was inside the main house—the alarm pad was already beeping, which made it easy to find—and thirty seconds after that he had cut the dedicated alarm phone line and then used a jammer to suppress the auxiliary wireless signal. It took him a while to figure out the code sequence that disarmed the system. The worn-down buttons were a giveaway, but the *order* in which they had to be pressed was challenging.

He had to work through the permutations and the box shrieked at him whenever he got it wrong, making him think of his poor dead mother—they had the exact same *tone*—but he persevered.

And the house was his.

After he had carefully restored the interlocking bricks on the driveway and scattered sand over them again, he went through the house in a practiced and competent manner, since he had a great deal of experience with how people arranged their secrets, and knowing people's secrets was a powerful advantage in his trade.

He found three pistols in different locations—by the sliding doors to the deck, near the back door, and in a night table in the master bedroom. He found but was unable to open a gun safe in the basement, next to a workbench that seemed dedicated to gun maintenance, which puzzled him.

He had been told that the subjects he was to process were retired financial people, although the man had demonstrated a degree of skill in self-defense. Yet this organized and squared-away work space suggested a military mind-set. Or perhaps, like many bankers, he was just an obsessive-compulsive, unable to deal with disorder in any way.

He noted this and moved on through the rest of the house, discovering nothing inconsistent with the profiles he had been given, a wealthy retired money changer, and his third wife, a pretty dark-haired creature of some ethnic extraction he did not care to discover. He inferred from an examination of their closets that they were living here more or less full-time, and that the dark-haired girl had left to run an errand, since she had not taken anything with her to suggest a lengthy absence. The husband, he presumed, would turn up eventually, since his car, a black GMC Yukon, was still in the garage.

Once he had them under control, he would contact his clients and invite them to attend the procedure. Tito did not approve of this aspect—it was much too public and he did his best work in private—but that had been an added element of his employment, a nonnegotiable one, and he had agreed, so there it was.

Satisfied with his afternoon's work, he went into the kitchen and found a bottle of Pellegrino. He opened it and poured himself a glass and sat down at the kitchen counter to wait for the owners to come home. He set his backpack down at his feet, laid the pistol he had found by the back door onto the countertop, which seemed to be Italian marble.

He noticed a set of knives in a standing wooden block at the other end of the counter. He reached out and pulled one free of its scabbard. These were fine knives and would have been more than adequate for his purposes, had he not thought to bring along his personal tool kit, which allowed him to achieve effects not easily duplicated by knife blade, no matter how skilled the hand.

He drank the Pellegrino and breathed in the sea air, feeling that he had done a good day's work, and that there were not many obstacles in the world that could not be overcome by a slow and meticulous man who could occasionally approach . . . *finesse*.

The Reckoning

They got up early and spent the morning doing what needs to be done every morning when you live on a farm and have horses and chickens and cattle to care for. He saw to the horses in the barn, a lovely big Hanoverian mare named Virago, as shiny black as an obsidian blade, two Clyde broodmares, Althea and Jocasta, a two-year-old Clyde stallion named Traveler, almost as big as Jupiter, and a gawky Clyde foal they were calling Tanglefoot, for obvious reasons. After he tended to their needs, Danziger went to the rail fence and whistled Jupiter in from the fields.

Watching him come thundering across a chest-high field of wild flowers was like standing on a railroad crossing watching the Wabash Cannonball coming down the mountainside and cross the valley floor.

Jupiter came up to Danziger, his eyes full of recognition and wary half liking, his ears forward, huffing and stamping. Danziger gave him his apple and then another. He looked at Jupiter's teeth and checked his ears for mites and spent time washing him down, going over his hide for deer ticks, his hooves for thrush—he needed a new shoe on his rear offside—

that would have to be tended to soon. Afterward he patted him down with a big terry cloth towel and took a brush to his barrel and withers and cannons and currycombed the tats out of his mane and his tail and his fetlocks.

All in all, by the time he was through, Jupiter looked like a show horse and Danziger looked like a pile of dirty laundry.

At noon they ate hard bread and cheese and apples and cold cuts—cider for Glynis and lemonade for Danziger—and then they showered and changed, a green summer dress for Glynis, with a pale yellow cardigan over it, jeans and a clean white shirt for Danziger—one of John Ruelle's old shirts, collarless—over that Danziger's range jacket, and of course those famous navy blue cowboy boots.

They were talking about various practical issues when there was a knock at the screen door and they saw Albert Lee standing outside in the shade of the porch, resplendent in a black suit, a gleaming white shirt, and a charcoal-gray tie.

He smiled at Danziger as Glynis opened up the door and brought him in. "Charlie, you decided to stay, I see."

"He did," said Glynis, looking serious, now that Albert Lee was here. "I've . . . explained things to him. He's ready to help if he's needed."

"So am I," said Albert Lee, pulling back his suit jacket to show the butt of an old pistol tucked into his waistband.

"What is it?" asked Danziger with professional interest. Albert Lee pulled it out, a small-frame stainless-steel hammerless revolver. He checked the action, flipped out the cylinder, and handed the weapon, butt first, to Danziger, who turned it in the light streaming in through the kitchen door. It was in perfect condition, fully loaded, and had a shimmer rippling along the steel.

"Damn," he said, "A Forehand and Wadsworth. I haven't seen one of these in years."

He snapped the cylinder back into the frame, passed it back to Albert Lee.

"I had it from my daddy. He went to the South African war. It shoots thirty-eight. I got an extra box of fifty. Not good for long-range, but it will do very nicely up close."

Danziger looked up at Albert Lee. "You think it'll come to that?" he asked.

Albert Lee glanced across at Glynis, who looked as grim as he did. "I believe it might," he said.

Danziger took that in. "Glynis, I see you've got a Browning Automatic Rifle back there in the parlor. It looks to be in pretty good condition."

"It is," she said. "Ethan brought it back from the war, and he always kept his weapons well."

"Do you have any spare rounds for it?"

"Yes. During the troubles with the Teague Faction after the war, Ethan bought four more magazines and a box of bullets."

"Springfield thirty-ought-six?"

Glynis gave him a look. "What else would they be? I know weapons at least as well as you do, Charlie. Do you wish to bring that along this afternoon?"

"Well, it would sure help clarify the situation."

"That it would," said Albert Lee. "Although it's a heavy brute."

"I've fired them," said Danziger, "I know what they can do. They're well worth the carrying."

Albert Lee looked as if he had a question, and Glynis asked him if he did.

"Well, Miz Ruelle, I was wondering if Clara was going to attend, at all?"

Danziger got the distinct impression that Albert Lee was more than a tad sweet on Clara.

Glynis shook her head, patted Albert Lee on the shoulder, gave him a sympathetic smile. "No, Albert Lee. I'm afraid Clara has already been to the Harvest. If all goes well, she may come down to dinner, and I hope you'll stay? Clara is always happy to see you."

"Is she here now?" asked Charlie.

"She is," said Glynis. "But there is someone to be dealt with this afternoon that she wishes never to look upon again."

The men heard that, left it alone.

"Well," said Glynis, wiping her hands on a dish towel. "We might as well get ready. You men get your gear together. It's about time."

Ten minutes later they left the old house and headed down the slope toward the wheat field, Danziger on the right, because the BAR kicked its empty brass out to the right and they were as hot as coals. The BAR was the M1918 model, so it could fire either single-shot or 350 rounds per minute on auto. Either way, Danziger figured the BAR pretty much owned the day.

Glynis walked in the middle, carrying a midsized package, flat, rectangular, wrapped in an old Indian blanket, and Albert Lee on her left, his suit coat open, his Forehand & Wadsworth in his belt, and his pockets full of loose thirty-eights, jingling like coins.

Danziger looked back up the lane to the house and saw a lovely young woman standing at an upper window. She had long blond hair and an oval face, large expressive eyes with a greenish tint, and sadness in her aura. She lifted a hand to Danziger, and he smiled and then turned away, knowing that he had finally seen Clara Mercer. They crossed Little Cut Creek and came up a small rise, and they were there and the Harvest had begun.

It was right out of Danziger's dream, the one he'd had in his room at the MountRoyal Hotel.

They were standing at the western edge of a field of wheat that rose and fell away toward a dense stand of pines and willows. There were dark figures in the distance, working along the edge of the field, digging in what looked to be trenches, shovels and axes rising and falling, the figures bent and somehow beaten-looking. There was a wheeled cart being drawn by a brace of oxen. The cart was loaded with round white stones, or maybe cantaloupe.

Or skulls.

Now that he was closer, Danziger got the question answered. They were stones, river rocks, rounded by water for ten thousand years. They were using them to build a barrier wall along the edge of the pine forest. By the look of it, a damn big barrier wall. A wall works both ways. It keeps things out and it keeps thing in. Danziger had no idea which way this wall was pointed, but his money was on keeping things out.

But they were just rocks.

Not skulls.

Freud was right, thought Danziger, *sometimes a cigar is just a cigar.*

When they crested the hill, someone in the wheat field called out, and the people working along the edge of the pine forest began to gather in the center of the field, where a small hay wagon stood, sagging and ancient, once painted green.

Glynis led the way, moving through the wheat with a silky hissing sound, the package cradled across her breasts. The sun was past noon and her shadow ran ahead of her. The heat lay on their shoulders and Danziger could feel it burning through the heavy twill of his range jacket. He had the BAR on a combat sling over his right shoulder, twenty-one pounds fully loaded, four spare box mags—twenty rounds each—stuffed into his outside pockets, and his Colt Anaconda in his belt.

In a few minutes they were all gathered around the old hay wagon, a crowd of perhaps thirty or forty people, all middle-aged or old, some black, some white, some dark, some light, a mosaic of the Old South. No children.

The people from the Blue Bird were all there—Danziger recognized the careworn woman who had invited him to their "sing" as she was getting off the bus—and many people he did not know, but all of them were carrying an invisible weight and an air of sleepwalking fatigue.

But they were smiling and all of them greeted Glynis in a way that made Danziger feel that they had a strong affection for her. Albert Lee got a few hellos and friendly nods. They all avoided looking directly at Danziger.

Beyond the gathering, over by the tree line, Danziger could see four men standing apart, hard-looking, their faces grim. They were holding tools, picks and shovels, and were wearing dusty overalls and work boots.

They looked ... separate ... like gravediggers waiting for the funeral to be over and the mourners to depart so they could get the business over with. All four men were looking right at Danziger and he felt ... not a threat but a *warning* in their expressionless faces.

Glynis unwrapped her package, and the sunlight glimmered on an intricately carved gilt frame. As she turned it, the sun flashed out in a blinding white blaze from the pitted and worn glass of an antique mirror, medium-sized, quite old.

All eyes were on the glass as she placed it carefully on the floor of the wagon, leaning it upright against the slats, the glass facing the people. A silence came down and there was nothing but the wind hissing through the wheat field and, from deep in the pine forest, the sound of crows calling.

Glynis turned to look into the pine forest for a while with a troubled expression, listening to the crows, and then she came back to the gathering.

"Today the Harvest comes again. Are we all willing to do this today? Those of you who are not willing and ready need not take part. You see Albert Lee is here, with the Blue Bird. Those of you who wish may go back to your homes or to one of the towns. And there is always room in the Annex. The work of this plantation will always go on."

She paused, as if letting her words settle in.

"So, remember, this must be something you *wish* to do. Something for which you feel ready all the way down to your toes. No one should feel forced or driven to it. No outer influence should bring you to it. It must come from your own heart."

There was movement and murmuring—it ran in a ripple through the crowd. It passed and an air of imminence set in, everyone waiting for the first person to begin this, whoever it might be.

Glynis said nothing, seemed content to wait until sundown, perfectly still, perfectly attentive. Even the crows in the deeps of the pine forest were now silent. Danziger and Albert Lee studied each face in the crowd, but they all were staring into the glass, fixed and rapt.

"I believe I am ready," said a small voice, a woman's voice with a strong southern accent, pure Louisiana, and the crowd parted to let her come forward. She was a young black woman, not tall, very beautiful, a full and sensual body.

She was barefoot and wearing a simple smock made of unbleached cotton. Her hair was held back by a red ribbon and she had a necklace around her neck, wide rings of emerald-green and scarlet stones, each ring separated by a thinner ring of intense yellow. The effect was snakelike, and against her coffee-colored skin, it glittered like a ring of fire and light. Her expression was calm and she held her body upright, her hands folded.

"Talitha," said Glynis with a note of surprise. "Are you sure?"

Talitha looked down at the wheat, as if considering. Then

she raised her head, a clear light in her topaz eyes. "I am, Miss Glynis. I feel my time is come."

Glynis looked both pleased and worried. Danziger got the idea that Talitha had come to the mirror many times before and it had not gone well.

"You must not be downhearted, Talitha, if it is not yet time."

"I will not be downhearted," she said.

Glynis came forward, gave her a kiss on the cheek, and then stepped away. "Here, come and look."

Talitha hesitated and then came up to the wagon. She took a breath, let it out, and then leaned forward, bringing her face close to the glass. Danziger, standing beside the wagon, his eyes roving over the crowd and then on to the edge of the pine forest, to those four waiting men, and then moving on to search the pines, could not see what Talitha was seeing in the mirror.

Everyone waited in silence.

After a minute, the girl straightened up, tears on her face. She looked at Glynis. "I am to go," she said in a trembling voice. "Second Samuel will meet me on the other side of the woods."

A low murmur ran through the crowd.

"Do you wish this?" asked Glynis. "You are welcome to stay."

"I truly wish it," she said in a small voice. "I been pining to see my daddy for a long time."

"Then go, Talitha, with all of our love."

Talitha smiled then, a sudden flash of joy and release. She turned for one last look at the rest of the people, performed a graceful curtsy, and then set off across the wheat field in the direction of the pine forest. Danziger noticed that as she moved through the wheat she made no sound and left no trail. Halfway to the tree line she faded into a misty outline and then she was gone.

A sigh ran through the crowd.

And that is how it went. Someone would step forward and look into the mirror. Their reactions varied—some seemed relieved, some seemed saddened—and some who looked into the mirror backed away and shook their heads and drifted off into the comfort of the crowd. Everyone who said they were to go left the same way Talitha had, moving silently away through the wheat, slipping into a veiled shape and then slowly fading away before they reached the pine forest.

In one hour Danziger counted nine people who took that walk. Glynis stood and waited, and the time rolled on, but no one else came forward.

She straightened herself, glanced back at Danziger and Albert Lee, a brief look full of warning, faced the people again. "Well then, now we come to the Reckoning."

She paused, let the moment stand.

There was a whispering ripple and then the crowd grew quiet. Waiting and attentive.

"The Reckoning . . . is not a gift we place into a man's hands. We are not the keepers of the Reckoning. We do not own it. It is not ours to give, nor ours to withhold. No priest trades in it, no judge commands it, no lawgiver defines it. It is a part of the living world, as much as the moon and the stars and the rivers. The Reckoning is forbidden to no one and open to all, but without it there can be no peace in this life, nor ever in the hearts of living men or dead."

There was a murmur of assent and the crowd stirred uneasily.

"It is now time for Abel Teague to come forward and face the Reckoning," she said in a carrying tone that was stern and full of judgment.

"Mr. Teague has been given six months here at the plantation to consider the days of his long life and how he has chosen to live among his fellow men and women. The hour has come for him to stand and tell us what he has come to know about himself, and what he might now have the grace to regret, and how he might see his ways differ from what they were. If this is honestly and willingly done, he will find that he is eased and unburdened. He will free himself. If it is not, if he refuses, he remains bound in chains of his own making, and he will be returned to his confinement to consider his ways for another season. Those who wish to witness Abel Teague's attendance are welcome to stay. Those who prefer not to should leave now."

The people shifted and stirred, a restless alteration, and many of them began to move away through the wheat toward the fence line.

In the end three men and one woman stayed, all of them with something hard showing through their sunburned faces, resolution in their stance and the set of their bodies.

Glynis raised a hand, waved in the direction of the four men standing apart. "Will he come willingly?"

All four men shook their heads.

Glynis sighed, looked back again at Danziger, and then spoke to the men again. "Then you must compel him."

They looked at each other, and one man answered, his voice strained and tense. "Ma'am. We are sorry. He will not come."

Glynis looked at Danziger and Albert Lee. "Then you two men must go and bring him."

Danziger smiled, started to move.

She stopped him with her hand. "Be careful. He looks old, but he is quick and strong and cunning. And the crows? You heard them? There may be guardians near. Be watchful."

They walked across the wheat field, a distance of fifty or sixty yards. On the way Albert Lee offered Danziger a sip from his flask, and Danziger accepted, savored it, handed it back.

As they got closer, they saw what looked like an open pit in the earth, a trench wide and deep, only a few yards from the edge of the forest, running along a section of the river-rock wall that was under construction. The four men were standing around it, staring down at something in the trench. Danziger and Albert Lee came up to the edge, Danziger covering the trench with his BAR. Albert Lee had his revolver out.

There was an old man sitting in the trench, a powerful old man, but weathered with age, as gray and seamed as barn boards. He had his back up against a bank of dirt and willow roots. He was broad and strong-looking, with a blue-skinned face made up of harsh planes and sagging flesh, the haggard sunken-cheeked face of a man who has spent his life doing exactly as he damn well pleased. He had a crater-shaped scar in his right cheekbone, and his right eye was blood-rimmed and bulging.

He slouched there in what looked to Danziger like a muddy formal suit, a dirty shirt that had once been white, thick black boots covered in muck. As their shadows fell across him he looked up, squinting into the sunlight, seeing them only as black figures against the sky.

He showed his teeth, big and yellow as piano keys, blood-red gums, thin lips, and flat-dead eyes like the eyes of a shark. "Who are these sorry-looking bumpkins?" he said in a grating voice, his accent Deep South, Louisiana or Alabama. His sleeves were filthy, and his knees too, as if he had been kneeling in the muck, digging the trench with his bare hands. His fingernails were cracked and bloody.

"He was trying to dig under," said the man with the shovel.

"I *had* dug under," growled the old man in the trench. "I was almost through. I asked you who you were," he snapped, looking up at Danziger and Albert Lee. He squinted more closely at Albert Lee.

"I know *you*. You were the darky from last spring. In the duel. You loaned me your pistol."

"I did. I loaned you this very one I have in my hand. Should have shot you myself," said Albert Lee in a hard flat voice.

The man in the pit grinned up at him. "But you didn't have the sand. Not then and not now. You darkies never do. It just ain't in you. Born to tote and carry and then go under the harrow with the rest of the manure. And who're you?"

This to Danziger. "Never mind who I am," he said, centering the BAR on the man's dirty shirt. "Get up or die in a ditch. I don't give a personal damn either way."

The man leered up at him. "But *she* cares, cowpoke. This is all *her* show. And you *can't* kill me, you ignorant lout. Not with that ugly damn thing, anyway."

Danziger appeared to think this through. "Well, I can probably shoot you into a lot of bits and pieces," he said with a big carnivorous smile. "How'd you like to get scattered all over this ditch in chunks small enough for the rats to eat? You'd still be *alive*, according to you, every greasy twitching bit, but the rats would have you down in their guts, and there you'd stay forever."

The old man's face changed. Danziger had reached him. He was shaken by Danziger's ferocity, and by the truth inside his threat, and it showed. "Who the hell are you?"

"My name is Charlie Danziger. Remember it."

The man put his head back against the dirt, sighed, and got slowly to his feet, making an irony of his obedience, staring at the men around the edge of the pit, coming back to Danziger. Hate came off him in waves. He stank of dead meat and sewage, not on him, but *in* him, like he was made of it.

"And my name is Abel Teague, Mr. Danziger. I will not ask you to remember it. You will have no choice."

He showed his teeth, looked past the men at Glynis Ruelle, standing by the hay wagon. "Mr. Danziger, let me share a confidence with you, one gentleman to another. Someday I'll buy a new straight razor," he said, his voice sliding into a reptilian hiss, "and I will gut that poxy cunt over there like a fallow deer."

Danziger clubbed him with the butt of the BAR and he went reeling backward onto the rim of the trench, blood spraying out of his mouth. He wiped his jaw, grinned through the blood. Two of his front teeth had been smashed in. The man shook his head, suddenly cheerful, smiling through blood.

"What time you figure it is?" he asked in a conversational tone.

Albert Lee had his watch out. "Three seventeen."

This seemed to please him. He stood up again, reeled a bit, put his head back, looked up into the sky, spread his arms wide. Crows were wheeling along the top of the tree line, a huge flock. Danziger heard Glynis shouting, calling his name.

Teague grinned up at them. "Mr. Danziger, all you wild-wood boys, please welcome my dear companions."

Three hard shots cracked out of the pine forest. The man with the shovel pivoted like a dancer, blood flying out of his shattered skull. A second man went down, falling into the trench, his pitchfork clattering on stones. Albert Lee was crouching, firing, steady and slow, aiming into the shadows of the pine forest.

Danziger raised the BAR, squeezed the trigger, the weapon thudding, the sound of it thunderous, the muzzle flare lighting up the tree line, his body taking the recoil. He could see figures in there, pale white figures, manlike, but not quite right. They had weapons, and they were *many*.

Danziger cut them down one by one, calm and methodical shooting—acquire the target, steady on it, squeeze the trigger, move on to the next—one after the other, firing semiauto, like taking out a row of clay pipes, four, five, six of the guardians, pale figures jerking under the impact of the slugs, coming apart, falling away into the shadows under the pines.

More shots came back and Danziger felt a round tug at

his shoulder, another at his cheek . . . he kept firing—killed
three more—and then the rifle stopped and he was reaching
for another box mag, ejected the empty one, stuffed it in his
pocket, slammed the new one home.

A ragged volley of mixed fire came out of the woods—
handguns, shotguns, maybe a rifle. He heard a solid thwack
and then saw Albert Lee falling backward into the wheat.

He racked the bolt and it locked. He punched the magazine home, lifted the BAR—aiming at a pale gray flicker in
the shadowy woods—felt movement at his side, half turned,
and Abel Teague was *right there*, swinging that shovel like
a lumberjack taking down a tree. Danziger flinched, felt the
heavy blow glancing off the side of his head, wild blue lights
exploded in his vision, he knew he was falling, going down,
going down *hard*—

It's Not the Drop, It's the Sudden Stop

Nick could hear Kate's voice and in some part of his mind he knew he was lying in a hospital room and that he felt pretty damn bloody awful, but he was also standing in an upstairs window in an old farmhouse, from the light it was close to sundown, and he was watching a crowd of people some distance away, a loose column of men and women, following an old green hay wagon.

The wagon was being pulled by a horse, a big chestnut horse with a long golden mane, a Clyde or a Belgian. The horse looked familiar, but Nick couldn't figure out why. Then he remembered.

It was the same horse that he had seen galloping along Patton's Hard in the moonlight six months ago. *Jupiter* came to him, but he had no idea what it meant. Maybe it was the horse's name.

Nick knew he was dreaming, but he was awake enough—and perhaps cop enough—to take an interest in the *quality* of the dream. It had been his experience that some dreams cheated on the special effects stuff, at least in areas that weren't all that important to the dream, but he had to admit this one was pretty damn convincing.

The details were exactly right, down to the raspy feel of the worn-down window ledge under his hands, and the heat rising up from the wood, and that rickety old barn across the lane, and the generator muttering, and the pine forest far away, a low black line that squared off and contained what looked to be a field of wheat.

Nick recognized the wheat field. He had seen it once, although upside down, projected through a small hole in a window shutter onto a basement wall in Delia Cotton's mansion, Temple Hill. Like a room-sized pinhole camera. Just as in the image on the basement wall, there was a sledge of some kind far off by the edge of the pine forest, piled high with small white spheres.

Rocks?

Or skulls?

He looked closely and decided they were rocks, river rocks, rounded by water, and they were being used to build some kind of barrier fence along the edge of the pine forest. It was all completely familiar to him. Nick wondered if there was a word for the reverse of *déjà vu*.

Jamais vu, he decided, admiring the dream with an outsider's detachment. The dream was a perfect rendition of a country farm from back in the days of the Great Depression. It even had a faint sepia-tinted coloring.

The people and the horse and the hay wagon were a long way off, maybe a quarter mile, but he got the idea, looking at them, that he was seeing some kind of procession.

As they got closer he could see the people were wearing clothes from the thirties, cotton dresses for the women and bib overalls for a lot of the men. Farmworkers and their wives.

Looked like them, anyway.

When they came through the cattle gate and turned into the farmhouse lane Nick could see that there was someone laid out on the wagon bed, cushioned by a pile of straw, a long spare figure in a black suit. Nick leaned out the window, trying to make out the details; since it was a dream he tried to conjure up some binoculars but had no luck.

"Nick, honey, please . . ."

Kate's voice. She was *close*.

He turned around, half expecting to see her standing in the farmhouse room, smiling at him.

"Nick . . . can you hear me?"

The procession was closer now, almost up to the laneway gate. Soon he could make out individual faces and one stood out, a middle-aged woman with long black hair, lovely even at this distance, a curved and sensual body, wearing a pale green dress, carrying a parcel wrapped in an Indian-pattern blanket . . . He knew her, of course, because he had seen her once before, in a way that had burned itself into his cortex. She was Glynis Ruelle. He scanned the group for Clara . . .

"Nick, honey, if you can hear me . . ."

As dreams do, this one flickered and faded, although Nick tried hard to file away the details.

He opened his eyes.

Kate was standing there, looking down at him, her face lit by the bedside monitors. She was pale and trying hard to smile, although fear was right under her skin, bringing out her fine-boned skull, her deep-set green eyes.

"I can hear you," he said in a dry croak.

Kate turned away, came back with a plastic glass half full of water. It had one of those bendable straws in it.

He started to sit up, but a sizzling bolt of white-hot pain lanced through his ribs. He kept as much of that off his face as he could. Kate tried to stop him, but he made it all the way to nearly upright, at one hell of a cost, but he hated being on his back. People in hospitals always died on their backs.

Kate held the straw up to his lips, but he took the glass from her gently, with a bruised smile. When the round had smacked into him he'd hit the tarmac on his right side and his cheek was a black-and-blue tattoo. He sipped the water.

It was better than blessed. It was exquisite.

"Thank you, babe," he said, in a slightly more human voice. Kate was standing by his bed and looking at him as if he were the Risen Christ.

"Jeez, Kate," he said. "Stop looking at me like that. I'm not dead yet."

His thirst eased, he blinked away the remaining wisps of the dream—something about a farm . . . Glynis Ruelle . . . Clara Mercer.

He looked around the ICU unit.

He was in the middle of a bank of monitors and IV feeds. He had something dripping into his arm, a kind of clip device clamped around his index finger, and there was a large rectangular package sitting on the chair behind Kate.

And he *hurt*.

His entire chest felt as if he'd been kicked by a horse. Several horses. Big horses. Big horses with grudges. And he had stitches underneath some kind of wraparound body bandage. He could feel them like fishhooks in his flesh. He took a deep breath and regretted that immediately.

Past the chair was a large glass wall, and beyond the wall was a group of people: Mavis Crossfire, Beth and Eufaula, Tig Sutter, Boonie Hackendorff. They were gathered around a doctor and listening to what he was saying so intently that Nick could almost feel it through the glass.

"Okay," he said, leaning back into the pillow. "What's this? A wake?"

Kate glanced at the window. "That's Dr. Ginsberg. He's the one who sewed you up. He's explaining . . . you."

"I'm glad somebody can."

Kate smiled, not persuasively. "Your heart rate was all over the place. They've spent hours trying to control it."

"And?"

"They think they've got it managed. For now."

"Good. Then I think I'll go for a walk."

"You will *not*!" said Kate.

"It's from Monty Python," he said. "That Holy Grail movie. Damn, I *do* feel like hell."

"Joan called me on the cell. She said you had woken up and were talking."

"Yeah. That's good, isn't it?"

"When I left you were . . . very sick."

He studied her, fighting through the pain. "I'm sorry, babe. I'm sorry I scared you."

She smiled at him. "You scared us all."

He looked at the monitors and then at the plastic sensor clipped to his finger, and he followed that lead back to the Vital Signs display.

"I know I got shot. They told me so in the ambulance. But it didn't punch through. I remember that too. Hurt like hell, but . . . if I'm not all shot up, why the machinery?"

"Your heart. I told you. The bullet sent a shock wave through your chest and it made your heart rate go all . . . funny. There may be tissue damage. Your enzymes are all out of whack, whatever that means. How do you feel right now?"

"My heart, you mean?"

"Yes."

"How does it look, on that?"

Kate studied it for a time. Nick realized she had probably become an expert on ICU procedures over the last . . . how long? It also occurred to him that in the last six months he had ended up in the hospital at least twice, once when a prison van he was riding in hit a deer and rolled over, and now because he had gotten himself shot.

Maybe I should have stayed in Special Ops, he was thinking. *It would have been safer than Niceville. This town is trying to kill me.*

"It's . . . steady," she said. "Finally."

She went all shaky and had to sit down in the chair. She shifted the package to the floor, leaned back, shook her head at him.

"I've . . . I thought you were going to die." She started to cry, serious racking sobs.

Nick tried to reach for her.

Bad idea.

The room went bright and the pain in his side went zig-zagging all through his body.

The duty nurse was there, all brisk and bustle, smelling of Old Spice.

Nick figured they taught that bustling thing at nursing school, along with the *glove* thing.

"You're in pain," she said, which Nick felt was stating the Stunningly Fucking Obvious.

"You think?" he said, in a grating whisper. He had his eyes on Kate, who was trying to pull herself together. The only thing she hated more than crying was being seen while crying.

The nurse reached up, fiddled with an IV, handed him a gray plastic remote.

"This controls the morphine pump," she said, smiling at him. "Don't overdo it. You die now and I lose the pool."

"What's the prize?"

"It's split by outcomes. Your not dying has wiped out most of the night-shift players. But I'm still in. You live, but you're a drooling gomer, I only get fifty dollars. If you regain all your bodily functions, I get a hundred."

"How will you be able to tell? You volunteering?"

"No. Not that I wouldn't enjoy that. But I think we'll just ask your wife."

She backed away and stood by the curtain, hovering.

Beyond her the people were gone, shooed away by a floor nurse. Nick looked down at the parcel on the floor. Kate followed his look. "What's in the package?" he asked.

"Oh, nothing," said Kate.

Nick peered down at it. "Oh, come on. The mirror? Really?"

Kate straightened up a bit, set her face. "I thought you were going to die."

"So you were going to send me to Glynis Ruelle?"

"Yes," she said, thinking of the strange talk she had had with Glynis just a while ago. "I was."

And she was so dead serious that Nick couldn't even smile. It hit him that she was in worse shape than he was. "You know what?" he said.

"What?" she said with an edge.

"I could use a kiss."

She smiled.

"Where?"

"Let's start with the lips. Then we'll see."

She stood up, came in, leaned down. "Maybe I should pull the curtains?"

"Maybe you should get me the hell out of here. Then you can kiss me anywhere you like."

The staff didn't like it, not one tiny bit—neither did Kate—but they finally agreed to move him from the ICU into a standard room.

Kate managed to make it a private room. He took his morphine pump with him. He figured he was going to have to buy one that he could carry around with him on the job. He was never going to be without one again. *Morphine: It's not just for sissies anymore.*

Kate got him settled down into the bed. They were still

monitoring his heart rate, and he had the morphine pump, but the morphine pump reduced the chest pain to a minor irritation surrounded by a rosy glow. This in spite of the fact that he was wrapped up in bandages from under his arms to his hipbones and basically felt like a grilled bratwurst. With stitches.

Kate was at the window curtains, pulling them back. He was shocked to see it was almost sundown.

"What day is it?"

"It's Sunday evening."

"I've been out for twenty-four hours?"

"They had you sedated. They were pretty worried about you."

"So were you, apparently."

"I don't want to talk about the mirror."

"I can understand that. Where is it?"

"I locked it in the car. Are you feeling okay to talk?"

"Yeah. Starting with how's Reed? How's Mavis? And Lemon and Frank?"

Kate sat down on the chair, pulled it over close. Nick watched her face. Out in the hall nurses were gliding by and the PA system was asking for housekeeping in Room 307, with an edge of hysterical urgency. Nick said a silent prayer of thanks that he wasn't downstream from Room 307.

"Okay," said Kate, facing up to it, "Reed wasn't hurt. He's doing a PISTOL Shooting Report right now. Mavis is up and around. She has a cast on her ankle. Lemon's over in the Haggard Wing, with nerve damage in his arm. He's going to be needing a lot of rehab. And . . ."

Her face had gone pale again, and she looked as terrible as a woman that beautiful could look.

Nick had an idea what was coming.

"Frank . . . honey . . . about Frank . . ."

"Kate, what is it?"

She looked at her hands, took in some air. "Okay. Lemon

got Frank to the ER, and they gave him blood, stopped the arterial bleeding, got him stabilized. He was in the Annex ICU until three this morning. They figured he was okay to move to a standard room—all the ICUs in town are full and they needed the bed . . ."

Her voice trailed off and she looked as miserable as he had ever seen her look.

He waited.

"He was conscious . . . but he was agitated. Upset. He was looking for something, couldn't find it. Getting angry. They wanted to sedate him, but he refused it. He was thrashing around, aggressive. So they held him down and . . ."

"Tranked him?"

"Yes. When he was out, they put an orderly in the room with him. There was a shift change, the orderly was asked to help move a patient. Frank was still out . . ."

She lifted her head and looked at him. "When they came back, the bed was empty. The drawers had been rifled, the closet too, some of his clothes were gone. They looked for him everywhere."

Nick was feeling sick. He didn't know what was coming but he knew it was going to be bad.

"Did they find him?"

"Yes. In the east parking lot."

"How did he get there?"

"He jumped."

"*Jumped?*"

"Yes. They found his coat on the roof by the maintenance door."

Nick could not get his mind around this. "Where is he now?"

"He's . . . in the basement. The morgue."

Nick started to get out of bed, and his face went paper white, and the room began to disappear.

He got himself back in control. "Kate. Who's out in the hall?"

She found her voice.

"Beth and Eufaula went back to see about the kids. Mavis Crossfire is here. She's been in and out all day."

"Mavis. Good. Can I see her?"

"Are you sure?"

"I'm sure."

Kate went to get her.

In a minute they were back, Kate looking tight and worried, Mavis hobbling after her on a fiberglass ankle cast, but no crutch. She was in uniform, crisp and blue and gold. She looked as if she had lost weight, and some of her light had been dimmed, but she was still Mavis Crossfire. She came to the edge of the bed, looked down at him.

"Well, I'm happy to see you awake, my friend."

"How's the ankle?"

Mavis smiled, let it fade away. "Bugger my ankle. You know about Frank." A statement, not a question.

"Yeah. Kate just told me. How well can you get around?"

"Better than you."

"Have you looked at Frank's room?"

"The hospital room? Yes. I've been all over it. I was looking for . . . something. Anything that would explain . . . what he did."

"Did you find an iPod and some headphones?"

She thought about it.

"No. I didn't. I remember him wearing them last night before Yarvik showed up. I guess they took them away when they got him into the ER."

"Were they on his body? When they found him?"

"No. Not in his clothes either. I'd guess they're still somewhere in the ER downstairs."

"Kate says Frank was agitated. Anybody ask him why?"

Mavis gave it some thought. "They told me he was trying to get up . . . to look for something . . . and they wouldn't let him."

"So they knocked him out and left him alone."

"Yes."

"Without his Chopin," said Nick, mostly to himself, but they both heard it.

"Chopin?" said Mavis. "The piano player?"

"Yeah," said Nick. "The piano player. Mavis, can you go get somebody, bring him here?"

"Sure will. Who?"

"Jack Hennessey."

"The fire captain?"

"Yeah."

She thought it over. "No way he'll be free to break away. Too much going on. Got a fire at Saint Innocent Orthodox, a broken gas main at Bluebonnet and North Gwinnett. And a stuck elevator full of ankle biters at the Dial Tower. If you like I can try to get him on a cell, or Dispatch can patch me through."

"Got your radio?"

"I do."

"See if you can get him."

"Now?"

"Yeah. Please."

Mavis pulled out her mobile, keyed SEND, had a brief exchange with Central. Nick and Kate waited. A gurney went by, a body on it, covered with a sheet head to toe, one withered hand hanging down. The gurney was followed by two young women, both crying, and two men, the husbands, looking grim.

"Yeah, Jack, this is Mavis—have you got a minute?"

"I got thirty seconds."

They could hear a siren in the background, and men shouting, and machinery working, voices in the distance, a crowd of some kind. "I got Nick Kavanaugh here. Hold on."

She handed the radio to Nick.

"Nick. I heard you were shot?"

"Yeah. But only a little. Are you still wearing those head-phones?"

A pause. *"You called me about that? No offense, Nick, but we don't have nearly enough fans for all the shit that's flying around right now—"*

"Frank Barbetta's dead, Jack. He went off the roof here early this morning, and I think he went because they took away his headphones."

"Jesus."

"Do you still have yours?"

A pause. *"Yeah. Chopin. Got one bud in, 'cause I need to hear what's going on around me. It was Frank's idea."*

"I know. He told me why. Jack, my advice, you keep them both in whenever you can."

"I will. Fucking buzzing is like the worst migraine a man ever had. Look, you were there."

"In the tunnel? With Dutrow?"

"Yeah. Did you get it?"

"The buzzing? No."

"Lacy Steinert?"

"No. I don't think so."

"Barb Fillion?"

Nick looked at Kate, and the memory came back, the woman in a blue uniform touching the glass——*go wake them*——

Nick looked at Kate. "Kate, was Barb Fillion here last night?"

"She was. I was going to tell you—"

He went back to the radio. "Yeah, okay, looks like Barb Fillion was here."

"But her partner Kikki, he's dead, I hear?"

Nick looked at Mavis, who nodded.

"Man. I didn't know."

"*Well, there you go.*"

"What do you mean, Jack?"

"*Able-bodied guys.*"

"What, like she was *choosing* people?"

"*That's what Dutrow said, wasn't it? Down in the cave? Maybe the fucking thing, whatever she is, needed options. Spares. In case something went wrong.*"

"Why not me?"

"*No idea. Maybe you're immune. Who the fuck knows? But she got into Frank for sure, and me, and maybe Kikki Matamoros, and maybe it killed him.*"

"That what you are, Jack? A spare."

"*Maybe. She gets around to me, I'm going off a roof, just like Frank. That's hard, man. Hard. I really liked Frank.*"

"Yeah. Me too."

"*Look, I gotta run.*"

"Okay."

"*Nick. You got any idea what the fuck is going on?*"

"Yeah. I think I do."

"*Good. Then do us all a favor?*"

"I'll try."

"*You're a cop. Go fix it, will ya?*"

If You Go Into the Woods Today, Go Full Auto

Danziger was riding through the pines, deeper and deeper into the forest, the Hanoverian mare moving well underneath him, branches slashing at him, the horse jigging and jacking around the tree trunks, hooves clattering on stones and then kicking up red earth over the flats, pine needles flying around like splinters.

The horse was in beautiful condition. Danziger felt she could run like this for miles, moving like a dancer, never wavering, ears forward, intent and eager, seeming to enjoy the chase, and up ahead a half mile those pasty man-things were running and running, not even stopping to get off a hazing shot as Danziger closed in on them.

They had gotten a good long start on him because he had stopped to check on Albert Lee—*I'm not hit too bad, Charlie, go get the man*—and then racing to the barn to saddle up Virago, galloping back up the lane, passing Glynis, who turned to watch him go, calling after him, something he couldn't hear over the drumming of the horse's hooves and the jingle of her harness.

"I'll bring him back," he called to her as he drove through

the wheat field and put the horse to the stone wall. Virago rose up like a big black bird, and Danziger, soaring with her, felt a rush of sheer joy in his chest as Virago came down like silk on the other side, caught her footing, snorted, and accelerated into the trees.

And a half mile in, Danziger had spotted the guardians, a tight pack of them, pelting down the sloping forest floor, less than a quarter mile away, the pine trunks soaring up all around like temple pillars, like being in a massive green cathedral filled with amber light and striped with long black shadows.

On better ground, the trees thinning out, he kicked the mare into a flat-out gallop, risking it all—his neck, the horse's legs, both their lives—thundering over the needle-thick earth, jerking the reins left and right, the horse snaking around the pines like a black ribbon.

Three of Teague's men stepped out of a blind at a range of two hundred yards, lifting up their long guns. Danziger saw the flames erupt from their muzzles, heard buckshot pattering through the branches at his left, and then the sounds of the shots, muted explosions deadened by the forest pressing in all around.

He put the reins between his teeth, still moving fast, closing the gap, one fifty, one forty—they were men, or looked like men, pale and staring, expressionless, motionless, watching him ride in. The ground was an easy slope here and a good gunhand on a steady-going horse could fire on the full gallop more accurately than at a rocking canter—the three men fired at him again and Danziger felt a cloud of buckshot go zinging past his cheek and something stung his left ear.

He steadied the BAR and put out ten rounds—calm and steady single-shots—and the three white figures went rolling and writhing down, falling away as Danziger thundered up a small slope, crossed a stretch of flat ground, got to the bush blind, and rode through them.

A teenage boy, his chest a bloody pit but still moving, clutched at Virago's harness. Danziger pulled out his Colt and shot the kid point-blank. The blast took the boy's face off and he fell away. Danziger glanced back to see him on his knees, hands cupping his shattered skull, and then he went down onto his belly.

Danziger looked ahead and spotted another cluster of them, moving through the trees, maybe three hundred yards—seven or eight small figures in white and blue shirts and black trousers, and in the middle of them Abel Teague, black coattails flying as he stumbled over a fallen trunk. Danziger wished for a scoped sniper rifle as Virago balked at a sudden ravine and he had to rein her in. No matter. He had iron sights, a rear notch, and a blade up front. *Use what you've got.*

Halted now, with targets in sight, he dialed up the rear sight wheel to three hundred yards—*a shot any deer hunter could make*. He changed out the half-empty magazine, pocketed it, slammed in a full one, switched the fire-select button to A for auto, steadied the mare, and braced the BAR in a pine notch, centered it in the middle of the pack, on Teague's running figure.

Too many trees.

The BAR had an effective combat range of five hundred yards and those men were running away fast. He took his time, checked his sights again, concentrated on that tiny black figure; they were running toward a clearing in the forest, so he'd have no time for a second burst before they were back into the trees again . . . all or nothing.

Wait for it . . .

Wait for it . . .

Now.

All of them were out into the clearing, a ragged line of running figures, Teague out front. He let half a breath out, held it, squeezed the trigger; Virago, tight to the pine trunk, didn't buck or flinch—a perfect cavalry mount. Danziger emptied the box magazine—twenty rounds out in four seconds, spent brass chattering away to his right, casings clanging on stones, fire and blue smoke erupting from the flash suppressor, the gun jerking and pumping, his body braced against the recoil. A chain of copper-jacketed slugs—each weighing a third of an ounce and delivering a thousand foot-pounds of force on impact—went sizzling away at twenty-eight hundred feet per second. They covered the distance between Danziger and the running men in less than a heartbeat.

And hit them *hard*.

Danziger saw the blood flying and the black flowers sprouting on the backs of their shirts, their skulls bursting into shreds of bloody flesh, arms flailing as the heavy rounds ripped through them, and the tall black figure going down into cottonwood brush.

Then . . . nothing.

Silence and stillness.

No wind.

No birds no animals no brooks running.

Danziger's ears were stunned from the gunfire, and the world around him was wrapped in silence. He could feel Virago's barrel heaving under his legs, the mare blowing and jerking at her bridle, and the faint jingle of harness brass. He could hear his own breath rasping in his throat, his heart pounding, and when he touched his left ear, his fingertips came away bloody.

Across the valley floor he could see a scattering of dead men at the edge of a cottonwood stand, little doll figures, arms and legs every which way, blood spatters and splinters of white pine showing across the black tree trunks.

The light was fading. If they were smart, if any of them were still alive, they'd go to ground and wait for him to come to them. As soon as he started across this valley he'd be wide open. But this was a hunt, and there was nothing to do but go in and finish them off.

Danziger kicked out the spent magazine, racked the bolt back, slipped the half-full mag back in, slapped the base to set it in solid, flicked the fire-select button to F for semiauto.

Then he reloaded the Colt, stuck it into his belt, patted the horse's neck, and gently eased her forward. They worked down a sudden gulley, came up on the other side and out onto the valley floor.

The pines here were farther apart, and the ground was smooth, a carpet of pine needles, a few rocks here and there, some deadfall trunks rotting under the needle beds.

Beyond the forest the sun was going down, the golden rays slicing up the hazy forest air, and the sky up above was glowing violet and turquoise. The sound of Virago's hooves was muffled because of the dense blanket of pine needles and because Danziger was nearly deaf from the BAR.

As he moved toward the cottonwood stand and the scattered dead men he watched his flanks and he watched the branches overhead and he turned often to see if someone was coming up behind him.

It was entirely possible—even likely—that someone had lived through that terrible fire and Danziger could be riding into somebody's muzzle right now, the man tracking him from behind a cottonwood, his finger on the trigger, one eye closed, breathing, breathing.

Nothing he could do about that.

He got across the valley. No one shot him. Or his horse.

He reined Virago in about fifty feet away from the cottonwood stand, slid out of the saddle, and got his boots on the ground.

He led the horse forward and tied her—loosely, in case he got shot dead—to the upraised branch of a fallen pine, the branch sticking up out of a thick mat of pine needles.

Danziger, his nerves on fire, thought the spindly branch looked like a dead man's arm sticking up out of a shallow grave.

He raised the BAR up, covering the cottonwoods, and slowly moved forward, finger on the trigger, letting the rifle lead him.

Twenty yards on, right at the base of the stand, he reached the first dead man. He was lying on his belly, his legs splayed out, his head gone, bone fragments scattered in front of him like bits of broken crockery. Danziger used a boot to roll him over, bent down, and put a hand on the man's belly, feeling bones and gristle under his hand.

The body was cold.

He'd been dead for only five minutes, and he was stone cold. Danziger moved on through the others, checking each one, finding six men, and they were all dead, all shredded up by the BAR.

And a few yards up, another one.

A middle-aged white man, bony as a stick, skin as blue as skim milk, lying on his back, his entire belly gone, his intestines scattered around him like blue rope.

His chest was rising and falling. His eyes were open and he was blinking slowly at the sky.

Danziger stopped beside him, his Colt in his left hand, the BAR steady on the dying man.

The man—the guardian, the creature, whatever the hell it was—turned his head and looked up at Danziger. His lips moved.

Through the soundless bubble he was wrapped in, Danziger was barely able to make out what the . . . thing . . . was saying.

"I . . . can remember . . ."

"Remember what?" said Danziger, his own voice too loud inside his skull.

The creature closed its eyes and Danziger thought it was gone, but in a moment it opened them again. The thing had gray eyes and blue-white skin and black hair. It looked like a man. Maybe he was.

"I think there was . . . a yellow house." Closed his eyes again.

"What *are* you, anyway?" said Danziger.

"I . . . I'm not . . . not this." Opened his eyes, stared at Danziger. "What . . . what are *you*?" he asked.

"Charlie Danziger. A man."

"A man? So . . . was I . . . She's out of my skull now . . . and I can remember some things . . . I had a name . . . and a yellow house . . . and we had land . . . *She* got into me . . . but now she's gone . . . I remember I had a wife . . . and we had a yellow—"

He just *stopped*, his eyes still open.

Danziger eased into the cottonwood stand, as quietly as he could, pushing the branches aside with his Colt hand, keeping the BAR up, ready to fire. There was blood spatter on the cottonwood leaves. A few yards into the stand he came on a bundle of black cloth, Teague's suit jacket.

He picked it up—it stank of the man himself—and saw that one side of it was speckled with blood. He touched the blood. It was cold.

He searched for Teague's body all around the cottonwood stand and never found it.

On the far side of the cottonwoods the pines began again, and he could see where a man had run away across the forest floor, a crooked track cutting through the carpet of pine needles, the forest floor sloping gently away toward the tree line a mile down the hill.

He walked back to Virago, got in the saddle, moved out, skirting the dead things, picked up the foot trail. He slung the

BAR over his left shoulder, shifted the Colt to his right hand, kicked the horse into a trot, and followed Teague's path.

The last of the sunlight died and the dark came down on the forest, but Danziger knew exactly where he was, about a mile north of Belfair Saddlery, what was left of it.

That's where Abel Teague was going.

Had to be.

Otherwise, why was he running? Just to get ridden down and dragged back? Which meant Teague thought someone was already there, waiting for him.

Down on the slope, on better ground, Danziger put Virago into a canter again. In the fading light he could see the end of the forest about a half mile away, and beyond that an open space—the burned-out clearing where the Belfair Saddlery had been. There was a faint glitter through the trees, red lights. A car, a truck, something waiting.

And there, almost at the clearing, a patch of dirty white over black—Teague, staggering through a gap in the tree line, a tall figure stumbling, arms waving. Danziger twisted the BAR around, pumped out three quick shots ... Teague flinched but didn't go down, and now he was out of the woods. Danziger kicked Virago into a flat-out gallop and came pounding down the slope, the trees rising up in the half-light, swerving to clear a tangle of deadfall—putting Virago over another downed trunk, three hundred yards, two hundred yards. He saw the taillights flicker, dimly heard a heavy door slam. He was almost at the tree line and he could see a big boxy shape, pale, with letters on the side; it was rolling, he could see it moving through the clearing. Headlights came on, a blinding white cone that cut through the night. He heard the sound of wheels on gravel and the knocking rumble of a big diesel engine moving fast, lurching away down the forest lane that led out to Side Road 311.

Danziger broke out of the forest, reined the mare hard right, and pounded down the lane after those receding taillights. The truck—it was an ambulance, a Niceville EMT unit—was moving faster, bouncing and swerving over the narrow rutted lane, pine branches scraping the sides, pressing in all around, the head lamps making the trees look like a gray tunnel of hanging branches.

Danziger lifted the Colt and fired three aimed shots, saw sparks flaring off the bumper; one taillight shattered and went dark.

The ambulance heaved left, the brake light came on . . . a pause . . . Danziger coming closer—and then the engine roared up again, tires churning. The EMT truck was flying now, receding into the distance. Danziger fired three more shots and saw a section of rear window break into a spray of glass. It rounded a turn, bounced off a hedgerow, swerved again, almost out of control, and then it was out of sight around the curve, and he could feel Virago under him, heaving and unsteady, slowing down, winded.

He pulled her back to a canter, hearing her harness jingle and her breath chuffing like a steam engine. She was still good to go, not totally blown, but like the athlete she was, she needed a breather. He cocked his head and listened as they came down the turning of the lane.

There was a gate there, and beyond it the smooth blacktop of Side Road 311.

He could hear the truck accelerating, going away north, into the rising hills of the Belfair Range. He pulled Virago to a halt at the edge of the highway. Far away up the rising slope, he could see the truck in the distance, a moving patch of white, one red taillight glittering in the dark.

It cleared a rise and winked out, and he was alone on a horse by the side of the road, and the stars were coming out.

He sat there for a while, thinking it over, while Virago got her breath back, her head low, now cropping a bit at the sweet grass by the side of the highway. She'd need some water soon, and so would he. *North*, he was thinking.

What's north on Highway 311?

Gracie is north.

And what's in Gracie?

Candleford House.

Virago was tossing her head and snuffling at the air. Smelling water, probably. He gave her some rein and she clip-clip-clopped across the highway to the far side and found a brook running there, inside the sweet grass along the verge.

He let her drink—not too much—slid out of the saddle and knelt down to cup up a few handfuls of water. It was clear and cold and better than pinot grigio, at least right now.

He gave her five minutes.

No cars came by, no traffic at all, just a country road in the Belfairs. The stars were all out and there was a hint of a rising moon along the western slope of the hills.

Back to Glynis and work out a strategy?

Or saddle up and go north to Gracie, a distance of forty-seven miles by the highway, and a bit less cross-country. Better than a full day's ride, and when he got there, then what?

Much as he admired Virago, he needed a car.

He looked up at the night sky. It was now a sweep of stars, shimmering and clear. And the moon glow was rising in the west. The sweet-grass perfume was all around him, the stalks hissing in a night breeze. The road was a black ribbon with a solid yellow line down the middle. He looked off to the north, beyond the hill, and saw a red flicker against the sky.

Emergency lights. Police or ambulance?

Okay, decision time.

He saddled up and went north at a steady canter, staying on the side of the road, ready to ride down into the ditch if he heard a car coming.

Fifteen minutes later he cleared the crest and looked down a long slope where the highway ran into a covered bridge across Little Cut Creek.

Two vehicles were stopped on the far side of the covered bridge, some kind of pickup truck and the ambulance. Its roof rack and side strobes were churning red and white, lighting up the valley, sending flickering red fire rippling across the grassy slopes of the hillsides.

Danziger rode up to it, pulling up twenty feet away. He dismounted, led Virago down the ditch and up the far side, tied her off on a fence post.

He walked up to the ambulance, Colt in his hand, coming quietly up on the passenger side.

He checked the ambulance, saw a blond woman in an EMT uniform slumped over the wheel, blood on her neck and chest, blood spattered all over the dashboard, obviously stone dead. Other than the EMT tech, the ambulance was empty. He heard soft voices coming from the pickup—country voices, thin, querulous, male and female, an argument.

He came back around the end of the ambulance and stepped up to the driver's side of the pickup, an ancient blue Ford. He saw an old man sitting behind the wheel, faced away, barking at his passenger.

Danziger tapped on the glass and the old man jumped a yard, turning to goggle wide-eyed at Danziger. He had a sunken weather-beaten face and a ragged white beard, watery blue eyes. His passenger, a pear-shaped pink-skinned woman wearing a churchgoing hat and a frowny face, leaned forward to glare at Danziger from the passenger seat.

The old man rolled down the window. The smell of whiskey and cigarettes came off him in waves. "Jesus, son, you scared me silly."

"Sorry, sir," said Danziger, slipping into cop mode. "What's going on here?"

"You kin see for yourself, deppity. Coming down from Gracie, we see this ambulance off to the side of the road, stop to look, we kin see the girl just sitting there. Cora, she useta be a nurse, goes to check on her. Dead as a dog, she is. Looks like she been shot. In the throat. Bled out fast, like a hog on a hook. Cora and me are wondering what to do about it. And you come along."

He didn't seem to be worried about seeing a badge. He *was* wondering about Danziger's ride.

"You patrolling on a horse?" he said.

"Yes, sir. Have you seen any other vehicles on the road?"

They both nodded, and the woman answered. "Yessir, we have. Just this minute. Big old SUV was parked beside the ambulance, did a yoo-ee soon as we come down the hill. Went past us going like a bat out of . . . heck. Went back up toward Gracie. You think they was the shooters?"

Dear God. Probably watches CSI Miami.

"No idea, ma'am. Can you two just pull forward a bit and get off the road. Wait there a minute?"

"Yes, sir," they said in unison, and the old man put the truck in gear, eased away twenty yards, tires growling on the gravel at the side of the road. Danziger looked up into the hills all around and decided that Teague wasn't up there.

He was in that SUV.

He opened up the driver's side door, looked at the girl. He put two fingers up against her carotid, got nothing, tilted her head back. The right side of her throat was torn open, a grazing wound from a big weapon. Probably his Colt. There was a big star-shaped hole in the dashboard where the round had smacked in. She had a Streamlight in her vest pocket. He pulled it out, shone it into her eyes.

Fixed and dilated.

Like the old guy said, dead as a dog. She'd caught his round in her carotid and managed to get this far before she bled out. He put the light on her ID badge. FILLION.

Danziger vaguely remembered seeing her around from time to time, back when he'd been with State. How she came to be helping Abel Teague escape from the Ruelle Plantation he had no idea.

He looked at her com set, saw that it had been switched off. Reached over and flicked it back on, and got a lot of faint chatter on the emergency channel, frantic cross talk, bordering on hysterical, but a long way away. The truck was marked CITY OF NICEVILLE EMT, so he was likely getting heterodyne signal bounce off cloud cover from seventy miles down the valley.

He put the flash on the passenger side, saw mud marks on the floor, pine needles as well, and some blood streaks on the back of the seat, not much, but some. Teague, in the passenger seat.

He went around to the back, opened the gates. The gurney was a heap of rumpled sheets and a tangle of blankets. It looked as if someone had been lying on it. Probably not Teague.

Then who?

He closed the doors, walked back to the couple in the pickup. The old man was drinking from a bottle wrapped in a brown-paper sack. He tucked it between his legs as Danziger came up to his window, swallowed hard, tried to look innocent.

"Can I ask you for some ID, sir," said Danziger. The old man looked at his wife, who poked around in the glove box and came up with a battered leather wallet, handed it across to Danziger.

He looked at the ID, driver's license, and insurance, an address that ended in RR. Country people, from right around here.

He handed it back. "Mr. Coglin, my name is Charlie Danziger, I'm with the State Police, and I'm going to ask you to do a favor for me?"

Mr. Coglin nodded and said he'd be happy to do anything for law enforcement.

"I've called this in and I'm going to have to stay here until we get some units here—"

"Got to protect the crime scene, ayup," said Cora, and Mr. Coglin agreed. "Just like in *Gangbusters*, Cora."

"That's right," she said, smiling and nodding. "Or *The Adventures of Ellery Queen*."

"Ayup."

Ellery Queen?

"Yes, that's right. Do you folks know the Ruelle Plantation?"

"We sure do," said Mr. Coglin. "Miss Glynis owns it. A real fine lady. It's just a couple miles east of here, up along Little Cut Creek side road."

"I'm going to need someone to take this horse back up there. Do you think you could hitch her up to your truck here and take her to Mrs. Ruelle? Tell her what happened here, and tell her that Charlie Danziger was still hunting, and that he will be back as soon as he can."

"Told you that was Virago," said Cora with a vindicated air. "No other horse like her in the twin counties."

"Surely can, Officer Danziger," said Mister Coglin. "Guess you heard about all the troubles up there, eh?"

Danziger gave this a moment. "What sort of troubles, Mister Coglin?"

"There was some shooting, people are saying. Cora and me, we heard some of it not too long ago, back there in the pines. You didn't hear it, sir?"

"Yes, I did," said Danziger.

Mr. Coglin tapped the side of his nose. "Figured that's why you was on horseback. You catch the feller?"

"Not yet," said Danziger.

"Too bad. Shot a good man up there, a Mr. Albert Lee, who drives the Blue Bird bus."

"Salt of the earth he was," said Cora, "even though he was a cullud man."

Mr. Coglin gave her a censorious frown. "Don't know as he's dead yet, Cora. Only that he got shot. And cullud folks is as good as anybody," Coglin said with a prim smile, "and better than some what live right around here."

He came back to Danziger. "She meant no offense, officer."

"None taken."

"Well . . . you go on now, Officer, and you catch that man. I hear he is a bad one."

"The worst," said Danziger. "His name is Abel Teague. He looks like an old man in a white shirt and black trousers. Has a scar under his right eye. He's quick and he's strong and he's dangerous. If you see him, don't let him get close to you."

Mister Coglin reached under the seat, pulled out a large single-action Colt .44 revolver, held it up so Danziger could admire it.

Danziger, a little on edge, barely managed not to shoot him.

"Got this with me all the time."

"And he's good with it too," said Cora. "Stanley was a sharpshooter in the wars."

"Long time ago," said Mr. Coglin.

"Yes it was," said Danziger, keeping an eye on the Colt until Mr. Coglin put it away.

Shaking his head—*getting rusty; should have thought about the gun*—Danziger went back to the mare, patted her flanks, unbuckled her girth strap, stripped off her saddle and the sheepskin pad under it, carried the saddle and the pad over to the back of Coglin's pickup and stowed it, got the BAR, and the box of .30-06 rounds from the saddlebag. Went back and stroked her neck, talking horse talk to her, and she whinnied back at him. He got the impression that she had enjoyed the chase and was sorry to see it end. A real fine horse, fast, steady under fire, and damn brave, one of the finest horses he'd ever met.

Then he watched as Mr. Coglin got Virago roped to the passenger side of the truck, where she'd be clear of the engine's exhaust pipe. She whinnied a bit, but seemed happy enough to go along.

"Well, you two have a safe night," he said, as Coglin put the truck in gear. "And don't stop for any hitchhikers."

"We surely won't," said Mister Coglin. "Good hunting, Deppity."

Coglin, thin lips pursed—probably glad not to have to account for the bottle in the brown paper sack—pulled away at a crawl and was still going away at a snail's pace, Virago clip-clopping calmly along beside the passenger door, when Danziger went back to the ambulance.

He gathered the EMT tech up and carried her back around to the rear gates, lifted her on to the gurney. She was a pretty girl and he felt damn bad about killing her, no matter how poor her life choices had been.

There was a bicycle lashed up against the other wall of the ambulance, a Gary Fisher, whoever he was, red and gold, with big fat tires. Looked expensive and it meant not a damn thing to him.

He covered the young woman up with a red blanket, strapped her down, got some wipes off the crash cart, and spent a few minutes cleaning blood off the front seat and the dashboard.

Then he got behind the wheel, shut off the emergency flashers, put the truck in gear, and headed north up Side Road 311 with Gracie on his mind. He told Glynis he'd bring Abel Teague back, in the saddle or across it, and he was going to do that if it killed him. Whatever the hell *that* meant around these parts.

Well, come to think of it, based on recent experience, it sure as hell meant *something* serious, because he'd left a whole litter of dead men behind him. He may not be through the looking glass, but getting killed was obviously still very much on the table.

The Third Man

La Motta was trying to concentrate on the soccer game, but that fucking dog was going nuts, moaning his stupid strangled moan and snapping at the air. Delores had Frankie Twice's vocal chords snipped so he couldn't yap, but Jesus Christ, that dog could still bitch and moan.

He was in Frankie Maranzano's media room, wearing wrinkled boxers and a hula shirt, lying back in a red leather recliner chair, a pitcher of Stella propped up on his fat belly, staring at a flat-screen television bigger than Nebraska.

Italia was playing those Greek pansies and fucking *losing*, which was bad enough in itself, but La Motta had laid down a heavy load on Italia by two and right now they were down by three!

Three!

What the fuck is this, basketball?

Nobody racks up high numbers in a soccer match, and sure as shit not those fucking Greek—

Frankie Twice just would not stop. He was out there in the living room, moaning and snapping.

"Delores! Will ya shoot that fucking rat dog, will ya just?"

In a moment Spahn was at the door, his clothes all messed up. He had a headache or the flu or some fucking thing, and he was pissed.

"Mario, will ya shut the fuck up?"

La Motta looked at him, his anger rising up. They had been cooped up in this stinking pink palazzo for weeks now—okay, it was *white*, so fuck you very much—waiting for the all clear to start moving around the state again, and to be honest he was starting to miss his prison cell. At least he'd had some privacy.

"Where the fuck's Delores?"

"She's over in her wing, taking a shower or shaving her legs or something," said Spahn, who was twice as sick of Mario La Motta as La Motta was of him. "And Desi's down inna gym."

"Will ya go see what the fuck is eating that dog, Julie?"

"I missed the part where I got to be your butt boy," said Spahn, and then he started coughing, a wet racking cough, working his mouth like he was going to spit up.

"Jeez, Julie, you hork up a loogie in this room I swear I'll fucking—"

"Fucking *what*?" said Spahn, with ice and steel in his voice. Although he looked like a plucked chicken, Spahn was a killer several times over, a skill he'd picked up as a street kid in Bed Stuy. He always had a ceramic flick knife on him somewhere and he was as quick as a mongoose with it.

"Jeez," said La Motta, prying himself off the recliner with an asthmatic wheeze. "You're as cranky as fuck these days."

"I'm sick as a dog, Mario, and the phone's ringing and you're in here watching those pixie farts playing with a soccer ball. I gotta get outta bed and answer the fucking phone."

"I didn't hear it. That dog keeps—"

"Talk to the hand, Mario. Talk. To. The. Fucking. Hand. I'm going back to bed." Spahn said something in a muttering grumble as he made his way back down the hall.

La Motta followed him out. "Hey, Julie. Who was it? Onna phone?"

Spahn turned and glared at him, the pot-light in the ceiling making his vulturine face look like a skull. "Chi-Chi Pentangeli."

"Who is?"

"Jeez, Mario. Tony Tee's operations guy.",

"Yeah, okay. Chi-Chi Pentangeli. I remember him now. What'd he want?"

"To say thanks. From Tony Tee. He says Tony Tee says thanks."

"Thanks? For what?"

"For the *favor*. Remember?"

La Motta worked it through.

"You mean, the thing with Tito? That done already? That was fast."

"Not done yet," said Julie, coughing into a wad of Kleenex, holding it up to consider the results. "Not done yet, but Tito called him and said if he still wanted to, like, get in on it, then he should pick up Little Anthony and come on up. *The table is set*, was what he said. Tito, I mean. That's what he said to Chi-Chi."

"*The table is set*, hah? That's Tito for you. Well, I hope Tony Tee and his kid like what they're gonna get for dinner, and they better wear a big fucking napkin, 'cause the juices are gonna be flyin', that's all I got to say."

He waited for Spahn to get the joke.

Lately, Julie Spahn didn't get jokes.

"Yeah, well, whatever," said Julie Spahn as he turned away. La Motta heard his door slam with a solid thud—this was a well-made building—and he decided to call his lawyer tomorrow and see if the Do Not Associate With restrictions had been lifted yet. Because if they hadn't, he was going to try to pressure Munoz and Spahn to find somewhere else to coop up. Or maybe turn Tito loose on both of them.

He came back around the corner and out into the tennis-court-sized living room. The floor-to-ceiling window wall ran right across the whole front of the suite, ending at the other side of Frankie Maranzano's office, which was set apart from the main room by a wall of tinted glass.

It was a hell of a nice room, although right now a pigsty, but Delores had hired another housemaid, a guy this time—well, not really a *guy*, a blond-haired marigold named Raylon Grande. Delores had brought him around earlier this afternoon, and the deal was him coming in twice a week to dust and vacuum and shimmy-shake and all that nancy-boy horseshit.

La Motta shuffled across the carpet and stood in front of the window wall for a minute, staring out at the city lights at the last of the sunset going down off there in the west.

He sighed and belched and rubbed his hairy belly, feeling a bit melancholy. Maybe it was time to change things up around here. They were all getting stale. Like in that airline commercial. They needed to feel free to move about the—

And the dog went nuts again, howling now, back on his bony haunches, head back, screeching at the sky like a coyote. La Motta grabbed a pillow off the couch and winged it at the dog, missed, and knocked a lamp and the phone off the table by the end of the sectional.

"Christ," he said aloud, because it was one of those old-fashioned phones all tricked out in solid gold trim and white enamel, where the old-timey handset rested on a golden cradle and you had to dial the numbers in a circle thing using an ivory stick thingy.

Delores had told him once that it cost Frankie Maranzano six thousand dollars, and if that was true, then Frankie Maranzano was a bigger putz than La Motta had ever suspected.

He waddled over, bent down with a grunt to pick up the phone. Shit, it was all busted up, the handset speaker hanging off, the insides all spilling out like electronic intestines—

What the fuck! La Motta knew what he was looking at. A bug.

He leaned down, peered at it through his half-glasses. It looked like a tiny black bedbug, all scrunched up inside the mouthpiece.

La Motta had been exposed to so much electronic surveillance in his career that he felt he could read by the light coming off his own skin like one of those glow-in-the-dark crucifixes his mother used to hang over his bed so Jesus H. F. Christ could suffer down at him all night long.

So he knew exactly what the fuck he was looking at.

Frankie Twice was still whining, but at a safe distance. La Motta put the phone thing down, turned and stared at Frankie Twice.

That little fucker is in pain, he thought. *And what hurts dogs enough to make them howl?*

Sound does. High-frequency sound.

He went back to the window wall and looked out across the glittering expanse of Fountain Square at the Bucky Cullen Memorial Federal Building. Home of the Cap City FBI.

He spent some time considering the darkened windows of the FBI office across the square. He reached the inevitable conclusion.

"Fuck. Me. Blue," he said aloud.

"What'd he just say?"

"What'd who just say? Spahn or La Motta?"

The FBI guy sitting next to him at the monitor table shook his head, lifted a hand.

"Gimme a moment."

They were sitting in a darkened office on the seventeenth floor of the Bucky Cullen Building, a good two thousand yards away from the window wall of Delores Maranzano's suite on top of the Memphis. They were Pulaski and Gerkin, known around the office as the Picklers, a couple of FBI electronic surveillance techs that had been choppered in from Chicago to run the Maranzano surveillance, Cap City being short-handed due to the fact that weird shit was bubbling up out of the sewers.

They were a matched set of FBI techno-geeks, both of them pasty-skinned with close-cropped brown hair and steel-framed glasses and the bulging steroidal torsos of chronic heavy lifters.

Pulaski had the headphones and was running all the video recording gear and the laptop, and Gerkin had the laser mike and the digital spotter scope and a whole bunch of related techno-geekery.

The spotter scope was linked to an HD monitor that was giving them a shaky image of a large fat man in boxer shorts silhouetted in the third window from the left in the Penthouse Suite.

Night was coming on and the lights of Fountain Square were making the humid air all misty, so it was hard to make out the details.

But the laser mike was working fine. It registered microscopic variations in the window wall glass and somehow or other—neither Pulaski nor Gerkin was entirely clear on the details—turned those vibrations into the sound of people talking inside the suite.

Lately all they'd been getting was that fucking Chihuahua snapping at the window wall. They got bits of some kind of conversation between Spahn and La Motta, but that was deeper into the apartment, and all they could make out was something about a guy named Chi-Chi Pentangeli, who was one of Tony Tee's people, and Tito somebody, and the table being set.

"The table is set?" asked Gerkin. "What's Tito, the fucking butler?"

"Sounds like a code or something," said Pulaski.

"You *think*?" said Gerkin, doing an ironical eyebrow twizzle at him. "And who the fuck is Tito? Is he in the files?"

"I don't know. We'll have to listen to the tapes and check with Boonie. You're distracting me, okay? Just now, the fat guy in the boxers was yelling at the dog and throwing something at him—broke a lamp, I think. And then nothing."

Gerkin was watching La Motta in the window while he was talking. "And then the fat guy—La Motta—he comes over to the window, his hands on his hips, and stands there for a while, and then he says three words. What'd he say? Did you get it?"

Pulaski paused to think about it. "He said—I think I heard—Fuck. Me. Blue. Giving it the periods, like. *Fuck. Me. Blue.* The dog stops moaning, and then he starts up again." Pulaski took the headphones off.

"Yeah. That's what I heard too."

"Fuck. Me. Blue."

Gerkin frowned into the spotter scope. "What's that mean?"

Pulaski adopted a professorial tone. "In your community of goombahs, it's a phrase that is usually connected with an unhappy surprise or an unpleasant shock of some sort. Normally it has negative connotations." Pulaski put the headphones back on.

"He's just . . . standing there." Gerkin looked through the spotter scope. The guy was right there, big as a bear, a black shape. "I don't know," he said, mostly to himself.

"What?"

"I got a bad feeling."

Pulaski had worked with Gerkin for eight years now. Surveillance was all they did. They worked out a lot to keep the exterior look of a pair of FBI muscle guys, but under the beef they were pure geek. They might as well have been wearing matching plaid pajamas and living in a basement apartment on a diet of mac and cheese. "What's the bad feeling?"

Gerkin was shaking his head. "I think . . . I think that fucking dog just burned us."

Pulaski went back on the headphones. "Dog is still there."

"Yeah. And now La Motta is gone." Gerkin reached over, turned the power output on the laser mike down a couple of bars.

"Shit," Pulaski said. "The dog just stopped whining."

They were quiet for a minute while the implications sank in.

Finally Gerkin said, "I hate that fucking dog."

Coker sat back in the booth and stared at the laptop on the table in front of him. He was in a nice and private tuck-away booth at a coffee shop called Bean Me Joe across the Mile from the MountRoyal Hotel. It had a good view of the front door and the fire exits. He was looking quite bankerly in a dark blue suit and a white shirt and a long blue overcoat that was too warm for this unseasonable season but did hide the SIG pistol he was carrying in a Bianchi shoulder rig.

The coffee shop had free wireless and strong coffee and a wild-looking barista with fantabulous free-range bazongas inadequately constrained by a thin cotton tee with a picture on the front: Che Guevara wearing a Che Guevara T-shirt with a picture of Che Guevara on it.

One of her nipples was poking into Che's right eyeball, but the other one was way off by itself in a field of red fabric.

Maybe it was sulking.

From where he was sitting the coffee shop was packed

full, with one exception, of Tin Town hipsters, skinny guys in tight-legged jeans with baggy crotches and trick facial hair talking to morose dead-eyed chicks with piercings and tats. Being avant-garde and *ay-pat-aying les bourgeoisie* must be depressing as hell.

There was only one guy out of place, a big slouchy-looking mutt in a long brown overcoat that looked like it was made out of dead bath mats. He was sitting alone at a table near the front, his long hair hanging down, white earphone wires sticking out of his hair, staring into a gigantic cup of latte something and talking to himself. Although the place was crowded, nobody was sitting anywhere near him. He had that *do not feed the animals* look about him.

Coker, still very much a cop, was keeping an eye on him and on the street outside.

Tin Town was just getting up to speed. Niceville squads were prowling up and down, the blocks were filling up with Sunday-night partiers. Gypsies, tramps, and thieves. A few minutes ago, a few blocks away, he had heard the poppity-pop-pop of semiauto pistol fire, and then sirens.

Out on the sidewalk a couple of homeless guys were squaring off for a fight, from Coker's POV a knife fight. There was already a crowd forming. Money was changing hands. By the curb a short guy in a newsstand was talking into a cell phone.

Coker was trying to remember the short guy's name. Joko something. Frank Barbetta's snitch.

Barbetta, wounded and in the ER; Lemon Featherlight too; and Mavis and Nick. Coker hoped they were all okay. But yes, they had trouble, and there was trouble in the air tonight too. Right around here. He could feel it. He'd asked Boonie about it, about what was wrong with Niceville, and gotten the back of Boonie's hand for it.

Well, whatever it was, it wasn't his problem.

He was here to tidy up the ledger and then go back to the beach house and pick up on his retirement again. He had called Twyla's current throwaway to get an update on Bluebell and generally touch base, but the call went to her voice mail, so he left a brief message saying he was fine and he hoped she was fine and say hello to Bluebell. *Probably out shopping.*

Coker figured it would take max two days to settle the Maranzano file. Twyla could handle the home front okay, and anyway he didn't really want to hear Bluebell moaning and bitching about her life.

But she was Twyla's family, and Twyla was his family, so it looked like Bluebell was his family too. He'd have to think about getting her relocated eventually, but right now he was happy to be out of the beach house and away from all the drama.

The laptop beeped at him.

He was looking at a blue screen with the crest of the Federal Bureau of Investigation floating in the middle. Under the medallion was a line of bright red letters:

FBI CJIS ENTER PASSWORD AND AGENCY

Coker had a Moleskine notebook beside the laptop. He flipped it open to the page marked by the black elastic band, and read what Charlie Danziger had written there over six months ago.

Coker if you ever need this, first, I sure hope you don't because you suck at this stuff, and second, if you're the one doing it then I'm either dead or in prison. After the Gracie thing I went in to see Boonie and I gave him a flash drive with a list of all my employees. Looks like Boonie stuck it in his mainframe because now I've got a back door into his CJIS database if we ever need it. So if you do, the password is:

1stBtn2ndMarinesTarawa
and the agency designator is
SAIC FBI CAP CITY UNIT 298701
By the way if I am dead, I always wanted to let you know you
were a good friend and I'm real sorry about all those times I boinked
Twyla's brains out behind your back.
Just kidding.
No, really.
Trust me.
Semper Fi
Charlie.

Coker held the notebook up and carefully typed in the
password and agency ID, sat back and waited, half expecting
the machine to blow up in his face. It didn't, and after a few
more keystrokes he was looking at Boonie Hackendorff's Cap
City FBI case file for MARANZANO, F.

It was damned instructive.

It was particularly instructive in those parts that touched
upon the Community of Goombahs.

Boonie, smarter than he looked, seemed to have estab-
lished what Coker already knew, that Harvill Endicott had
been sent down to Niceville six months ago to collect on what
three Mafia goons had decided was their share of the Gracie
bank job, operating under the delusion that Byron Deitz had
pulled the job and that he had the money stashed away somewhere.

According to Boonie's analysis, after talking it over with
Nick Kavanaugh, after Nick and Coker had taken Deitz out
of the picture at the Bass Pro Shop, Harvill Endicott had
consulted with the goombahs—three guys named La Motta,
Munoz, and Spahn, who had a serious grudge against Deitz—
and the goombahs had told him to go ahead and find the
money, wherever the fuck it was, and get it for *them*, on the

basis of it was owed to them on account of karma and fate and because—like all made guys—they were greedy fucks who could eat the whole world and still wake up hungry.

Somehow Endicott had gotten on to a kid named Lyle Preston Crowder, the only weak link in that Gracie thing; Coker had wanted to kill the kid but Charlie had gone all Saint Francis of Assisi on the issue. Anyway, Coker already knew the rest.

Luckinbaugh had been tailing Endicott for them and reporting in, so when he let them know that Endicott had cornered Crowder in a Motel 6, Coker and Danziger had come in for a look and been duly burned by Endicott.

Like a pair of prancing putzes.

And Harvill Endicott had pulled together a team from Delores Maranzano's operation and sent them up to Danziger's ranch to get the money, and in the following clusterfuck Charlie Danziger took two in the chest while saving Mavis Crossfire's life. Much as Coker admired Mavis Crossfire, if anybody had checked it with him, he'd rather have Charlie Danziger alive and Mavis a dead hero.

But that's not how it went.

Anyway, it was all there, like a conga line of clowns doing the fucking cha-cha of Destiny. Mario La Motta, Desi Munoz, and Julie Spahn.

And the *goo-mai*, Delores Maranzano.

They were why Charlie Danziger was dead.

And Charlie Danziger was Coker's partner.

And when somebody killed your partner, you had to go do something about it. It was as simple as—

Noises up front, chairs flying around, tables going over, coffee mugs smashing, chicks screaming—and a big hoarse voice over it all, bellowing *Shut the fuck up please just shut the fuck up I'll do it I said I'll do it* in a hoarse ragged bray like he was losing his mind to *sheer fucking crazy*.

Coker saw the big goon in the bath-mat coat shoving the baggy crotch guys out of the way while he was reaching into his coat, coming out with . . . *an AK, where the hell would a mutt like him get an AK?* The guy had it out now and he was bringing it to bear right on the barista with the free-range bazongas—*ah shit*, thought Coker, who was halfway out the side door, *not her not those fantabulous tits.*

So he stepped back into the coffee shop with his Sig in his right hand and he lifted it up and he drilled the guy twice in the side of his fucking ugly head from a distance of maybe twenty-five feet, and through a sea of bobbing heads and screeching hipsters, which, he had to admit, was pretty cool shooting, all things considered.

The guy went over sideways, like that Kodiak bear at the Bass Pro Shop, crashed down through a pile of overturned chairs, bounced once, lay still.

Everybody was silent, staring at Coker, including the barista with the free-range bazongas.

"Is he dead?" asked Coker into the silent room.

One of the baggy crotch guys stepped in, stared down at the guy, looked back at Coker. "Yeah, I think so. His skull's all broke up and there's squishy shit running out of it."

"Okay," said Coker. "Well, it's been lots of fun and you all have a real nice evening."

He was headed for the side door with his laptop under his arm when the barista called to him. "Hey, you, Marine Corps, what's your name?"

"Harry Lyme," said Coker for some demented reason, giving her his wolf grin, and he was gone.

He had the coat off and he was jogging to his rental Town Car down the block with the echo of the gunfire still ringing in his ears and he was thinking as he slowed to a walk, *Now why the hell did I do that?* And the answer came back right away.

Free-range bazongas.

Much Ado About Nothing

They got Lemon out of his hospital room, they had to bluff down a duty nurse to do it, hurried him down the hall to the Haggard Lounge. There were people already in it: a pack of jabbering tweens, a random intern sleeping off the night shift, and the farm couple from Grant Wood's *American Gothic*.

Reed, who was in uniform, told them it was a police emergency, and they all hustled themselves out of the lounge and Reed shut the door behind them. They all stood there, looking at him.

Finally Nick, still in his bathrobe, sat down on one of the armchairs, taking a while to do it, and the fact that he was moving seemed to free up everybody else.

Nick had called a meeting, and this was *it*, as far as he was concerned, the last tango in Niceville.

Frank Barbetta was dead because Nick wasn't taking this problem seriously enough. He had made the decision, internally so far but he was about to make it clear to everyone else, that they either figured out something useful right now and then went out and did it and had some success doing it, or he was taking his wife and his family and anybody else who wanted to come and he was getting the *fuck* out of town as soon as he could walk ten yards without passing out from the pain.

Sitting around the room in silence, aware that something major was coming from Nick, were Reed and Kate, along with Lemon and his entourage, Lemon bound up like a mummy, his left arm wrapped tight against his chest, shirtless, and still somehow managing to look like a GQ model.

Beth and Eufaula were taking care of the kids and Mavis was back out on the streets, trying to cope, trying to keep the lid from flying off.

There was coffee, stale but hot, on a side table, and a flat-screen TV with the sound off was showing a Cap City CNN report from a coffee shop down in Tin Town, where there had been some kind of shooting—VIGILANTE SHOOTER SAVES THIRTY AS SMALL SOUTHERN TOWN SLIDES INTO CHAOS was the crawl—under a video of a well-developed girl in a red Che Guevara shirt talking to Sarah Band.

Everybody got their coffees and sat themselves in a rough half circle around Nick's armchair, where he was leaning back, stone-faced, arms on the rests, pale and tight.

He sighed, looked at Kate, who was eyeing him warily, and then he looked around the room. "Okay. Here it is. There is something wrong with Niceville and it isn't going away. Lemon knows it, Reed knows, Doris knows it, and I know it. I have no idea what the hell it is. And if we can't figure out a way to deal with it, we should all get out of town."

"Okay. Out *when*?" asked Reed, cool but intense.

"Out as soon as I realize there's not a fucking thing we can do about it."

"Then you should go now," said Reed, "because I've seen the thing up close and what I did about it was to back myself out of a fourth-floor window and hit every branch on my way to the ground."

"Candleford House," said Lemon, who had heard the story.

"What is this Candleford House?" asked Helga.

Reed gave it a moment, did a check-glance at Nick, took a breath, and laid out the history of the place in a few words, leaving out the part where Clara Mercer's ghost had told him that Rainey Teague needed to be killed before Abel Teague could take over his body and live another hundred years. He ended with the story of what happened to him when he got up to the top floor and ran into *nothing*. Helga listened, thought about it.

"You all call it *nothing* but it is very much *something*, yes?"

"Yes it is," said Doris Godwin, "my people have always known what it is. It is a demon. My people call it the Kalona Ayeliski."

"The Raven Mocker," said Lemon.

"Yes. The Raven Mocker. Because it imitates the sound of a real raven, and its presence is signaled by ravens. It has been in this part of the world long before our people came here. Would you like to know what it does?"

"Very much," said Helga.

"It's a spirit, invisible, but sometimes it takes the shape of an old woman. When people are weak, dying, she comes in at that hour and *feeds* on the soul of the dying person. Each soul she sucks in gives her another year of life. She feeds on suffering, on pain, on anguish. The sharper the suffering, the longer the dying, the more she is satisfied. That is the Kalona Ayeliski."

"We too had stories," said Helga, "in Reykjavik, similar stories. The *draugir*, my father told me of them, they would come to eat the souls of the living, but they were only the bodies of dead men come back to life."

"Well, the Raven Mocker is a fuck of a lot more dangerous than some dipshit Viking zombie," said Doris with an edge. Helga stayed cool.

"I see that it is. This spirit, this Raven Mocker, how did your people fight it? With spells? With other spirits?"

"No. With a sing. And with smoke. There were people who hunted the Raven Mocker. It was what they did. They knew she was coming because of the ravens or crows that were flying around her."

"Like the crows on Tallulah's Wall," said Kate. "Doris, tell us where the name Tallulah came from."

"There is a pool on top of that wall, the Niceville people call it Crater Sink. But we, my people, called it after an eater of souls who lives in it, and her name is Tal'ulu. It is where the name Tallulah comes from."

Doris turned to Lemon. "Do you have your cell phone with you?"

Lemon did. He fished it out of a pocket in his robe and handed it to her. Doris flicked through to his photos and handed the phone over to Helga, who looked at the screen. Pictures taken by the camera's flash in the middle of a forest at night. In each photo there were people standing under the trees, staring back at the flash, hundreds of them, men and women, some in ordinary street clothes, but varying in fashion as if they were from different eras.

"What are these?" Helga asked.

"Doris took those shots two months ago, on top of Tallulah's Wall. She was helping me get a kid down from there, and she could *feel* something out there all around us. In the forest, in the dark. She had a camera. This is what she got."

Helga looked down at the phone again, paging through the shots, frowning. "These people . . . they are from different times, different ages . . . I see soldiers from your Civil War, I see Native Americans, people who look like villagers from a long time ago, people from the Depression, others look like they are from the fifties . . . and they all look . . ."

"Dead," said Nick.

"And these people . . . are they ghosts?"

"We have no idea," said Doris. "Images, maybe, just images burned into the air around Crater Sink. Like the images of ash people that were burned into the walls in Hiroshima and Nagasaki. But whatever they are, the old forest around Crater Sink is full of them. There may be thousands of them. If this is hard for you to understand, then stop trying to understand it. It is what it is. No amount of science is going to explain it."

She glanced at Kate, as if considering whether it was cruel to carry on. But she did. "We believe, Lemon and I, that they are people whose souls have been eaten by Tal'ulu."

Helga stayed on point.

"Is this Tallulah—"

"*Tal'ulu*," said Doris.

"Tal'ulu . . . is she the same spirit as the Raven Mocker?"

Doris thought about it. "Our people did not think so."

"But, according to what Lemon has told me, about this entity he is calling *nothing*, doesn't this entity behave exactly like your Tal'ulu spirit?"

"Yes," said Nick, remembering Jordan Dutrow's death. "This thing enjoys human pain. Suffering. Grief. She gets off on it. She eats it and drinks it."

"And you have *seen* this?"

This got under Nick's skin. "I have seen what happens to people she gets control over. Would you like to hear some specific details, because—"

"Nick," said Kate, "no need to do that. I think Helga was just asking for confirmation."

"Yes," said Helga. "Please. You do not need to give me . . . details. I do not want to hear the details. I can see them in all your faces."

She went back to Doris. "So your people, when they fought the Raven Mocker, they did what you call a *sing*? I know of such things in many cultures, but I do not assume to know what it is in yours. Can you describe it for me, what is this *sing* in the Cherokee world?"

"What it sounds like," said Doris, but with some of her edges smoothed off. "It's a chant, a very specific chant, and it has to be sung exactly right. There are other things that are a part of it, sharpened sticks, a call for the Red Warrior and the Purple Warrior, and smoke. But the chant is what has the power to drive away the Raven Mocker."

"So you fight the Raven Mocker with *sound*, in other words?"

Doris, along with everyone else but Lemon, was surprised by the question. "Yes. A song is made of sound."

"And did it work?" asked Helga.

"Yes. According to the stories, if the singer was skilled and came in time, then the Kalona Ayeliski was driven away."

"This is all lovely," said Reed, "but if our plan here is to take the choir from Holy Name up to Crater Sink and lay some Handel's *Messiah* on her, you can count me AWOL. I've locked horns with this bitch, and trust me, Handel isn't going to cut it."

"Chopin did," said Nick.

Reed didn't know about that part, so Nick filled him in on Blue Eddie's advice to Frank Barbetta, about Chopin.

"I saw that. Frank had headphones on when he came to see us at the house."

"Yeah, and when somebody took them away, Frank killed himself rather than let the . . . buzzing . . . take him over."

There was a silence.

"Then he was a brave man," said Helga.

"Yes. He was," said Nick.

"And listening to Chopin, this had an effect on the . . . the buzzing?"

"Frank thought so."

"But this sound in his head, has anyone else heard it?"

"Yes," said Nick. "I heard it when we were down in the storm drains."

"And what was it like?"

Nick thought about it.

"Like . . . radio static. A cross between hissing and buzzing. High-pitched—"

"Was it steady, or did it rise and fall?"

"It . . . varied."

"Did it ever start to sound like speech?"

Nick shook his head.

"I never gave it a chance. But a kid named Jordan Dutrow got infected by this thing, and he said it talked to him. So, yes, I'd say it could sound like speech. Where are we going with this?"

Lemon spoke up. "Helga has a theory, about this whole thing."

"I'd love to hear it," said Nick.

"We all would," said Kate.

Helga looked at Lemon and then back to the other people in the room. "You know about the bone baskets? That Lemon found?"

"Nick and I both found them, Helga."

"Yes. Sorry. They were in a riverbank, yes?"

"Yeah," said Nick. "Along the Tulip."

She looked over at the coffee table, saw the white plastic box with the digital panel. "That is a microwave. What happens when you leave something in a microwave for too long or set the power too high?"

"You get crispy critters," said Reed.

"Crispy critters?"

"Reed means you get stuff that's burned to a crisp," said Kate.

"Yes," said Helga, "and burned by what?"

"Microwaves put out radiation," said Nick. "The wavelength comes in somewhere between radio waves and infra-red radiation. The waves cause molecules to vibrate—to heat up—"

"Yes," said Helga, "because heat is really just molecules in rapid motion."

"Okay," said Reed. "And?"

"We do not yet know how Lemon's bone baskets were made—this will take many years to understand—but I believe that they are whatever was left after this entity consumed all those people."

"Jesus Christ," said Reed.

"This is not a matter of God and Satan. This thing is a *being*, an entity. I believe it is made of radiation. It exists as a type of wave that comes somewhere on the radiation spectrum. Where we do not know yet, but—"

"Helga," said Nick, "this thing *thinks*. It plans. It *operates*. It's a thinking being. It's a lot more than just a string of electrons. It reasons. It remembers. It makes plans. It's *alive*."

"Yes. It is alive. It thinks. It makes plans. And so do you. So do we all, yes?"

"Okay," said Reed. "Not tracking you here."

"We do all those things too, and we too are really nothing more than a string of electrons."

"Oh, Jeez," said Reed. "Here we go, down the rabbit hole. Quantum mechanics?"

"Yes," she said, with heat. "Down at the quantum level, we are all just . . . energy waves—"

"Or energy particles," said Nick, who had read his physics texts. "Nobody knows which."

"The theory is we're *both*," said Reed. "But this thing, it doesn't have a form, a body."

"We do not know that," said Helga. "I have Googled the geological charts for this area. You have this big lake under-neath us here, it is called the Sequoyah Aquifer?"

"Yeah," said Nick, remembering Arnie Driscoll's lecture at the Dutrow scene. "It runs from the Belfairs all the way down to Cap City."

"And does this Crater Sink connect to it?"

"Yes. At least, we're being told it does."

"So there is your *body*, Reed. The entire valley of the Tulip River. From Gracie down to Cap City. The limestone shelf that lies underneath the earth right here. That is the *body* that this entity lives in. What is the one element that is present in all of these places?"

"Water," said Kate. "The Sequoyah Aquifer. The Tulip River. Crater Sink. The storm drains under Niceville. Water is the single common element in all of this."

Helga looked at her with approval. "Yes. That is correct. Water is a great conductor of sound, of electricity, of waves. I believe that *nothing* lives in water. That it uses water as a conduit to project itself."

"There's no water in Candleford House, Helga," said Reed. "And it was sure as hell *there*."

"Look, Helga," said Nick, who had heard enough. "I get it about the radiation. I get it about *waves* and water. I think you're about as right as we're going to manage. I'm still not hearing what the hell we can *do*. How do we fight this thing?"

"*You* don't," said Doris. "I will fight it."

"Fight it *how*?"

"With a sing. I will go up to Crater Sink and I will drive her back down into the earth. Lemon will come with me, if he can."

"I can move. I can't drive, but I'm going."

"You're not going anywhere," said Nick. "You just got out of surgery."

"So did you," said Kate.

Nick looked at her, and then at everyone. "This is nuts. No

disrespect, Doris, but we go *sing* at this creature? This is the *best* we can do?"

"It's nuts, okay," said Reed, "but I'm damned if I can think of anything else to try. Can you?"

Nick didn't have a good answer for that. He looked at Helga. "Anything, Helga?"

"I was thinking that energy waves can be canceled out by other energy sound waves. This may be why Chopin's music had an effect on the *voices*. But I cannot think how we would do such a thing."

"Such a thing," said Doris, "is called a sing."

Helga worked that through. "I think you may be right. And I can think of no better course right now. When do you go?"

"Now," said Doris, standing up, looking at Lemon. "There are things we need to gather."

"May I go with you?" said Helga.

Doris gave her a long hard look. "For a sing to work, everyone has to have a strong belief. If you're weak, if you waver, if you think like a scientist, if you try to reason through it, she will get inside you. You'll end up like those things in the forest. You must have a very strong mind to keep her out, a *quiet* mind."

"I won't waver," she said.

"I'll go too," said Reed.

"There is no point in *all* of you going," said Kate, an edge of impatience in her voice. "If Doris and Helga can do this— God help you, but I think you're crazy to try—and Lemon will back them up, then there are other things that need doing too."

"Like what?" asked Nick.

"Like finding Rainey."

Nick managed not to say what first came to his lips on the

Finding Rainey question. He was looking for a phrase that was slightly less inflammatory when Reed cut in.

"Kate's right," he said. "We need to find him right now."

"Why right now?"

"Here's why," said Kate. "Rainey is gone because somebody has plans for him. Remember what Reed saw in Candleford House? What Clara Mercer told him?"

"Man," said Nick. "A ghost story."

"You're drawing the line at *that*," said Reed, a big grin, "but you're *fine* with the rest of it?"

Nick had to smile at that. Reed was right. The whole thing was absurd, a fever dream.

"Okay," he said, "I'm in. Where do we start?"

"Find Barb Fillion," said Kate.

"Why her?"

"Because she's got Rainey. Find that ambulance and you've got Rainey."

"How do you know this?"

"You know it too," said Kate.

And then Nick remembered, the blue girl behind the window, and the thoughts in her head that came drilling through the glass . . . **go wake them**

That wasn't the girl in the EMT uniform. That was the thing inside her head.

It was the voice of Nothing.

"God . . . you're right."

"Yes, I am."

"Reed, can you go down to the ER and ask them if Barb Fillion's EMT truck had a GPS transponder?"

"They all do," Reed said on his way out the door.

Nick looked at Kate. "I'm going with him."

"No you're not. You can't. What help could you be? You're practically a cripple. You're in no shape to go anywhere but back to your room."

"Kate . . ."

"What?" she said, with steel.

"Do you *really* think I'm going to go lie down right now? Watch some football? Maybe have a nap?"

"Nick—"

"Kate?"

They locked on for a while.

"Fine," said Kate. "But I'm going too."

"Kate—"

"Not one more word, Nick. Not. One. More. Word."

"Man," said Lemon, "if I were you, Nick, I'd shut up right now."

Nick shut up.

The Running of the Rats

They held a summit in Julie Spahn's bathroom because it was at the back of the suite and farthest away from the window wall overlooking Fountain Square, and because Julie Spahn, who had his very own electronic bug detector, had swept the rest of the suite and, other than a contact bug they found underneath the number plate on the front door, declared the place clean.

They had not swept Delores's master bedroom, because she was still in it, with Frankie Twice, watching a movie, and the door was closed and probably locked, which she had taken to doing lately, after Desi had tried a couple of times to stop by for a grope and a tumble.

Spahn, now sicker than two dogs, got the spindly gold-wire and white-fur decorator chair that stood next to the Jacuzzi—the same Jacuzzi, by the way, that had been stuccoed with a variety of Harvill Endicott bits a couple of months back.

Desi Munoz, still in his workout gear and smelling of A535 rub and greasy sweat, was sitting on the can, breathing heavily through his open mouth, since his adenoids were a burden to him and to anybody else within hearing. He and Spahn were sitting quietly and watching Mario La Motta's temper boil over and run down the side of the pot.

"That fucking spic skank—"

"You already used that one," said Spahn, whose head was pounding. "Get to the point, will ya. I feel like shit here."

"We ought to bring her in here—"

"Keep your voice down," said Munoz. "She hears us, she'll call 911 in a New York minute."

"Where is she?" asked Spahn. "Right now?"

"She's in her bedroom," said Desi Munoz, "watching *Pride and Prejudice*. Again. Every Sunday, that's what she does. Mr. Fucking Darcy, in her red silk pajamas. Let me go get her, we can all have some fun taking her apart."

"No. Leave her alone. We gotta *finesse* this, Mario," said Spahn. "You can't just chop her up inna Jacuzzi. They got surveillance on us, they got a laser mike on the windows. And we're not supposed to be associating, remember?"

"Fuck finesse," said Munoz. "Finesse is for little Jew-boy *maricones*!"

Spahn studied Munoz for a while, marking him with a Best Before date, and went back to La Motta.

"Mario," he said in a low but carrying voice, "here's what we gotta do."

"Get that bitch in here and—"

Spahn stopped him with a raised palm. "No. She's for later. Maybe for Tito. Right now the most vulnerable thing we got is all of us sitting here in the same place."

"They've already got us for that," said Munoz. "Probably got us on film, so we're fucked."

"Maybe they do," said Spahn, "and maybe they don't. Right now, all we gotta do is split up. Mario, how long you figure they had a laser on us?"

"Jeez," said Mario, "how long's the dog been whining and snapping? Maybe twenty-four hours?"

"Okay. And the bug inna phone—"

"Wasn't attached," said La Motta, "I shook the handset and out it drops."

"So that Raylon guy, he didn't have time to attach it. And the fact that they had to send him in like that tells me they didn't have any choice. Why? Because the bug in the number plate wasn't working good enough. The rest of the place is clean. So far, my bet is, they got a few pictures and some voice. The fact they haven't made a move on us tells you what?"

The other two thought about it.

"We're not the targets?" said Munoz.

"That's right. I mean, we haven't made any moves, we're just visiting the widow of a business colleague. Haven't left the building other than to get some meatball sandwiches and a beer. Even the associating beef is little-league bullshit. This is all about Tony Tee and his Miami crowd. They rolled up three of his operators last spring. Now they're here sniffing around, looking for more."

They liked the sound of that.

"So . . . what do we do?" asked La Motta. Spahn liked being asked. The power balance was shifting his way. All he had to do was put his thumb on the scales a bit. "We're out of here, right now. All of us."

"Where'm I supposed to go?" said Munoz. "I got all my stuff here."

"You got money?" asked Spahn.

"Yeah . . . money I got. A few Gs and my Mondex card. Maybe fifty large."

"Then you go throw some shit in a bag and find a hotel."

"What if they got people watching me? They'll see me coming out of here."

"So leave your Caddy down in the parking level. They'll be looking for it. Take the fire stairs, leave by the loading-dock gates. I already scoped it out. Dark back there, nothing but Dumpsters and a Porta-Potty and stuff. You walk a few blocks, make sure there's nobody on you—you can do that in your sleep—catch a cab, find a nice hotel somewhere close. There's a Westin a couple blocks over. You still got your Hermenegildo Garcia ID, all that shit?"

"Yeah. It's still good. Came down here on it, haven't used it since."

Spahn looked at him.

La Motta looked at him.

"So?"

"So what?" asked Munoz.

"So go."

"What, right now?"

"Yeah," said La Motta. "Go check into the Westin. Right fucking now."

"We'll be right behind you," said Spahn.

Munoz looked at them, trying to figure out why he was getting a slithery feeling up and down his back. Was he being handled?

Either way, time to get some distance here.

"Okay," he said, getting up. "I'll go shower, get the fuck out. But I'm with Mario. We gotta do that bitch."

"We will. Just not tonight," said Spahn.

"We're gonna put Tito on her," said La Motta.

"Man," said Munoz, "I'd hate to miss that."

"We'll see how it goes," said Spahn. "If you can't be here, we'll film it, send you a clip."

"How'll we know Desi got clear?"

Spahn thought about that. "Got a throwaway phone?"

"Yeah. A couple."

"Just phone here. Soon as you're clear. Ring three times, hang up."

"They'll pick up the number."

"That's why they call it a throwaway."

They went back and forth for a while, but in the end Munoz showered and changed into some dark clothing and jammed some stuff in a valise and took the fire stairs all the way down to the freight floor. He hopped down off the Dumpster dock, checked for people in cars or vans or hanging around. There was nobody. He jogged up the alley, reached the corner—still nobody—did some jigs and jags trying to bring out any watchers.

Still nobody.

He hailed a cab on Nathan Bedford Forrest Avenue, threw his valise in ahead of him, hopped in, told the cabbie to take him to the Westin, and was gone in sixty seconds.

He turned around and looked out the rear window a couple of times, saw nothing. Just typical traffic, cars and trucks and vans and cabs, people strolling around, cops on the corners, sirens in the distance, downtown Sunday night in Cap City.

Did not pick up on the black Lincoln Town Car that eased out into the block and fell in six cars back, like a big black shark, just gliding along, smooth and silent.

An hour later Munoz was safely in his rooms, a corner unit at the Westin with city views north up Garrison and east along Cannon Palisades, sitting on the edge of the king-sized bed with a miniature bottle of Johnnie Walker Red clutched in his paw and having a crisis of belief.

He had made it to the hotel and that puzzled him, since it had been his experience that once the feebs had their teeth in your ass they were as hard to dislodge as herpes, and Munoz knew better than anyone what a sore trial that affliction could be to a man of his delicate sensibilities. But nobody got in his way or even showed a tail, and he was wondering if maybe he wasn't being *handled* just a bit by Mario and Desi.

Well, he made the call anyway, three rings and a hang-up, but as he redialed to order up a steak-frites and a cheese plate and a bottle of Barolo, he resolved to address these issues in a more forceful way, perhaps by bringing in some of his own people to add weight and muscle to his—

Three knocks at the door, done with a key, which usually means room service or a maid.

A maid.

He had ordered turndown service because he liked the little foil-wrapped chocolates and he also liked having a young maid in his room so he could fantasize about grabbing her by the—

The door to the suite opened and a tall silver-haired hardcase in a long blue coat walked straight across the carpet and had the muzzle of a large stainless-steel pistol—maybe a SIG—zeroed on the spot between his eyes where his eyebrows would have separated if his eyebrows separated, which they did not. Munoz frowned into the muzzle, which made his unibrow bunch up like a caterpillar.

"Who the fuck—"

Behind the stranger the door slid quietly shut on its spring-loaded hinges.

"In the bathroom" said the guy, a sort of cowboy edge in his voice. The guy looked vaguely familiar, and it occurred to him, while he was regretting the fact that his little black Sigma pistol was in his bag across the room, that he had been right, that he had been set up by La Motta and that little Jew bastard.

Apparently, in the view of the tall guy with the face like a canyon wall and weird yellow eyes, Munoz was taking too long to comply, because the guy, quick as a snake, raked Munoz across the left cheek and the bridge of his nose with the barrel of the SIG. Munoz, blind from pain, reeled back and rolled away and got to his feet, thinking *Okay, this is a shakedown or a hit, but either way a guy as smart as me could always—*

"Into the bathroom," the guy said.

Munoz steadied himself on the wall, shook his head. His nose hurt like hell and he could feel blood all over his shirt.

"Look, whoever the fuck—"

Got himself raked with the barrel again, across the right eye and right cheek, and now he was almost fucking blind and a little worry-worm crawled into his lizard brain as he reeled down the hall toward the bathroom.

Got to think got to think of something got to make a move right now—

"Stop right there," said the guy.

They were at the door into the bathroom, a big lush space all chrome and slate and a Jacuzzi the size of a Vegas hot tub.

"Turn around."

Munoz turned around, blinked one eye half open—he *knew* this guy from somewhere—and what he saw in the guy's face let him know that if he was going to make a move, it had better be—

"Charlie Danziger," said the guy, and he pulled the trigger. Munoz, who had no fucking idea who Charlie Danziger was, never heard the shot, just a flash of blue light as the round went through his forehead, tumbled a bit, plowing a trench into the middle of his brain, chugged straight on through and blew out the back of his skull and it took all of Desi Munoz with it and he went straight down to his knees, tottered— Coker gave him a little shove with his wing tip—and fell onto his back with a meaty thud.

Didn't bounce, not even once.

Coker looked down at the guy, put a safety shot through the bridge of his nose and another into his chest. Looked down and noticed he had some blood spatter on one of his Allen Edmonds wing tips.

Got a towel and wiped that off, checked himself in the mirror, straightened his collar and cuffs, and took the fire stairs eight flights down, his long blue trench coat flying out behind him like the wings of a messenger angel.

Spahn and La Motta were packing when the phone rang. Spahn looked at the clock on his bedside table—fifty-eight minutes. He watched the phone while it beeped at him—*what if Delores picks up? . . .* but she didn't. Too busy with Mister Darcy and Pemberley and all that Brit shit.

One ring, two rings. Three rings.

And it stops.

Okay, he thought. *Desi got through, which means there's no serious surveillance. Good to go.*

Now get La Motta gone.

"Why do I have to go next?" said La Motta. He didn't like being pushed out the door. He'd been resisting it ever since Munoz had called in. It was in the back of his mind to leave last and spend some quality time with Delores before he closed the door.

"Because you're gonna kill Delores and fuck us all in the ear," said Spahn. "I know how your mind works. You stay back, there's no way you're not gonna go in there and shred the bitch."

He could see the truth of this on La Motta's face. And La Motta knew it.

"So why don't we? She's a fucking snitch."

Spahn was losing his patience. He felt the knife on his belly skin, it was *talking* to him.

"Which is exactly why we can't do her. Right now the feds are just poking around us, trying to get info on Tony Tee. You heard the phone. Desi got clear, he's sitting in the Westin right now, ordering up dinner service, a couple of hookers. So they may be on us but not a lot. But we kill a CI who's snitching for the feds? Then we are fucked, my friend, well and truly fucked."

"So she fucking skates?"

"For now," said Spahn, thinking *Get the fuck gone before I can't help myself*. He stayed on point. "For now, Mario. For now. We lay back, bring Tito in, take her off the street in a couple of days—we'll have a nice quiet place all set up—we do the bitch right. We don't cowboy it by ourselves with the fucking feds sitting on the other side of Fountain Square, listening? She gets one screech out, they'll come running. Seriously."

La Motta didn't like it. But he went.

Finally, thought Spahn, closing the front door after La Motta was gone.

Just you and me, bitch. Just you and me and my little black blade.

Thirty minutes later Spahn was standing outside her door. He was naked—not for sex; women weren't his thing—but so whatever he got sprayed or splattered on him he could just shower off, and he had his knife and he had snorted the last of the coke so he'd be all bright and focused for this long-awaited party.

One the other side of the door Delores Maranzano had *Pride and Prejudice* playing, but she wasn't watching it. She was sitting in a chair about fifteen feet from her bedroom door, holding a cell phone and Frankie Maranzano's Dan Wesson .44, resting it on her lap, because it weighed a fucking ton. Frankie Twice was watching her from her Bottega Veneta bag, blinking at her.

She could feel someone standing outside her door. She was reasonably sure it was Julie Spahn because Mario had an iPhone she had given him and Find My iPhone was telling her that Mario's iPhone was down in the alleyway behind the building. It could be Desi out there, but she had taken Desi's measure a long time back—literally and figuratively—and whatever else he was, he wasn't a lurker. Desi would be hammering on the door saying *Hey, babe, come on, I just want to knock off a piece of that righteous ass*, because to Desi this was courtship in the Continental Style.

What was outside the door was a lurker, and the only lurker she knew was Julie Spahn.

She had counted on them all buggering off as soon as they figured out the surveillance, but she had laid down some contingency plans, and one of them covered this, Julie Spahn at the door with that black knife in his hands. She had seen it in his eyes from the first day. So if he came through that door she'd blow his nuts off with Frankie's revolver, step over and give him three more in his head and chest. Then dial 911.

Self-defense, and she had an undercover FBI agent to back her up. Sooner or later he'd either come through the door and die or he'd give up and leave, because he didn't know how much time he had before the FBI came knocking at the front door.

She was golden.

All she had to do was wait.

The Picklers were clock watchers, and all they had been doing was *waiting* and it was thirty-three minutes to the end of their surveillance shift. They had the laser rigged up to the hard drive and set up to record, which meant they could spool up a good eight hours of whatever went on up there in the penthouse suite at the Memphis, which over the last hour and a half had amounted to zero.

Silent as the grave, except for somewhere in the distant recesses of the house maybe somebody was watching *Masterpiece Theatre*—was that still on?—because Pulaski, whose wife was addicted, had been forced to sit through so many of them that his subconscious mind had the theme music burned into it like tribal scars.

"Fuck this," said Gerkin. "Where's Boonie?"

"Out looking for that Coker dude, along with everybody else. Office is empty. We're the only people here."

"Typical mooks," said Pulaski.

"Waddya think?" said Gerkin, fishing for it.

"I think," said Pulaski, "that it's Miller Time. Set it up to record and we are out of here."

And they did and they were.

And so they didn't find out until the next morning, when they were sitting in Boonie's office with their hands in their laps as Boonie, his voice reaching decibel levels approaching permanent ear damage, laid out for them what *precisely* had happened next, over there in the Pinnacle Suite at the Memphis.

Spahn had the key to the master suite in his hand. He figured Delores might be waiting for him on the other side, with a gun in her lap.

She was that kind of snaky bitch.

And any minute now the feds could come through the door. She could be calling them right now. But he wanted to cut her *so bad*.

What to do?

The carpeting in the hallway outside the master suite was as thick as polar bear fur. Coming down it, Spahn had not made a sound, as silent as mist on water, his bare feet gliding along, toes curled, feeling the air on his naked skin, cocaine pulsing like blue fire behind his eyes, his mind as cold and clear as a vodka martini.

So the voice came as a shock.

"Hey there, buttercup."

Spahn pivoted, his face twisting into a grimace. He took a step, stopped himself—saw the tall silver-haired man in the hall, a harsh sharp-planed face, yellow eyes, a blue suit like the feds wore, a long blue coat over that, and a SIG pistol in his right hand, steady as a stone, the black hole of the muzzle lined up with Spahn's left eye, behind the pistol a killer's face, nothing in it but sudden death.

"The knife. Put it down."

Spahn thought about throwing it.

"Don't even think that," said the man.

Spahn looked at him, dropped the knife, kicked it away, cutting the sole of his foot on the point. Pain, but he ignored it. Now his blood was spilling out onto the white carpet.

The guy. Who was he?

Spahn *knew* him, that killer face, those yellow eyes, the Marine Corps haircut. "Fuck me. The *banker*."

The man's expression didn't change, but something flickered behind his yellow eyes.

Spahn saw his death coming. *But not yet.*

He had *information* this guy was going to need. He had some vig. Traction. He could *deal*.

"You know who I am?"

"Yes. You're . . . *the name the name* . . . Sinclair. The money-changer guy. From Florida."

Coker considered the man while he added it up. Twyla's cell phone not being answered, going to voice mail three different times. Nate Kellerman's ripped-up knee. Little Anthony and the Tony Torinetti connection. His chest went cold.

Things are one way.

Then they're the other.

"What have you done?"

"Not me," said Spahn. "It was La Motta. Gotta talk to La Motta. Not me. Wasn't me."

"La Motta's dead. Munoz is dead. There's nobody left to talk to but you."

The door to the master suite opened, Delores Maranzano in the open door. Her hands were empty.

"I know what they did," she said. "But I don't know how to stop it."

"Who does?"

"He does."

Spahn shot her a look of pure ninety-proof hate and she swatted it right back at him, with a thin smile.

"It was his idea," she said.

Coker looked at her for a while and she felt something cold and slithery run up her back and curl itself around her throat.

"Don't try to handle me," the guy said mildly, but in a way that left a lifelong impression deep down in her amygdala.

"No, sir," she said, her eyes meek and her voice soft. Julie Spahn watched the exchange and decided that the guy was just a fucking banker after all, and his best defense was a good offense.

"Yeah, it was, my friend, I sent a guy down to your beach place, and the guy I sent is your worst fucking nightmare, so if you ever hope to see your little Puerto Rican girlfriend alive again I'm the only guy who can make that happen. What you need to do, banker boy, is sit down and listen up."

Coker looked at him for about a minute without saying anything. Spahn tried to read the expression in his eyes and decided there *was* no expression in his eyes. It came to him that perhaps in this case a conciliatory approach might have been more appropriate.

What happened next was what the Picklers should have been around to hear, what they were treated to the next morning in Boonie's office. It went on for quite a while.

Because the Memphis was a very solid building and because the Penthouse Suite had no next-door neighbors, nobody but the participants knew what all the fuss was about.

At the end of it, Coker knew all there was to know and Julie Spahn went out the bathroom window and got about eleven seconds of free fall to come to a deeper understanding of the world and his place in it, which, when he finally hit bottom like a chicken-skin meteor packed full of guts, turned out to be right smack on top of a Porta-Potty in the loading alley behind the Memphis.

The impact utterly destroyed the Porta-Potty and would have killed the guy sitting in it at the time if the guy didn't already have a bullet hole in his forehead and two more in his chest. Together the two old friends, Julie Spahn and Mario La Motta, gave a whole new meaning to the term *inseparable*.

Candleford House

The ambulance was parked down by the 7-Eleven, just where the GPS said it would be. The same 7-Eleven where Reed had left his Mustang the last time he had come to Gracie. He and Nick and Kate looked at Candleford House as they cruised past it in Reed's patrol car.

It was a tall forbidding building made of gray stone blocks. It had two towerlike bays rising up on its wings, each tower topped with Norman turrets. Leaded casement windows, a center balcony with twisted pillars, an upper balcony under carved stone arches, a massive wooden front door under a stone portico, the whole building stained by time, as grim as an open grave.

It had been left to rot behind a chain-link fence. All the glass in the lower floors had been broken by neighborhood kids or their fathers or their grandfathers, long years before. On the top floor there were a few unbroken windows, stained-glass arches that reflected the streetlights. Massive live oaks crowded in all around it and loomed above it, casting it into the shadows.

Reed wasn't ready to leave his Interceptor stuck out by the side of the road, so he put it into the 7-Eleven lot beside the Niceville EMT truck. He called in his position and status to Dispatch, and said he'd be ten-seven at this location with Detective Nick Kavanaugh of the Belfair and Cullen CID and Kate Kavanaugh, a lawyer with Family Services.

"Roger that," said Dispatch. "Reason for stop?"

Reed looked at Kate, who smiled back at him.

"Your call," Nick said from the backseat, "unless you've got a radio code for ghost-hunting?"

"We're ten-seven for dinner," said Reed. "We'll be on the portable."

"Ten-four, Pursuit. Enjoy."

Reed clicked off, tugged his belt into place, popped the door. He got out faster than Nick, who despite his meds was still moving like an old man. Kate waited by the curb as the two cops got themselves together. She was looking at the ambulance, which was locked up and dark. She put a hand on the engine cover. It was still warm.

"Reed, have you got a light?"

Nick, in civvies, a charcoal suit and a white shirt, his chest still wrapped tight, his Colt in a belt clip, pulled a Heider compact out of his inside pocket, handed it to Kate. Reed was unlocking his shotgun and checking the load.

Kate shone the light into the driver's side window. "Keys are still here. There's blood on the dashboard. And I see a bullet hole," she said.

She went around to the back gates.

One of the rear windows had been shot out, and she put the light into the open frame, saw a human shape under a red blanket, strapped down on the stretcher. And a Gary Fisher mountain bike up against the other side of the cabin.

"Nick . . . come here," she said, and he caught the tone in her voice. "There's a body."

Nick and Reed were right there, Reed pulling out his Maglite.

"Not Rainey," said Nick. "Look at the shoes. Those are

paramedic boots. And too small. Rainey's got feet like the Sasquatch."

"Stand clear," said Reed, reaching in through the broken window and popping the inside lever. The gates swung back and Reed stepped up into the cabin.

"It's Barb Fillion. Throat's gone. Looks like a grazing wound, hit her carotid and she bled out."

Kate moved back.

"That's Rainey's bike," she said, a slight tremble in her voice. "He was here. I can feel it."

"Not now," said Reed, looking at Nick.

"I should call this in," he said.

"We have to get inside Candleford House," said Nick. "We can't have state troopers all over us when we're doing it."

"That's a dead body—"

"We'll take care of her. Just not yet. We have to do this thing."

Reed closed the ambulance up, got the keys out of the ignition, locked the truck up. Nick was looking at a big gray Lexus SUV that was parked beside it. There was a pattern of tiny droplets on the driver's window; in the fluorescent glare from the 7-Eleven, they looked coppery and wet.

He put his Heider light on the driver's window and saw blood spatter on the dashboard. He moved to the rear window and saw two bodies, a young man and a little girl half stuffed into the backseat like a couple of bags full of bones.

"Two more bodies," he said to Reed.

"We already decided," Reed said. "Let's go do this. We'll call it in as soon as we're done here."

The three of them walked back up the block toward Candleford House. The street was deserted, most of the lamps were out, and garbage littered the empty lots on either side of the building. The neighborhood had long ago come to a verdict about the old asylum. Leave it alone, keep your distance.

"Last time I was here I popped the lock on the chain-link. It's around the back."

The lock was still popped, the chain hanging down. The gate was slightly open and it groaned like a dying thing when Reed shoved it back.

"There's a summer kitchen in the back. That pile of bricks up against the wall."

They found it, moving carefully over the litter and junk that had gathered inside the fence. The summer kitchen was now just a sagging ruin made of bricks and tin and rotting boards.

Inside a rusted steel door, a flight of stairs rose up into the gloom of the interior. The stairs were marble, worn smooth by time, and they led up to a main floor landing.

Nick, first up the stairs, stood in the doorway at the top of the staircase, thinking that the interior of Candleford House looked exactly the way Reed had described it.

Like walking onto the deck of the Titanic *after a hundred years at the bottom of the ocean.*

There was a huge central hallway with a checkered tile floor. The ceiling far above them was lined with decorative tin tiles, and a large chandelier, rusted and ruined, dominated the air space.

The atrium went all the way up to a domed skylight made of stained glass, the bowl of it illuminated with city glow bouncing off the cloud cover, sending a pale blue shaft down the atrium, dust motes drifting inside the column. The atrium was lined with galleries on all four sides, buried deep in purple shadows, supported by carved wooden pillars. There were four levels of galleries. They receded into the dimness far above.

The three of them stood there, oppressed by the weight of all the emptiness, the pounding silence.

And there was an odor in the air, not just rot and mold and dead things.

Something else, something strange.

Cordite. Gunpowder. Fresh and acrid.

"Somebody's been firing a weapon in here," said Reed. "Not long ago."

"Yeah," said Nick. "I can smell it."

"What now?" said Reed.

"Your call," said Nick. "You know the place."

"Abel Teague had private rooms on the top floor. If Rainey's anywhere, he'll be up there."

Kate was looking at the staircase. "Can we trust the stairs?"

Reed gave her a smile.

"How do you feel about waiting down here alone while Nick and I check them out?"

Nick sensed a figure standing in the shadows on the far side of the main floor, pulled his Colt out and heard Reed rack a shell into his shotgun, the sound bouncing around the atrium and fading into the upper dark. He felt Kate move in close to him, heard her rapid breathing.

"Rainey?" she said. "Rainey, is that you?"

"Reed, you put that shotgun away," said a voice out of the dark, a man's voice, a familiar deep voice with a cowboy tone. "I'm too pretty to die."

The figure stepped out of the shadows and into the faint pool of light from the glass dome, boots grinding on broken plaster and rotting wood, a tall man in jeans and a range jacket, boots, long silvery hair down to his shoulders. Reed lowered the shotgun. Kate took a step forward, stopped.

"Charlie?"

Danziger moved farther into the light. There was something in his hands, a long heavy rifle. His face looked haggard and weary and he had a bloody wound on the side of his head.

"Yeah, it's me. You folks try not to get all spooked about this, okay?"

"Charlie," said Nick, not surprised by much of anything these days. "I heard you were in town."

"Yeah? From who?"

"Frank Barbetta."

"Yeah, me and Frank sorta got into it Friday night, ended up at Blue Eddie's. He here with you?"

"No," said Nick. "He's not."

Danziger caught Nick's tone. "What happened?"

Nick told him.

Danziger listened and was quiet for a while. "That's too damn bad. That bitch gets into everybody eventually, doesn't she?"

"No offense, Charlie," said Reed, "but what the *hell* are you?"

Danziger looked at Nick, shook his head.

"Gotta love the young," he said. "They don't tap-dance around the main question, do they?"

"It's a good question," said Kate.

"Yeah. I've been giving it some thought for a few days now."

"Come up with anything?" asked Nick.

"Yeah. You know the expression *one foot in the grave*? I think that's the position I'm in. Can I ask you a question back, Kate?"

"Please."

"You look around you right now, what do you see?"

Kate looked. "I see the inside of a prison, a terrible place, an abomination that ought to be burned down to the ground and the ruins sown with rock salt."

Danziger looked around the main floor and then came back to her.

"You don't see eight dead things? One of them about a foot from where you're standing?"

Kate stepped back. "No, I don't."

"Look harder."

She stared down at the floor and saw . . . something. A man-shaped stain on the wooden slats.

"I see . . . what is it?"

"Well, before you three got here, that's what I was doing. With this."

He held up the BAR. "They're Abel Teague's . . . guardians. The last of them, I think. I tried to clear them out. I've been killing them all day, ever since I left the Ruelle place. I think I got them all. I hope so, anyway. I guess you found the ambulance and the SUV beside it?"

"Yes," said Reed. "And three dead bodies."

"Yeah. Why I turned on the GPS. I figured somebody would come. I'm glad it was you. I feel bad about the EMT tech. She came for Teague down by the Belfair store. No idea why. In that ambulance. I tried to stop them, put a round through the back window, got her and not him. I figure Teague hijacked the SUV so he could get up here. So I took the wagon and came on up. I figured—"

They heard a sound, a kind of low whispering sigh that turned into a hissing slither like air rushing in through an open window. It got bigger and louder until it seemed to fill up the atrium, float down from the roof, pour out of the walls, rise up from the floorboards all around them, invisible, a pressure wave, a vibrating *presence*.

Reed knew what it was because he'd felt it once before. He tried hard not to run for the stairs, the street, the cruiser, the highway, another state.

"Don't run," said Danziger. "She's not here for us. She's here for the boy."

"Rainey?" said Kate.

"Yeah," said Danziger, his voice low and soft, watching the dust motes in the light column, seeing them move and drift as something invisible passed upward into the dark. It got easier to breathe.

"Is Rainey here?"

"I haven't gone upstairs yet. I had to deal with his helpers. But he's nowhere else, and he sure as hell heard me shooting up his people."

"He'd be in his rooms," said Reed. "Top floor." Danziger looked at him.

"You've been here before?"

"Yeah. Once. I left by an upstairs window."

"Well," said Danziger. "I got to go up there."

"I know," said Reed. "Clara Mercer told me."

Danziger's smile went away. "Then you know what we have to do? Kate, are you up to this? I know you were on the kid's side."

"I still am, if we can get *her* out of his head. Maybe there's still some way to do that?"

"You think there is, Charlie?" said Nick.

"Tell you the truth, Nick, I don't think we've got a chance in hell. I think we're all gonna die here or maybe worse. And now that I've given you my pep talk, who's dumb enough to come with me?"

Nick looked at Kate, and she gave it right back.

Not one word, Nick. Not one word.

"I think we all are," she said.

Danziger gave Kate his best smile.

"I wish Coker were here. He'd love this part."

Crater Sink

They took Lemon's truck up the access road that led to the parking area near Crater Sink. The road had been cut and the parking lot put in many years ago, when the city council had decided to make a tourist destination out of Tallulah's Wall and Crater Sink, call it the Haunted Mountain or something like that, put up a railing around the pool, build a concession stand, sell tickets.

That hadn't gone well.

All that was left now was a broken-down winding ribbon of corroding tarmac pressed in and crushed down by the old forest all around it, and at the end of the road a cleared space in the pines and willows that used to be a parking lot. At one end of the lot a meandering gravel path had been laid down, now almost entirely overgrown with weeds and covered in fallen leaves. A chain of footlights led off into the darkness under the towering canopy of willows and pines and live oaks. At the far end of the path a low circle of yellow lamps defined the perimeter of Crater Sink, a near-perfect circle of moss-covered limestone walls surrounding a pool of water a hundred feet in diameter, a thousand feet deep.

Doris stopped the truck at the end of the path, left the engine running. She looked over at Helga, who was in the passenger seat, and then back at Lemon, leaning at an angle in the bench seat, his left arm strapped to his body, a leather jacket over his shoulders, his chest bare, his face wet with pain and sweat.

"Lemon, do you want to wait here?"

"Wait for what?" he said, showing white teeth in the dark, a pin light in each green eye.

"We have to confess something," said Doris.

"Yeah, we do," said Lemon.

"What?" said Helga.

"We don't actually know a chant for this," said Lemon. Doris nodded, looking solemn.

"Then why are we here?"

"Because we *think* the chant was only to keep the singer's mind calm," said Doris. "Music was what counted. Every plains tribe had a different chant for different spirits—"

"But in many ways they were all the same," said Lemon. "The point was that the singer be clear so that the power could come into him and he could be stronger than the spirit."

Helga gave that some thought. "You *think*, but you don't *know*?"

"Nope," said Lemon.

"Okay," said Helga, "so we need music, then?"

"Yeah," said Lemon, holding up a Bose speaker in a black case and his iPhone.

"What is the music?" Helga wanted to know.

Doris and Lemon exchanged a smile.

"It's a recording of a Shoshone spirit song, a chant for the healing of a sick soul. We found it on the Smithsonian website."

"Do you think it will work?"

"We're about to find out."

Helga laughed at that, and they all smiled.

Doris said, "Okay, time to do this."

"Will this really work?" asked Helga.

"Hell no," said Lemon. "We're all gonna die."

"He is joking, no?" said Helga to Doris.

"We'll see," she said.

They cracked the doors and got out.

The night was cloudy but they could see the lights of Niceville spread out below them, a carpet of glowing jewels covered in mist, except for the dark oblong of the Confederate Graveyard and the broad back of the Tulip snaking through the heart of the town.

Helga walked to the edge of the lot and looked out over the town. Music was rising up faintly from the glittering bars on the Pavilion, and traffic was streaming north and south along the riverside drives, a ribbon of red and a river of white, a dull rumble from the avenues and cross streets. Below them the lights of the mansions in The Chase neighborhood rose up against the foot of Tallulah's Wall, pressing into the trees along the base of the cliff. In the northwest an airplane was lifting off from Mauldar Field and the searchlight on the radar tower was making a slow circuit, flaring up blue-white as the spot came around.

Over the music from the Pavilion they could hear the pop-pop-crackle of semiauto gunfire, and sirens, some in the north, more down in the crowded streets of Tin Town, a mile below the Pavilion. A sparkle pulse of red and blue lights was arcing and flashing halfway down the Mile, a police helicopter was hammering south toward Cap City, and a couple of fire trucks were bulling their way east across the Armory Bridge, driving cars onto the sidewalks. They could hear the heavy bass blare of their horns from a mile away.

"A lot going on," said Lemon, standing behind her. Doris

was waiting for them at the opening of the pathway, facing into the forest.

"Yes," said Helga. "The city is all stirred up, like an angry hive. Is it always like this?"

"No," said Lemon, looking grim. "It's not."

"Let's go, kids," called Doris from the edge of the forest. They turned and walked across the lot and followed Doris into the woods.

Riders on the Storm

They went up into the dark, the stairs creaking and moaning under their weight. Each flight ended at a gallery, and the next one began at the far end of that gallery, so they had to make their way through the shadowy halls, following Reed's flash, a harsh cone of light as they passed by open doors leading into rooms that had once been bedrooms for patients. The rooms on the first gallery were large and airy, with casement windows, although barred. The rooms on the second less so, smaller and more cramped, one window only, and that one covered in crossbars, and on the third gallery there were no windows at all, only tiny cells with chains and manacles attached to the walls, twenty cells to a side and four sides on each gallery. They passed by these open rooms and could feel the grief, the pain, the fear seeping out of each tiny room. On their left the atrium fell away to the ground far below; beside them the chandelier hung motionless in the cone of blue light, coated in dust, draped in webs.

As they went up they heard the building breathing in and out, a low bass note that growled and hummed in the air itself. The air was getting thicker around them, as if the pressure were being pumped up, and they could hear voices now, some rising up from below, faint cries and whispers, and other voices coming from the top floor, a man's voice, deep and strident, and another voice, much less clear, more like a hissing vibration.

Danziger had the lead, with the BAR, Reed behind him, keeping the light moving, Danziger following the cone with the muzzle of the BAR, Kate next, and Nick following last, with his Colt, turning and watching, looking up and down and left and right, down into the atrium, up at the dome of the skylight, getting nearer, his skin crawling and his chest muscles tight, his stitches on fire, his head pounding from the slow fading away of his pain meds. He had popped two amphetamines—a standard Special Ops tactic. He had wanted to be clear, and he was clear, but he was paying a high price.

They reached the top floor. Here there were no cells or holding rooms. The stairs led up to a landing fenced in with balustrades, and another landing that branched up from the main one, where a flight of smaller stairs led up into the rafters and a door that probably opened onto the turreted platforms on top of Candleford House.

"In there," said Reed, pointing the light to a large sitting area with a stained-glass window. It had once been a pretty room, and the air here was cleaner and less smothering. There was a carpet in the middle of the room, faded oriental patterns now coated in mold and dust. A large industrial light in a green tin shade hung over the center of the carpet. Reed put his light on the carpet, picked out the four indentations in the general dimensions of a bed frame. It was directly under the bowl of the factory lamp, clearly intended to shed a glare down on whatever, whoever, was in the bed.

No one had to be told what the bed and the light had been used for. Danziger stepped across the carpet, Reed close behind, Kate and Nick back a few feet, Nick watching the door they had come in through. He looked at Kate and saw, in the light streaming in through the stained-glass window, that she had gone into herself, as if listening to a voice only she could hear.

She felt his eyes on her, looked at him, gave him a smile that did not reach her eyes. "She's here," said Kate in a whisper.

Danziger and Reed had stopped at a section of wall that had been kicked in. A broken board with a window cut into it lay shattered on the other side of the wall, half resting on a large armchair, covered in dust. Beside the armchair was a smoking table, and a footstool had been shoved into the corner of the little space, which was really not much more than a cupboard.

Its purpose was also clear.

Whoever sat in that chair would have a comfortable view of whatever took place in the sitting room and on the bed under the light, and he could enjoy a cigar and a glass of brandy while he watched. There was a second door on the other side of the space, set into a wall of unpainted spruce boards. They could hear voices coming through the thin wooden slats, a murmuring bass rumble and something else, something not really human at all.

Danziger stepped over the shattered board and into the space, moving the armchair as he did so, the BAR across his chest, his boots crunching into broken wood splinters and bits of glass.

The voices stopped.

There was a pause, something heavy sliding across the floor on the other side of the wall. The inner door popped open slightly, as if a catch had been released. A band of pale light showed along the open edge of the door.

"That you, cowboy?" said a hard voice from inside the room. "You just come right on in."

Danziger checked Reed, Nick, got a nod, lifted the BAR, braced himself, slammed the panel with his right shoulder, sending it flying back. He stepped through it as the panel bounced off the wall and came swinging back. Danziger stopped it with his shoulder, covering the room with the BAR.

It was a large master bedroom lined in wood paneling, with a wall of stained glass running the length of the room. City light streamed in through the window wall, but the rest of the room was in shadows, dim corners and darkness above, black shadows in the rafters.

In the middle of the room, under a large brass chandelier that had five lit candles glowing in it, was a four-poster bed frame, mattress and spring long gone, resting on a large carpet that had been eaten away by mold and rot.

On the far wall by another door stood a four-drawer dresser, and on the dresser was a set of crystal glasses and a decanter of something that looked like cognac in the flickering light from the candles. Three chairs were arranged in an arc in front of the dresser.

Sitting in the largest of the three was Abel Teague, a shotgun resting in his lap, the muzzle pointing at Rainey Teague's head, Rainey's white face staring back at the door, his body rigid with fear, his eyes dark holes in his face with a flickering pinpoint of candle glow reflected in each eye.

And in the middle chair, upright, dressed in a long silky blue gown that covered and revealed her lovely body, sat a woman who was neither old nor young, neither pretty nor plain, unmarked by age but magisterial, radiating power and a cold intelligence. She ruled the room.

Her hair was very long and very red and it fell in rivulets and curls down past her shoulders. Her long-fingered hands were folded in her lap, her legs crossed at the ankles, her feet bare. Her eyes were as black as polished ebony, and in them the same candlelight flickered and danced, but with a greenish tint. She was looking at them, perfectly still, utterly motion-less, staring back at them without any emotion showing on her face.

Danziger moved out of the way and Reed came in, and then Kate. When Rainey saw Kate, he started to get up as if he wanted to go to her, but Teague had the shotgun and he moved the muzzle enough to keep him there.

"Kind of a standoff, isn't it, cowboy," he said, talking to Danziger. "I'll give it to you, son, you can ride and you can hunt and, by Jesus, you can shoot. You cut my boys to pieces, you surely did."

"We're here for the boy," said Nick.

Teague showed his gravestone teeth. "The boy is mine," he said. "My son. My own blood son."

"Kate," said Rainey. "I'm sorry—"

"Shut up," said Teague, lifting the shotgun. He came back to the rest of them.

"I don't want to have you in my head," said Rainey. "I know what will happen to me."

"*Nothing* will happen to you," said Teague. "And we'll all have a wonderful time together. You'll see things, boy, and do things and experience things that few living men have ever done. You're a young lad, be patient, you'll grow into your money and your size—"

"And I'll be dead and you'll live in my body like . . . like a worm in a corpse."

Teague smiled. "Boy's got a gift for melodrama," he said. "But the matter is already decided. You folks don't believe me, why just ask the lady here."

The woman had not spoken, had not moved.

Kate stepped forward around Nick and into the room and walked over and stood in front of her. The woman's head moved to track her, but nothing else in her seemed alive, except for the black light in those bottomless eyes.

"I am Kate Walker," she said.

"And I am who I am," said the woman in a voice that seemed to come out of the walls all around them.

"I know who you are," said Kate.

The woman smiled then, a terrible thing to see.

"No one in this world knows what I am," she said. "I am Nothing. I am No Thing."

"No," said Kate, her voice trembling.

"No?"

"No, I know your name. You are Branwen."

There were crows in the trees that hung down over the surface of Crater Sink, and they were not happy to see Lemon and Doris and Helga walk out onto the open ground that surrounded the pool. They screeched and flapped and fluttered and cawed, growing louder and more threatening.

Doris walked to the edge of the pool, looked down into the black water and then up at the branches. The crows in the trees glared back at her, tiny red lights in their eyes, heads cocked and beaks clacking as they puffed themselves up and twitched and shifted on the branches.

Doris kept her eyes on them and said nothing. Their chatter grew and spread and they became more agitated. They started to dart and flutter and skim just above the surface of the pool.

Some of them flew at Doris's head, clawing at her, one or two coming close enough to catch at her hair, but she did not flinch or move.

She lifted a hand and Lemon put the Bose down on a shelf of rock, touched the iPhone. The first notes of the Shoshone healing chant floated out into the night, a sinuous human voice rising and falling and under that the pounding of drums.

At Candleford House, Kate and the woman stared at one another. The woman tilted her head slightly, like a raven, and seemed to listen to a sound no one else could hear. And then, faintly, from a long way off, they all could hear music, a man's voice singing a Native American chant, rhythmic and snake-like, and under that the bass beat of drums.

The woman went away, went inward, and then flared back at Kate. "You have sent people to my gate. I can hear them at the door. This will serve no purpose. I will not tolerate it. I do not intend to be alone for another age of your kind. I will take the boy and we will use him together."

"No, you will not. Mr. Teague will go to the Reckoning and you will go on being Branwen."

"How do you know my name is Branwen?"

"Your sister told me your name."

"I have no sister."

"Yes, you do. Her name is Glynis."

The crows withdrew, clacking and fluttering, higher and higher into the branches around Crater Sink, as if driven away by the music.

Helga and Lemon came to stand near Doris, and they all stood there, listening to the Shoshone singer chanting. Other than that, the forest was silent. The surface of Crater Sink was as still as black glass. And then it wasn't.

The woman stood up. She was taller than Kate, almost as tall as Charlie Danziger, and she seemed to grow as she towered over Kate, bearing her down. "Glynis has nothing to tell me. And if those people do not leave my gate I will go back there and take them and keep them in torment forever."

The sound of Shoshone spirit chant was filling the room. Teague stood up and started to pull at Rainey, as if to take him away from the sound, but the woman lifted a hand and froze him in place, never taking her black eyes off Kate.

Kate, shaking and shivering, struggled to find her voice again. "Glynis told me about the storm."

Figures were emerging from the darkness under the trees, the burned souls that Doris had seen in her pictures. They came forward in silence, as faint as wisps of fog, drifting slowly through the trees, gathering in around the pool as if they were being called upon. The surface of Crater Sink was rippling and shimmering and its color was changing from a bottomless black to a cobalt blue, and a green spark was showing down deep, a green fire rising up.

And now Doris and Helga and Lemon felt the fear, the dread, felt it coiling around them, tightening on them, squeezing the air out of their lungs. Doris gripped the railing, feeling the panic coming, fighting it. She looked down at her hands and saw the skin over her knuckles go white.

She heard Helga gasping for air and saw Lemon on the other side of her, his eyes closed, body stiff, vibrating like a tuning fork. The shadow figures pressed in around them, a cold clinging mist on their skins, whispering and clutching, and now, in the depths, Crater Sink was filling up with a terrible blue light.

"She told me a story," said Kate. "About a storm. She said it wasn't the way it happened, but she had to tell it in a way that made sense to me."

The woman had her fixed and caught, pinned like a dragonfly on a card, her eyes boring in on Kate's, and Kate could feel her prying at the gates of her mind, pulling and twisting her, trying to force her open, trying to get inside her and infect her.

There was a bottomless well of hate and cruelty and rage inside those black eyes, but Kate closed her mind and she told the story the way Glynis had told it to her in the mirror while Nick was in the ICU and she was alone in that awful night.

"Two sisters lived by an ocean. They spent their time making things out of the sand that was there, shaping it into mirrors and other necessary objects. One sister was lighter and the other was darker, and in the land behind them lived other twins just like them, all of them doing other things, making other objects that were beautiful or necessary, and sometimes they met to exchange them or just to sit together and watch the ocean.

"One evening a storm came from the land behind them, the worst storm the sisters had ever seen, and it caught them both up and carried them away across a huge dark ocean. The storm came from the other side of their world, from the blue sun that lit it, and the storm flared out over the endless ocean, taking them away with it into the darkness.

"After a long time the storm died and the sisters were alone in a new place, but it was not yet finished being made and the ocean was too wild and they could not live near it. But there was calm water in caves beneath the surface of the land. It was dark but it was quiet and they got used to it. They had their mirrors to see each other when they were apart and to travel from place to place, and the light from the mirrors kept the dark away.

"One morning the lighter sister discovered that the world above their home had changed and there were living things moving on the surface, and she became interested in the lives of these creatures.

"The sisters disagreed about the creatures and they had a falling-out and the sister who was interested in the surface world and the lives of those creatures spent more and more time with them. The other sister was left alone, and she learned to hate the things her sister was caring for.

"So the day came when they had a terrible fight, and the other sister left her, alone in the dark, and went to live in another part of the world."

She stopped and waited.

The woman was as still as death, and around her an aura, a halo of dark light was spreading out in a fan. The pressure in the room was immense and suffocating and she loomed over Kate like Tallulah's Wall, but Kate held her ground.

"There is more," the woman said finally.

"Yes," said Kate, "she took something with her."

The woman's shape was changing. The dark light was swirling around her, spreading out into the room, dimming the candles, pulling the shadows in from the dark corners of the room, down from the rafters, up from the floors, and a high-pitched buzzing whine drilled into their hearing.

"She took the mirrors," said the woman in a spidery buzzing voice that seemed to come from everywhere, "and she left me alone in the dark, alone in the deep, left me to go and care for her pets. As if I were nothing."

Crater Sink cracked around the rim and the railing gave away and the three of them went into the pool. The railing and the stones that held it dropped away from them and down into the deeps. Lemon could not move his arms to tread water and he slipped down deeper into the pool, sinking, looking up and seeing the two women above him on the shimmery silver surface, treading water, legs kicking, getting smaller and smaller as he dropped down into Crater Sink, and the music got fainter and fainter. He knew he was going to die down here and he remembered what people said about Crater Sink. *Things go into Crater Sink, but nothing ever comes back out.*

The woman stopped, half turned and looked away, seeing something that only she could see. Then she came back to Kate. The Shoshone healing chant was everywhere around them now, the drums almost drowning out the sound of her voice, but they could still make out what she said.

"They are in my house."

And she was gone in a hissing rush, and the dark went with her. They were alone in Teague's rooms on the top floor of Candleford House, with the lamplight streaming in from the stained-glass windows. The silence pressed in on them, making their ears ring. Teague was the first to react.

He stepped in close, put the muzzle of the shotgun up against Rainey's temple. "She'll be back. If you folks want to see another morning, best to run now."

Charlie Danziger leveled the BAR and blew Teague's left arm off at the shoulder. Teague went down, writhing, screaming, the shotgun clattering away. Rainey backed into the wall and Kate went to him, took him by the arm, looked at Nick.

"Teague's right. She'll come back."

"Get him out," said Nick. "Reed, go with her."

Lemon felt hands on him, grasping, pulling. He looked up and the women were there, rising up with him. He looked down and saw a shape flying up out of the deep, a woman, her red hair streaming behind her, rising up in a swelling halo of blue light. He kicked and struggled, his lungs bursting, his vision going. The surface was only a little way off, a rippling silvery wall, and beyond it the yellow glimmer of the perimeter lights.

Doris and Helga dragged him upward, their hands tight around his chest. Around them the blue light got brighter and more intense and now they could all hear the high-pitched hissing whine that came out of the limestone wall.

They broke through the surface, kicked for the edge of the pool. Lemon looked back down and saw the woman in the water, less than ten feet down, floating there in the light, hair streaming, her silky robe spreading around her like a blue dahlia, motionless, perfectly still, staring up at them.

Kate and Reed were gone with Rainey. They could hear them going down the stairs, the sound fading away, and then it was just the three of them, Charlie Danziger and Nick Kavanaugh, in the attic rooms, standing over Abel Teague, who was staring up at them, blood flecking his gray skin, holding the shattered stump of his left arm, his shark eyes on them. He licked his lips, spat out blood.

"I told you I can't be killed."

Danziger looked at Nick. "Seems to be true," said Danziger. "Should have bled out by now."

"Yeah," said Nick, "what's the deal?"

"Glynis said that *she*, that other bitch, she keeps him around, like a pet. Can't kill him."

Nick gave the matter some thought, watching Abel Teague struggle into a sitting position and back himself up against a wall, clutching his bloody stump, glaring at them. Still not dying.

"Waddya think?" said Danziger. "We could just cut him up in little tiny bits and leave him here for the rats."

Nick considered that, worked it through.

"No," said Nick, "She might know how to stitch him back. I have a better idea."

The woman floated there, looking up at the three intruders. A male, injured, maimed, of no utility at all. But the other two, she could see them clearly against the shining silver surface of the pool, two females. One made of the dark and one made of the light.

She hovered there, between the upper world and the lower one, looking at the two women, feeling a terrible pain growing inside her, anguish and grief and loss. She floated there, looking up at the two women—the *sisters*—and she did not know what to do. Doris and Helga pushed Lemon up onto the rim, and then they slipped back into the pool and drifted there, looking down at the woman in the water, surrounded by the blue light.

"Are we going to die?" said Helga.

"Definitely," said Doris, looking into the woman's eyes, seeing the green spark inside them, the red hair like flame around her, "but not yet."

They drove Teague down the stairs, along the galleries, and down more stairs, Teague stumbling and staggering ahead of them, Danziger prodding him with the muzzle of the BAR as they went down and down. They reached the main floor and walked Teague out into the center of the space.

"What now, boys?" said Teague, weaving, breathing hard. Danziger looked at Nick.

"The basement," said Nick.

Teague looked at the two of them, a terrible understanding coming into him.

"No," he said.

Danziger worked it through. "The furnace?"

"Yes," said Nick. "The furnace."

After that, Teague fought them, and he was a strong man, large and determined. It took the two of them to force him through the cellar door and down a long flight of stone steps into the basement of Candleford House.

It was a low cavelike space, stone and concrete and wooden

beams supported by pillars of river rock and concrete. The cellar was dank and reeking of rats and vermin and running water. There was a storm drain in the middle of it, covered by a steel grate, and they could hear the sound of water rushing and gurgling far down a stone shaft.

"Candleford House's connection to water," said Nick, but Danziger didn't ask what he meant.

At the other end of the basement, up against a wall, lit only by the glow coming in through a slit window, stood a gigantic iron furnace with a massive barred grate. The furnace was cold and slick with mold and rust and the iron grate stood wide open. Behind the grate was a black hole.

"There," said Nick, giving Teague a violent shove that sent him stumbling over the dirt floor. Teague fought them all the way over to it, and when they got him there he was trembling.

"It won't fire up," he said, his voice vibrating, his eyes wide, his face full of fear.

"We're not going to fire it up," said Nick.

"Then what?" said Teague, looking back and forth between the two men.

"You used this as a crematorium, didn't you?"

"No. It was a furnace. Nothing more."

"Reed met a woman in Gracie," said Nick, talking to Danziger. "Her name was Beryl Eaton. She was a kind of archivist. She knew all about Candleford House, what this man and his people did there. They used this furnace to burn the dead."

"A lie," said Teague. "It was . . . sanitary."

"Were they always dead?" asked Nick.

"What do you mean?" said Teague, but his eyes flicked away and they knew he was lying.

"You son of a bitch," said Danziger.

"You burned them alive sometimes, didn't you? Did you bring down a chair, and sit and watch as they went into the fire?"

"No," said Teague, backing away from the furnace, away from that awful black hole behind the grating. "They were always dead. I swear it."

"On what?" said Nick. He pushed the grate open wider. It groaned and moaned against the hinges. Nick lifted the heavy bar that locked it in place.

"Get in."

Teague shook his head, backed away, tripped and fell into the dirt. "No, I . . . I won't. I can't."

Danziger jerked him to his feet, shoved him up against the side of the furnace, held him there.

"He won't die in there," said Danziger. "We can lock him in, but she'll find a way to free him."

"They're all in there," said Nick to Teague, and Teague flinched away from his words. "Everybody you burned alive, every soul you and your people tortured to death, they're all in there. And they're waiting for you, Teague. They've been waiting for a long time. Put him in, Charlie."

And they did. They slammed the locking bar down and Danziger found a rock to hammer it with until the bar bent down into a hook. It would take a cutting torch to burn through that. The last they saw of Teague was his face pressed up against the grating, trying to force his flesh through the bars.

Reed was standing by the side of his cruiser, the engine running, Rainey and Kate inside. Reed cocked an ear and listened. It was Teague, screaming. Faint, but he could still be heard.

"Jeez. What'd you do with him?"

Nick told him.

"Lovely. But Charlie's got a point. Sooner or later she'll find a way to free him."

"Doesn't matter," said Nick. "What she wants is his *mind*. In a little while, he won't have one."

Nick looked up and down the street. It was long after midnight. "Charlie, you want a lift somewhere?"

Danziger set the BAR down at his hip, reached into his range jacket, pulled out a cigarette, lit it up, pulled in a long breath, grinned at them, his head wreathed in a cloud of cigarette smoke that glowed in the downlight from the streetlamps.

"No, but thanks. I'm good right here. I'm pretty sure there'll be a bus coming along soon."

And there was.

Firth Things Firth

By the time Coker had reached the street he had phoned Twyla's cell phone over and over again and on each call it had chimed seven times and then gone to her voice mail. So now he was half crazy and he was running to the Lincoln wondering what the hell to do—call this Chi-Chi Pentangeli guy, call Tony Torinetti himself, call the Florida State Patrol and get them down to his—

"Coker, stop it right there."

He skidded to a halt and had his SIG up and he was less than six feet away from Mavis Crossfire, standing in the dark beside his black Lincoln Town Car. She had her service piece out and it was zeroed on his forehead. Mavis wasn't a great shot, but she was good enough to drill him a new eye from that distance and they both knew it.

"Mavis," said Coker, his chest clamping up, breathing through his teeth, trying to fight down the panic. "Mavis, I can't do this right now."

"Boonie should have figured that you'd show up here," she said, not getting his tone yet. "He's got all his crew up in Niceville staking out Charlie Danziger's ranch."

"Danziger's? Why?"

"They think you hid the money there."

"Jeez, Mavis, you saw Charlie's Mondex card."

"I know. Boonie thinks you had some reserve funds stowed away in cash, and now you need it, which is why you're back in town."

"I don't need any goddamn cash," said Coker. "I came back to—"

"Settle with the Italians. Because they killed Charlie. I know. That's why I'm here. I know how your mind works. You get them all settled?"

"Yes. But now I've got a complication—"

"You usually do. Tell me about it in a minute. I gotta know, why'd you do that thing up at Bean Me Joe?"

In spite of everything, Coker had to laugh. "I told you, Mavis, you'd never believe it."

"It was the tits on that barista, right?"

"How'd you figure that?"

"Am I right?"

"Put your piece down and I'll tell you."

"You first."

"Mavis, I'm not gonna shoot you."

She thought it over.

"Probably not."

She lowered her gun, and Coker did too. The air went a little slack. The rain was coming down now.

"It was her breasts. Right?"

"Free-range bazongas, Mavis. It was my civic duty to save those amazing free-range bazongas."

"For posterity?"

"Yeah. They were a national treasure. How'd you know it was me."

"You made an impression on the barista. When the guys put it out on the net, I knew it was you. So I came down here and waited."

Coker put the gun back in his coat. "I can't get arrested right now, Mavis."

"When's a good time?" she said, with a big Coker-like grin. "Does Tuesday work for you?"

"I gotta be three hundred and fifty-nine miles down the road by sunrise, Mavis. It's a matter of life and death."

"It always is with you. What's happening?"

Coker told her.

"Jesus, Coker. How do you get into these situations? Call the local cops. They'll get right in there."

Coker shook his head.

"I just had a talk with a guy named Julie Spahn. He says they're waiting for me, that nothing's gonna happen until I show up. They want to do the whole family. *The table is set*, Spahn told me."

"You believe him?"

"Mavis, I have to. I gotta believe him. Otherwise, I'm just gonna eat my gun right here."

"Four dead cops," said Mavis. "I can't forget that. Nobody can."

"How many live hipsters up at Bean Me Joe?"

"It doesn't work like that. It's karma. It's your karma that Twyla and Bluebell are paying for."

"Yeah. It probably is. And how I feel right now is karma too. I'm getting more fucking karma than I can handle. Mavis, truly, I gotta leave right now, got to leave right this second."

She looked at him for a while.

"How far did you say?"

"Three hundred and fifty-nine miles."

"Crow flies or interstate?"

"Interstate."

She looked at her watch.

"Sunrise is in five hours. You're never gonna cover that distance in five hours."

"I will at a hundred and twenty miles an hour."

"You'll have every patrol cop and county sheriff in the southern states on your ass. You'll have choppers buzzing around you like bumblebees."

"Nothing else I can do. I don't have a chopper and there's no private jet around I can hire."

"You need a cop car. Lights and sirens."

"Don't have that either."

Mavis looked at Coker for a time. Coker felt her look and it stung. He wasn't used to caring and he didn't like it one bit. Finally she spoke.

"I do."

Delores Maranzano was sitting in her master bedroom in a cobalt-blue nightgown made mostly of curved air and sinful intentions and having a glass of white wine when Mavis Crossfire appeared in her doorway. She jumped so high her wineglass hit the ceiling and then bounced across the room. She sat up in the bed, clutching the sheets around her free-range bazongas.

"Settle down, Delores," said Mavis, who was dog bone tired. "I'm not here to arrest you."

"Sergeant Crossfire, isn't it?" said Delores, whose mood was greatly improved by the news that she wasn't about to get shoved into a squad car.

Besides, she had always kind of *liked* Mavis Crossfire, who was actually very pretty in that big dangerous Nordic Valkyrie kind of way.

"Then why *are* you here?"

"Well, it might have something to do with the naked old buzzard who took a tumble from your bathroom window a little while back."

Delores said, "Oh dear," and made big eyes and let the

sheets drop away from her breasts just enough to raise the room temperature a few degrees. Mavis watched her do it and sighed to herself.

"Where's your damned dog?" she asked.

"Frankie Twice? He's in the bathroom. He has a bed in there. He's had a trying night."

"So have I," said Mavis, stepping into the room. She was carrying a large plastic cage with a large nonplastic cat inside it.

"Whose cat is that?" asked Delores, sitting up and leaning forward, giving Mavis a panoramic view of her bona fides. Delores had very fine bona fides.

"Her name is Mildred Pierce. She was in my squad car. I've got to call a cab."

"What happened to your squad car?"

"I loaned it to a friend. Can I put her in the bathroom with your dog?"

"Well, that might upset Frankie Twice."

"He'll have to cope," said Mavis, walking across the room. She still had her ankle wrapped, but she was managing pretty well. She opened the door and set the cat carrier down inside it and closed the door.

Delores did not like that. "She can't get *out* of that cage, can she?"

"If she can, we'll sure as hell hear about it," said Mavis, turning to look at the huge flat-screen that took up most of Delores Maranzano's bedroom wall. "What are you watching?"

"*Pride and Prejudice*," said Delores.

"The one with Colin Firth and Jennifer Ehle?"

"Yes. It's my favorite."

Mavis took off her uniform jacket, laid it across one of Delores's bedroom chairs.

"Mine too," she said, and sat down in the chair.

Delores studied her for a while, making a little frowny face, because she always did that when she had to think something through. "You look pretty tired, Sergeant Crossfire."

"I am," said Mavis. "I am very damn tired."

"Are you still on duty?"

Mavis looked at her watch. "No. Technically my shift ended at midnight."

"Then perhaps you would like a drink?"

"I would," said Mavis, and Delores got out of bed and walked across the room to get another glass. There were few women in this part of the state who could cross a room like Delores Maranzano. She came back to Mavis and leaned way down and over to hand her a crystal flute full to the brim with ice-cold white wine. Mavis took the glass and the Magical Maranzano Boobs of Doom and the obvious hint.

"It's pinot grigio," said Delores, standing in front of Mavis, looking down at her.

"Then may I propose a toast?" said Mavis.

"Certainly," said Delores. "To whom?"

"To Charlie Danziger. He loved this stuff."

"To Charlie Danziger," said Delores. "He died, didn't he, Sergeant Crossfire? A while back?"

"Yes he did. Charlie Danziger was a good friend of mine, Delores. A very good friend."

Delores felt a little shiver of fear slither up her spine. She couldn't read the woman at all.

"How did he die, Sergeant Crossfire?"

"He got shot. Saving my life."

"How *awful*," said Delores, putting a hand to her throat and dropping to her knees in front of Mavis, her nightgown slipping partly off her shoulders. A tableau of sympathy, with fabulous breasts. "How awful. Do you have any idea who did it?"

"Yes, I do. They used to work for your husband."

"Oh, no. Not that awful shooting in the hills?"

"Yes. That awful shooting in the hills."

"I had *no idea*. My nephew, Manolo, was behind that. A bad person, he was. Full of rage. And he was crazy with grief about Frankie. If only I had known, Sergeant Crossfire. I might have stopped it, and you would still have your friend, Mr. Danziger."

"Yes," said Mavis. "If only you had known."

Delores sighed, put a sympathetic hand on Mavis's left knee, let it rest there. "I do feel your loss," she said.

"Well, all dead but one," said Mavis.

Delores leaned in closer. "I know what you're going through. I too have lost a loved one. My own dear Frankie. I feel his absence every night, right here, deep in my bosom." She put her left hand over her right breast and sighed a weary sigh. Plus there was lip tremble.

"And . . . are the police still hunting for that last . . . person, Sergeant Crossfire?"

"No," said Mavis. "That's all taken care of."

Delores seemed to find that reassuring. "Closure," she said. "It's so important. In these last few weeks, since poor Frankie passed away, I have learned so much about closure and the grieving process," Delores said in a breathy whisper, sliding her hand up Mavis's thigh. "And there is great comfort to be found in sharing grief. Grief is a lonely burden, but sharing it with another person so heals a troubled heart, Sergeant Crossfire, don't you think?"

"I couldn't agree more," said Mavis. "I'm always ready to share some grief. Matter of fact, I'm kind of known for it."

Delores gave Mavis her very best up-from-under. "And do you think you might . . . share your grief . . . with *me*?"

Mavis smiled, reached out, and held her cheek. "Oh yes," she said. "And call me Mavis."

Istrians Really Value Their Eyelids

Coker covered the 359 miles between Cap City and St. Augustine in four hours and seventeen minutes, including two stops for gas and coffee, and it was lights and sirens all the way. He had to talk his way through a whole lot of deputies and state patrol guys who wanted him to pull over and explain what all the rush was about, but he managed to convince them that his mission, which was top secret and had to do with Homeland Security and was being monitored by an Argus drone, was way too important to stop and chat about.

In the final ten miles between St. Augustine and the beach house in Shore Road he got Mavis Crossfire's Suburban up to speeds that GMC didn't like to talk about in public, but then Mavis had her own mechanic working on the truck and he had done some things to it that Coker was sure the Niceville PD wouldn't approve of.

The sun was just tugging its big glowing red ass out of the eastern rim of the Atlantic Ocean and a flock of late-season pelicans were flying in a single snaky line a few inches above the waves when Coker shut the smoking machine down a hundred yards up from the beach house. He covered the ground at a soft trot, carrying Mavis Crossfire's Defender shotgun at port arms, trying not to think about what he was almost certain to find.

He stopped a few feet shy of the shore road gate, crouched down beside the wall, and took out his iPhone. It had an app that allowed him to make a Bluetooth connection with the security system inside the house. He flicked it on and thumbed the tab that said HEARTBEAT. He waited a few minutes, watching the screen. It blipped and bopped and then he was looking at a schematic of his beach house.

There were five little red beating hearts in the schematic. Three were in the basement, and two more were out on the front deck right now.

He hit the button that said SILENT DISABLE and killed the perimeter alarms.

Take the assholes out front first.

He moved through the gate—there was an alien rental van in the driveway, beside a black Benz with Dade County plates. The house was dark and silent, but he could hear faint music coming from the deck out front.

He ghosted down the side of the house, the sand cold and silky on his ankles. Out on the shore the waves were booming in, crashing and falling and then pulling back with a sliding sandy hiss.

The sun was in his eyes as he rounded the corner of the deck, but he was moving fast and he had the shotgun down on the two people sitting in the deck chairs before they even noticed him.

The two people were Twyla and Bluebell, in bathrobes, sipping what looked like margaritas.

Twyla saw him, jumped up with a squeal. "Coker, where the *fuck* have you been? Do you have any *fucking* idea how *worried* we've been?"

Coker came up onto the deck, checking out the window wall, seeing nobody in the main room.

"There's three fucking heartbeats in the basement, Twyla."

"Of *course* there are, you asshole. I've been calling and calling—"

"Who's in the basement, Twyla?" asked Coker, unnaturally calm.

"Little Anthony Torinetti and his fucking mobster daddy and a piece of shit Istrian named Tito Smeraglia."

"I know who they are," said Coker. "How'd you get on top of them?"

Twyla took a deep breath, looked at Bluebell, who sipped at her margarita and smiled at him.

"I came back from Jacksonville with Bluebell and I checked the iPhone app for heartbeats."

"And there was one," said Bluebell. "In the kitchen."

"So I switched on the Halon fire suppression thingy."

"She knocked him out. It was the Istrian."

"When he came around we asked him a bunch of questions."

"He didn't want to talk to Twyla at first."

"But he changed his mind when Bluebell tried to cut off his eyelids. It turns out Istrians really value their eyelids. We had him call Tony and his kid and tell them everything was good to go."

"Twyla told him to say *The table is set*. Like a code, huh? He wasn't going to do it except for the eyelid thingy. I knew how to cut off eyelids from being a nurse," said Bluebell.

Coker didn't think to ask her why a nurse would know how to cut people's eyelids off, but he got around to it later, after things had calmed down. "My question," he said, riding over the chatter, "is why the *fuck* haven't you been answering your cell phones? I've been calling and calling."

"We never got any . . . oh, shit," said Twyla, her voice trailing away. "I might have maybe forgot . . ."

"To change the SIM cards?" said Coker.

Twyla made a squinting face. "Oh, Coker . . . don't be, like, all mad and stuff."

Coker sat down in the deck chair. Heavily.

"Can I get you a drink?" said Bluebell.

"That would be just . . . lovely," said Coker. "What about the goombahs?"

"The what," said Twyla.

"Torinetti and the rest."

"Well, they're in the basement."

"I get that. What'd you *do* with them?"

Bluebell came back with a gigantic blue margarita in a flower vase and handed it to Coker.

"We tied them up with some plastic cord cuffs."

"And then Bluebell cut their ankle tendons," said Twyla, looking at her sister with a degree of sibling satisfaction that was, Coker thought, unique to Cherokee women whose ancestors may have invented the whole idea of scalping and skinning prisoners.

"Yes, I did," said Bluebell proudly.

Coker took a serious belt of his margarita. He looked at Bluebell. "How'd you know how to cut ankle tendons and eyelids?"

"From being a nurse, silly."

"What do you want to do with the goombahs?" asked Twyla. Coker found his heart rate slowing down to something between *hummingbird* and *eggbeater.*

He had some more of the margarita.

"Something massive," he said, and he put his head back on the deck chair and closed his eyes.

Six Months Later

When Two Mirrors Look Into Each Other, What Lies Between Them?

The Niceville Disappeared finally stopped reappearing by the following spring. Boonie Hackendorff's best count for missing people had been set at a hundred and seventy-nine over a period of fifty years. Of that number, only thirty-four actually reappeared, which came as a great relief to their loved ones, not to mention the overworked and overwhelmed Psych Ward staff at Our Lady of Sorrows in Cap City.

None of the Returned had any idea where they had been or how they had been Disappeared in the first place. Human nature being what it is, some of the Returned got a little cranky when they realized that their loved ones had adjusted pretty well to their absence.

In particular, younger relations who had inherited homes and money after the missing person had been declared legally dead were highly resistant to giving it all back to Aunt Lobelia now that she had turned up on the front porch looking dazed and confused but utterly persuaded that she wasn't dead and who were these damned strangers living in her damned house.

There were some ugly scenes and the Niceville PD and a phalanx of social workers and lawyers had to spend a lot of time racing about Garrison Hills and The Glades and Saddle Hill and Upper Chase Run trying to put a damper on a lot of domestic strife.

And, as was noted above, there were plenty of Aunt Lobelias and Uncle Reynards who finally ended up in the Psych Ward at Sorrows, since there seemed to be no better place to put them.

One happy exception to this was the arrival one soft June afternoon of Kate's father Dillon Walker, who turned up on the landing at Nick and Kate's townhouse looking like he'd been dragged through a hedge backward—very unlike him— and utterly convinced that he had only that day set out to drive down from VMI to assist Kate in her researches into Rainey Teague's history.

The fact that it was Rainey himself who opened the door when he knocked was rather upsetting for both of them, and it took Eufaula a while to get things calmed down and the old gentleman into a spare room so he could lie down and take in the new circumstances, which over time he managed to do.

He and Rainey became accustomed to each other and even found a shared interest in Niceville's genealogy, although for very different reasons.

Rainey by this time was growing into a broad-shouldered and athletic young man, acutely handsome, and he had managed to develop a few friends at Regiopolis Prep after he made the junior football team as a middle linebacker.

If Axel Deitz bore Rainey any sort of grudge for shoving him into the Tulip River, he kept it hidden and they seemed on the surface to get along reasonably well, although now that Beth and Hannah and Axel lived in a very nice home across the river in The Chase, they only really saw each other at school, which suited Beth very well, since she and her brother Reed retained a deep and abiding distrust of Rainey Teague and all his works and days.

Nick and Kate eventually stopped trying to get her father to reconstruct where he had been and what had happened to him, and he never inquired openly about the mirror, although he had figured out where it was and he thought about it more than anyone knew.

He did the same amount of thinking about Rainey too, and he kept that to himself as well, at least he did for many months, until he had reached some important conclusions and felt he needed to share them with Nick and Kate before he died.

Tig Sutter, the CO of the Belfair and Cullen County CID, retired shortly after the events of that terrible weekend in the fall, and Nick got promoted to CO in his place.

Beau Norlett got his legs back and he and Nick went back to being cop partners again, as they were in the beginning of all this, and Nick enjoyed watching Beau turn into a very smart and very skilled street cop.

Mavis Crossfire never told anyone about lending her Suburban to Coker on that complicated night, but she wasn't surprised when a Kenworth Car Carrier pulled up at her home a week later with her Suburban lashed down to the flatbed, freshly waxed, detailed, and gleaming, fuel all topped up, and a *thank you, all is well* note from Coker taped to the dashboard. Although she knew that Coker might have been no more than 359 miles away—it was equally likely that Coker and Twyla and Bluebell were in Bali or Borneo—she never went looking for him, nor did she ever give Boonie even a little hint.

Nick managed to piece a lot of it together over the following weeks, but since Mavis Crossfire was a dear friend and a good cop and Nick was experienced enough to know when to leave well enough alone, that's pretty much what he did.

Mavis did develop an unlikely association with Delores Maranzano, who after the timely deaths of all of her competitors finally took over most of Frankie's interests in trucking, real estate, waste management, and recreational drug trafficking all over the Southeast from Cap City to Miami.

They found each other useful, and Mavis Crossfire, being a smart cop, appreciated useful people wherever they might be found.

Lemon Featherlight got his Air National Guard chopper pilot papers and ended up doing a lot of air cover and coordination work with the state and county cops. Doris Godwin kept her job with the Peachtree Lines and they both kept in close, perhaps even intimate, contact with Helga Sigrid, who had gone back up to the University of Virginia to head a new division of the Forensic Anthropology Department devoted to the full-time examination of what had become known around the global scientific community as the Featherlight Ossuary.

By the late spring what her people were finding out about the bone baskets drew the attention of assorted three-letter agencies in the government, but so far they were merely observing. From a distance.

What exactly had happened that night up at Crater Sink and at Candleford House remained a secret all who had been involved kept very close.

The lady in the well gradually descended into the deep, never taking her eyes off the two women as they floated there in the cold blue light. She eventually faded from sight, and in the following six months the aura of malice around Crater Sink seemed to dissipate.

Nick and Kate and Reed never talked about that night with anyone other than Lemon and Helga and Doris. Rainey seemed to have no recollection of it or of the events preceding it, or at least he said so with every sign of sincerity. For a long time Nick didn't push the issue, until he had to, but when he had to, he did.

At the Ruelle Plantation the winter passed and the spring came on and Charlie Danziger ran the horses and the stock and helped Glynis with the crops. The Blue Bird bus made sure that people who didn't know where they were going managed to get there safely, and he and Albert Lee stood by Glynis for the Reckoning in the spring.

Abel Teague wasn't there.

Abel Teague was still in that furnace in the basement of Candleford House, still mostly alive, still in torment, his mind utterly shattered.

But he wasn't alone.

Timeline of Niceville Families

———

1763

Thierry Sébastien Mercièr–Sylvie Rose Didier-Beauchene

✳

Their seven children establish marriages
to lesser nobility in Anjou, Paris, and Corsica.

✳

1793–1794

The French Revolution
Thirty descendants and relatives of the Mercièr line are guil-
lotined during the Terror. Four Mercièr children survive and
flee to Ireland.

✳

1795

Dublin, Ireland
Beau Mercer–Mary Margaret Mullryne

✳

1798

Nine children and several relatives in the Mercer–Mullryne–
Gwinnett family are murdered during the Irish uprising when
the families are denounced to the English by Lachlan Teague.

✵

1800

Surviving Mercers, Mullrynes, and Gwinnetts flee
to the Carolinas.

✵

1801

Because of his service during the Irish uprising, the English
Crown rewards Lachlan Teague with a trading franchise in
the West Indies.

✵

1803

Lachlan Teague deserts his wife, Maureen Catherine Kincaid,
and takes up residence in Hispaniola with his son,
London Teague.

✵

1807

London Teague–Celestine Garza Cremone

✵

1820

Lachlan Teague dies. His son London Teague, age forty-
three, inherits Lachlan's slave-trading franchise in Hispaniola.

✣

1822

The West Indies slave trade is suppressed by the Royal Navy.
London Teague deserts Celestine Garza Cremone and flees
Hispaniola for Louisiana in America.
He establishes Hy Brasail Plantation.

✣

1825

London Teague–Cathleen Marr
Jubal Teague, born 1827
Tyree Teague, born 1828

✣

1830

Cathleen Marr commits suicide.

✣

1833

London Teague–Anora Mercer
Despite strong opposition from John Mercer Gwinnett
Eleanor de Lacey Teague, born 1834
Cora Evangeline Teague, born 1835

✣

1840

Anora Mercer dies from the bite of a harlequin
coral snake. John Mercer Gwinnett accuses London Teague
of murdering Anora Mercer.

✣

1841

London Teague and John Mercer Gwinnett fight a duel at
John Mullryne's plantation in Savannah, Georgia. Both men
are maimed but survive.

✣

1841

Cora and Eleanor Teague are taken under the protection of
John Mercer Gwinnett.

✣

1862

Tyree Teague is killed in action at Front Royal in the
Shenandoah Valley.

✣

1866

Jubal Teague–Sensibility Mullryne
Savannah, Georgia

✣

1865–1870 (date uncertain)

London Teague dies of syphilis and opium addiction in a
brothel in Baton Rouge.

✣

1865

Cora Evangeline Teague dies of influenza in Niceville.

✻

1870

Eleanor de Lacey Teague–Clete Bluebonnet Ruelle
Two female children, Lorelei Ruelle and Daphne Ruelle

✻

1888

Lorelei Ruelle–Albemarle Mullryne Mercer

✻

1890

Daphne Ruelle–Lucas Gwinnett Haggard

✻

1891

Glynis Mercer
Born to Lorelei Ruelle and Albemarle Mercer

✻

1893

Jubal Teague and Sensibility Mullryne have a son named
Abel Teague. Sensibility Mullryne dies in childbirth.

✻

1893

Clara Mercer
Born to Lorelei Ruelle and Albemarle Mercer

✻

1893

Lilla Haggard
Born to Daphne Ruelle and Lucas Gwinnett Haggard

✻

1895

Lucas Gwinnett Haggard dies in a duel. Daphne (Ruelle)
Haggard and daughter Lilla move to Niceville.

✻

1907

Glynis Mercer–John Ruelle (third cousin removed)
They inherit the Ruelle Plantation from Lorelei and
Albemarle Mercer. Clara Mercer (fourteen) comes to live at
Ruelle Plantation.

✻

1910

Abel Teague courts Clara Mercer.
Niceville Families Reunion
Mullryne Plantation, Savannah, Georgia
The Mercer family strongly objects to no avail.

✻

1913

Clara Mercer goes to Sallytown under the care of the
Palgrave family. She delivers a male child, March 2, 1913.
Abel Teague refuses to marry Clara.

✻

1913–1917

John and Ethan Ruelle repeatedly demand satisfaction from
Abel Teague. Teague avoids a stand.

✳

1917

Abel Teague and the Teague Faction use their influence with
the conscription board to have John and Ethan Ruelle drafted
into the American Expeditionary Force.

✳

JULY 1918

John Ruelle is killed in action at the Battle of Soissons,
France. Ethan Ruelle is severely wounded.

✳

DECEMBER 24, 1921

Ethan Ruelle is provoked into a duel with Lieutenant Colin
Haggard and killed.

✳

1925

Daphne Ruelle Haggard–Jubal Custis Walker

✳

1926

Dillon Walker is born to Daphne Ruelle Haggard and Jubal
Custis Walker.

✳

1947

Lenore Mercer is born to Sybilla Mullryne (Savannah) and Gwinnett Mercer II (Charleston).

✳

1966

Dillon Walker–Lenore Mercer

✳

Three children:
Elizabeth (Beth) Walker, born 1979
Katherine Rosemary (Kate) Walker, born 1986
Reed Walker, born 1988

✳

1994

Lenore (Mercer) Walker is killed in a rollover accident on Interstate 50.

✳

APRIL 1999

Abel Teague–Unknown Rape Victim
They produce one child, Rainey Teague, who was born in January 2000.

✳

2008

Katherine (Kate) Walker–Nicholas Michael Kavanaugh

✳

2012

Abel Teague shot dead in a duel at the Gates of Gilead Palliative Care in Sallytown.